Chronicle of Destiny

Thanks!

Chronicle of Destiny

A novel by

Etta Jean

Hydra
Publications

Hydra Publications
337 Clifty Drive
Madison, IN 47250

www.hydrapublications.com

Dedication

Dedicated with love to my mother Cheryl for her unquestioning support and copious supply of peppermints.

Part One

Tariah

Prologue

Dear reader,

I was born in a normal city, at the edges of a normal country, on the normal world of Lucksphere. I was a normal girl, with normal Magi powers, and I had a normal life. My parents were normal, one an Air Magi and the other a Water Magi. They had grown up normal, in normal cities, inside normal countries, on this normal world.

But during my thirteenth year of life, all that normality changed. I woke one morning and discovered that I was destined to die.

You see, my body had changed overnight. My skin had developed lines. Far from normal, these brown lines patterned me in a wide array of swirls and loops. They covered me from my face and down over my body and all the way to my toes. They swept down only the right half of my face and then expanded across the entirety of the front of my body, and then down only the outside of my left leg.

I was marked as a Chronicle. I was a member of the most hated race on the world. I didn't even know why they were hated! When people spoke of Chronicles, they spoke of Dragons and evil pacts. And yet, Dragons themselves were not so frowned on. On the contrary, Dragons scorned Magi as bigots and murderers.

I knew nothing about Chronicles, yet during my thirteenth summer, I became one. Before I started developing a figure, I developed lines.

It was law. All Chronicles were to be put to death instantly upon discovery. Children had been murdered for centuries just because they were different. My parents . . . let me live. They loved me no matter what I was. But how would I hide? The answer came from an unlikely source. There was a SunKin Faerie within our city who took pity on me. She sensed my awakening and came to my home. She used her magic to make my lines invisible.

There was a price to be paid. I could not let myself become passionate about anything. In temper, in amusement, or in love, I had to remain dispassionate about it all. If I ever grew passionate, my Chronicle body would respond and all her magic would disappear. Even the Kin cannot stop a Chronicle's power forever.

So. There I was. Thirteen years old, still waiting to grow breasts, and I was doomed to death if I ever let my emotions show. I could never fall in love, could never marry. Tell me honestly. Which is better? To be doomed to choke on my own emotions, or to die?

Well, I did not die. I continued to grow and age. I choked on my emotions, never let loose the feelings that welled so often inside me. In some ways, in my efforts to stay alive, I think I forgot how to truly live.

Then, in the summer of my twentieth year, it all changed. And that is the summer where my story begins.

Tariah M. Chronis

Chapter One

The sun was devilishly hot. Even the Magi with Air powers could not keep cool enough breezes blowing to prevent the sun from trying to bake them all. Any storm that was summoned to block the sun only managed to make the air humid and increase the discomfort of all. Even the SunKin, the Faeries and Elves who existed on the light of the sun, were feeling the effects.

Tariah Chronis lifted her visor for a moment long enough to squint at the distance, then lowered it again. It was the only thing keeping her silver eyes from straining in the bright light glaring off every reflective object. Thanks to the full desert clothes that were considered casual summer wear of the citizens of Symphony, she wasn't completely melting either.

She glanced down at the thought. 'Full clothes' was really a misnomer. By the standards of other cities, she might be considered barely dressed at all. On top, she wore a piece of cloth crossed over her breasts and tied both behind her neck and around her chest. On the bottom she wore a pair of cloth shorts that vividly displayed the length of her long legs. Her feet were encased in sturdy boots to protect them from the harsh desert sand.

Her long auburn brown hair was coiled on top of her head and her visor helped keep the weight in place. The visor was designed to shield her eyes from the sun and to also provide a soft cooling breeze down the length of her body. Unfortunately, the breeze was currently not working.

She let out a hard breath and pulled gloves on her hands. She was standing in front of a large cliff face outside the edges of her city. At the top of the cliff were several scraggly bushes with Knockback berries on them. So named because they were so sour that they knocked back any who ate them, she thought in wry amusement.

With lithe strength, she began to climb the cliff face. She had made the climb so many times that it was child's play. Her body was lean and strong, well honed from survival in the hottest desert on Lucksphere. Only the hardiest of people made Symphony their home, but she couldn't imagine living anywhere else.

Halfway up the wall, a cloth bag filled with water struck the wall beside her head and exploded, sending warm water spraying into her face. Muttering curses, she shoved up her splattered visor and twisted slightly to look back at the ground. Her hackles rose as she saw the three teenage males standing there with nasty grins.

She had to order herself not to get angry. She stepped on the anger, choked it, and nearly choked physically as she forced herself to ignore them. For seven years, it had been her way of life. All her emotions had to be choked and stifled. If she ever let them free, her fate would be sealed and the world would sentence her to death.

"What do you want?" she called down to the boys. "I'm busy here."

"See?" one said. "I told you she didn't get angry. You can do whatever you want and she won't get mad at you. It's not normal. Hey, *poka*!"

"*Poka*, my ass," she muttered. *Poka* was an insult that implied the person being referred to was as slow and stupid as a Pokagale bird. The birds were so stupid that they often died falling out of their own nests because they forgot they could fly.

"Tariah's a poka!" The chant came from all three boys as they started lobbing more water balls.

She jerked her visor down again and started her climb once more. She ignored their taunts as fiercely as she ignored the water balls that kept narrowly missing her head. Finally, more disgusted than angry, she turned and made an elegant gesture with one hand. It was an exceptionally rude gesture, and it also harnessed her power. "You want Water," she muttered, "you get it."

A large tidal wave lifted out of the sands and began to chase the boys as they ran screaming back toward the city. They didn't make it in time, and the wave swept them up and sent them tumbling through the center of town. Even from the cliff, Tariah could hear the city laughing.

With a little satisfied smile, she worked her way up the rest of the wall. At the top, she unsheathed the dagger on her hip and began to harvest the berries. They were really sour and really disgusting, but their medicinal properties couldn't be beaten. The doctors made poultices and remedies out of the berries and leaves both.

When the satchel around her waist was full, she climbed back. As she jumped the last two feet, the ground under her feet shook and rumbled. It nearly knocked her over before she was able to catch her balance. It ended fairly swiftly and she let out the breath she was holding. Quakes on the continent of Choral were always more annoying than detrimental.

The rest of Symphony was of like mind. In size, the city covered a ten-mile diameter and boasted a population of nearly ten thousand. The buildings were made of red brick and hard-caked mud, but colorful tapestries and awnings brought the place to life. The streets were mostly sand but wooden tracks had been laid down for carts to roll on. Street sweepers made sure the tracks were kept clean every day.

Tariah loved Symphony. The heat, the color, the land, and the people. With a spring in her step, she hurried toward the doctor's office at the end of the main street. Inside was cool and comfortable, a welcome change from the midday heat. "Doc!" she called. "I'm back!"

"Ah there's my favorite Magi." The doctor was a MoonKin Elf of Dark power, and his skin was smooth chocolate. His eyes were silvery-gray like the moon and marked his MoonKin heritage as visibly as the little silvery tattoos on his arms.

He was not very big, only around five-six, so Tariah never felt exceptionally small beside him even though she was only five-two. She was a little fascinated by him too. Most Kin did not leave their homelands, but Maxim had done just that. He claimed it was to sew back together impulsive Magi, which amused her immensely.

She took off her satchel and set it down on the table. "Here you go." She gratefully took the glass of water he handed her and nearly finished it in a single gulp. "Whew! I needed that." She smiled. "A Water Magi, and I still get thirsty so fast."

"It's part of your power, and you know it." He began to sort the leaves and berries. Casually he said, "I noticed the three terrors come tumbling through town.

3

Were they harassing you?"

She lowered her lashes slightly. She knew Maxim knew what she was though neither had spoken of it. The Kin always automatically sensed and recognized power in all other beings. It was one of their gifts. "Yes," she finally said. "But it didn't mean anything."

"I wish there was another way for you," he said softly. "You are one of the most giving young women I've ever known. To be condemned . . ."

"It can't be changed." She shrugged one shoulder then smiled. "If anything, it gives me an edge. They think I'm a Master Magi, and that's enough to make them wary."

Master Magi were as rare as Chronicles but not nearly as loathed. Masters were simply Magi of exceptional skill. Tariah was willing to endure the slightly awed looks of people when they witnessed her strength with her powers; strength well beyond her years. It was better than to see them looking at her with hatred and murder in their eyes.

"What makes a Magi different from a Chronicle?" she whispered. "I don't feel any different. I'm just stronger, and I have lines over my skin."

Maxim sighed. "Like all creatures, a Magi uses lightning from birth. At puberty, they develop powers related to a primary element. Either Air, Water, Fire, or Soil. Then, during second puberty, they specialize with a secondary element related to the first."

"Yes, I know." She pulled a face. "Believe me, I went to school, and I was Magi the first part of my life. What makes a Chronicle *different?*"

"Well, I couldn't say precisely," he said. "They were wiped out over a thousand years ago, and all since have been put to death. But if the tales of my fellow Kin are true, then Chronicles were basically Magi that developed secondary elements at the same time as primary, and during second puberty they gained wholly new powers that were unique only to Chronicles and Furies."

Her heart gave a soft thud. She had never heard of a Fury before and yet something inside seemed to suddenly awaken. It strained and reached as if looking for something. "A Fury?" she asked softly.

"A Fury is a Dragon Lord." He watched her intently. "A Dragon Lord is not always a Fury, just as a Dragon is not always a Dragon Lord, but Furies are always Dragon Lords. They are the other half of a Chronicle. They are perfectly balanced and matched. When the correct Chronicle and Fury meet, they form a powerful bond and become Dragoons. The Fury will feed on the power of the Chronicle, and in turn the Chronicle can use Dragon majiks."

Tears burned the back of her eyes as she thought of finding the Fury meant for her. Someone that would accept her and love her for everything she was. She would not have to live in fear ever again. Somewhere in the world, she thought, there was probably a Dragon who felt the same as she. "I don't care for the majiks," she whispered. "I just want someone to understand me."

He had to smile. "I suspect that is how Chronicles always felt, and Furies as well. The Dragons still wait for Chronicles, or so they say. Legend states that they would protect any Chronicle they found, Fury mate or not. Legend also states that the lost continent of Dragons would welcome any Chronicle that was able to find them."

She frowned. "But how would I find them?" she asked. "I mean . . . Dragons aren't seen as commonly as Kin, and their continent has been lost for centuries, right?"

"That's what I've heard as well. Supposedly it lies at the place where the edges of

4

the world meet." He smiled. "Perhaps someday you will find it. They say a Chronicle always knows. Maybe those lines on your body make the map leading you to them."

With a soft sigh, she put the thoughts of Furies and Chronicles out of her mind. Thinking about it just made her want it more, and if she let herself feel too deeply for it, then the aforementioned lines would become visible on her body. "Maybe someday," she agreed softly.

"Go home, little one," he said gently. "Don't stress yourself out."

She felt tired in the soul and heart so she had no problems agreeing with such a thing. With a sigh, she left the doctor's office and walked back outside into the oppressing heat of the afternoon. She pulled her visor lower over her eyes and headed down the dusty road toward her home.

Her parents owned the town library. They collected and stored books for the entire city so that they could be accessed by everyone. They worked in conjunction with other city libraries to provide copies to each other. In this way, the entire continent of Choral had access to all the books they could want. Transport between continents was long, and trade with the other lands was only just starting.

Sheer curiosity filled Tariah and she went over to the bookshelves to get out the giant book of maps. It was recent as of five years; the newest edition was being worked on since the mapmaker was trying to convince a Dragon to fly her over the countries, and there were rules against Dragons flying over cities.

Tariah opened the book and flipped to the center where there was a world map. Laid out flat, the world of Lucksphere looked like a mass of blue with spots of brown and some green and only a little white. Most of the world was desert; toward the north there were some forested and plains lands and to the very north there was a land of ice.

The primary islands of the MoonKin and SunKin were located scattered in an atoll around the edges of the forested country known as Carnelian. Tariah traced a finger lightly over the map. There were huge chunks of ocean. More than enough space to hide an entire continent, but nothing felt right.

Her right shoulder began to burn. She winced and pressed a hand to her skin and felt the heat underneath. It had happened once or twice before in her life, but never like this. It felt as if something was moving under her skin. Her lines itched horribly.

Her eyes fixed on the map. "At the place where the edges of the world meet," she whispered. She pulled the map out of the book and began to fold it into a sphere shape. There were cuts in the paper for just such a thing, and in a few moments she was holding a global representation of her world.

She turned it around until she was looking at the seam where the two sides had come together, and she felt a little shiver go down her back. In this shape, the two halves of ocean met at the seam and the two spots of deepest ocean came together. She measured it with her fingers. Based on the scale of the globe, the spot of deepest ocean was about the size of a medium continent.

It was a little unnerving. She quickly unfolded the map and put it away. The Deepest Ocean was a sailor's nightmare. It could not be traversed at all. If you came within a mile of the dark waters, your ship was immediately assailed by winds and torrential waves. Many ships had been lost, and hundreds killed, in the centuries since its discovery.

"And what are you up to?"

She jolted, then turned with a smile as her father wrapped an arm around her shoulders and hugged her. He was barely taller than she was and had the same sparkling silver eyes. His hair, however, was gold in color. He was an Air Magi of average strength but sensitive to the fluctuations of other powers.

She rested her head on his shoulder. "Well," she said, "I was looking at the maps."

"Thinking of abandoning your poor parents and traveling the world?" Dublin Chronis pulled a saddened face. "You ungrateful child."

She just laughed. "You would like to have time alone for you and Mom, and you know it, Dad." She turned her head with a smile as she sensed her mother's approach. "Right, Mom?"

"Guilty," Persia Chronis said ruefully as she walked over. She was taller than her mate by about four inches, and her hair was the same auburn as her daughter's. Her eyes were smoky blue and she was a Water Magi of stronger power.

She picked up the book of maps and flipped through the pages. Her heart was aching. She had wondered how long it would be before Tariah's Chronicle blood demanded she seek out the Fury meant for her.

When she had learned her daughter was a Chronicle, she had scoured every book she owned for more information. All she could say with certainty was that a Chronicle was compelled, by the very power that made them, to seek out the land of the Dragons and to find the Fury that matched them. "Where would you go if you could go somewhere?" she asked softly.

"I don't know." Tariah rubbed her hands over her arms, still feeling cold even in the warm weather. "Just somewhere. Somewhere I would not have to live in fear. Doc told me that legend speaks of Dragons guarding Chronicles. A part of me wishes to find out if it is true. The rest is more afraid it isn't."

Dublin and Persia looked at one another and unspoken messages passed between them before both nodded slightly. "We stand behind you," Dublin said quietly. "No matter what. If you want to set sail for the primary continent, we'll help pay for the ticket."

Tariah looked at him in surprise. "Really?"

"Really. You know we just want you to be happy."

She did know. Her parents had always done everything they could to help her adjust to the burdens she lived under. "I'll think about it," she decided.

There came a commotion from the street, and they all walked over to the doorway. "It's the Militia," Persia whispered, recognizing the soldiers on horseback. "What are they doing here?"

The Militia was the primary military force of Lucksphere. They originated in Spectrum, the primary continent, and had outreaches on all the other Magi continents. Magi were ruled by one kingdom on Spectrum, the Kin were ruled by one on their main land, and the Dragons . . . well, they were ruled by their own kind but no one knew where. They adhered to the laws of the land they were in at the time they were in it.

It was very rare to see a fully armed Militia unit in a city unless the continually shifting magic in the land had mutated the wildlife nearby into something that posed a threat. "We aren't under attack," Tariah said softly. "What's going on?"

Maxim often spoke on behalf of the city, and he walked forward to address the captain riding at the front. "Is there something amiss?" he asked calmly. "We were not expecting you."

"Rumor reached us that this city might be harboring a Chronicle." The captain was grim in face and tone. "If this is true, the entire city will be fined and the Chronicle must be immediately eliminated."

"Go back inside, Tariah," Dublin said quietly. "Now."

"I must know," someone called. "Why are Chronicles always killed?"

The captain glared at the speaker. "You question the law?"

"No," the man said hastily, "I just was wondering."

"Fair enough." The captain's eyes were restless as they moved over the crowd, as if he was trying to determine who might be the Chronicle. "Several thousand years ago, there were two kinds of Magi on this world. The normal kind, like us, and other Magi known as Chronicles. Chronicles were like Magi but developed differently. There was something weird about them. They were able to bond with the Dragon Lords known as Furies. When bonded, the Fury and Chronicle became far superior in power to the rest of their races."

"What's wrong with that?" Tariah asked defiantly.

The captain glared at her. "It is unnatural."

"Sounds like it was very natural," Maxim countered. "If what you say is true, this was something dictated by the nature of their respective species. Particularly if you look at the evidence that even after the race was destroyed, some are still born." His silvery eyes were sharp as glass. "What do you fear in Chronicles, Magi?" he asked softly. "Or is it jealousy that drove the Magi to massacre the entire race and send the Dragons into hiding?"

"Enough!" the captain roared. He drew his sword and dismounted. "All those between first and second puberty, please come forward!"

Tariah, at the cusp of second puberty, was part of them. She had faith in her hidden lines, but her stomach still quivered as she slowly walked forward with the rest of her peers. She could not hide away. If she hid away, it would give her away.

The females in the Militia examined the girls, and the males examined the boys. There were a couple hundred Magi of the right ages in the city's entirety, but only twenty or so present. The rest would be examined at their homes.

As it came her turn, Tariah just stood and waited. She was wearing clothes that revealed most of her skin so it was obvious she possessed no lines. Yet the soldier examining her seemed to sense something odd because she kept squinting at Tariah's shoulder. "What are those faint traces on your skin?" she asked.

Tariah squinted at her shoulder and felt her stomach dip as she saw the faintest hint of lines. Thinking quickly, she said, "I had an accident at the cliffs. I got burned when I smacked into the rock."

"They don't look like burn marks." The soldier shook her head. "But then again, they don't look like what a Chronicle's lines are reputed to look like either." She moved on down the line and Tariah let out the breath she was holding.

Once they were satisfied, the Militia got back on their horses to begin knocking on doors. Dublin and Persia wasted no time in hustling Tariah back into their home. Maxim went with them as well. "Tariah needs to leave the continent," he said bluntly as the door shut. "She needs to seek out a Dragon who can take her to safety."

"But it's a legend!" Persia almost cried.

"What other choice is there?" Dublin demanded. "This was far too close for comfort. If they find her out, they'll kill her."

Tariah slowly sank down to sit on the edge of a chair. She felt dazed and lost. But what choice did she have? Stay or leave, she was in danger either way. But by seeking out a Dragon, she might just have a chance. "I'll go," she said softly. "I'm not sure how much good it'll do, but I'll go." She straightened up with a smile. "Either way, the worst that could happen is that I die, and I've lived with that for years now."

"That's our girl." Maxim smiled and opened his mouth to say something more when a shocked expression suddenly crossed his face.

Tariah blinked. "Doc?" Her gaze slowly lowered and she saw the silver bloodstain spreading across the front of his cloth tunic. As he crumbled to the floor silently, the other three turned and looked at the doorway where the female soldier of before stood.

She slowly lowered her bloodstained sword. "I knew there was something odd about you," she said in satisfaction. "You are the Chronicle. All of you are hereby sentenced to death."

Tariah couldn't look away from Maxim's body, and tears welled in her eyes. "Why?" she whispered. "Why kill them? For loving me? For wanting to protect me? Why kill me? For jealousy? I didn't ask to be a Chronicle."

The ground began to tremble under their feet in the familiar pulses of uncontrolled power. Pain and anger welled inside Tariah. It choked her throat and made her blood burn. Maxim had been her friend. He had always been there. She had been a little in love with him, as if he was a part of her family. And now he was dead because he had loved her in return.

The soldier stepped back sharply. "Captain!" she barked out the door. "Hurry!" She moved into the room further for space to fight, and she kicked Maxim's body out of her way.

Tariah saw red. All her years of learning to resist her emotions came to be worthless. Water power erupted in the air around her and began to swirl dangerously. Shards of Ice power from her secondary skills formed at her feet.

Golden lines suddenly blazed into appearance on her body. They started at her scalp on the right side of her face, traveled down to her shoulder, crossed over her chest and stomach, then down her left leg. They traveled down the outside of her right arm to her hand, and the mark for the character 'chron' appeared on her palm.

The soldier was so terrified in that moment that she could not speak. She whirled to run and nearly tripped over her own feet in her mad dash for the door. Even Dublin and Persia were afraid. They did not know if their daughter had any control, and they feared she might destroy herself.

The shards of ice broke into pieces that floated up into the air. They quivered violently and the sharpened ends glinted. They fired through the air with lethal accuracy and impaled the soldier in the back. She was flung out into the street and screams lifted on the air. The sound of pounding hooves became distinct, and Dublin turned to Tariah. "Run!" he ordered her. "Get away from here!"

Tariah looked at him and her mother and realized both were ready and willing to die if it meant she got away. She couldn't stand it. And yet her lines burned, urging her to the north beyond the city. She *felt* it. She felt the road ahead of her. In that moment she knew her lines were indeed a map. She had to follow it even if she did not know where it led.

She turned on her heel and fled out the back of the building, snatching her cloak off the wall as she went. Her odds of surviving in the desert were small, but if she could make it to the next city, she might be able to find a Kin who could help her. They were neutral to Magi and Dragon alike, but they had soft spots for Chronicles if her past experiences were anything to go by.

The sun was low in the sky as she raced across the glowing desert sands. Her lines burned against her skin, urging her on. North. All she knew was north. Perhaps going north would eventually lead her to the land of the Dragons.

Perhaps there she could find out why she had been born a Chronicle and been destined to die.

Chapter Two

The sun was burning hot. Even for a SunKin Faerie like Sparkle, it was almost unbelievably hot. She had to stay in her Sylph form just to keep from being smothered in the heat. The only downside to her Sylph form was that she was now barely an inch big and it was hard to fly accurately across the land because of even the smallest winds.

She was looking for pitcher crabs that lived in sand dunes. They had the softest and tastiest flesh in the desert and could be sold for a fortune in Carnelian where they had no deserts. Kin like Sparkle lived on the Outposts built just for trading and went to the nearest continent to do their harvesting.

As she was angling down toward a dune that looked promising, she caught sight of a piece of dark against the white sand. For a moment she thought it was a crab, but as she got closer she realized it was a Magi.

With a little glimmer of magic, she went back into her natural form and angled down to land beside the figure lying in the sands. In natural form, she was not even a foot high but it was more than big enough to stop beside the girl and check her pulse.

Shock filled Sparkle. The girl was still alive. On the heels of that shock came a second one as she realized the girl was covered with Chronicle lines. She had to get her out of the desert, *fast!*

She looked around and spotted a nice dune nearby. Soil power pulsed around her feet as she pointed at the dune then ribbons of green light flowed down her arm and over to the dune. The dune pulsed and then began to rise up into the air until it formed a tall golem. Crabs scuttled away across the ground as their home was disturbed, and the golem lumbered over to Sparkle.

"Carry her," she ordered as she flew up to sit on the golem's shoulder.

The golem obligingly picked up the girl and carried her gently as it turned and began crossing the desert under Sparkle's direction. She had built a cabin under the sand using her Soil power so that she was sheltered from heat and cold alike. It was also completely undetectable by any Magi, with or without Soil power themselves.

Once at the cabin, the golem carried the girl inside and gently put her down on the floor. Sparkle dismissed her pet, who went outside and turned into a dune again, then turned her attention to her unexpected guest.

The girl was of smaller height and weight for a Magi, and her hair was thick and auburn brown. Her skin was light brown from the sun, but the Chronicle lines were golden as they went down her body. She was really very pretty.

Sparkle flew over and grabbed a jug of water. Since she needed to cool the girl down and get rid of the heat in her skin, the quickest way was to simply pour cool water over her. So she flew over the girl and did just that.

The water was absorbed instantly by her body. "Oh." Sparkle stuck out her lower lip. "A Water element." Well, that would make things a little easier.

Tariah awoke to a raging headache and pains in her whole body. She also awoke to a SunKin Faerie hovering over her. Her eyes widened swiftly and she tried to sit up, terrified she might be in a town. Immediately the Kin hugged her around the neck comfortingly. "No, no!" she said. "It's okay! You're safe!"

Tariah looked around slowly. The cabin was about the size of a large bedroom, but it was a full home with a privacy room and a kitchen. Her power was very low because she had been drawing on it hard to survive in the desert, but she felt the pulse of water close underneath her and knew she was underground.

Sparkle let her go before flying over to get a canteen. She brought it to Tariah and watched like a hawk as the young woman sipped carefully. "My name is Sparkle," she said. She landed on Tariah's knee and bowed gracefully. "A Soil secondary SunKin Faerie."

SunKin were Light primary, just as all MoonKin were Dark primary, so they only referred to their secondary when introducing themselves. Tariah had to smile. "I am Tariah Chronis, a Water Magi."

Sparkle tilted her head and her green eyes were thoughtful. "Technically, I'd say you're a Water Chronicle."

Her gaze lowered. "Yes," she said softly. She drank more from the canteen. Both her body and her power needed the water very badly to recover. She couldn't help but wish for a pool or a spring to simply immerse herself in.

With a sigh, she looked at her rescuer. She was definitely SunKin because her skin was pale. And she was definitely Faerie because she was tiny and had wings. Her hair was pale lavender and there were tiny flowers in it, as was not uncommon of Soil powers. Her eyes were grass green and there were little gold tattoos on her face and arms. "You're cute," she decided.

Sparkle blinked then smiled. "Well, you're cute too, for a Magi." She tilted her head. "Hey, Tariah, is there water near us?"

Tariah nodded. "I can feel it, yes. Why?"

"Let's make ourselves a spring!" She flew over to one of her walls and began gathering her power. The wall obligingly opened and made a doorway. She began to make a hall as well and stretched it about ten feet away from the cabin itself.

Tariah frowned thoughtfully. "Why?" she asked.

Sparkle grinned at her. "Why not?" She snorted delicately. "Don't tell me you Magi don't use your powers simply for fun sometimes. Why have them if you don't play with them once and a while?"

Tariah began to smile. "You're right." She very carefully got to her feet and walked over to Sparkle by holding onto the furniture and the wall. Her legs felt like rubber. She followed Sparkle down the hall she was making and then stood in the doorway while her new friend formed a new room and began making a basin in the ground. "Make sure it's really deep at one end, but shallow at the other."

"Oh good idea!" Sparkle did as requested before getting fancy and lining the bottom and sides with smooth stone to keep everything clean. "There! Now, Chronicle girl, where's our water?"

Power flowed around Tariah and the room began to pulse blue. Water began to pour out of the walls and flowed across the ground toward the spring. It was so sweet and pure that Sparkle felt it tingle in her lungs when she took a deep breath. There was nothing like fresh desert water.

Once the pool was filled, Tariah stopped the flow. She stopped long enough to take off her shoes before she slid into the spring, clothes and all. Sparkle wasn't surprised; when she was too low on Soil she had a tendency to dive into a mud hole without changing clothes first. She stripped off her clothes, flew up in the air, and dove down directly into the middle. Despite her size, she made an impressive splash that hit Tariah.

Tariah sputtered for a moment. She then smiled and dove under the surface. She could breathe underwater because of her powers, and she let herself sink deeper until she was at the bottom of the deep end. It felt incredible. It was as if her body was actually soaking up the water around her, and some of the aches began to fade. When she surfaced again, she slung her hair out of her eyes and saw Sparkle skating across the top of the water. "You're good at that," she praised.

Sparkle laughed. "Well, sure!" She twirled around on one foot and let herself sink back into the water. She was watching closely, however, as Tariah moved to the edge of the spring and began to undress. She had been hoping the other girl would be comfortable enough to get naked. She had never seen a Chronicle, and she was immensely curious.

Tariah felt a little nervous as she put her clothes to the side. They were both females, and Sparkle was a Kin, but a part of Tariah was still ashamed of her lines. She ducked back down underwater as quickly as she could and let only her head stay on the surface.

"Talk to me," Sparkle said curiously as she paddled closer. "Was it your lover who blabbed on you? I mean, you're alive and definitely older than first puberty, so obviously your parents didn't have you killed."

Tariah smiled. "I haven't started second puberty yet. I should be doing that sometime this year though. So no lover."

For all species, first puberty was where their bodies developed and began to grow in ways that defined them as male or female. It was also where their natural lightning abilities began to develop into a primary element (or secondary for Kin). Second puberty was where they began to develop hormones and urges related to sexual development, and began to develop secondary skills related to the primary. It occurred anywhere from ages sixteen up to twenty-one.

Sparkle nodded sagely. "It'll be hard for you. I mean, you won't be able to experiment or learn about your body or stuff like that because you won't be sure if you can trust anyone."

Tariah smiled wryly. "Tell me about it." She sighed and sank down in the water to her chin. She was not looking forward to second puberty. She never had been, really. Even with the ban lifted on her excessive emotions, Sparkle was right. "I'd rather be dead I think." Moments later Sparkle dunked her. She surfaced again with a sputter. "Hey!"

"Hey yourself!" Sparkle poked her in the nose. "I didn't go saving your Chronicle butt just to hear you wish to die. You owe me, so you have to live." She scrambled back hastily as Tariah reached for her. "Whoa!"

Tariah caught her firmly and dunked her in retaliation. Sparkle surfaced, her hair hanging in her eyes, then she began to giggle. Tariah couldn't help but begin to laugh as well. She smiled as Sparkle shot forward and hugged her around the neck again. Gently she hugged her back. "Thanks Sparkle," she said softly.

"Anytime. Hey! Make this a hot spring, okay?" Sparkle released her to dive back under the water as Tariah obligingly heated the water with magic. Contented, she floated on her stomach with her arms on the side of the spring. Tariah joined her and Sparkle said, "Let's be friends."

"Okay. Friends it is." Tariah pulled herself up out of the water and sat on the side. She pulled her hair forward over her shoulder and began to work the tangles out. Unbound, her hair fell to her waist and was very thick.

Sparkle studied her and smiled. "You'll make some Fury a very happy man."

Tariah was startled. "Furies are male?"

"Not all of them." Sparkle shook back her three-tiered flowery wings. "See, Chronicles and Furies are always perfect opposites. Always male-female, and always opposing elements. So I can say with certainty that your Fury is a male and a Fire power." She frowned. "It's so sad."

"What?" Tariah wished longingly for a bar of soap as she looked at her still grubby fingers.

"Well, that you are a Chronicle and don't know anything about it." Sparkle was of like mind and flew down the hall to fetch some soap. She returned and plopped it down beside Tariah along with a piece of cloth. "Here," she offered, "I'll scrub your back."

"Sure." Tariah pulled her hair forward over her shoulders as Sparkle scrubbed soap over her back. She was thoughtful as she looked across the room. "I guess it is kind of sad," she agreed after a moment. "But I don't mind it, really. The only thing I really want to know is why Chronicles are hated."

Sparkle's nose wrinkled. "Kin talk of jealousy. Magi were jealous that Chronicles were much more powerful so they spread rumor and destroyed them. We fought alongside the Dragons and Chronicles in that war, but we did not win."

"Fought?" Tariah looked over her shoulder. "Kin are neutral."

"And pacifists," Sparkle reminded her. "We will side with anyone we feel is being slighted. If it had been the other way, Chronicle after Magi, we would have sided with Magi. That is why all Kin will help you now, Tariah. Because you are being wronged. You would have sanctuary on any Kin outpost or in our homeland."

Tariah drew a long breath. "Will you help me?" she asked softly. "Help me find the land of the Dragons?"

She nodded firmly as she handed Tariah the cloth. "Absolutely." She giggled as Tariah began to scrub her clean. "It tickles!"

Tariah just smiled and rolled into the spring with her wiggling, slippery friend. They were both rinsed clean and Tariah got to work on her hair. "Thanks, Sparkle," she said softly. "Do you think you could hide my lines like was done when I was little?"

Sparkle shook her head. "Nuh-uh. My powers don't delve into that sort of thing. But . . . I bet I can come up with a better idea. We'll just tell everyone we're traveling entertainers, and I made you look like a Chronicle so everyone knows what to be wary of!"

It was simple enough that it had to work. Tariah smiled. "I like it." She rinsed off fully and pulled herself out of the spring. She was feeling better already, although she was now starving. "I don't suppose we could make ourselves some dinner."

"Sure!" Sparkle flew out of the water and used her powers on the sand once more to weave two warm blankets, one of the right size for each of them. She wrapped herself up, then flew over to land on Tariah's shoulder once she had done the same. "I'm glad I met you."

Tariah rubbed her cheek against Sparkle's gently. "Me too," she said softly. She stretched. "Let's have some dinner."

Sparkle had some pitcher crab for her own consumption, and Tariah cooked it up for them. Sparkle was fascinated. She had never really learned to cook Magi food. She was used to the pre-made dinners that the Kin had fashioned. They were full meals, but they were missing an element. A person with that element could add it and instantly have a ready meal. Tariah, for her own part, was equally fascinated by the Kin method. They were such timesavers!

They both slept in blankets on the floor with a fire for warmth. The following morning had Sparkle circling Tariah to study her critically. Since Soil powers could make cloth from sand or grass, it was easy to make new clothes for her friend. But to make sure they fit, she needed to know Tariah's measurements. "Let's see . . . Wow, you're not very busty."

Tariah crossed her arms with a glower. "Be quiet."

"I didn't say you weren't pretty."

"That doesn't take the sting out of your words. I've always wished for more curves." She poked her friend in the stomach gently. "Besides, you're pudgy."

Sparkle gasped. "I am not!" She stomped a foot in the air indignantly then dissolved into giggles. "Okay, I am! I like sweet things! My auntie makes the best snacks in the whole world." She studied Tariah again then decided that her friend was beautiful for a Magi and really ought to show it off. She was also a desert girl and would hate confining clothes. With those thoughts in mind, she drew the sand down from the walls and used her power to weave first cloth and then weave that into clothing.

Tariah shortly found herself in snug cloth leggings, a top like the one she had been wearing before, and a sturdy cloak to protect her from the hottest parts of the day. They were all in dark green and looked really flattering against her skin and lines. "You're really good at this!" she praised.

"Aren't I?" Sparkle gave a saucy curtsey before starting to pack up her tiny backpack for the trip to the port. When Tariah returned from fetching her boots, Sparkle brought down the wall to the spring and shut it off protectively. "It's our secret."

Tariah smiled. "Sure." She picked up one of the visors that Sparkle had been storing and waited as it recognized the species holding it. It obligingly grew big enough for a Magi and she pulled it on and down over her eyes before pulling her hood up. The visors were made predominately by Kin, and again were of a technology far surpassing most Magi.

Once they were ready, they set out into the desert to begin walking toward the port that was a good thirty miles to the north. Sparkle rode on Tariah's shoulder, and she was covered protectively by her own visor and cloak. "The outpost where I live," she said, "is forested."

"Oh really?" Tariah considered that. "I've always lived in the desert. I can't imagine trees everywhere."

"It was hard to get used to no trees at all for me!" Sparkle smiled. "I'll take you there. The outpost is between Choral and Carnelian, but closer to Carnelian which is why it is forested. The Kin that live there will help you too, I'm sure of it. And if Dragons go anywhere off their isle, they go there. I bet they'll definitely be willing to help."

"Do you think there's a Fury out there for me?" Tariah asked softly, longing in every word. She wanted to find the one person meant for her. "I just want to find a true friend. You're the first I've ever had, but I want more. Someone to share my heart because we're the same."

"I'm sure of it!" Sparkle was *very* sure, and her tone reflected it. She was also hiding a little smile because she knew more about Dragoon bonds than Tariah did. Tariah would get her friend, but unless she was one of the rare exceptions, she would also be getting a lover to help her explore all of her second puberty curiosities.

~*~

Harmonica was bigger than Symphony by about fifteen miles and it boasted nearly three times the population. In appearance, however, it bore a strong resemblance. The buildings and homes were built the same, and most of the people dressed with the heat in mind.

The streets were paved with strong stones that were easier to traverse with wagons and carts. Some buildings got as tall as three stories, a feat that was highly impressive to Tariah and Sparkle alike, both country girls at heart. "Wow," Tariah breathed, looking skyward.

"It's really tall." Sparkle was sitting on her shoulder as she had for the last five days of walking. "Someone told me once that the cities on Spectrum have buildings as tall as six stories."

"That's amazing!" Tariah felt eyes on her and pulled her cloak tighter closed. She was wearing her hood far over her head and keeping her arms carefully covered. Still, she knew she was being stared at. Any Magi worth their salt was going to sense she was powerful. "How do Master Magi act?" she whispered.

"I think they're kind of anti-social," Sparkle whispered back. "I think you should be doing fine."

She drew a long breath and composed herself as they began working their way through the town toward the center square where the market was. Other entertainers of all kinds were present as well, showing off and trying to earn coin through free shows.

There was only one open spot left. Sparkle claimed it by making a stone stage with her power. "Okay," she said softly. "All you have to do is make the biggest and most showy and grandest displays possible."

Tariah nodded then climbed up onto the stage. Sparkle began to fly around the market. "Come one, come all!" she called. "My friend is a Master Magi and through my power of disguise I have made her look like a Chronicle! If you've ever wondered what the purest race of evil looks like, now's your chance!"

The word 'Chronicle' alone gathered attention. People immediately began to move toward the stage where Tariah stood. With a touch of defiance, she took her cloak off and dropped it on the stage beside her. Her lines blazed brilliantly in the sun and gave her already lovely features a rare and unforgettable beauty.

"This is how you recognize a Chronicle!" Sparkle flew around Tariah. "These golden lines are veins of Dragon power! According to the legends of the Kin, when a Chronicle and a Fury meet and bond as Dragoons, the Fury grows matching lines of Chronicle power. This is how they can harmonize through one another!"

Tariah was startled. She had no idea if Sparkle was blowing hot air or if she was sincere. She did know, however, that the few Kin in audience knew she truly was a Chronicle. They had little smiles on their faces as if they enjoyed seeing the Magi be fooled by their own rumors.

"What kind of powers do they have?" someone called.

"I'm glad you asked that!" Sparkle spun in the air then landed on Tariah's head. "Master Magi and Chronicles are not that different in power. Observe! My friend here has not yet entered second puberty."

"Pity," came a male voice from the back of the crowd and made everyone snicker.

Tariah was beginning to get into the spirit of things and she blew the speaker a kiss. "I'll write you a letter when I do," she called back, and it made the crowd laugh.

Sparkled giggled. She absolutely adored Tariah. "Now watch! Show them your stuff!"

Tariah let the Water well up inside her and it flowed around her feet as it became tangible. As she lifted her hands, the water flowed up her body and into the air over her hands where it began to become the shape of animals and people. Over her hands, she actually recreated the city in water.

"She's good!" a woman murmured to her friend.

"Ah but that's not all," Sparkle said as she heard the comment. She flew around the stage. "As we all know, Magi develop secondary skills while in second puberty. But Chronicles and Master Magi are different. Watch this!"

Knowing what Sparkle was asking, Tariah dissolved the city and the water flowed back down her body. Ice suddenly formed at her feet and shards began to float in the air. A gasp traveled through the crowd as they realized she had secondary skills with or without puberty. She smiled and the ice formed over her hands as a cloud that grew and surrounded the market. And then, softly, snow began to fall.

"What's that stuff?" a kid asked.

"It's called snow," another said. "Wow it's cold!"

Sparkle grinned. "And there you are! When looking for a Chronicle, this is what you're looking for!"

A Militia soldier was in the crowd and he nodded succinctly. "Your timing is good. I received word from my superiors that the rumored Chronicle in Symphony is no rumor. He or she escaped the city after killing a soldier."

A murmured panic began to run through the crowd and Tariah's heart beat hard inside her chest. She was nearly holding her breath as people began approaching the stage. But to her surprise, and relief, they simply offered the little ivory coins that served as currency on Lucksphere. "For showing us what we need to be wary of," a lady said.

As more people came forward, Sparkle quickly made a bucket from the stone and it was into that that the people tossed their coins in passing. While that occurred, a few of the children ran over to where Tariah was sitting down on the edge of the stage.

One reached out to touch the lines on her arm then smiled in delight. "They're warm!" She smiled shyly. "I think they're pretty." She and her friends hurried off before they were caught, and Tariah let out a little breath. Even if the kids thought she was fake, their words warmed her.

Within ten minutes, the crowd had thinned and gone back to observing other displays. Sparkle peered into the bucket and her eyes slowly widened. "Oh my. Tariah, look at this!"

Tariah scooted over to look inside and her eyes widened equally. The bucket was half- full of money, and someone in the crowd had tossed in a few bronze coins as well. The bronze was worth five times the value of the ivory. Tariah looked up swiftly and her eyes met those of a SunKin Elf at the back of the crowd. The Kin bowed gracefully then turned and disappeared into the crowd.

Sparkle quickly wove two bags for them to carry the money inside; she gave one to Tariah and kept the other. Both bags were on the heavy side, but it reassured them because it meant they could afford ship fare and inn stays as needed, and any supplies they could not make. Tariah could provide water, and Sparkle could make shelter, but food was something they lacked the ability to create.

"Where are you going next?" the Militia soldier asked as he approached them.

Tariah shoved her nerves down and found a casual smile. "Well, we thought we might stay here a while then go to Carnelian."

"Carnelian is a good idea," he said. "The captain is on his way to this town too. Apparently they fear the Chronicle might try and catch a boat."

Sparkle sat down on Tariah's head. "Hmm. Maybe we ought to go to Carnelian now then. Maybe we can beat them there and warn the people." Her stomach was quivering too. She had gotten the whole story out of Tariah and knew that the captain would recognize her.

"Good luck," the soldier told them with a salute. He paused a moment then noted, "You know, I didn't get your names."

"Sparkle," the Faerie offered easily.

Tariah didn't want to give her first name and said only, "Chronis."

"Well, farewell to both of you." The soldier watched them hurry off and frowned thoughtfully. The name Chronis was familiar. If he wasn't mistaken, he could have sworn it was the name of the first Chronicle on record. It was the name from which 'Chronicle' was derived. The irony was interesting.

Chapter Three

The next ship out of Harmonica was scheduled to set sail in an hour and was due to arrive at the harbor on the southern side of Carnelian in two weeks. Tariah had never been on a boat before, and she could barely hide her excitement as she followed Sparkle up the gangplank and onto the deck. The ship was as big as a large Dragon and had enough cabins for the over one hundred passengers it was carrying.

Because it had served them well before, they kept up the façade of being traveling entertainers. And, even keeping up that façade, they still kept to their own cabin almost exclusively. Because everyone thought that Tariah was a Master Magi, no one found it to be out of the ordinary.

Dinner was served every night in the restaurant on the ship. The first night out, it was a formal dinner. Upon hearing that, Tariah and Sparkle were slightly ashamed. Neither of them possessed any clothes that could possibly be considered formal, and there was no sand for Sparkle to use to make them.

"Well, damn it." Tariah sat down cross-legged on the bed. "Now what? I mean, that would take anti-social too far. We have to go, at least tonight."

"What're we supposed to do?" Sparkle asked. She was flying in agitated circles around the room. "Put on a sheet?"

"The other question is," Tariah noted, "formal by whose standards?" She pointed at her clothes. "These *are* formal by the standards I grew up with. They cover more than half my body."

Sparkle blinked then began to giggle. "You're such a desert girl."

"Watch it, woody." She flopped over onto her back and lifted her right hand to study the lines etched across the back and the symbol on her palm. She had never realized just how little the Magi knew about Chronicles despite their hatred of them. How could you hate something you knew nothing about?

Her lines began to burn and a fierce and powerful longing welled up inside her, so strong it literally brought tears to her eyes. For just a moment she thought she had felt him. She thought she had felt her Fury, and even that tiniest touch made her longing to find him worse. Her lines burned. *North.* She had to go north.

Sparkle watched the glow that rippled down Tariah's lines and saw the pained expression cross her face. Her lips tightened. She did not like seeing her friend hurt, and as long as she was on this stupid journey, she would. She knew that Chronicles of the old days had supposedly sometimes taken years or more to find their Fury, but she wanted Tariah to find hers *now*.

Someone knocked on the door and she flew over to open it. "Yes?" she asked.

One of the ship crewmembers was standing outside the door, and he had a large bag in his hands. "This was sent to you by your fellow Kin," he said. "I was asked to give it to you."

"Oh." She smiled. "Thanks!" It was hard to determine which the sender was. There were several other Kin on the ship. She thought it might be the Fire secondary SunKin Elf she had sensed. Kin could always feel one another if they walked in the same place within a short time. The bag definitely felt fiery.

The sailor put the bag down inside the door then took his leave. Sparkle shut the door, and Tariah kneeled beside the bag to open it. It promptly overflowed and pure white sand spilled onto the floor. It was freshly made and of incredible quality. Tariah's eyes widened. "Where did they get this?"

Sparkle swirled her hand in the sand softly. "She made it. She must have! That's how the best sand is made, you know? A Fire/Smoke user can break down glass into the purest grains. This is the high quality stuff, the stuff sold in cities for Soil weavers and such." She smiled at Tariah. "She's giving us her support in the best way she can."

Tariah lowered her gaze. "All of you Kin . . . you've done so much for me." Her voice broke. "I had a friend who was a MoonKin. His name was Maxim. He was a doctor in the town and he . . ." Tears slid down her cheeks. "He died to protect me."

Her Faeric friend's face darkened slowly. "Who killed him?"

"The Militia." She wiped at her eyes, unaware of Sparkle's sudden alertness. "It was just so stupid. I lost him and my parents just because they loved me. There's no reason to hate me, let alone them!" She turned, startled, as she realized Sparkle was sitting on the air and drawing shapes in the air. "What are you doing?"

"Writing to the MoonKin Elder." Her fingers glowed as she sketched and wrote in the characters that made up the Kin language. "Telling him what happened. The Militia made a big no-no. Kin are neutral. Killing one of us when we did not instigate the fight is against the boundaries of the treaty."

Tariah watched in fascination. "Kin can communicate across the world without letters?"

"These are our letters. See, we each put out a different kind of energy. It's like your lines. It's completely unique from person to person." Sparkle was still writing. "And once we meet, we can write to each other by writing with an energy that matches the person we're writing to."

"That's amazing." She scooted closer to watch, and she could see what Sparkle meant. Sparkle's power and energy always seemed, to her, to look and feel like a bunch of little dancing sparks. The energy she wrote with looked and felt like sparkly blue stars. "Can you teach me to read this?"

"Probably but it might take a while. We have over five hundred characters in our language."

"Five hundred!" She sat back. "Well." The language of the Magi only had one hundred. "That's . . . that's a lot."

"That's nothing." Sparkle stopped writing and the letter seemed to vanish into thin air with a small pop. "The Dragon language has over one thousand." She giggled and flew over to land on Tariah's stomach as her friend fell over on her back in shock. "Theirs is easier though. It's one thousand different characters instead of our five hundred that can be used in ten different ways."

Tariah put an arm over her eyes. "I'm beginning to feel like the naïve desert girl you called me."

"That's okay. You're nice, and you're smart. You learn things fast." Sparkle flew over to the bag of sand once more. "Let's make a bunch of guys really envious and annoyed that you're still not in second puberty."

Tariah considered that and decided the idea appealed to her. She sat up with a grin. "Sure. Why not?"

When they entered the restaurant for dinner, they got what they had been aiming for. Every Magi bachelor in the place stared at Tariah with a comical combination of dismay and longing. The Kin males were no less appreciative, but they were more amused than dismayed. The Faeries also made a point of indicating it was Sparkle that they had their eyes on.

Going on the assumption that formality was determined by your birthplace, both females wore what was formal from their homelands. Tariah, a desert girl, wore a dark green skirt that tied at each hip and fell open along the outside of each leg. On the top she wore a piece of matching dark green cloth that wrapped around her neck, crossed down to wrap around her bust, then continued to wrap around her in a cross pattern until her hips, where it fell in with the rest of the material. Underneath both she wore a dark gold bikini that very nearly blended in with her skin in the candlelight.

Sparkle was a forest girl. In stark contrast to desert dwellers, forested people tended to wear clothes that covered most of their bodies. Forests were both slightly cooler than average and infested with bugs that liked to nibble on exposed flesh.

Tonight, Sparkle wore a tunic the color of roses just blooming. It had a collar that she turned up rakishly to protect her neck, and the sleeves went down past her hands where they flared like rose petals. The tunic went to her knees, and underneath it she wore a matching skirt of a slightly darker color that went to her ankles. Around her tiny waist she had fastened a leather belt. She looked, very much, like a little rose with wings. And though, yes, she was slightly plump in places, it only added to her delicate loveliness.

The Faerie males were enchanted. "Hey!" one called across the room in the language of the Kin. "Read my energy!"

It was the Kin equivalent of the Magi pick-up line 'write me a letter.' After translating it for Tariah, her Chronicle friend could only snicker and take a seat at a table. Her long hair was pinned up on top of her head, and her lines were like golden ribbons as they flowed over her skin. There were many present who couldn't help but think that even if she had been a real Chronicle, she would have still been very beautiful.

Dinner passed peacefully. The entertainment for the night was a Magi storyteller, and he wove fascinating tales from even the most common of prompts. If someone told him they wanted a tale about sand, he wove a tale about a type of sand so rare and beautiful it grew like a waterfall in an oasis only seen by children.

As Tariah was enjoying her dessert, she became aware that she was being stared at. It was not an uncommon occurrence, but for some reason this gaze made her skin crawl. The power that flowed in her blood seemed to sting suddenly as if warning of danger.

She looked around with a frown. A lot of eyes were on her, but there was only curiosity or interest in their gazes. Nothing felt threatening . . . until her eyes fell on a shadowy corner of the room. Something sent a chill down her back.

There were five people sitting in the corner. All were wearing heavy white cloaks that covered their bodies entirely. The Magi chalice symbol was emblazoned largely on the back of their cloaks, and it was an unusual shade of black—the symbol was typically blue. A black dagger lay across the base of the chalice, and something about it made Tariah very nervous.

Sparkle followed her gaze and her brows drew together. "That's the Black Magi Elite," she said softly into Tariah's ear. She was sitting on her friend's shoulder in an effort to avoid ordering dessert and getting pudgier; sweets went right to her waist and hips, dang it. "They're really powerful Magi that travel the world looking for more to join them. I think they're trying to get recognized as their own race or culture, but they're no different from other Magi, except for their power."

Tariah frowned. "I don't like them."

"Few do. They're really, well, *elite*. They snub anyone who is less than they are." She looked longingly at the custard Tariah was eating. "Just a bite?" she asked.

"No." Tariah smiled and took a bite herself. "You're on a diet, remember?" Still, even with the distraction, she couldn't help but feel a chill along her power. She was disguised as a Master Magi, and the Elite were watching her. Though she might have assumed she would be safe with them, something about them terrified her.

Time passed slowly on a boat, she discovered, as the first week drew to an end. There was not much to actually do on a cruise. At least, not much that she wanted to do. There were games and entertainment and all manner of activities for the passengers, but none of it interested her. She was a Water Chronicle, but she missed her desert. She missed the stark sands and the hot sun. She missed her life.

With another week looming in front of her, she began to get bored. In her boredom, she began to experiment with her powers. She was working on learning to manipulate her ice as easily as she did her water. She had the freedom to do it now, so she went ahead and practiced. She wanted to be able to make cities of ice that were more real than reality itself.

She was enough busy with her shaping that she didn't notice the glow in the room at first. When it did trigger, she turned her head and saw that there were symbols appearing in the air. Since Sparkle wasn't present, she could only assume it was a letter. It was definitely Kin language. "Whoops!"

She quickly hurried out of the cabin and up to the top deck where Sparkle was visiting with one of her fellow SunKin. Tariah promptly grinned when she saw the scene. Since flirtations tended to be a bit universal, she was pretty sure she wasn't wrong that the handsome male Faerie was smitten with her friend. He was hovering much closer than was polite, and Sparkle was giggling. "Am I interrupting?" she asked as she approached.

"Chronis!" Sparkle beamed at her and hoped her cheeks weren't as flushed as they felt. Daylar was one of the handsomest Faeries around, and he was *flirting* with her. Her, of all people! By Kin standards, she was actually kind of plain. "You're not interrupting at all," she told Tariah.

Daylar grinned. "Yes, she is." He touched his wings and bowed gracefully in a sign of respect. "Daylar, Air secondary SunKin Faerie at your service. You are Sparkle's friend?"

She smiled. "Last I checked I was." She really liked him. He was quite handsome, even by Magi standards, and his wings were like wispy clouds. The light in his eyes underlined his cheerful spirit. "Are you flirting with my partner?"

"I might be." He studied her intently and was not disappointed to realize she was indeed a genuine Chronicle instead of merely the pretender she professed to be. Word had traveled fast among the Kin about the rumors of a Chronicle. He would make sure the rumors were confirmed with his kind so that they knew to watch for her. "Are you here to take her away and break my heart?"

"I'm afraid I am," she apologized. "She has a letter waiting for her." She drew her thumb over her cheek and nose in the Magi sign of respect. "Come visit any time."

Sparkle knew she was blushing even more as she landed on Tariah's shoulder to return to their cabin. "It was nothing!" she announced. "He was just flirting with me. He does that. Daylar's one of the handsomest Kin around. He wouldn't be flirting with me."

Tariah covered a smile. "Sparkle, you're nervous."

"I am not!"

"Yes, you are. You're chattering, and you're contradicting yourself." She linked her hands behind her back. "I liked him. And despite the fact that you 'might be a little pudgy,' you're cute as a button."

"Oh."

She opened their cabin door to let Sparkle fly inside and then shut and locked it behind them. The letter was still waiting, and she followed Sparkle curiously. The Faerie sat down on the air and began to read. After a few moments, the letter rippled and different writing appeared. Tariah wondered if it was like a second page.

A few more pages later, the letter disappeared completely. Sparkle drummed her fingers on her arm thoughtfully. "See," she said, "I wrote the MoonKin Elder and told him about Maxim. Apparently the Militia contacted them and said you were the one who did it."

Tariah bristled. "That's outrageous!"

"That's what the Elder had thought, and my letter confirmed it. He and the SunKin Elder have conferred and want me to bring you to the mainland for the Kin. If they offer formal sanctuary, then the Militia can't touch you there." She looked at Tariah. "Maybe we can keep you safe long enough to contact the Dragons. Seems they've had no luck so far. It's summer. They very rarely leave their lands at all during summer."

Tariah let out a long breath. Though her lines burned and urged her north, something equally told her that it would be good to go to the Kin homeland known as Kindred. It was a series of islands around the edge of Carnelian. It was not really a deviation from their current heading. It just meant they would have to catch another boat at the harbor and go back out into the ocean for a while. "Okay," she said. "Let's go. Seems like everything I do is by instinct these days, and at least among the Kin I would feel safe for once."

Sparkle flew over to hug her. "You've just got to promise to either let me visit, or come visit me, once you've become a Dragoon and are living with the Dragons."

"You have a deal." Tariah hugged her in return then looked at the door as there was a light knock. "Who is it?" she called as she got to her feet.

"I am of the Elite." The voice was male and emotionless. "I wish to speak with the Magi known as Chronis."

Tariah and Sparkle exchanged a frown then Tariah walked over and eased the door open a crack. "I am she."

"My name is Soh." The man pulled down the hood on his robe to reveal a grizzled face and deeply set brown eyes. His beard and mustache were the same gray and black as his hair, and his skin looked like tough leather from exposure to the sun without proper care.

There was nothing unappealing about him, and nothing remarkable. But Tariah felt her power stinging again and sensed danger. "Hello, Soh," she said formally. "What can I help you with?"

"I wish to speak with you of joining the Black Magi Elite." His eyes held a sharp gleam that could have been power, intelligence, or madness. It could have been a frightening combination of all three. "You would do well in our ranks, young Chronis. We need power such as yours."

She summoned up a kind smile even though her stomach was jittery. "I thank you, but I am just a traveling entertainer. I don't really like belonging to any group. Your offer is gracious but I decline."

"I will ask again later." He bowed and walked away.

She shut the door quickly and let out a soft breath. "That's bad, isn't it?"

Sparkle nodded slowly. "I get the sneaking feeling it is. We better get to the Kin, and fast. The Elite come and go from there, but they would not dare touch you under our protection."

The next day another Elite member came to speak with Tariah. She gave her the same response. On the following day it was a third member. On the fourth it was the next. On the fifth day, Tariah spent most of her time staring at the door and waiting. She knew damned well that they would try again. The Elite was clearly not used to being turned down.

They were only a few days out of Carnelian's port town. They would be docking in two days if the weather held. It didn't seem likely at the moment. The sea was dark and turbulent and the sky was covered with clouds. Lightning rippled across their base. The waves were choppy but relatively stable for the time being.

The knock on the door made both females jump slightly. Composing herself, Tariah opened the door. "Yes?" she asked.

It was Soh. The gleam in his eyes at that moment was more madness than intelligence, and it sent chills down her back. "Why do you refuse us, Tariah Chronis? Do you think you will be safe among the Magi?"

Her back stiffened. "How did you learn that?" she hissed softly. Anger began to mingle with her fear, and ice shards sparkled in the air threateningly. "Tell me!"

He laughed nastily and held up a pair of wings between his fingers. They were covered with gold blood but very recognizable with their cloudy, wispy shape. "He didn't want to tell me willingly. But he did eventually tell."

Sparkle went white. "Daylar!" She shot through the air past Soh and down the halls, shouting Daylar's name in the language of the Kin.

Fury bubbled under Tariah's skin so hard that the ice condensed. The ocean waters around them began to grow more violent. Storms on Lucksphere always seemed to be like a living creature, and they fed off the power of anyone they touched. "You bastard," she said thinly. "For this alone I will never join the Elite!"

She took off down the hall to help Sparkle find Daylar, and Soh shouted behind her, "How many more Kin will die because of you, Tariah Chronis? Eventually even they will grow to hate you!"

She ignored him and followed Sparkle's trail as it wound around the ship toward the deck. The entire boat was shaking and shuddering as the storm opened almost over their heads. Though she had cut it off, her power had been enough to bring the storm to the forefront. The crew was ordering everyone to their cabins and preparing to battle the waves.

She found Sparkle on the deck, and the Faerie was desperately dragging at some crates thrice her size. "He's behind here!" she shouted. "I hear him! Tariah, help me!"

Tariah lent her strength, and they dragged at the boxes until they moved aside. Tariah swiftly knelt and scooped up the prone form that lay behind them. He was covered in bruises, and golden blood seeped from the wounds on his back, but he was still alive. "Daylar!" she said softly. "Can you hear me?"

His eyes opened and he managed a little smile. "I'm sorry, Tariah."

"No, don't be!" She looked at Sparkle. "How can we heal him?"

Tears ran down Sparkle's face. "We can't. Not without wings. Our bodies can't heal without them. It's like ripping out your heart." Her stomach churned for a moment then her back straightened and she clenched her hands into fists at her sides. "Take mine. Take two of my wings and give them to him."

Tariah's breath stopped. "Sparkle . . ."

"Don't," Daylar whispered. "Not for me, Sparky."

"Yes!" Sparkle's knuckles were almost white and tears burned her eyes. "He won't win! I won't let him!" She took his hand and held it to her cheek. "I'm sorry you got involved," she whispered. "This is the least I can do. Please, accept my wings, if you can."

Understanding filled Tariah. More than her wings, Sparkle was offering her heart. She had said it herself. A Kin's wings *were* their heart. Tariah held her breath as she waited for the answer. She loathed the idea of hurting her friend, but she loathed even more the idea that Daylar would die. He was guilty only of liking Sparkle and befriending Tariah.

"Okay," he finally said. His eyes closed as a little smile curved his lips. "Now at least I will have an excuse to stick around you."

"Idiot. You didn't need one." Sparkle let go of his hand and turned to Tariah. "Please. Take my top two wings and put them on his back. It's that easy."

"Easy!" Tariah swiped away her tears with her free hand. "Damn it, if both of you die, I'll be pissed!" She set Daylar down on her lap then gently grasped Sparkle with one hand. Before she could tell herself not to, she grasped her friend's top two wings and pulled. They were shockingly easy to remove, and they came off as easily as pulling petals from a flower.

Golden blood welled and began to flow, but Sparkle's other wings glowed and began to creep up her back to seal the wound. Her stomach churning, Tariah took the two wings and pressed them against Daylar's back. She had no idea what she was doing, but it proved to be the right thing. Light flared with an odd sound, and the wings were jerked from her fingers as they attached to his back. The blood flow began to stop.

She gathered both Kin in her arms protectively and lurched to her feet as the boat shuddered wildly. Staying was out of the question with the Elite still there. She looked around desperately, and she thought she saw the outline of an island to the west. It had to be either an outpost or a part of Kindred. With her powers, they might make it. She ran swiftly to the edge of the railing and climbed on top.

"Tariah Chronis!" Soh shouted behind her. "There is nowhere your kind belongs except with the Elite!"

She shot him a look over her shoulder out of glittering silver eyes. "I belong with my Fury, wherever he may be!" she shouted back. "And not you, or anyone else, is ever going to keep me from finding him!" Holding tight to her two precious companions, she dove over the side of the ship and into the waiting ocean. There was no going back now.

Chapter Four

With the turbulence of the storm above the surface, the best thing Tariah could do was use her powers to encase herself and the two Kin inside a bubble that would allow them to breathe underwater.

She let go of them only long enough to rip strips of material from the bottom of her leggings and turn them into shorts. She tied the strips together into a long loop then wrapped it around her body crosswise like a sling. Gently she tucked the two Kin into it so that she had her hands free.

Once they were secured, she shrank the bubble down to just the two Kin. It gave her the freedom to start swimming, which she was surprisingly good at despite living in the desert. Few Water elements didn't find a way to learn how to swim considering how much time they spent in water.

She stayed five feet under the surface. It protected her from the storm but allowed her to rise easily if she needed. She could only curse herself mentally; the storm wouldn't have even gotten that bad if it hadn't grabbed her power.

After half an hour of swimming, she was tired. She rose to the surface to rest, and she saw that the ship was nowhere in sight. The island she was aiming for still seemed like a line on the horizon.

"Tariah?" Sparkle whispered.

She looked down swiftly to see Daylar also looking up at her blearily. "It's okay. Go back to sleep." She hugged both Kin gently and only loosened her grip when she saw they were asleep once more. Both were very pale, and even their tattoos were dull. Fury churned inside her heart. If she got her hands on Soh, she was going to rip his arms off.

She rested for a few more moments before swimming again. The storm had lessened finally, but it still lingered. She didn't dare use her powers to make them move faster; the storm would drink them up faster than a thirsty desert madman.

She lost track of time. The clouds overhead made it impossible to tell what time of day it was. Exhaustion tugged at her ankles but she kept going. If she fell asleep, the bubble on the Kin would disappear. She swam as long as she could and floated to rest. She didn't let herself think about anything except reaching safety.

The island steadily grew bigger and bigger. She was finally able to see the edge of the beach and the darker line behind it that indicated trees. If she looked to her right, she was able to see an even longer and far fainter line on the horizon. Her vague memory of the maps she had seen told her she was approaching either Kindred or Carnelian and the other was the line in the distance. Size told her she was likely closer to Kindred, and she really wanted to be right.

More time slipped past. She didn't know how long she had been swimming. A day? It had to have been at least that. She was finally less than a mile from the island. The storm had eased entirely and the clouds had dispersed. It was nighttime, and it would have been horribly dark if two of the four moons hadn't been full.

The beach was a strip of white and the trees beyond were an ominous, dark shape. They were very big, and she thought they might be nearly as tall as her cliffs back home. Through them, even at this distance, she could see the lights that indicated a village lay ahead.

Encouragement brought a surge of strength to let her keep swimming. Her muscles were aching. She was thirsty, hungry, and so tired that her eyes were blurry. If she managed to get to safety, she was going to sleep for days. It felt like she hadn't slept well in weeks.

When she was finally able to put her feet down and walk out of the waves, relief made her lightheaded and she stumbled up the shore. She fell to her knees on the sand and stared blindly at the distance. Daylar stirred slightly and asked faintly, "Are we safe?"

"I think we are. Stop talking and rest." She lay down on the sand and closed her eyes. She just needed a few moments to rest before making her way to the village. She could sense Light and Dark power and knew that there were more Kin than Magi around. She was safe enough.

When she opened her eyes the next time, she was staring at a wooden mobile turning slowly over her head. It was clearly carved by a Soil/Wood master for each wooden animal seemed real enough to come to life.

She was lying on a soft bed and there were warm blankets tucked around her. She was completely naked, but that didn't wholly surprise her. After everything that had happened, her clothes had been wrecked. She held the blankets to her chest and sat up to look around.

It looked like either a guestroom or an inn room. Nothing spectacular made it stand out, and there were no indications that anyone had personalized it with their power. Daylight poured in the open window and filled the room with light and warmth. Beyond the window, she could hear the sounds of a village busily at work.

Realizing that she couldn't sense Sparkle or Daylar, she looked around swiftly. There was no sign of them. She swathed the blanket around herself like a dress and got out of bed. She hurried over to the door, but as she was reaching for the knob, it was opened into the hall. A slender SunKin Elf with arms full of clothes stood on the other side. "Oh!" The Kin smiled, her blue eyes sparkling. "You're awake now."

"Yes." Tariah clutched the blanket closer. "Where are Sparkle and Daylar?" she asked urgently. "Are they alright? Please, tell me!"

"They are fine," the Kin assured her. "Both are recovering nicely. Sparkle woke and was able to tell us everything that happened. Daylar's body is adapting just fine to her wings." She smiled. "Sparkle can't believe that he loves her, but it's very obvious."

Tariah found a smile as relief made her feel lightheaded. She was more than willing to let the Kin escort her back to the bed so she could sit down. "She seems to think that because he's handsome that he wouldn't be interested in her. But she's the sweetest person I've ever known."

"She is, at that." The Kin set down the clothes she was carrying. "I am Rumidia, a SunKin Elf, Fire secondary."

"Tariah Chronis." She hesitated for a moment then said softly, "A Water Chronicle."

Rumidia stepped back and studied her critically. The young Chronicle was surprisingly lovely, especially with her Chronicle lines swirling over nearly a third of her body. Rumidia wasn't used to seeing such short Magi, but she was delighted nonetheless. Kin Elves were on the shorter side as well. Few were ever over five-six in height. "I'm glad to meet you."

Tariah looked down at her hands. "Even though it was my existence that resulted in Maxim's death, and nearly in Daylar's as well?" she whispered. "Soh was right about that. If you all keep protecting me . . ."

Rumidia propped her hands on her hips and tossed her blue-black hair out of her eyes. Her sharply pointed ears quivered as a sure sign of her anger. Kin Faeries were marked by their wings. Kin Elves were marked by their ears. Rumidia's happened to be the ears of a feline, and they acted as such by showing her displeasure. "Now look here, little one," she scolded, "Soh is a fool. Moreover, the Magi are to blame for trying to kill you. We Kin stand up for those being wronged."

Tariah digested that. Then, "Okay. And . . . thank you."

The door flew open with a bang. "Tariah!" Sparkle shot into the room like a little bullet and plowed into Tariah with enough force that she almost managed to knock her back. "Tariah! You're awake!" Sparkle was crying as she clung onto her neck. "I was so scared! You didn't wake up for three days!"

"Three!" Tariah's eyes widened. "I was more tired than I thought." She eased her friend back and held her on her palms to study her.

Sparkle's tattoos were still slightly faded, indicating she was recovering, but her wings seemed to have settled fully into their new position. They were currently folded against her back and there were bandages wrapped around her body to keep them in place. There were no bloodstains, thankfully. Either they had stopped bleeding or they were well padded.

Tariah asked, "Faeries can fly without wings?"

Sparkle nodded and wiped at her eyes. "For small distances. We use our Light or Dark powers for it." She hovered woozily over to Tariah's shoulder and sat down. She was dressed in a loose sleeping gown and she almost slid off her friend's shoulder. To anchor herself, she wrapped a lock of Tariah's hair around her waist. "Want to see Daylar?"

Tariah smiled. "Yes, very much so!" She looked down suddenly. "But, er, first I want clothes."

Rumidia chuckled. "As we assumed you might." She gestured to the clothes she had set down. "You're not acclimated for the forest, desert child. You'll want to wear some of our style of clothing in order to protect your skin and to keep you warm."

Tariah studied the clothes in resignation. "I figured you'd say that," she said on a sigh. As Rumidia left the room, she gently put Sparkle down on the bed. She walked over to where the clothes were waiting. She would just have to learn to adjust.

The clothing consisted of sturdy cloth leggings and a snug cloth tunic that clung to every inch of her body from her neck to her wrists. The collar came up around her neck but there were diamond patches of skin visible on her shoulders where the material was deliberately not sewn together. To go underneath the clothing was a matching cloth bikini specially designed to help keep her warm and support her figure.

Sparkle was delighted as she saw how her friend looked. "Wow! You look really pretty in our clothes!" She saw Tariah preparing to braid her hair and swiftly hovered over and grabbed onto the brown locks. "No! Leave it down! I like it!"

"It gets in my way." Tariah plucked the Faerie out of her hair and set her on the table. As a compromise, she braided the thickest part of her hair down her back but left several locks in the front loose. "There, better?"

Sparkle hovered over to land on her shoulder and wrapped herself in Tariah's hair happily. "Yup!"

Tariah just shook her head slightly and left the room. She was definitely at the inn, she saw, so she headed for the stairs down to the bottom floor. Rumidia was behind the desk and waved cheerfully as the two partners headed outside into the cool morning sunlight.

Tariah immediately shivered. The air wasn't strictly cold, but it was vastly cooler than she was used to feeling. She crossed her arms around herself tightly, then looked up in surprise as a MoonKin Elf draped a cloak around her shoulders. "Oh! Thank you."

The man smiled. "It's not a problem. We've gone to a lot of trouble to keep you alive. We don't want you getting sick." He headed off toward the woods with a whistle, an axe propped on his shoulder as if there was nothing at all unusual in having a Chronicle in his village.

She slowly looked around. It was hard to determine the size of the village because of the way it was settled in and around so many trees, but an instinctive sense of the area and the feel of the power told her that it had to be at least the size of Symphony. The buildings were made of stone and wood, and the ground was covered with lush grass while the roads were hard packed dirt.

Trees loomed everywhere, towering high in the sky to touch the clouds. Sunlight filtered down through them hazily and cast sunbeams everywhere. Kin walked and worked everywhere, in shops and in homes, Faerie and Elf alike. This part of the village was almost predominately SunKin, something that made her ask, "Do the MoonKin live in the more shadowy parts of the woods?"

"Yeah." Sparkle smiled. "Since their power is Dark, they like the shadows more, just like we're Light and like the sun more." She studied Tariah. "You're Magi raised. Do you know what Light and Dark are?"

"Vaguely." She began to walk down the road, slowly taking everything in. "I remember in school that they said Light encompassed both elements of Water and Air, and Dark encompassed both elements of Fire and Soil. Seems sort of simplistic, especially since you all do still learn the four elements, regardless of your primary element, and some even learn secondary. Or tertiary as it may be."

Sparkle nodded sagely. "To be literal, Light is the element of the sun and Dark is the element of the moon. *Technically* you could say they encompass the other elements since Dark basically works like Soil and Fire, and Light like Air and Water, but they're not actually the same thing. They have a similar application in use, though Light and Dark are a lot more in-depth and powerful. Like, as a Light primary, I could use really powerful destructive blasts. And the MoonKin are *really* strong healers. They can almost raise the dead. Ah, turn here!" she added.

29

Tariah obligingly turned and headed down the road her friend indicated. She could see now where they were going; there was a large building ahead with the universally recognized white water drop that indicated a place of healing. "It's sad," she remarked. "I'm learning more about Kin than I even know about myself as a Chronicle."

"Elder Juniper said he would be willing to talk to you," Sparkle noted. "He's been around a really long time and might know more about what you are."

"Sparkle!" a MoonKin Faerie scolded from the doorway. He was hovering in mid-air, his gray dove wings holding him aloft. His soft dark ruby skin was lightly covered with the silver markings of his race, and his hands were propped on his hips. "I told you not to wander off."

Sparkle ducked down behind Tariah's shoulder and hid in her hair. "But, but, I wanted to find Tariah! She was worried about me too."

The Kin sighed. "You're three and you act like this still."

Tariah's brows went up through her bangs. "Three?"

"Well, by Magi standards." Sparkle smiled. "Faeries of either Kin blood mature really fast for our first two years then age really slowly from there on. Elves of either Kin blood mature really slowly in the beginning, but once they're like fifty or something they age at a normal rate. So, you at twenty are the equivalent to a two or three year old Faerie and a fifty to sixty year old Elf."

The MoonKin smiled and bowed. "I'm ten myself. I suppose I'm not *that* much older than Sparkle." He waved a finger at Sparkle. "I'm still your doctor! Get in there, right now, missy."

She sighed. "Yes sir." She hovered through the air woozily then disappeared into the building.

Tariah looked at the doctor and smiled before lifting a hand and drawing her thumb over her cheek and nose. "Warm greetings," she said. "I am Tariah Chronis, a Water Chronicle." It was getting easier to say, she noticed with some surprise.

The Kin smiled and folded his wings around himself as he bowed in an equal sign of respect. "Warm greetings, young Chronicle. I am Poplar, an Air secondary MoonKin Faerie. I am also one of the doctors for this town." He flew over to land on her shoulder gracefully. "I'm glad to see you are well."

"I'm more glad that Sparkle and Daylar are well," she countered. She smiled. "May I see Daylar?"

"Naturally." He flew off her shoulder and into the building. As she followed, he headed for the next floor down, leaving a little trail of energy that she was able to follow easily.

The intensive care room was located under the main floor. It was a place that had been specially built to block outside energies and majiks from getting inside and interfering with those who were badly wounded or sick.

Sparkle was sitting on the side of a Faerie-sized bed and sulking as a SunKin Elf checked her temperature. She was sulking because checking someone's temperature meant that another person of like element had to surround the patient with their power and it tended to cause an either uncomfortable or stuffy sensation. It was the only accurate reading possible though since, as an example, Fire elements tended to always be on the warm side.

Daylar was also sitting up on a bed and he was also wearing a sleeping gown. His new wings were folded against his back and bandages were wrapped around him as well. His markings were even paler than Sparkle's, but his eyes were full of plenty of liveliness. The fist around Tariah's heart eased as she saw that he would be fine.

He spotted her and brightened. "Tariah!" He waved his hands at her happily. "Guess what!"

She walked over and knelt beside him. "What?" she asked with a smile.

"Sparkle's going to bind her energy to mine!"

Sparkle gave a gasp. "You tattletale!" She shot over to him and poked him repeatedly in the chest. "I was going to tell her! You promised not to blab! Dang it, she was my friend first and I wanted to tell her!"

Tariah tilted her head. "Bind your energy?"

Poplar was smiling as he flew over to land on her shoulder. "You Magi refer to it as 'linking your elements.'"

She began to smile as delight spread through her heart. To link your element to someone was to tie your life to them for eternity. "Oh that's great!" She scooped up both Kin to hug them gently. "I'm glad that something good happened from all this," she said softly, but fiercely.

"I'd have convinced her eventually anyway," Daylar said confidently, his brown eyes twinkling merrily. "But now she *has* to believe me that I love her." He pointed over his shoulder to the wings. "If I didn't, my body would have rejected her wings."

Sparkle was blushing. "I think you're crazy."

"Probably."

Tariah nuzzled both with her nose and made them laugh and giggle. "You're both crazy but I'm very glad you're my friends. Daylar . . ." She held him on her palm and lifted him to eye level. He was only an inch or two taller than Sparkle so he was still only around a foot in height. "I truly am sorry. I promise, I'll make Soh pay."

He shook his head. "As long as you find your Fury, I'll consider us even." He thought about it then amended, "No, actually, I won't. You have to come back and give me and Sparkle a ride on a Dragon's back. *Then* it'll be even."

She smiled. "Deal."

"Okay, that's enough," Poplar scolded them all. "You two need rest, and Tariah has a meeting with the Elder. Let's go." He ushered both Kin back over to their beds. "Stay put or I'll have you tied down. I want another day of rest from both of you, at the least!"

"Yes sir," the soon-to-be-couple obediently chorused.

Tariah covered a grin and hurried from the room before she started laughing. Once back outside she gave a long stretch with her hands over her head. She was still going to drown Soh if she found him, but she'd make sure it was quicker since it was nice to see Daylar and Sparkle happy.

With a little help from a few Kin, she was shortly on the path that headed to the Elder's house. She had to assume he was expecting her since both Sparkle and Poplar had said he wanted to talk to her. She was nervous. Despite what the others said, she couldn't help but feel a lingering guilt for everything she had caused.

The Elder was waiting for her on the front step of his home. He was an average sized SunKin Elf, possibly only an inch or two taller than Tariah, and his hair and eyes

31

were matching yellow. His skin was pale blue and the gold markings sparkled in the sun. He looked young in appearance, as most Kin did, but his eyes spoke of many years.

He studied Tariah as she stopped in front of him. He was not displeased with what he saw. She was both lovely and strong, and her power was so strong that one could nearly taste it. Her Chronicle lines were vivid against her skin, a sure sign that her Fury did exist in this world at this very moment. "Welcome, Tariah Chronis, Water Chronicle." He touched the finned ears on his head as an Elf sign of respect. "I am Elder Juniper, an Air secondary SunKin Elf."

She returned the gesture of respect. "Warm greetings, Elder. You wished to speak with me?"

"Come inside, my dear." He held the door for her before following her inside.

She liked the interior immediately. It was warm and cozy, filled with wooden furniture and soft cushions everywhere. It was also much warmer than the outdoors. She loved everything she'd seen of Kindred, but she missed the heat of her deserts. "What did you wish to speak of?" she asked.

He took a seat and gestured to the one across from him. When she had also sat down, he leaned back in his chair and crossed his arms comfortably. "Well," he began, "there are many things. To begin with, I wish to know of Maxim. The MoonKin Elder, Sage, and I have discussed what the Militia told us as well as what Sparkle brought to our attention. I want your side."

Her hands clenched together in her lap. "Maxim was a doctor in Symphony. He was my friend. When the Militia came looking for a Chronicle because of some rumors, he and my parents wanted me to escape. A soldier overheard us and just . . ." A tear slid down her cheek. "Just stabbed him from behind. Like it was nothing. His only crime was protecting me." She swiped at her eyes. "They wanted me to run, to escape. So I did. And I'm going to live." Her eyes glittered fiercely. "If only because people died to see that I do." She looked at the Elder. "Why? Why do the Magi hate Chronicles?"

"Jealousy." He sighed quietly. "I am old, my dear. Not old enough to remember the Chronicle War, but my father had fought then. He spoke of it to me. So, too, have others spoken. We Kin keep detailed records, especially of times and people lost."

"Then tell me, please." She met his eyes. "Tell me what I am, and where I am from." "Very well." He sat forward. "No one knows," he began, "the exact reason or place Chronicles and Furies come from. It just happened one day, a few thousand years ago, that a set of Magi twins developed lines on their bodies during first puberty and were capable of using secondary elements as well. No one really thought much of it. But at the same time, in the Dragon race, another anomaly was occurring. What do you know of Dragons?"

"Not much."

"I see. Well, at that time, the Dragon race lived mostly on their island. About half of the race are known as Dragon Lords because they can take a shape other than their natural one; shapes such as a Kin or Magi form. These Lords primarily lived and walked among Magi. But then two Dragon Lords discovered that they could use secondary elemental skills from first puberty."

Her eyes widened. "Like Chronicles."

"Precisely. The Dragons dubbed these Lords 'Fury' because it is a word in Draconic that means 'evolution', which is what they assumed they were. Well, long story short, when the twins encountered the Lords, something happened. The Furies developed lines that matched their Chronicle, and the two formed a bond that was even deeper than a Linked couple. The Chronicle could use the Fury's majiks as their own, and the Furies could use their Chronicle's ability to manipulate the same. They completed one another. We have always assumed it was the lines."

She touched the lines on her face softly. "So these *are* lines of Dragon power. And they gain lines of Chronicle power."

"We believe so." He closed his eyes. "In honor of the twins who were known as Chronis, the new Magi were called Chronicles." He smiled and opened his eyes when he felt her surprise. "We do not know if you are related, but it is certainly coincidental."

"I'd say."

Continuing, he said, "For a few thousand years everything was fine. There came to be many Chronicles and Furies. About the time of second puberty for the Chronicle, they would be driven to seek their Fury somewhere in the world. Their lines would lead them for their lines contained the power of their Fury. These lines would act as a map and take them to their final destination, wherever it may be. It was usually wherever the Fury was."

"They could not seek us?"

"No. They know when their Chronicle is born and when they die, but they do not know where they are until they have bonded as Dragoons." He smiled, sensing the next question. "A Dragoon is the name for a Fury or Chronicle when they bond." He got to his feet and walked over to the window. "About a thousand years ago, the Magi began to show their jealousy. Chronicles were, after all, more powerful and more advanced. They were also, once bonded to their Fury, immortal.

"Magi began to spread rumors that Chronicles were hosts and Furies were parasites. You see, in exchange for the share of majiks, Furies needed to feed on their Chronicle's power. That was the other difference between a Fury and a normal Dragon Lord. A Fury has only a set amount of power and must therefore feed from a Chronicle who, unlike Magi, has nearly limitless power.

"In either case, warfare eventually broke out. The Chronicles were driven into hiding. And, eventually, they were slaughtered. In the years since, they have been killed upon discovery. Any Fury that feels their Chronicle die . . . well, Dragons are immortal. Rather than suffer endlessly, the Fury is mercifully released of this life."

There was silence as he finished speaking. Tariah had hundreds of questions but she did not ask them. She knew they were questions the Elder could never answer. To understand, she would have to find her Fury and get her answers firsthand. More than ever she felt the burning of her lines. *North.* She still had to go north.

"We have tried to contact the Dragons," Juniper suddenly said as he turned around. "To tell them we have a Chronicle. But after the slaughter of the Chronicles a thousand years ago, even the Dragon Lords stay mostly on their island. Especially during summer, the time when most Magi enter first and second puberties, and the Militia is sharp to find Chronicles. The Lords know they could never find their Chronicle before they are killed."

"The Magi are the only ones not suffering over this," she whispered. "It's so unfair." "You would seek vengeance on them?" he asked softly.

"Of course not!" She shot to her feet indignantly. "I don't care what they do as long as I can live how I want. Chronicles and Furies are normal parts of evolution. If we weren't, we wouldn't still appear! The Magi will have to deal with it!"

He nodded. "As long as you hold to that feeling, the Kin will aide you."

There was a knock on the door and a SunKin Faerie flew in. "Elder," she said, "there is a soldier from the Militia here. Rumor reached them that we are sheltering a Chronicle."

Tariah took a sharp breath and Juniper gently touched her shoulder as he went past. "The Militia would not dare do anything to us. We may not outnumber them, but we far exceed them in power. Moreover, it would upset the balance of the land and destroy many islands, as it did before the treaty."

She followed him even though she would rather have hidden. "Is that why there is a treaty at all?"

"Precisely. The Magi decided that they wanted to get rid of the Kin to take their land. In the destruction of so many Kin, the land was sunk. We lost many more before the Magi got smart and offered a treaty." He smiled. "So, you see, you are quite safe with us. Go rest, my dear."

She reluctantly went back to the inn but she waited anxiously for word as to what would happen. As evening was settling, she heard voices downstairs and snuck down to listen. Rumidia was talking with Poplar, and she hoped one or the other knew what was going on. She did not want to be the cause of more death.

"So the Militia knows we have Tariah," Rumidia murmured. "And what can they do about it?"

"They're going to station soldiers at every port and city. If she even goes near it she will be killed." Poplar's voice reflected his disgust. "They hope to keep her from following her lines and finding her Fury. They won't succeed."

"What about a formal offer of sanctuary?" she wondered. "If we make her honorary Kin, the Magi don't dare touch her at all."

"Juniper and Sage are discussing it as we speak. They're also sending word out to every Kin on Magi lands. We want everyone looking for the Dragons. If we can find even one, then we can get Tariah to their island where she can surely find her Fury. On the isle, she should be free. There's just one catch."

"What's that?"

"Well, the Militia have made it plain that if a Kin is caught assisting Tariah on Magi lands, they will consider it a breach of treaty. And we both know what that means."

Her voice went flat. "Death to the one breaching. They can't just manipulate the treaty however they like!"

"Until we make Tariah an honorary Kin, they can. But finding a Kin who can mark a Chronicle is nearly impossible because of their lines." He sighed. "We'll just have to do whatever we can."

Her throat tight, Tariah went back upstairs. So she couldn't go to Magi land. That was fine. She would find her Fury herself. She would find the Isle of Dragons on her own. She was a Water element. She could survive on the ocean. She was sure of it.

She waited until it was dark. Once the village was quiet, she snuck out of the inn and to the docks. She left a few coins for apology then untied a small boat and began to sail it out into the ocean. Her lines were burning so she couldn't feel that this was wrong. She was tired of always needing to be protected. She was tired of the stupid jealousy and fear that was driving the Magi. And most of all, she was tired of following anyone's whims but her own.

She would find the damned isle by herself, and then she was going to give her Fury a piece of her mind for not looking for her when he had felt she was alive more than a few hours!

Chapter Five

Dominic Whisperer was a Fire element Dragon. Or, at least, that was the appearance that he let the rest of the world see, though any Kin who met him sensed the truth. Dominic was a Fury.

He had been hatched by his parents, both Fire element Dragon Lords, nearly three centuries before. Like most other beings of the element Fire, regardless of race, he was fierce and protective and very quick to temper. It was matched by a deep loyalty and sense of life that made him loved by his entire race.

When he had entered first puberty (an occurrence that came around the age of one hundred for Dragons), many females who had been waiting with their hopes held for him to eventually reach second puberty had found those same hopes dashed. Dominic had not just developed Fire powers, but he had also developed Smoke and shown his Fury blood.

It was a grim and cruel fate for Dominic. Not only did he have to watch his majiks usage for fear of draining it too low, but there was no telling when his Chronicle would be born. Once he felt her birth, it would be a ticking time bomb to the day when she would be killed and Dominic himself would need to be put out of his misery.

As he studied a window display in a large city on the main Magi continent of Spectrum, he smiled wryly to himself. He had felt his Chronicle's birth over twenty years ago. Either she was an exceptionally slow bloomer, or something had occurred to keep her alive.

It hurt. Oh, did it hurt. There were times when he would feel his throat close and his heart clench and his eyes burn with the overwhelming longing to find the one person who would understand him. The one person who would love him no matter what he did. But unlike Chronicles, Furies were not given the ability to track their chosen partner. He had tried. For the last ten years he had been trying. And he could not find her.

It was summer now. Summer was the time when nearly all races would begin first or second puberty. He had grown to loathe the summer. Each time it arrived he felt as if he was waiting with his breath held for his world to fall apart. And then, when summer was over, there was always the lingering despair that perhaps his Chronicle was hiding her identity and being forced to live a lie. That, more than anything, broke his heart.

Prismatic was the capital of the Magi continent Spectrum. It was the capital of the entire race and by far the biggest city. It was nearly twenty miles in size, not including farmlands, and boasted a population of nearly two hundred thousand. It was the Magi center and the source of the most commerce and trade.

It was situated in the middle of the desert and well isolated from even the next closest town, some two hundred miles away. Dominic liked Prismatic if only because it allowed him to disappear in the crowds. Like Kin, Dragons could not hide their heritage. Though Dominic could walk in the form of a Magi, his hair was black with red streaks. The streaks were the mark of his Dragon blood.

Well past even second puberty, he wasn't worried that any Magi would ever know he was a Fury. He had no idea how they would react, and he wasn't particularly interested in finding out. He did not hate the Magi for what they had done, but he sure as hell did not trust them.

As he was passing some women gossiping on the corner, he very nearly ignored them entirely. But as he was going around the corner of a store, he heard the word 'Chronicle' very clearly. Shocked, he froze for a moment. He swiftly doubled back and stayed out of sight to listen.

"It was just speculation," the older woman was saying softly, "but the Militia is now being assigned to every port city on every Magi continent. It's got to be true. There's a Chronicle out there, alive."

"Unbelievable," the younger woman murmured. "Why wasn't he or she killed outright?" "Well, there are lots of rumors about that. Some people claim she manipulated the minds

of the people around her." The old woman snorted in derision. "If that were true, we wouldn't even know of her now. No, I suspect her parents loved her more than they feared her."

"And it still got them killed," the younger woman said curtly. "They'd have been better off killing her themselves than let her go through what she is now."

Dominic's fingers lengthened into claws and left gouges on the stone behind him as he grabbed the wall to control his temper. Smoke emerged from between his teeth as he hissed softly. His instincts told him that the woman was thinking of self-preservation more than the terror of a child.

Underneath the anger came the first stirring of hope. A female Chronicle had survived past first puberty and was only now being discovered. His Chronicle would be twenty now. It was more than slightly possible that the survivor and his Chronicle were the same person. In fact, he was nearly one hundred percent certain they were. The odds of two Chronicles surviving at the same time were smaller than a desert resident's swim clothes.

"No matter the reason, the Chronicle is alive." The older woman sighed. "I feel sorry for the child. She has no hope for a normal life."

Dominic had heard enough. He began walking quickly through the city toward the transportation district. It was the only place that Dragons were allowed to land when in natural form or to take off from in the same. He was not allowed to fly over Magi cities, but he had no objections to going the long way around. He would do whatever it took.

"Dragon! *Ashti ke!*"

He stopped and turned around, his brows drawing together over his gray eyes in confusion as he heard someone speaking Draconic. At first he thought it was a Magi calling for his attention, which would be almost impossible, but he realized immediately that it was not. It was a SunKin Elf, and he was running toward Dominic as fast as he could. "What is it?" Dominic asked warily.

The Elf looked around, realized there were far too many Magi, and switched to the language of the Dragons, something he was sure no Magi would know. "The Kin have the Chronicle in our possession."

Dominic's eyes widened sharply. "You do? Is she well?" For the same reason, he also spoke Draconic.

"From what the Elders tell us, yes. Word has been flying among the Kin. We've been trying to locate even one of you to tell you. If you could take her to your isle then surely she could find her Fury and be safe." The Kin studied him. "Although . . . you are a Fire Fury yourself. And she is a Water Chronicle. Perhaps she is yours."

"Whether she is or not is not a concern to me." His eyes were fierce. "I will take her to the Isle whether she belongs to me or not. If not mine, she belongs to one of my fellow Furies. Where is she?"

"On Kindred, on the island furthest south. The Elders are discussing making her honorary Kin to protect her from the Magi, but we're still trying to locate a Kin that can harmonize with her. It's nearly impossible with her lines." The Elf touched his ears as he bowed. "Swift flight, Fire Fury. Please hurry."

Dominic didn't need to be told twice. He turned and made his way even quicker to the area affectionately termed 'the airport' because Air Magi would create portals to protect people while Dragons were taking off and landing.

Ten minutes later he was flying across the sky as swiftly as he dared. He had to circle around the outside of the city and impatience surged inside him. With it was a heavy dose of fear. He had been raised knowing that a Fury and Chronicle were always well matched, sometimes opposites and sometimes identical.

Knowing that he would not be happy with a weak-willed female, he realized that he would therefore be blessed, or cursed, to be partnered with a strong-willed Chronicle. If this Chronicle was his, then she would hate being cooped up and protected. She would be more likely to set out onto the open sea in a boat with full trust in her power.

Normal Dragons had nearly limitless power. They could push themselves to fly as far and as fast as they wanted and cover miles in minutes with only the slightest drain on their power. Furies were different. Their powers had a limit, and without their Chronicle to feed from, they had to watch their majiks use lest they risk being severely injured or even potentially dying.

He was pushing his luck and his limits as he shot across the sky like a red and black bullet. It wasn't something he would have dared if he hadn't felt utterly certain that this mysterious Chronicle was his. He wouldn't even consider any other thought. It had to be her!

It was for this reason that when he reached Kindred two hours later, he fell straight to his knees when he changed into Magi form upon landing on the beach. He shook his head and fought the sickness churning in his stomach. The sand was turning very interesting blurry shades of color that did nothing to help his nausea.

"Oof, you're in bad shape." The MoonKin Faerie that was hovering near had his hands on his hips. "Well, I've never treated a Dragon of any kind before, but there's a first time for everything."

Dominic turned his head and tried to bring the Kin into focus. "You're a doctor?"

"That's me. Name's Poplar." He flew over and hovered anxiously as Dominic forced himself to his feet. He staggered, and Poplar swiftly grabbed his cloak to keep him from falling over. "I don't know a lot about Furies, but I do know enough to be capable of scolding you for pushing so hard!"

Dominic planted his feet, closed his eyes, and reached for his reserves of power. To his surprise, he felt a warm hand on his arm and realized someone was offering their Fire element to help him. He opened his eyes and turned his head to see a lovely SunKin Elf beside him. With a smile, he covered her hand and accepted her power to bolster his. "Thank you."

"Naturally." The Elf touched her ears as she bowed. "I am Rumidia." She propped her hands on her hips as she studied him then she sighed. "By the moons, I hate to be the bearer of bad news, but . . ."

"But . . .?"

"We, ah, seem to have lost the Chronicle." Poplar sighed when Dominic covered his face with a hand. "We were trying to keep her safe but she thinks that we'll be hurt if we do. She seems to have stolen a boat and set off into the ocean."

Dominic cursed softly in Draconic. "When?" he asked curtly.

"Last night some time. Her partner, Sparkle, says that she always was feeling a burning to go north, so she likely went that way."

Shock reverberated through him. Up until this morning, he had been north of these lands. This Chronicle *was* his. She wasn't looking for the Isle at all; it lay to the far west in Deepest Ocean. She was looking for *him*. "I'll find her," he vowed softly. "And take her to the Isle where she will be safe."

Rumidia and Poplar shared a smile. They had been hoping the handsome Fury was the one for their Tariah, and both were fairly sure now that he was. He was Tariah's elemental opposite, and his personality would fit with her nicely. "Send us word when she is safe," Rumidia said. "Please. We all love her very much."

"Gladly." With the boost to his powers, it was not difficult for him to take Dragon form again and begin flying across the ocean to the north. How far could a small boat get, even piloted by a Water Chronicle?

Farther than he thought because it was a good twenty minutes and ten miles of ocean before he spotted the little boat floating on the waves. He had been flying as fast as he dared without missing anything, and yet it had felt as if he was crawling across the sky.

The small boat was simply drifting on the waves. He angled downward and changed into Magi form when he was close enough to land. It was a tricky thing to do when the boat was barely five feet wide and he was ten feet from nose to tail, but he managed.

The Chronicle was lying on the bottom of the boat, motionless, but he could feel the surge and snap of her power and knew she was only unconscious. He carefully knelt beside her and reached out a hand to tenderly brush her hair from her face. She was stunning, he realized in wonder. Her golden lines flowed down her skin like rivers, and he felt as if he could read every curl like a map to her soul.

A hot fist grabbed his heart and held on tightly as he gently lifted her into his arms and held her close. His throat was so tight he could barely breathe. *Finally*, he thought in wonder and relief. Finally he had found her. The one person meant only for him. He tenderly pressed his lips to her temple. "You'll be safe now," he murmured.

He held her for a few more moments then forced himself to put her down again. It was the hardest thing he had ever done. He jumped backward off the edge of the boat and turned into his Dragon form again just before he hit the water. He gathered his Chronicle in his claws as carefully as if she was glass, and he held her protectively where she wouldn't fall. He turned to go west, to head for the Isle . . . and realized in a sudden shock that he could not remember how to get there.

Praying it was only because of his diminished majiks, he turned and began to fly across the sky back toward Kindred. Until his Chronicle awoke, and until he could determine why the hell he had forgotten the route back to his own damned home, they would be safe among the Kin.

Rumidia and Poplar were both startled when they saw him flying over the island, but they were also relieved because they could see he carried someone or something in his claws. They hurried quickly down to the beach where they could see the light strafing off his scales as he landed.

They reached the shore just as he turned back to Magi form. Tariah rested in his arms, deeply unconscious with her head lying against his shoulder. Poplar scrambled through the air and touched her forehead gently. His breath came out in a relieved whoosh. "She's just asleep. She must have been sailing all night."

Rumidia was watching Dominic's face as he looked down at Tariah. The knots of fear in her stomach began to unwind as she saw the expression in his gray eyes. It was a combination of awe and wonder, coupled with an emotion so strong that she was wary to even label it love. "She's yours," she said softly.

"Yes." He buried his nose in Tariah's hair, delighted with the way it smelled like the desert. "She's mine and I am hers. Where should I take her?"

"I run the inn." Rumidia smiled. "You can bring her there. Poplar, why don't you go tell Sparkle and Daylar that everything will be okay?"

"Just because you're older than me," Poplar grumbled as he flew off, "doesn't make you my boss."

Dominic followed Rumidia as she worked her way back through the village, and he noticed immediately that everyone who saw him with Tariah looked instantly relieved and delighted all at the same time. He had to smile. His Chronicle had more friends than she likely realized.

The room Rumidia escorted him to was a much more private one on the second floor at the back. He carried Tariah over to the bed and gently set her down on it. It took considerable willpower to ignore the sight she made. Her physical beauty stole his breath, but her power was what truly attracted him. It was *his* power that sensuously flowed in lines down her body. His fingers trembled as he ran them down her cheek.

Hunger prowled through him. A hunger for her soft lips and graceful curves. It was also a hunger for the power that flowed through her body. He could nearly taste it, and it was a surprising realization. He had not realized that his need to feed on her power would be a literal need, like food or water.

The door squeaked open and he turned his head just as a little lavender streak shot in the room. With lightning reflexes, he shot a hand out and caught the little Faerie when she was a foot from Tariah. "Hold it there, firefly."

Sparkle wiggled indignantly. "Lemme go!" She aimed a sulky look at him as she crossed her arms. His grip was gentle around her body but implacable. "Tariah's my friend!"

"Tariah." He repeated the name slowly, enjoying it. It reminded him of *tarinah*, a word in Draconic that meant storms in a desert.

She wanted to be annoyed but couldn't retain it, not when she saw the way he looked at her friend. So this was Tariah's Fury. She decided she liked him merely because she liked the way he looked at Tariah. "Her full name is Tariah Chronis. What's yours?"

"Dominic Whisperer." He brought her up to eye level and held her on his palm. He smiled as she shook out the sleeping shirt she was wearing then he frowned intently as he saw the bandages wrapped around her body. "What happened?"

She held onto his thumb for balance. He was of average height for a Magi male, she supposed, since he was two inches shy of six feet in height, but his hands seemed bigger. They were almost twice Tariah's size, but, then again, her friend was little. "Well," she said slowly, "I had to give some of my wings to another Kin."

He smiled. He knew as much about Kin as they themselves did. "Congratulations, I assume, are in order."

She blushed a little. "Well, yes, but . . ." She looked at Tariah sadly. "The Black Magi Elite are after Tariah. They know she's a Chronicle and want her to join them. They ripped off Daylar's wings to make him tell them. Tariah blames herself but it's not her fault."

Anger beat upward in his heart. "No," he said as evenly as he could, "it's not."

She suddenly giggled. "When you're mad, you breathe smoke!"

He lifted a brow then smiled and blew a swirl of smoke around her. "Sometimes," he agreed. He gently put her on his shoulder where she sat down companionably. "You're Tariah's friend?"

"Uh-huh. I found her in the desert after she fled Symphony." She looked at him seriously. "Please, Dominic, make sure she's happy. She keeps having bad things happen to her just because she's different. But I love her, a lot."

"I'll do my best." He rubbed his thumb gently over Tariah's cheekbone. He wished they were already bonded fully. He had heard tales of Dragoons who could share their dreams, and he wanted to share Tariah's and make sure she knew she was no longer alone. For the time being, it would have to be enough to hold her as she slept.

Sparkle cleared her throat. She was past her own second puberty, and she was far from blind. It was quite obvious Dominic wanted Tariah badly; it was also both expected and perfectly natural. It was also bad timing. She felt *really* bad for him. "Dominic?"

"Yes?"

"Tariah hasn't started second puberty yet."

It took him a few moments to realize what she had said. He closed his eyes in a combination of dismay and horror as he realized what he was about to endure. Frustrating wouldn't even be the word for what he would go through until Tariah was ready to take him as her lover. She wasn't even ready for him to kiss her let alone touch her as he craved. "*Kekle.*"

Sparkle had to assume that was a particularly nasty Draconic word. "I thought I'd just, you know, warn you."

"Yeah, thanks." He sat back with a sigh. "I can't decide whether I'm annoyed at needing to learn self-control when it's my right to claim her, or exceedingly grateful that no one else has touched her at all."

She muffled a snicker then coughed when he glowered at her. "Sorry. I just find it sort of sweet." She kissed his cheek. "I had wished she would find you soon. I'm glad she did. Now, no matter what, she'll be happy. Right?"

"We both will." He drew Tariah's hand to his cheek and rubbed against her fingers slowly. It was her right hand and he felt the pulsing of her lines against his skin. It fascinated him. Her lines were made of his power, and yet they were filled with hers. The combination was heady and nearly made his mouth water. His majiks were so low that he either needed to go into hibernation for a while, or feed. He was really leaning toward the second. He could sense now just how amazing it might be.

"I wonder why she hasn't woken," Sparkle remarked suddenly. "I mean, she's not low on power. It's kind of funny actually, but she seems to be *over*-producing power. I can feel it in my wings. It tickles. I half expect to see her dissolve into a puddle or something."

"That is because our Dominic is here," Juniper said from the doorway. "To cement the bond, a Chronicle and Fury must make their first exchange. To that end, the Chronicle will suddenly produce an exorbitant amount of power, and the Fury will be drained. After that, the exchange will be more of an 'as needed' basis. Or whenever they are in a, ah, particular mood."

Dominic's smile was wry. "Indeed. How did you know?"

"I was contacted a short time ago by another of your race, another Fury. She informed me of what to expect and said that she would tell the rest of your kind about Tariah." He lifted a brow. "You cannot do this yourself, I take it."

Dominic cleared his throat. "I seem to have forgotten the way back to my isle. And I can't seem to lay a successful hand on the energy output of any of my kind. Would you mind contacting my clanmate and telling her this? See if perhaps she or the Elders know what is going on."

"Gladly." Juniper smiled. "Come, Sparkle. When Tariah awakes, she will want some time alone with Dominic. Let Nature take its course. It has rules for us all. And you shouldn't be out of bed, missy."

"Oh come on!" She was indignant but obligingly flew over and rode on his shoulder as he left the room and shut the door behind them.

Dominic looked back down at Tariah's peaceful face. His Chronicle. He had thought he would never find her. With a soft sigh, he reached out and gathered her close so that he could feel her heartbeat. He was never going to let her go again.

Chapter Six

Tariah awoke to a blinding headache. In fact, it wasn't just her head. Her whole body ached to the point of nearly being real pain. She knew she wasn't in her boat on the ocean anymore; she felt a soft bed beneath her and the familiar feeling of Kin near. She knew someone had 'rescued' her, which annoyed her slightly, but the annoyance was faint in the face of the way her body hurt.

Her fingers curled into the sheet beneath her as sweat broke out on her skin. What was wrong with her? She wanted to unleash her power in a wild torrent, to rage and seethe like the seas. She felt as if she was choking on her own Water element. A faint whimper slipped past her lips.

"It's alright." The voice was soft and male, and the hand that covered her cheek was the same. "Just open your eyes and look at me."

The voice and the touch reverberated through her body and touched a deeply buried inner instinct she hadn't known existed. *Mine*, a part of her soul whispered. *This man is mine*. Shock echoed inside her. Hers? Her Fury? Her eyes flew wide and she found herself staring up into the storm gray eyes of a man she had never met before but recognized on a cellular level.

He was, without exception, the single most beautiful man she had ever seen. His face was rough edged without being hard, and his black hair fell into his eyes. Red streaks curled through the black, and she wondered if he would mind if she ran her hands through them.

A slow smile began to spread as she carefully lifted a hand to touch his face. It might have been a sign of second puberty. It might have been merely him. Something inside made it impossible to resist the urge to touch him. If it *was* just him and whatever was between them, then second puberty was bound to be interesting.

Dominic's breath caught. Her smile had to be one of the most beautiful things he had ever seen. "Hello," he said softly. "I think I belong to you."

Some of the pain was erased in sheer joy. Tears burned her eyes. "Really?" she said just as softly. "Because I think I belong to you too." His presence curled around her and seemed to sink into her heart. She wasn't alone anymore.

The pain returned with a vengeance and rippled through her body. Her fingers tightened on his face, and he gently covered her hand. "It's because we need to bond."

"Okay fine." Her breath hitched as a spasm seemed to rip from her stomach outward. "No offense, but if this is going to happen every time, I'd sooner find a way to drown myself."

"Don't you dare!" He gently lifted her onto his lap and held her possessively close. As if responding to his presence, pale blue light began to emanate around her skin. Her lines rippled like waves. It was unbearably beautiful, and hidden instincts rose inside him with a hunger he could not fight.

He bent his head and pressed his lips to the patch of skin bared on her shoulder. He breathed in, as if drinking, and her power flowed into him. It was like the freshest of water, pure and sweet, but there was a flavor to it like rare fruit.

The pain almost immediately lessened inside her body as he fed on her power. She relaxed against him and closed her eyes slightly, savoring the knowledge that someone needed her. Obligingly, she tilted her head to the side as he pressed his lips to her neck.

Though he would have liked nothing more than to cover her entire body with kisses and feed from her power everywhere, he knew better. She wasn't ready for him, and he wasn't a fan of self-inflicted torture. A thousand emotions seemed tangled inside him, welded together with a lust more powerful than he had imagined. It nearly overshadowed his hunger. Or perhaps they were the same. He couldn't tell, and he didn't care.

"I'm going to kiss you," he warned her as he cupped her face in his hands.

She smiled. "It's my first one, so be nice."

Talk about putting a man on the spot. Yet he wasn't worried. It was wonderfully easy to be gentle with her when she trusted him unthinkingly. Deep inside, he could feel the same thing. A bedrock trust that he had never before experienced. If he needed her, she would be there. If she needed him, he would be there. The feeling tightened his throat with overwhelming emotion. "Tariah."

She didn't get a chance to respond before his lips were covering hers softly. She had nothing to compare it to, but she had the feeling he definitely knew what he was doing. His lips were warm and soft as they moved over hers, and the feeling of him drinking her power this way stole away even the last vestiges of pain.

As the last of her power flowed into him, it was as if they were suddenly breathing inside each other's bodies. Where she had her hands resting on his chest, she could feel the skin heat underneath his cloth shirt. Her palms itched and tingled as she felt power, his or hers she didn't know, building under his skin.

He lifted his head slowly and realized that he could feel her inside him. Almost curiously, he reached out with his mind as if to touch her. She sensed him and mentally shied away. He frowned. "You don't want me in your mind?"

She turned her face away. "I don't want to share my memories," she said. "I don't want even you to know. Especially you."

He said nothing. Her emotions were clear as they flowed along the lines connecting them. She was ashamed of something, and there was a heavy dose of terror mixed inside. He ran his hands gently up and down her arms, and his fingers tingled as they skimmed along her lines. "I won't pry," he said at last. "But I eventually want to know. You can peek into my mind anytime."

Rather than immediately peek in his mind, she actually leaned forward and peeked down the collar of his shirt. His brows lifted in amusement. "If you want me naked, you only have to ask."

She stuck her tongue out at him briefly. "I was just curious if you have lines now, and it seems you do." It belatedly dawned on her that for all the intimacy between them, for all the ease she felt, and despite the fact that she felt as if he was a part of her soul that she had been missing since birth . . . she didn't know his name.

An odd look crossed his face. "I'm not sure which of us felt it first, but I agree that we're in a very odd situation. I don't normally kiss a woman before we've been properly introduced."

Her lines suddenly burned so hot that he had to hastily release her arm. He stared at her in surprise as her chin set and her lips thinned. Even without peeking into her mind, he could read her emotions clearly. She was feeling a level of jealousy unusual for someone not in second puberty. "Tariah?"

She got to her feet and walked away a few steps. She felt perfectly fine physically now that she had fed her Fury. Her emotions were another matter. She was being eaten alive by jealousy. She *hated* that he had been with other women, and she knew it was a stupid feeling. She knew damned well that he had been an adult long before her *grandparents* had been born. She struggled to find the self-control she had lived with for the last seven years. It felt strangely unnatural now. "I guess I'm a jealous woman." Her tone managed to be flippant, but there was a note underneath that gave her away.

He tried to put himself in her shoes. Say she had already finished second puberty and had been with at least one lover. How would he feel? The answer came as a surge of feral anger. Ripe jealousy briefly stole his voice. It was entirely illogical. Having a lover was perfectly normal and natural, but he could not deny that he understood her feelings. "I guess I'm a jealous man," he said ruefully.

She looked at him in surprise before smiling wryly. "I guess we both have a lot to learn about how this relationship will work. I didn't think friends could be this possessive."

He ran his tongue over his teeth. "Before I address that, maybe we should get the formalities out of the way. My name is Dominic Whisperer." Introducing himself to someone who knew him inside and out felt very odd.

She felt no less silly, particularly because his mind *was* open to her. He didn't consciously think about his name—no one did—but all she had to do was dig in his memories for instances of people who had addressed him. She shook her head with a smile. "Tariah Chronis, but obviously you knew that since you've been calling me by name."

"I did." He held out a hand to her. "Come back here."

She immediately walked over and took his hand. He drew her onto his lap and she let out a contented sigh as she rested her head on his shoulder. She had never felt that complete in her life. As long as she was with Dominic, she knew she was where she belonged. Tears burned her eyes as she wrapped her arms around his shoulders. "I'm not alone anymore."

"Neither of us are." He rubbed his cheek over her hair softly. "I've wanted to find you for so long." He cleared his throat. "Tariah, I need to explain to you about Dragoons."

She reluctantly straightened up. She liked cuddling him; he was bigger than she was by quite a bit but she was discovering she enjoyed it. She liked being small enough to snuggle on his lap. "Explain what precisely?"

He ran his fingers through her hair, then drew his touch forward to trace over her lines. He wanted to follow every curl with his lips but firmly reigned it in. "Dragoons . . . their bonds are not just friendship, not as a rule."

It took her a few seconds but it sank in finally what he was implying. Her eyes widened and she blurted, "But I'm not in second puberty yet!"

"Trust me," frustration leaked into his voice, "I'm aware of that. If you were, that kiss we shared would have created steam between us." He framed her face in his hands, enjoying the tingle of her power teasing his skin. "You're going to be poking around my mind, and you're going to be feeling my emotions. I wanted you to know what you'd be seeing and feeling and not understanding."

She thought about it to herself for a long time. A part of her was a little flabbergasted that it could be that simple. Being a Chronicle meant she didn't have to struggle with falling in love. She didn't have to question if her feelings, or her lover's feelings, were real. Her Fury was everything she could ever want. She would be able to love him without question and he would love her the same. What they had was something more precious than the world around them would ever understand.

She smiled suddenly and her silver eyes sparkled like the rarest of coins. It stole Dominic's breath and heart all at once. "Well," she said with an impish note to her voice, "at least it reassures me about one thing. I had been worried that I would go through second puberty without ever once getting to explore my new feelings. But now I have you." She threw her arms around his neck happily. "Just remember to be patient with me."

"I'll do my best," he murmured huskily. "But be gentle to me, Tariah. If you turn out to be a tease, I'm going to go mad. I'm having enough trouble keeping my hands to myself right now." He nuzzled her neck gently. "You smell like the desert."

"I ought to. I'm a desert girl." She eased back and pulled a face. "I hate these clothes Rumidia made me wear. I hate confining clothes. I prefer my desert clothes, and the sun on my skin." She tilted her head. "What kind of weather is on the Isle of the Dragons?"

"It depends on where you live. We have a little bit of every landscape. The mountains are the warmest other than our desert. The valleys are where we get the coolest, but even then it doesn't get too bad." He cleared his throat. "We have a small problem about the Isle, Tariah. I seem to have forgotten how to get there."

She groaned and dropped her head on his shoulder. "Why me?" she wailed. "Why do I always have to have things the hard way?!"

For just a moment, he got a glimpse in her mind of her mad dash across the desert. His fingers tightened on her waist for a moment and then he clutched her close. "The big difference," he said urgently, "is that you are with me now. You're not alone anymore. I promise." He groaned as he felt the heat of her tears on his skin. "No, don't you dare. Stop it, right now."

"Are all men such babies about crying?" she sniffled.

"I don't know about other men, but I can't stand to see *you* crying. It breaks my heart."

She lifted her head to study him for a moment. She smiled and wiped at her tears. "You're a big baby. You're a softy at heart. The big, bad, Fire Fury is a sucker for weeping women and cute kids. You cry at linking ceremonies." Laughter lurked in her voice as his cheeks warmed. "You made everyone think you're this badass Dragon and you're completely not!"

He tweaked her nose gently. "You love me anyway, and you know it." His breath was held. He knew that they had been born to love one another, but he still wanted to hear it. He *needed* to hear that she loved him even though he was soft-hearted and bad-tempered all at the same time.

Her smile filled with wonder as she cupped his cheek. "You know what? I do love you. I can see it. You hate losing and you would argue with me until the end of time if you thought you were right . . . but I love even that. I don't know why, but I do. Everything about you seems perfect to me." She curled closer. "If this is what it means to be a Dragoon, then I'm really glad I am one."

He held her for a moment then eased her back. His gray eyes moved over her face slowly to memorize every feature. At the same time, his power and his soul memorized that which was hers, wanting to ensure he would always know her. Tenderly, he curled his presence around her mind, blanketing her comfortingly because he could not get inside.

She closed her eyes as she felt him inside. Without hesitation she reached for him in return, memorizing him so that he was stamped on everything that made her. The steady flow of power back and forth between them was the most wonderful thing she had ever known. She *trusted* him. Why was she holding anything back?

He took a quick breath as he felt her mind reaching out for him. She wasn't hiding anymore. He didn't immediately go looking even though he wanted to know everything. He waited until she let him in, until she had blended their minds and shared willingly everything she was and had been through.

It surged past his mental eyes in a riot of images and sounds. It was hard to pick out anything specific, and he knew that it was because of the trauma she had endured. Everything had blurred together and most of the details had been lost. But some stood out. Some were in horrifying clarity. His stomach churned and his heart broke. He struggled to keep himself calm, and all he could manage to say was, "It was *not* your fault! Stop thinking that!"

She looked at him sadly. "Tell me my existence didn't cause Maxim's death. If I hadn't been here, he would be alive."

"He would also have been greatly lonely and depressed without ever knowing why." He cupped her face in his hands and softly brushed kisses over her eyes even as his mind softly caressed her in a similar embrace. Both seemed to be weeping inside. "I know I would have been lost without you."

"Is it true?" She closed her eyes. "Do the Dragons really have to . . . to kill Furies who feel their Chronicle die?"

He let out a long breath. "Yeah. You see, Chronicles are driven to find their Fury, but they don't feel them until they connect. Furies feel their Chronicle, but cannot track them till they connect." He rested his forehead against hers. "My brother was a Fury too," he said quietly. "Fifty years ago, he felt his Chronicle born. Eleven years later, he felt her die. He just seemed to . . . disappear. He didn't eat, he didn't sleep. He just suffered. He never spoke a word to anyone. It was like watching him bleed out one drop at a time. And worse still, it would never end."

She gently framed his face with her hands. She didn't need to hear the rest. She could see it inside him. To end his brother's misery, Dominic himself had taken an enchanted saber and struck his brother down. "If it had been you, you would have thanked him," she said softly. "Now in the Underrealm, he and his Chronicle are together."

He nuzzled her hands softly. "Someone else around here is soft at heart." He smiled when she pulled a face. "Deny it and I'll call you a liar. You also have a nasty habit I'm going to need to work on."

She narrowed her eyes. "What's that?"

"No more hiding your emotions." He leaned in and softly touched her lips with his. "In fact, I insist that you give me whatever you've got. If it means you like to shout and throw things when you're in a temper, be my guest."

"I am not violent by nature," she muttered.

"Never fib to the man who can see inside you. Given half an opportunity, I think you would sooner kick me than give in, even when you're wrong."

She gave him a half-hearted punch in the shoulder. "I've never really lost my temper," she confessed. "Or cried. Or had a *really* good laugh. I only recently was able to even express my emotions. I'm going to have to learn as I go."

He studied her. "Are you ticklish?"

Her eyes widened. "You wouldn't!"

He would. She swiftly tried to get off his lap, aiming to get across the room. Her Fury, however, was much faster and he caught her wrist. Quick as a blink he had her pinned to the floor, and his fingers mercilessly zeroed in on the sensitive skin of her waist.

She wiggled and squirmed but couldn't get away. He was tickling her from the inside out and it felt so ridiculously funny that she couldn't stop the laughter welling up from some hidden place inside. She was breathless with it as she fought him to get free. "Stop it, you meany!"

He grinned at her and kept up his relentless assault. "Nope." His throat closed with overwhelming emotion as he heard her laughing. It was the most beautiful thing he had ever heard. There was a burning well of life inside her that he hadn't immediately noticed. Restraining her emotions had not just insulted her nature, it had insulted life itself. His Chronicle needed to always be laughing. "Say please."

"I'm going to drown you!"

"That's not a please."

"Dom-in-ic! Let me go! I can't breathe!" She gulped air as his fingers stilled. She could barely see for the tears in her eyes, and she was wildly happy. She had never played with anyone like this before. There was so much she had never gotten to do that she was free to do with Dominic. She was free to do whatever she wanted.

He was experiencing a similar feeling. He'd had friends for a long time. He had brothers and sisters that he had more than once gotten to play with and wrestle with. And yet he had never been as incredibly happy as he was when wrestling with his small Chronicle.

"Small!" She glowered. "I am not . . . much."

"But I like it. You're the perfect size for me. Of course, I might worry that you'll fall off my back while we're flying. I might have to carry you." He smiled as he felt the sudden surge of delight inside her. "You want to fly. Well, then I'll be sure to teach you."

"Teach me?" She tilted her head. "How?"

"Chronicles can use a much more extensive range of powers by drawing on their Furies' majiks. I've heard about everything from summoning to transformation to

48

conjuring to extremely strong mental skills like Telepathy and Telekinesis. Of course, you'd have to feed me afterward." He nuzzled her again, loving her scent. "You might even be able to turn into a Dragon shape."

She was tickled at the very idea. "When do we practice?"

The door opened and they turned their heads to see Juniper standing there with Sparkle on one shoulder and Daylar on the other. Both Faeries were dressed a little more normally, but both still had their wings bound. Juniper covered a smile. "Are we interrupting?"

"Not completely. I was tickling Tariah without mercy." Dominic let Tariah sit up before getting to his feet to assist her as well.

Sparkle giggled. "Her waist is the worst."

"Tattletale."

"Now, girls," Juniper chuckled, "behave. Come, Dragoons. Let us go to my house where we can talk formally. We Kin have an offer to make to Tariah, if you are both willing to accept it. We hope that it might negate some of the bad effects of the Magi."

Tariah felt Dominic reaching for her hand and automatically slipped her fingers into his. The ease of the gesture and the belonging that went with it was exhilarating. Contented, she rested her head against his arm as they walked. "Does this have to do with the honorary Kin thing that I heard mentioned?"

"Eavesdropping is not nice," Daylar scolded her.

She stuck her tongue out at him. "So is keeping secrets from friends. I'd like to have an illusion of control over my life, thank you." She smiled when he hovered over to land on her shoulder, and Sparkle followed to land on her other. She softly rubbed her cheek against both. She was glad they would be happy.

Inside the Elder's home, they all took chairs and got comfortable. Dominic's idea of comfortable was to have Tariah on his lap. She had a different idea and they finally compromised by sitting together on the couch with her snuggled up against his side.

Juniper covered a smile as he walked over to his own chair. "We Kin," he began, "want to offer formal sanctuary to Tariah and therefore bring her under the protection of the treaty. The only way to do this is to make her an honorary Kin."

Dominic frowned. "Chronicles, I thought, had too erratic a power for that."

"Normally this is true. But we think that we have found someone who can get around it." He gestured to Daylar. "Our Daylar. His own power is quite erratic now because he had his wings removed and then replaced with someone else's. His body is sustaining two different elements for the time being. It might be enough."

Tariah frowned. "I'm not sure I understand what you mean about erratic."

Dominic skimmed a hand down her hair. "Erratic in that a Chronicle, or a Fury for that matter, develop in ways different from the rest of the world. Where others develop slowly and steadily, we develop faster and with a greater range."

"It is fairly simple for a Kin to relate to a Dragon or Magi," Juniper said. "We are born with Light or Dark, then develop a secondary element, then a tertiary. Dragons and Magi are born with Lightning, and then develop a primary element, then a secondary."

It dawned on Tariah then. "But Chronicles and Furies develop secondary at the same time as primary, and then develop completely new skills unrelated to any other

49

race. Daylar has a chance because he has technically gained another skill on top of the natural."

"Precisely." Juniper touched his arm where his tattoos were. "We of this world . . . our bodies are made by our power. We Kin bear these marks because of our Light and Dark powers. You Chronicles bear your lines because of your connection to a Fury's power. Our bodies cannot be changed. Our marks cannot be removed, nor can new ones be added, unless the power itself is changed."

Tariah nodded. "What you're telling me is that in order to place a mark on me that shows I am under Kin protection, Daylar has to be able to mark my power, and he couldn't do that if he wasn't capable of resonating with me."

"Precisely." Juniper smiled at Dominic. "She has a curious mind."

"I know." Dominic nuzzled his nose through Tariah's hair. "I enjoy it."

She lifted a brow at him. "I'll remind you of that when I start second puberty."

Sparkle fell off her chair laughing and Daylar was nearly right behind her. Juniper coughed, but his eyes twinkled merrily. "If you are in agreement, let us see if Daylar can make you one of us. He will claim you as family, just as you will need to claim him."

She smiled. "Well, if Daylar doesn't mind, I don't. I think he's a bit young to be my father, though. Maybe a brother."

Daylar smiled in return. "I have six big sisters. I wouldn't mind a little sister too. Because I'm *technically* older than you, after all."

"Technically." She straightened away from Dominic and got to her feet. She held out a hand and Daylar hovered over to land. "I would be honored to be accepted by the Kin," she said softly. "Thank you, Daylar."

He bowed gracefully. "I thank you, Tariah. I owe you my life, and you brought Sparkle to me." He closed his eyes and began to glow with soft white color as he opened his power and reached for hers. She began to glow softly blue as she reached for him in return, and the two colors seamlessly meshed.

It fascinated him. As he felt Tariah's power, he felt equally Dominic's presence. Changing one would change the other. He began to wonder then if perhaps the erratic patterns of a Chronicle or Fury had less to do with their unusual development and more to do with the endless cycle between Dragoons. He could nearly see the power flowing back and forth between the two.

He didn't want to mark her in a way that wouldn't be flattering, but he always wanted it to be visible. His first thought was to place a mark on her back shoulder; she was a desert girl and therefore tended to wear very little clothing. Much to his surprise, however, the decision was taken from his hands. His power was magnetically drawn to where her lines flowed over her arm. Even just a little touch from his Light power caused her lines to ripple like water.

Her lines abruptly moved. The curls shifted and reformed and flowed together to form a wing shape on her shoulder. It was as if the wing was a part of her lines and yet still distinct. It was followed by a flickering glow from underneath Dominic's shirt as his own lines shifted to form the same mark, defining him as well.

Daylar and Tariah stopped glowing and both smiled. "I always wanted a brother," she said as she hugged him gently close. She laughed. "Now I guess I get Sparkle too!"

Sparkle shot over to hug her as well. "Naturally!"

"Welcome to our land, young Kin," Juniper said with a smile. He started to add more when he noticed that there were symbols appearing in the air. "Ah. She finally responds. Let's see."

Dominic leaned to the side to see the letter. "My clanmate?" He straightened back up and gathered Tariah close against him once more as she returned to his side. His fingers smoothed over the newest design to her lines. He *really* wanted to trace her lines with his lips and taste her power there.

She elbowed him lightly. "Behave. Patience is rewarded."

"It better be."

Juniper decided that he greatly enjoyed their relationship and the way Tariah always seemed to be smiling. Turning his attention back to the letter, he began reading through what his contact had to say. It was interesting, to say the least. As the letter disappeared, all he could say was, "Well."

"Well what?" Sparkle asked.

"It seems that the Dragon Elders believe that Dominic's memory loss is because of his Chronicle. A Chronicle must follow the map within their lines. It is their journey of discovery and power. The map is supposed to lead a Chronicle to their Fury and the Isle. Dominic has found Tariah before she has followed her lines."

Dominic sighed. "My memory of the way to the Isle has been taken away to ensure that Tariah is capable of finishing her journey."

"There is some suspicion that if she does not, she might risk destroying herself. Her lines will continue to develop but the power will have nowhere to manifest. It could drive her mad."

"Let's not." He held Tariah closer protectively.

Her nose pressed to his shoulder, she sighed. "Oh well. I knew it couldn't get better." But, then again, things *were* better right there. Maybe not easier, but certainly better. She rubbed her cheek gently against Dominic. She would be happy just to stay on Kindred with him, let alone travel with him.

Her lines suddenly began burning. The fierce longing tightened her throat. *North.* She needed to go north still. There was something else to the north that was pulling at her. It wasn't just Dominic. "I guess I go north," she said, trying to smile.

Dominic tenderly framed her face with his hands. He knew as well as she did that the only two lands to the north were the three continents belonging to the Magi—Carnelian, Spectrum, and Glacia on the top of the world. "We'll figure something out," he said softly. "I promise."

"I believe you." She closed her eyes and rested her cheek on his hand. "I guess we leave tomorrow morning." She opened her eyes and found a real smile. "I suppose I should look at it as a chance to learn what flying is like."

He smiled and softly touched her lips with his. He couldn't have asked for a better Chronicle.

Chapter Seven

They had dinner with Daylar, Sparkle, and both their families. It was probably, Tariah remarked dryly to her former partner, the only time she had ever felt big. Both SunKin families were made entirely of Faeries, and Tariah towered over them all. Dominic took it in stride even though he himself was even taller; he was more used to it.

After dinner, the Dragoons returned to the inn where Rumidia had assured them they would always be welcome to rest. As they were walking together, Tariah commented half to herself, "I should be ashamed of myself."

She felt more amused than ashamed. He just smiled. "Why?"

"I'm about to spend the night with a man I haven't known even a full day." She sent him a smile. "I mean, even in second puberty that's considered slightly tacky, and I'm not even in that yet."

Her Fury gave a quick laugh then swung her up into his arms and in a quick circle. "You know what, Tariah Chronis? I think I'm absolutely crazy about you." He rubbed his cheek against hers softly. "Even if you hadn't been my Chronicle, I suspect that I would have loved you."

Her brows shot up. "Is that possible?" She linked her hands behind his neck and hooked her knees around his waist to hold on as he walked. She held no fear of falling. In fact, she was enjoying herself because she was able to see his face clearly. He smelled incredible, like the smoke that curled through the night sky during a good bonfire. She liked it a lot.

He carried her into the room they would share, then sat down on the plush chair in the corner. It automatically grew larger to accommodate his size, and then it got slightly larger still as it read Tariah's presence. The result was plenty of room for both of them. She *really* liked Kin inventions.

"There are two kinds of Dragoon pairs," he told her. "What's considered the primary kind, and then there is what is considered secondary because it happens rarely. The primary kind is what we are. The simplest term I can think of to describe it is 'lovers' but it's so much more than that."

"I can tell." She smoothed her hand over his chest unconsciously. She just needed to feel his heat and strength. "What's the secondary?"

"The simplest term for that would be 'twins.' It's the exact same sort of bond as a primary, but there is nothing romantic about it. Twin Dragoons, however, tend to remain single. It is very hard for a Twin Dragoon to find someone that they care about as much as their partner. When it does happen, the other Dragoon will often experience similar feelings for the mate, especially when it comes to protecting them."

"Oh I see." She smiled. "So if you *had* been with another Chronicle as a twin, and then fallen for me, the Chronicle would have loved me too and wanted to keep me safe if only because I made *you* happy. That's really beautiful." She leaned forward and rested against him. "I think I'd have loved you too. There's just something about you."

He nuzzled her hair. "I'll take that as a compliment."

She softly giggled. "Dominic, why are you always nuzzling me like that? It's so sweet, and you want so badly for people to not know you're a softy."

"It's the Dragon in me." He snuggled her closer. "Nuzzling each other is how Dragons show affection. We're very tactile creatures. And besides . . ." He buried his nose against her shoulder and breathed in deeply. "I like how you smell."

"What do I smell like?" she asked curiously.

"Like fresh water." He smiled. "Specifically, fresh water in the desert. Pure and clean but really sweet." He kept his arms around her waist as he got to his feet then gently helped her balance until she was standing on her own as well. "We should get some sleep. Tomorrow will be a long day."

Tariah, inexplicably, felt shy as she looked around the room and realized that she didn't have a night shift. She would have to sleep in her clothes or naked. The embarrassment puzzled her. Why was she embarrassed? She knew she had a beautiful figure, and she trusted Dominic implicitly. She knew him as well as she knew herself. Why was she nervous? Her heart was pounding hard.

"Is something wrong?" he asked. He softly smoothed his hands down her arms to comfort her. He could feel that she was unsure but he couldn't seem to pinpoint the source.

She turned to frown at him. "I'm nervous. I don't know why. I'm not self-conscious but I am now. What's wrong with me?"

His eyes softened and his fingers were tender as they rubbed over the lines on her cheek. "Welcome to the first stages of second puberty, *ishke*. You're suddenly becoming aware of the difference between male and female."

She glowered. "I know the differences, thank you."

"Ah, but now it's personal. Focus on your feelings. Are you nervous because you think you're not attractive, or because you want me to find you attractive?"

She wrinkled her nose. "I know I'm attractive. I'd be silly if I didn't know it." Saying it, she realized that he had hit it on the head. She was nervous because she wanted him to find her beautiful. She wanted him to look at her and see her as everything he had ever wanted. The frustrating part was that she *knew* she was what he wanted and yet she couldn't make the nerves go away. She crossed her arms. "I don't like this," she muttered.

His hands were gentle and confident as he began to calmly help her out of her clothes. He felt her determination to ignore her nerves, and his heart melted. There was nothing more beautiful than getting to watch firsthand as his Chronicle finished blossoming like a desert flower.

"Don't be poetic." Her cheeks were warm with embarrassment. "I'm trying not to lose my nerve. Why does this stupid second puberty make confident people skittish? It's stupid."

He hid a smile. "Is it stupid then?"

"*Yes.*" She crossed her arms over her naked breasts as he neatly absconded her bikini top. "I'd just as soon skip to the part where the curiosity begins."

53

He bit his tongue to keep from chuckling. It took all his willpower to keep his fingers steady as he got to work on her boots and leggings. She was the most stunningly beautiful creature he had ever seen. "You have to be conscious of your own body and how it works before you can consider how other bodies feel, and how they might work together."

Now naked except for her long auburn hair, she tapped a foot lightly on the ground. With a confidence that was purely bravado, she tossed her hair back over her shoulder and propped her hands on her hips, baring herself entirely to his eyes. "Reassure me so I get my confidence back and I can get over this." Try as she might, she couldn't keep the slight quiver out of her voice.

He stopped breathing as he stared at her. She was so utterly perfect to him that it should have been a crime. It could be debated whether he had been perfectly made to love her, or if she had been perfectly made for him. No matter the origin, the result was an encompassing hunger to taste every inch of her gentle brown flesh. The golden lines that flowed sensuously like water down her soft curves. His fingers itched to start touching and his body was hard and heavy with desire. "When I can manage to find a compliment," he said, his voice thick, "I'll give it to you. Right now I can barely remember my name."

Her nerves eased and her confidence returned. He wasn't doing anything to hide how he felt, though he was trying to shield his thoughts. She managed to get a glimpse, and her pulse fluttered in a way she hadn't felt before. She let it be; she would understand in time. "Is this the end of the first stage?"

He smiled wryly. "No. Unfortunately, it never quite goes away. You're always going to be more conscious of how you look to the person you want. You, however, have an advantage." He skimmed his hands over her hips gently. "I'll find you attractive no matter what you're wearing. Or not wearing."

"That's a consolation." She tilted her head. "Are you nervous about me?"

"Hell yes."

It was said readily and quickly and made her feel *much* better. She smiled. "You worry that I won't find you attractive?"

"Absolutely." He rolled his eyes and invited her to enjoy his situation. "Even knowing that eventually you're going to respond to me as deeply as I do to you doesn't make me less worried. We're all the same inside when it comes to how we want to appear to the person we want."

"It's not fun." She went over to the bed and turned back the covers. The sheets were soft and cool to the touch but warmed as she slipped under the blankets. "I'd just as soon go along knowing I was attractive and not caring about other opinions my entire life."

"Wouldn't we all?" Knowing she might be edging into the realm where she would be self- conscious about his body as well, he removed only his shirt and boots. He left his pants on as he walked over to join her. He nudged her lightly in the shoulder. "Scoot over and share."

"I got here first."

"I'm bigger." He slid under the blankets then caught her in his arms and snuggled her close. She turned over and cuddled even closer, her nose tucking against his chest. Her body perfectly aligned to his, all her curves fitting against him as if they were two halves to a complete being.

She let out a soft sigh as his arm draped over her waist. His warmth wrapped around her, and it was as wonderful as the desert sun. She felt his power curling around hers and couldn't resist reaching out to hold him as well. Her hand lifted and covered the wing mark within the lines on his chest. "You should go shirtless, like desert men," she said sleepily.

He lifted a brow. "It's a bit early for you to be interested in me naked."

"It's not that. I just want everyone to see that you're mine." Her hand smoothed over the lines. "You wear my lines. I want people to see." Her lashes fluttered closed. "But, eventually, I guess, I'll just want to admire you at my leisure. You're already beautiful to me."

Her power stilled its soft pulsing and he knew she was asleep. Smiling wryly as he thought of the time ahead, he buried his nose in her hair and let out a soft breath of contentment. It was going to be a long couple of months, but the end result would be worth it. He couldn't wait to claim his Chronicle as his entirely.

Tariah was awakened the next morning by the feel of someone jumping up and down on her shoulder. She cracked one eye open, saw Sparkle, and promptly closed her eye again as she curled more firmly against Dominic. "Go away," she mumbled against his shoulder.

"No." Sparkle's wings shimmered as she flew over and began to jump on Dominic's shoulder instead. "You too! Wake up, wake up! There's something very important happening in the Magi!"

"Someone find that bronze grows on trees?" Dominic asked sleepily.

Tariah giggled and Sparkle huffed out a breath. Indignant, she grabbed the blankets and jerked them off the couple. "Darn it all, both of you get up!" Her pale lavender brows lifted as she saw her friend. "You're naked."

"Give back the blanket and I won't be." Tariah reluctantly sat up and shoved her hair out of her eyes on a large yawn. "What's this about the Magi and something important?" Remembering how her hair liked to go crazy while she was asleep, she had to fight the urge to run to a mirror and fix it before Dominic saw her. She could only glower at herself. She was beginning to hate this self-consciousness.

He opened one eye to study her and his stomach quivered with fresh desire. Why she needed a mirror, he hadn't a clue. She was heartbreakingly lovely when she was flushed and rumpled from sleep. His fingers itched with the urge to make her hair even more tangled, and lust merged seamlessly with a hunger for her power. He rolled over and pulled a pillow over his head. "I hate my life."

She ignored him as she looked at Sparkle. "What's this important news?"

"You need to see it for yourself! Hurry and come to the Elder's house. I left clothes for you over there." She pointed to where there was a stack of clothing on the table. "You're going to Spectrum, and it's a desert too, so I made sure that they were your favorite kind of clothes." She grinned impishly. "They'll probably be Dominic's favorite too. Oh, and I left clothes for him. I had to guess at his size; they might be on the big side."

She sailed out the door and it swung shut behind her. With a sigh, Tariah nudged Dominic. "Up you go."

"No." His voice was muffled by the pillow.

Without guilt, she pounced onto his back and listened to his breath whoosh out. "Yes, damn it. If I have to suffer, so do you."

"Different sort of suffering." He suddenly twisted and dislodged her. Before she could tumble off the bed, he sat up and caught her safely in his arms. The instant his hands closed around her arms, her power began to flow over her like a soft blue veil. "Breakfast in bed is my idea of a treat."

She could only laugh as he buried his nose against her neck and drank her power from there. Contented, she wound her arms around his shoulders as he lifted his head and framed her face in his hands. He softly kissed her, drinking her power right from her lips. It was sweetest there.

As he reluctantly lifted his head, one hunger eased, he searched her eyes. There was still no recognition of him as a mate inside her. It was frustrating even though he knew nature had to run its course. With a sigh, he released her so that she could get dressed.

She slid out of bed and walked over to the table. She picked up an article of clothing and asked curiously, "Do you like kissing me, Dominic?"

His brows lifted. "I'm surprised you have to ask."

"You've only done it to feed." She shrugged her shoulders as she pulled on her cloth bikini. "I was just, you know, wondering."

Enchanted by the sign of nerves once more revealing themselves, he walked over to nuzzle her softly. "Trust me, *ishke*, once I have any sign that you are ready for your first real kiss, I will be right there waiting to claim it."

"How will I know?"

"You just will. I promise." He released her slowly and watched with interest as she pulled on cloth shorts and a cloth top that was little more than a bikini itself. His pulse spiked and he felt his Fire surging eagerly inside for her Water. "We'll have to live in a desert so I can see you this way all the time."

She looked down. "This isn't the least I've worn. Some of the hottest days in Symphony had me running around in a bikini and a piece of cloth tied around my hips." She stretched largely, rising up on her toes as she did. She felt much better now that she wasn't stuck in confining forest clothes.

With a curiosity more born of an interest in knowing everything about her Fury than an interest in him naked, she sat on the edge of the bed to watch him dress. Dominic, sensing her intent, discovered that he himself was suddenly very self-conscious. "Don't stare at me," he grumbled as he reached for the clothes provided.

She smiled. "Why not?"

"Because I want to impress you and I can hardly do that until you are further along in your development." He walked over and swiftly tossed the blanket over her head. Before she could do more than sputter, he had her all tangled up. "Have fun, *ishke*."

"You bully!" She wiggled and squirmed but couldn't seem to find where the edges had been tucked. Finally she gave up and sat in sulky silence as she listened to him dressing. As the blanket was finally unwrapped and pulled off her head, she narrowed her glower at him directly. "Next time I'm embarrassed about changing clothes, I'll get you stuck in a blanket, you jerk."

He smiled and leaned down to nuzzle her cheek with his. "But I can reassure you, remember?" He straightened up and stepped back. He held his hands out to his sides. "Well? How do I look? Will I pass for a desert dweller?"

She studied him critically, comparing him to the other men she had known. Comparatively, the open vest fit Dominic's wide shoulders and strong chest much better than most Magi men. It also revealed the golden lines on his chest, and that was a definite plus.

The pants were snug on the hips but loose around the legs so they fit him the same as anyone. The boots they were tucked into only went halfway up his calf instead of closer to his knee, meaning his legs were a little longer than most Magi. The sandy brown color complimented his coloring and especially his black hair. The little red streaks were much more distinct. "You'd pass," she decided with a smile. "It looks good on you."

Females only starting second puberty were hard on a man's ego. He smiled and scooped her up into his arms. She wound her arms around his shoulders and leaned against him with an absolute trust that touched something deep inside. "This must have been what Magi were jealous of," he said softly, burying his face in her hair.

She closed her eyes. "I know I would have been." She released him as he put her gently on her feet. "Let's go see Elder Juniper. I'm curious as to what the Magi are up to now."

They put on the cloaks they had been provided, then left the room with their hands linked. Watching them go past, Rumidia just smiled to herself and hoped she got to meet any child they eventually had. Dragon or Magi, the child would be spectacular with these two Dragoons for parents.

Sparkle was flying in circles in front of Juniper's door. "There you are!" she scolded as she saw them. "This is big, really big!" She flew over and landed on Dominic's shoulder then sat down. "You're never going to believe this."

"Magi discovered how to make boats fly?" Tariah guessed.

"No, better!"

Inside the Elder's home, Daylar was present as well and he was busily writing a letter to someone. Juniper was observing, but he stood with a smile as he saw who was entering. "Ah, there you are. Good morning to you both. Please, have a seat. Are either of you hungry?"

"A little," Tariah said as she sat on the couch.

Dominic grinned as he joined her. "I had breakfast."

"My power doesn't count." She elbowed him slightly.

"In that case, I suppose I could eat something." He skimmed his fingers through her long hair. He knew that she was going to put it up before they left. He wanted to take as much advantage of it as he could.

Sparkle flew off to fetch something for them and Juniper sat back in his chair. "Let me begin by saying that we have checked this information thoroughly and it is true. Daylar was quite busy this morning with that."

Daylar had finished his letter and he flew over to Tariah's shoulder. "Every Kin I know on Spectrum has confirmed it."

"Confirmed what?" she asked warily.

"The king of the Magi has sent out an order for a ceasefire to the Militia. They are to cease their blockade on the ports, and he has asked specifically that you come to

Spectrum as he wishes to meet you personally."

"What?" Her eyes slowly widened. "But . . . why? Magi hate Chronicles and they wanted me dead!"

"You are a Dragoon now," Dominic said softly. "If they kill you, they would have to kill me. Killing me would bring the Dragons down on them hard. My race has been waiting for an excuse to exact revenge and this would be the last straw."

"And," Daylar noted, "you are honorary Kin now as well. The treaty between Kin and Magi states that there will be no killing one another unless a breach of the treaty is made. As long as you obey their laws, they don't dare touch a hair on your head lest we have reason to come in and beat the hell out of them ourselves."

"A reason," Sparkle said as she handed bowls of savory rice and fruit blended together to both Dragoons, "that we will be happy to take. I mean, eradicating any of the three races entirely would completely destroy the world, but we could, you know, take out a few thousand or so."

"Sparkle," Juniper scolded. "That's not a very Kin point of view."

She looked at him fiercely. "If they touch Tariah, then I don't care."

Silence held for a bit as the Dragoons finished their meal. Dominic set his empty bowl aside and gently curled his hand around the back of Tariah's neck in comfort. He could feel the whirlwind of emotions inside her and he knew they were too turbulent for even her to understand let alone him. "It's your decision," he said softly. "Wherever your lines lead is where we will go."

As if called for, her lines pulsed and she felt the sharp tug inside. *North.* "I have to go north," she said softly. "I don't know more than that. But Spectrum is north of us so . . ." She set her bowl aside with a sigh. "I guess I meet the king. I don't want to, but I should, if only to prove I'm not some . . . monster."

"Speaking of monsters," Daylar said, "it may interest you to know that Symphony has had an outbreak recently. It's as if your disappearance disrupted the power flowing in the land. Crabs, dogs, cats, and even a few Magi, have been mutated into monsters. The Militia is keeping them at bay, but the city seems to blame them for driving you off. It looks like at least your home stands behind you."

Her throat closed. "I'm glad," she whispered. "At least that means I have somewhere I can visit that people won't think I am a monster myself."

"Indeed." Juniper stood even as they did. "May the moons guide you, Dragoons. Tariah, be sure to write to us." He smiled. "You are Kin enough now to at least be able to write to Daylar."

"It's a promise." Tariah hugged Daylar and then Sparkle when she flew over as well. "Both of you be good," she scolded softly. "And make sure to contact me when you're going to have your ceremony."

"We will!" Sparkle nodded firmly then wiped tears out of her eyes. "Be safe," she whispered as she watched the two Dragoons leave the house. Then, on a little sob, she turned and flew into Daylar's arms. She was going to miss Tariah something fierce!

Dominic and Tariah stopped only long enough to pick up supplies. She wore her share in a sack that was part of a belt she could wear around her waist. He opted for a regular sack he could carry over his shoulder. With a smile he said, "Of course, you'll have to hold onto it while we're flying."

"I can do that." She rested against his shoulder as they headed down to the dock where the beach was big enough for him to change form safely. She had yet to see him in his natural form, and she was very curious about it. She had never seen any Dragon up close; she had only seen images of them in books.

"Stay here," he told her as he stopped her at the edge of the trees. He handed her his bag then walked further away down the sand to where he had plenty of room. He knew that a lot of Magi, and even some Kin, found Dragons to be slightly alarming because of their sheer size. He was hoping that Tariah would not be afraid.

Red power flowed around him and fire blazed at his feet. It swept upward into an inferno for a few moments and obscured him from sight. When the fire faded away, there was a red and black Dragon standing where he had been moments prior.

Tariah's breath was held as she slowly walked forward. Somehow he seemed even more beautiful this way. His body was covered with scales that rippled like flames in the sunlight, and his wings were long and elegant. The skin between the ridges of bone was so thin that sunlight went through it and created reddish shadows. His golden lines still glimmered in the light as they flowed down the front of his body.

He was almost twice her height in his length from nose to tail. His face was hard and dangerous with sharp angles and wicked teeth visible when he opened his mouth even a little. The fins on his head were like small wings that curved upward to catch sound around him. His claws were long and wicked, made for rending metal and stone let alone flesh.

He was a terrifying, imposing sight, but she felt no fear as she crossed to him. She stopped in front of him, then smiled and held up her hands. He lowered his head toward her and nearly groaned as she began to softly stroke the scales on his face. Her hands seemed softer than ever against his Dragon skin. "You're not afraid," he said, and his voice was the same even though there was an echo of power in it.

"Why would I be?" His scales were *soft*, she realized in delight. More like feathers than skin. She gently wrapped her arms around his head and rubbed her cheek against his. She felt his surprise and smiled. "Dragons nuzzle each other to show affection, remember?"

He gave a bark of laughter and lifted her in his claws with a swiftness that startled her. She felt no actual fear, though. She held onto one of his fingers to maintain her balance as he opened his grip to let her stand on his palms. Now she knew how Sparkle felt! "Don't you dare drop me."

"I could never do that." He lifted her to eye level, fascinated at how tiny she seemed now. He felt as if he was holding a precious stone or something small and infinitely valuable. He would sooner tear off his wings than hurt her. "You want to ride or be carried?"

Her eyes glowed like coins with delight. "Ride! I want to feel like I'm flying too."

He lifted her toward his back and she climbed over easily. "Sit astride right above my wings. This way you will be balanced and not fall backwards no matter how fast we are going."

She did as she was told and felt her heart pounding with excitement. Hers, his, she didn't know. This first flight for them was the first real connection for them as Fury and Chronicle. Dragons *hated* to have passengers riding when they flew because the power of their rider clashed with their own. It made things uncomfortable for both.

But for Furies, their Chronicle was their other half. Their powers merged seamlessly. Flying together with Tariah riding his back was perhaps the single biggest statement they could make that they were Dragoons. "Hold on," he told her, and his wings kicked up sand as he flapped them and sent them flying into the air.

She clung onto his neck with a muffled shriek as they shot nearly straight up into the air. They hovered there for long moments and then he began flying across the sky at a speed she hadn't dreamed was possible. The ocean sped by below them ten times as fast as any ship ever made.

The feeling was indescribable. She straightened up to look around and felt the wind whipping through her hair. "It's incredible!" she said, wonder in her voice. "Dominic, this is incredible!"

He smiled. "I'll have to teach you how to take a Dragon form and you can return the favor. How does that sound?"

"It sounds like a deal." With a contented stretch of her arms, she leaned down until she was resting against his neck. If she got good at it then she would be able to take Sparkle and Daylar for a ride, just as she had promised. She didn't even worry about the rider thing; they were too small for that anyway. She could carry them in her claws. Even the idea of *having* claws tickled her. She couldn't wait to try everything in her new life.

Chapter Eight

The ocean flew below them like a streak of dark blue. Though the closest landmass was Carnelian, they could not fly over the top of it and straight to Spectrum. Dragons alone could disrupt the flow of power in the land where the cities were. A pair of Dragoons could disrupt the flow of the land as long as there were Magi somewhere nearby.

"Why is that?" Tariah asked as they flew along the edge of Carnelian more than two miles away from land. The continent looked like a strip of brown and dark green where plains and trees met. "Aren't we balanced?"

"We are," he told her, "but the Magi aren't." He smiled and swooped under a cloud to make her laugh. "Don't your Magi schools teach you anything?"

She ran her fingers through her hair to dislodge the Flutterlies that had gotten stuck. True to their names, they flew off in a flutter of white. Clouds on Lucksphere were made of thousands of the little creatures. Storms were a byproduct of too much Air or Water power, and they were made worse when Flutterlies started sucking up more from people on the surface.

"They do," she said, "but they never really go into detail. We only go to school for two years, Dominic. Long enough to learn about what Magi are and our role in this world. If we want to learn more, we need to learn it on our own time. And, I might point out, that there are few books about Dragons considering the, uhm, stressed relations between the two races."

"'Stressed relations' is a good term for wanting to beat the crap out of each other, I suppose." He angled down toward the ocean and just skimmed the surface. "Lucksphere is purely power, as you know. Power formed our world and then formed the three races that populate it. Magi are the power of the seas. Their presence prevents the oceans from overwhelming the land.

"Kin are the power of the land. Their presence is what allows lands to form and shift. Dragons are the power of the sky. Our presence is what keeps the sky from falling in and crushing those below. If any of these races were to be completely eradicated, then the world could fall apart."

She took a quick breath. "Like the war that instigated the treaty between Magi and Kin."

"Lucksphere, according to legend, used to have five continents the size of Spectrum. And now there's only one, Spectrum, the medium sized land of Glacia, the two smaller lands of Choral and Carnelian, and the island outposts of the Kin. The isle of the Dragons is smaller than Spectrum but larger than Glacia."

"So stupid," she whispered. "But I suppose it shows that Chronicles and Furies are not completely crucial to the world. Our destruction has had no effect."

"Hasn't it?" He let his power wrap around her as if in a gentle hug. "Two thousand years ago, when Chronicles were plenty, there were no outbursts in the land that mutated other beings. Look at Symphony. Your presence held it in line. When you were gone . . . it was a riot."

Tariah possessed an uncanny intelligence that she very rarely chose to exercise. She was finally beginning to understand her race, and with it came understanding of why they might exist. "There are too many Magi," she said slowly. "There is more sea than land or sky. That's why only Magi become Chronicles. Chronicles are made from the excess power in the world, and the Magi are the ones causing the excess because they are so clumped together onto minimal landmasses that the lesser amount of Kin can't keep things balanced. The presence of Chronicles gives the power a place to manifest and maintain the balance."

Dominic glanced back over his shoulder in surprise. "I had never considered that. Then why are Furies made from Dragons? We are not as numerous as Magi, but we are certainly more in population than the Kin."

"Because you are infinite. You are the sky, and the sky is infinite. No matter where you stand, eventually you will see an end to land or sea. But the sky is *never* gone."

Her mind was swirling through everything she had seen, heard, and felt, and it was a whirlwind that he didn't even try to attempt reading. Awe filled him as he realized that his desert girl had the intelligence of any ten scholars. Her uncanny grasp of little clues and ability to assemble them into a full story amazed him.

Everything she said made sense. To balance the output of Magi, Chronicles were made as power siphons. They took in the power of the world where it was excessive. Because it could in turn destroy them, Dragons, whose bodies were capable of infinite power, were made as Furies. But, unlike their brethren, a Fury didn't have infinite power. This gave the Chronicle a place to filter out the excessive power without upsetting the balance of nature.

"That's why," he said softly. "That's why erasing the Chronicles didn't stop them from appearing. And that's also why the children of Dragoons were not always Chronicles or Furies themselves."

"And," she said, smoothing a hand over his neck, "why we are opposite elements. If we were the same element, the same gender, or the same in any way, the generated power would be equally unbalanced." She frowned. "I can't, however, seem to figure out how our flying over land would be disruptive."

"That's simple enough. Power flows like waves in water. If you cross it slowly, you don't cause big ripples. If you cross it quickly, you make big waves. Dragons don't normally affect the land we fly over because we're out of range of the waves. But over cities, the power is much closer to the surface. As Dragoons, the opposite is true. You and I put out a power that is big enough to reach down to the land."

"Oh." She thought about it, then shrugged with a smile. "Well, as long as it is a law of nature and not a Magi law, I don't mind." She listened to his laugh then leaned down to gently hug him. "Are you alright? We've been flying for a few hours now."

"At this speed," he told her, "we should reach Spectrum by evening. But I will need to feed again. If you're tired, take a nap. I won't drop you."

"I know you won't." She lay against his neck and closed her eyes. "And I'm not tired. I'm actually enjoying this a lot. I never realized flying could be so much fun. We better not let the Magi know. They might try to build ships for the air or something."

The sun was sitting on the edge of the ocean to the west as Spectrum became more than a line in the distance. It had been a sliver of brown for almost an hour. Now it was steadily growing larger and larger. It was just like Choral in many ways since Spectrum was nearly one hundred percent desert but it did not get nearly as hot. Temperatures were more smothering than scorching, though visitors from Glacia rarely could tell the difference.

The nearest city to where they were approaching was still ten miles inland. It was not quite a port town, but it was still close enough to the beaches to catch the attention of travelers in their own boats and ships.

Dominic did not want to share Tariah with a city of Magi just yet. When he landed on the beach, he said, "Why don't we camp here tonight? I can't fly to the city, and it would be a few hours by foot."

"That's fine." She slid down off his back and landed gracefully on the sand. Her legs, however, were rubbery from lack of use and she stumbled several feet as she tried to walk. She would have taken a nosedive into the sand but Dominic was quick enough to catch her in his arms. She held onto him for balance as she waited for her legs to adjust. "How did you change back so quickly?" she asked curiously.

He gathered her closer to savor the feel of her in his arms. "It takes less energy to go into a Magi form than it does to go back to my Dragon one. I suppose because a Magi form is much more simplistic."

"I see." She smoothed her hands over his arms and discovered that she really liked the way his skin felt to her fingers. It was nearly as soft as his scales, but there was hard muscle packed underneath. It made her feel safer than she ever had in her life.

He cleared his throat. "Tariah?"

"Hmm?"

"Please stop petting me."

She frowned. "You don't like it?"

"It's more that I like it too much," he sighed. "When you're ready, I'll pet you all over and you'll find out what I mean."

"Oh." She stilled her fingers, suddenly realizing that the swirling emotions inside him were very volatile. The most overwhelming was the feeling that she felt inside herself for him. It was something the Magi might call 'love' but she felt it was too simple a word for the feeling. She also recognized hunger inside Dominic. It, his love for her, and a third emotion were all tangled together. She didn't recognize the third. "What *is* that called?" she asked.

He knew what she was asking. "The different races have different words for it. Magi call it 'desire.' But that seems too simple a term. Saying that I desire sleep when I am tired doesn't have the same impact as when I say I desire you every second of every minute of every hour."

Something deeply feminine inside her was thrilled at the idea that he wanted her that badly. "What do Dragons call it?"

"*Ishke.*"

Her eyes widened. "But that's what you've been calling *me* all this time. I thought it was an endearment."

"Well, it is." He leaned down and nuzzled her softly. Her scent was even stronger now, as if being in the desert that had given birth to her made her stronger. "It's a word encompassing all the wants, needs, and desires of the world. When I call you *ishke*, it means that you are the one thing I want, need, and desire more than anything. Even life."

That feminine emotion inside her was giddy. *She* was giddy. She warily pressed a hand to her heart. "I feel funny when you say that."

"Funny how?"

She tilted her head. "Like I had just won something that I'd been after as long as I was alive." She sighed at the look in his eyes. "Is this another puberty thing?"

"I'd guess so. I'd never felt that until meeting you, though, so perhaps it's a onetime occurrence." He studied her. "That's odd, though. It seems as though you are developing at a much quicker rate. I don't know if it is because you are a Chronicle, or because of my presence."

"I don't care which it is." She cuddled against him. "I'm just glad it won't go on for months!"

"Me too!" was his heartfelt mutter. He buried his nose against her neck and hunger roared to life. His majiks were very low, and her power had welled in response to his need. It flowed over her like a blue aura just begging for his attention.

He wanted to savor every moment. He had lived without her for centuries, and there was no reason to hurry. He lifted her right hand to his lips and pressed a kiss to the character on her palm. In Magi, 'chron' meant 'life.' In Kin, it meant 'strength.' In Dragon, it meant 'heart's keeper.' He thought it was the perfect symbol for his Chronicle.

He softly drank her power as he trailed his lips up her arm. It was sweet like wine and much more potent than it had been before. "Desert girl," he murmured huskily. "I didn't realize what that might really indicate."

She wasn't really paying attention to his words. She was trying to analyze the odd feelings inside her body. Her skin was tingling and sensitive, and she felt oddly lightheaded and breathless. They were not unpleasant feelings, but they were odd. "Dominic?"

"Hmm?" He drank her power from where her shoulder met her neck. When she was out of second puberty, he was going to drink his fill everywhere. Every curve and hollow had its own taste and texture. His control was strained as he fought the urge to go exploring.

"I feel odd."

He lifted his head quickly. "Am I hurting you?" he asked quickly. "Did I frighten you?"

"No." She frowned thoughtfully. "It's not a bad feeling. I feel slightly dizzy though. And my skin feels sensitive."

His pulse began to beat cheerfully throughout his entire body as the other half of his hunger for her surged forward. He ached and burned to possess her, to touch and caress and savor her body. His own Fire powers didn't make him that hot. "Well." It was the best he could manage around his tight throat. "It sounds like your body is trying to catch up to your emotions."

Oddly, knowing that it was perfectly normal made her wariness fade away entirely. She smiled. "I'm supposed to feel really good in more than my heart when you're touching me?"

"The moons save me from curious Chronicles in second puberty!" he muttered.

"Dominic, please. If I can't ask you, who can I ask?"

He cupped her face in his hands and felt her emotions with his. "Let's put it this way," he said roughly. "When you are fully matured, what you feel right now will be like a grain of sand compared to a desert the size of the ocean."

Her eyes widened to pools of liquid silver. The evening sun made them shimmer and ripple like molten metal. The sight took his breath. "That sounds a bit scary," she said softly. And yet, she wasn't scared. She could see and sense how the emotions affected her lover, and though they were almost frighteningly immense, they weren't truly alarming.

"It is," he agreed. "But it's very nice when it's shared." He leaned down and softly touched her lips with his to continue drinking her power. He let his emotions mesh with hers so that he would know precisely what she felt.

The lightheadedness was there to diminish her thought processes. Her lips were tingling and she was a bit flushed. None of it, however, was actually directed wholly at him. It was merely her body beginning to develop the proper sensations and signals. Her body was beginning to decide what it wanted. It was far more than he'd hoped to see for a long time. Feeding hunger appeased, he lifted his head slowly. "When you're ready to start experimenting, just let me know."

"Deal." She released him and smiled. "Let's see about feeding *me* now. I need dinner."

By the time the sun had fully sunk and the moons had risen in the sky, Dominic and Tariah were secure in the camp they had made on the beach. Dinner had been made from a desert rabbit that she had caught and he had cooked, and she was feeling very full and surprisingly content. She stretched out on her back and stared up at the sky, simply grateful that she could.

Dominic returned from disposing of the remains of dinner, and he sat down beside her. He smiled as she automatically shifted and put her head on his lap. He smoothed his fingers down her lines softly. "I didn't think anyone so tiny would be so dangerous."

She smiled. "I used to spend long hours climbing cliffs to get supplies. You build up a lot of strength that way. And I've always been fast, so my ice power makes a good projectile weapon."

"I'd noticed." He had been utterly fascinated as he'd watched her successfully track and roust the rabbit, only to kill it from almost two hundred feet away by using a single sliver of ice. "Remind me to never make you mad."

She muffled a giggle as she snuggled closer. "I keep wondering," she said softly, "when I might develop my secondary skills, like I heard would happen. I don't even know what they are."

He cocked his head. "That's a good question. There are three Dragoon abilities. They in turn will evolve into their own secondary abilities. But that won't happen for another fifty years or so."

The idea of being with her Fury for fifty years or longer pleased her greatly. "What are the skills?"

"Telepathy, which is the reading of minds. Telekinesis, which is the movement of objects using the mind. And Ultravision, which is the ability to touch something and see its history in your mind." He ran his fingers through her hair. "Are you going to put this up when we start traveling?"

"Of course. It's too hot to wear it down." Her finger drew absent designs in the sand beside her. "I don't know if I'd want to read minds. There are some things I just don't want to know or hear. I'd want to be able to control it."

"Maybe it's time to find out what we can do." He eased her up off his lap. "Let's just see. We can try applying our minds to something and see if anything happens. Here. Close your mind to me, and I'll see if I can read it even without our bond."

She obligingly, if reluctantly, closed her mind and cut off his presence. She immediately felt cold inside. She liked having him inside her mind at all times. The endless flow of power between them always made her feel warm and secure. "I'm going to think of something really silly," she said. "Something so outrageous that you'll start laughing the minute you see it. Then we'll really know."

He concentrated as hard as he could and probed at her mind. It remained firmly and stubbornly sealed. He pushed, he prodded, and he metaphorically shook, but the barriers remained firm. With a sigh, he said, "I don't think Telepathy will be my skill." He tilted his head. "What were you thinking about?"

She leaned up and whispered in his ear. Almost immediately he gave a shout of laughter. "Remind me never to doubt you again about your capacity for silliness." He let out a little breath as he felt her mind open for him. He had been lonely without having her there to touch at his will. He possessively gathered her closer mentally and with his power as well. It was just as good as having his arms around her. "Okay," he said. "Your turn."

"But I don't want to close you off again." She frowned and began to mentally poke around his mind. "Where's something you're hiding from me?"

"I'm hiding nothing," he defended himself.

"You are too. There's a big dark spot." She kept poking until she finally found the spot he had blocked off. It was part of his memories and she was immediately interested all the more. "Past lovers?" she asked. She poked again at the spot and waited for jealousy. It didn't arrive this time. It didn't take long for her to realize that it was her growing confidence that had erased the ugly emotion. She better understood how he felt, and that meant she knew nothing in his past was a threat.

He just sighed. "Stay out of those memories, *ishke*. They're hidden for your sake." The argument was for form only. He knew she would get inside; her mental strength felt unusually sharp and seemed to be growing stronger.

She poked and prodded at the barrier then tried pushing. Unexpectedly, she found herself on the other side. His memories were laid out before her, and they were indeed of past relationships. She gave them barely more than a cursory look. She really didn't care. It was enough to know she had access. "Who was the Kin Elf?"

He smiled as he took down the barrier. "I had a feeling you'd ask that. She was my first. Stayed friends up until she passed away a few years ago." He skimmed his thumb over her lower lip. "Telepathy must be your Dragoon skill."

"I don't want it." Her voice was as sulky as her face. "I don't want to read minds."

"You have to do it on purpose. You won't just hear what's inside people's

66

heads." He sighed when she got to her feet and walked away. He'd had a feeling she would do that. "Come back here. Don't sulk." She didn't respond and he got to his feet. "Tariah, come back here. It'll be just fine."

She shot him a look over her shoulder. "Stop trying to placate me. After everything I've dealt with, I've earned my sulk about being given the ability to read the minds of the people who want me dead!"

"You have to admit, that'd be useful."

"Hmph." She swung around to pace off her annoyance and suddenly felt something wrap around her. She gave a startled yelp as the invisible grip yanked her backwards off her feet. She landed on her ass in the sand with a thump. "Ouch!"

"Oh, shit." Her lover rushed to her side and knelt down. "Are you okay? Did you get hurt?" He ran his hands over her quickly. "That was *not* my intent, Tariah, I promise!"

"Don't touch me, you fiend!" She slapped at his hands. "I don't care what your intent was! If I want space, you have to give me space!"

He bit his lip to hide a smile at the evidence of her temper. He had been wondering if she would have one. Most Water elements were fairly even-tempered, but they could eventually be provoked. "Now, Tariah."

"Don't 'now' me!" She poked him in the chest. "Promise you won't do that again unless I'm in danger!"

"Alright, I'm sorry!" He was careful to keep his amusement hidden. "I won't do it again unless there's danger." Sensing her ire fading, he caught her in his arms and tumbled her down onto the sand. He braced his weight on his elbows to keep from crushing her but he remained close. "Feisty little thing."

She blinked then smiled. "I guess I am. It felt kind of nice to get mad for once." The anger evaporated quickly as she cuddled closer to his wonderfully warm body. His weight and scent was stirring up that feminine thing inside, but she ignored it. Until it decided to be *specific* about what she felt and wanted, she didn't really care.

"Are you falling asleep?" His voice was warm.

"No." She gave a little yawn. "But I think I could. I'm sleepy suddenly." She closed her eyes and curled up on her side as he released her and got to his feet. She heard him establishing a protective barrier to keep out other people and creatures alike before she felt him return and lay down beside her.

She promptly turned over and snuggled up tightly against him. His arms closed around her, and she gave a soft little sigh. "I can't figure out how I ever slept peacefully without you," she murmured, rubbing her cheek against him.

"Me neither." He pressed his lips gently to her hair. "Go to sleep now." He closed his eyes as he listened to her breathing even and her power go quiet. Only then did he let himself think about the future. He had a house on the Isle, but it was in the mountains. He would have to move it closer to the desert for her sake. It would have to be made bigger, too, just in case she wanted as many kids as he did.

Thinking about all the fun and terror it would be to raise a brood with his Chronicle's frightening temper and intelligence, he fell asleep smiling.

Chapter Nine

They broke camp the following morning right after dawn. "How far are we from Prismatic?" Tariah asked as they set out on foot across the sandy dunes.

Dominic glanced up at the sky where only two of the four moons were still visible in the rapidly lightening blue color. Since he was only able to see the moons to the west and south, he was able to pinpoint the direction to Prismatic. "We're about a week's worth of walking away at the minimum. Refraction is our first city and I believe it is almost exactly eight days away from Prismatic."

She sighed. "There's only one bright side in all of that."

"What's that?"

"I get to spend the time with you." She smiled at him. "When I was running across the desert from Symphony, it was worse because I was alone. But now I'm not."

He could find nothing to say to that that would possibly convey how he felt. The best he could manage was to gently curl his fingers around the back of her neck and draw her closer. No hair impeded his touch, and he eyed the top of her head balefully. Upon waking, she had promptly fastened her hair up on top of her head in an elaborate coil of braids. He *still* didn't know how she had done it.

She grinned. "Girl magic, as Sparkle called it."

"I won't deny that the females of any species have a strange and powerful magic over us helpless males." Laughter lurked in his voice. "But then again, perhaps it is simply our hearts that make us so helpless."

"Perhaps it is." She linked her hands behind her back. "I'm helpless to you, but I'm not attracted to you, so it must just be my heart." She tilted her head back to let the sun wash over her face. "Of course, I'm sure it will be both eventually."

"You could be bad for my ego if I let you." He tucked his hands in his pockets as the sun rose steadily higher and the air heated. In the desert, during the hottest parts of the day, physical contact was vastly uncomfortable because skin-to-skin generated heat as well. Much as he wanted to touch Tariah, he kept his hands to himself.

Two hours of walking later and they were seeing the shape of Refraction wavering in the heat waves from the sand. He was sweating and sweltering, but she didn't seem to be affected at all. It fascinated him all over again that she was so truly a part of the desert. He knew people who were truly 'of' the land were at home there, but he hadn't imagined just how much that entailed. "I'm a little envious."

She stuck her tongue out at him briefly. "It's just worse for you because you're a Fire element. Your internal temperature is higher to begin with. I'm much cooler so I can shed the heat of the sun. Actually, it's more like I soak it up. I *love* the desert heat."

As the city grew larger before them, she began to feel tension gathering inside. Refraction was not much bigger than Symphony but it was still bigger than she was comfortable with. It was built in a spiral direction to take advantage of the power in the land. The biggest concentration of people was in the very center, but there were still many along the outer edges where the two Dragoons were approaching.

They had barely reached the entrance when several men stepped into their way. "The Dragon can pass," one man said icily, "but the abomination stays out here."

Tariah said nothing. Dominic barely bit back a snarl. "You *did* hear there was a ceasefire, correct?"

"That's the only reason she's still alive." The man gave Tariah a onceover with his eyes, and disgust filled their depths. "If I had my way, she'd be dead where she stands. Chronicles are a revulsion of nature!"

"We're leaving." Dominic pulled Tariah closer protectively. "They can keep their bigoted hate to themselves and we'll keep our coin."

She shook her head. "We're crossing to Prismatic, Dominic. We need more than just a few supplies. You're going to want a cloak, too. You're not cut out for the desert. I'll be fine out here. You can get what we need."

He knew she was right but he didn't like leaving her alone. "Be careful," he said softly as he leaned down to press his lips to her cheek. "Call for me if they even look at you funny, understand?"

"I understand." Her heart squeezed tightly for a moment as she watched him walk into the city. It was wonderful to know someone loved her that deeply. She could count on him to be there for her no matter what.

Disinclined to remain near the idiots glaring at her, she moved away from the entrance and sat down on the sand. She had been expecting this from the beginning. Magi had been believing in the 'evil' of Chronicles for centuries. They wouldn't stop thinking it just because the king said not to kill her.

Sensing stares, she turned her head to see several small children peering around the side of a building. They were watching her with expressions ranging from awe to wonder. There was no fear in their eyes. She smiled and waved at them, and they waved back with happy smiles. It helped ease her heart. Maybe there was hope for the Magi race.

A hard hand closed over her shoulder and shoved her flat onto the sand. She rolled over and scrambled up to her knees, her heart pounding madly. Three men were looming over her, and they wore ugly smirks on their faces. Something disgusting was in their eyes that she did not recognize but despised anyway. "Go away!" she ordered.

"Sex with a Chronicle is supposed to give you power," one chortled. "Let's find out!"

Her eyes narrowed dangerously. "You're going to wish you'd never had that idea."

~*~

Dominic had just paid for a week's worth of supplies and transferred it to his backpack when four little kids came running up to him. "Dragon!" The littlest of the girls grabbed his leg tightly. "You need to hurry!"

"What's wrong?" he asked in surprise. The other three grabbed his hands and began to pull, and he couldn't figure out what had put such terror in their eyes. The answer came as a sharp stabbing sensation inside his soul that could only be Tariah's fear. Her voice ripped across his mind in a mental cry, and an explosion of Water and Ice erupted outside the city.

The roar that emerged from his lips came from the very bottom of his soul. It was the roar of a fully-grown Dragon who had been wronged, and it was a chilling sound. No one in the city had heard it before, and every adult cowered back in fear.

On the contrary, not a single child was affected. The four who had gone to Dominic were more relieved than anything. As he rushed through the city faster than any Magi could travel, they scrambled after him as fast as their legs could carry them. They wanted to make sure that the pretty lady with the nice eyes wasn't hurt.

She wasn't hurt yet. She was pissed off. The bomb of Water and Ice had rendered one of her attackers half-frozen. Another nearly drowned when she encased herself in water and he couldn't release her arm in time. The third was a Water Magi, and he was mostly unaffected by anything she could throw. He dug his fingers into her arm and slapped her sharply across the face. "Stop fighting! Be nice and we won't hurt you!"

Her silver eyes turned crystalline blue as Dominic's majiks poured into her body. "Funny. I could say the same thing!" She shoved her free hand hard against his chest, and her power punched him pointblank with enough force to send him flying backwards onto the sand. Astonished, she stared at her hands. She hadn't known she could do that with power.

All three men were struggling to regroup when the piercing roar cut across the air. They went very still and slowly turned around to see Dominic rushing out of the city. A blur of red Fire shifted him to Dragon form halfway, and he landed next to them hard. The ground rocked and sand flew. The men flew as well, like leaves in a wind. Dominic's claws lashed out and he grabbed them before they landed. His gray eyes had gone red with rage. "Tell me why I shouldn't kill you!" he snarled gutturally.

On shaky legs, Tariah walked toward him. Other than a few bruises and the red mark on her face, she was relatively fine. "Let them go, Dominic."

"No." His razor sharp teeth bared in a mockery of a smile. "I'd rather eat them."

"You'll get indigestion." She pressed against his chest and wrapped her arms around as much of him as she could. "Don't lower yourself to their level."

He technically had every right to avenge her assault, and that was a right that applied under every species' laws. On the other hand, it would get them in trouble with the Militia. Her pain made him want to start chomping into her attackers, but her fear made him hold himself back. With obvious and careful control, he turned and tossed the men toward the city. They landed with thumps, their eyes wide and white with horror. "Be glad my mate is more forgiving than I!" he snarled at them.

The men scrambled into the city, and Dominic turned back to Tariah. He lowered his head and nuzzled her softly to comfort them both. She wound her arms around his neck and rubbed her cheek against his scales. He was an awe-inspiring sight, and she was both proud and astonished that such a magnificent creature belonged to her.

Red light flared and he turned to Magi form. She held on through the change and found herself dangling from his neck. Her feet left the ground, but she didn't care. His arms closed around her waist and held her tight. The lingering majiks inside her faded, and his presence filled the space left behind.

The children came running forward and there were many more than just the four who had fetched Dominic. At least fifteen clustered around Tariah and Dominic, and all were talking over each other as they sought reassurances. "I'm fine," Tariah told them. "Really. Thank you for caring."

One of the older girls shook her head. "We're really sorry about what happened. You haven't done anything to us. Why should we hate you? We'll tell our parents what *really* happened. We won't let anyone blame you."

"Thank you," she said softly. "But we're leaving anyway to keep the peace."

"It's stupid!" a small boy blurted. "You're not a monster! You're just different! Why are we supposed to be scared of something that's just different?"

Dominic smiled as the children went running back into the city. "Out of the mouths of children, as they say." He turned and ran his hands over Tariah swiftly. "Are you sure you're alright?" He found the bruises on her arms and a low growl rumbled in his chest. "Damn them!" He leaned down and softly pressed his lips to the mark on her face. "I should have eaten them anyway!"

She bit her lip but a soft snicker escaped anyway. When he glowered at her, she softly framed his face with her hands. "You wouldn't eat them, and you know it! Kill them maybe, but not eat them." She pressed her lips to his in a comforting kiss. "I was never truly afraid," she said gently. "I knew you'd save me."

He enfolded her in his arms and wrapped his new cloak around them both as well. Heat of the desert be damned. He wanted his Chronicle to be protected from everything. She was the most precious thing he owned. "Let's leave," he said softly, touching his lips to her forehead. "And even if we pass another city, we're not entering it."

"Agreed."

They set out once more across the desert. They didn't speak much as they walked. They were simply content to keep the silence and listen to the endless flow of power that circled between them. It was perhaps the most comfortable silence either Tariah or Dominic had ever felt. They didn't have to speak to understand one another.

After a while, almost four hours out of Refraction, curiosity got the better of Tariah and she asked, "What are the Dragons like? Their society, I mean. They're almost never seen anywhere. The few books about them just describe their appearance, not their way of life." She glanced up at Dominic. "From what I've felt from you, I guess you're all very close."

"Very much so." He smiled. "We're sectioned into four clans, one for each element. We have more Elders than most because we're immortal, but one from each clan is elected every hundred years to sit on the Council of Elders. They keep the laws."

"I bet they get loud."

"Good bet." He chuckled softly. "When they fight, you can hear it all the way across the land!"

She grinned. "Who is the loudest?"

"Hmm. Tough one. Probably the Air Clan Elder. He's stubborn." He skimmed a finger down her cheek. "I'm sure they'll be thrilled to meet you. For so long we've wanted so badly to find even one Chronicle."

She glanced at him solemnly. "You don't need to feel guilty. None of you are at fault. How could you have known how it would end?"

He closed his eyes. "Saying it isn't the same as believing it, especially when you've been watching others suffer for a millennia. Dragons will inherit the memories and feelings of those who pass on. It's how we make sure that important things are carried on even when our immortal bodies fade."

She slipped her hand into his. "So that's how you know so much about Chronicles despite being so young."

"Yes. I inherited from a Fury who lived at the end of the war. His Chronicle had not yet been born." There was a combined sadness and bleakness in his eyes. "He felt her birth and death before I was born. The day that he was put out of his misery was the same day I hatched."

"Now we live in memory of all of them," she said. She stopped and held him tightly. "Chronicles . . . we've suffered too. My entire life I *knew* there was someone out there. But I had no name for the feeling until Maxim told me about Furies. If I'd never found you . . . I'd have died too."

"Tariah." He buried his face against her hair for long moments then reluctantly released her. "I'm getting you all sweaty. It's too damned hot in this desert."

"I like it."

"You're a desert girl. I'm a mountain Dragon." He looked around. "Are there any oases nearby? And, if not, could you make one?"

He looked so hopeful and adorable that she burst into laughter. "Okay, okay. Let's see if we can find one to camp at." She lifted her head and scented the air. She could smell the strong surge of Water power in the land. "There is one near. To the . . . east." She smiled. "It should be a nice one. The power is strong."

It took them less than ten minutes of walking toward the east to spot the oasis she had felt. They would never have seen it if they hadn't deviated from their route, but they were glad to be seeing it now.

Because Water power in the desert would gather close under the surface, oases were formed. They were little patches of trees and grass and water amid the desert landscape. They looked like little islands in a sea of sand. This one, in particular, was on the larger side. It had actually grown full size trees, and quite thickly too.

Dominic made Tariah wait at the edges of the trees while he prowled the interior to make sure they were the only ones there. Once he was sure, he returned to her side and escorted her deeper into the trees. "Wait until you see," he told her.

She almost didn't have to see anything. She could smell and feel the water. Still, her sigh was long and heartfelt as she saw the deep pool of water shimmering under the sun. "I think I've died and gone to the Underrealm." She hurried forward to drop her hipsack on the ground then only waited long enough to remove her boots. Clothes and all, she dove into the pool without a splash.

He started laughing. "And I thought I wanted a swim!" He hardly blamed her. There were times when he loved to take the smallest Dragon form he possibly could, barely a foot in length, and crawl into a fire pit. It had been his favorite napping spot as a kid. Anticipating a nice swim, he removed his cloak and shirt and got to work on his boots.

She surfaced and turned to tease him when she realized he was removing his boots. He had already removed his top clothing and the sunlight flowed over his smooth skin and cast fascinating shadows along his muscles. The lines on his chest seemed more golden than ever and gave his already beautiful form something else. It was something she could not name, and she had never noticed it before.

Her breath held, she watched him as he dove, still half clothed, into the pool with her. She felt flushed and breathless, her stomach fluttering in an odd way. In fascination, she lifted her hands and looked at them. She had never before had an urge to run her fingers over him, but now she wanted to so badly that her fingers seemed to itch.

A hand closed around her ankle and tugged her underwater. She muffled a yelp as she was dunked then she blew a stream of bubbles at her grinning partner. Indignant, she swam away and surfaced again. He surfaced behind her and she turned around to splash him. "Meany."

"You seemed distracted," he scolded her. "I wanted your attention."

She watched almost helplessly as water drops ran down his strong shoulders when he straightened up. The water went halfway up his chest where he was standing, and the part out of the water seemed to shine in the sunlight. She wondered why her mouth was dry when the air was moist. A bit disturbed by her body's sudden reaction, she turned away slightly. "You have it," she whispered.

He had no compunctions about tangling his emotions with hers to find out why she was acting so oddly. The feelings that then seemed to surge into him made his entire body tighten with stifled desire. "I see," he managed to say, but his voice was huskier than usual, "that maybe I won't be suffering for long."

She looked at him with a frown. "This is a puberty thing, isn't it?" she accused.

"Afraid so, *ishke*." He searched her eyes and saw the beginnings of her awareness of him as a mate. He slowly swam toward her to draw her into his arms. "Take your hair down," he said softly, his voice still husky with his desire for her. He wanted to see her hair flowing around them.

She felt a shiver that went from her bones outward at the sound of his voice. It was as if everything suddenly seemed sensual to her. Everything he did or said made little flutters of something skim along her nerves. It was a feeling of pure delight, and one that something inside her readily embraced. "I feel so odd," she murmured.

"You're getting twice the signal." He turned in a circle and let her float before him gracefully. "You seem to be skipping right over one of the primary stages of puberty. Normally what you're feeling would occur with anything that you liked. Everything would be sensitive to your developing senses." He lowered his head and softly nuzzled behind her ear. "But I guess because I'm here, you're zeroing right in on me as a target."

"Oh." She closed her eyes and let herself savor how it felt to feel him so close physically and emotionally. It combined with the cool feeling of the water to make her skin almost unbearably sensitive. A little afraid, she grabbed onto him. "I don't like this."

He sighed softly, his eyes tender as he carried her toward the shore. "That's because you're trying to convince yourself that something is wrong."

"Isn't it?" she asked curiously as he set her gently on the grass. She didn't let go of him and he was forced to sit beside her. For some reason, she simply couldn't bear the idea of releasing him. Her hands felt glued to him. "I'm going through second puberty in a *week* when it's supposed to take a *year*!"

He ran his tongue over his teeth. "Yes, but that's because of me I think." He lowered his head to touch hers. "What I feel when I touch you," he said softly, "is much more than I've ever felt before, Tariah. I breezed through second puberty because it seemed so comfortable and unimportant. But those feelings came back when I met you. The curiosity and the hunger to learn another's body. Not just anyone, but you. And it's a million times stronger for you."

"But it doesn't scare you," she said softly, searching his eyes. "Why not?"

"Because while I know that what is between us is bigger than before, I at least know what it is and what we're in for." He nuzzled her neck. "Take your hair down. Please? And take your time. I like it."

Her fingers were trembling slightly as she reached up and began to untuck the little twists she had made in her hair. As each tuck came undone, a braid fell down and unraveled from the weight of her soaked hair.

He was holding his breath as he watched her. He had always thought there was something very beautiful about a woman taking her hair down, but when it was Tariah it was downright sensual. Her silver eyes seemed deeper than ever, like a pool he could drown in. It took every drop of his willpower not to kiss her as he craved. For all her awakening sensuality, a true kiss would likely terrify her when she was still trying to adjust to the sensitivity of her body.

She was never looking at taking her hair down the same way again. Her heart and her stomach were quivering with an odd sort of desire as she watched the smoke of his eyes deepen. The feel of her own hair sliding over her skin was powerful to her senses, and it made her want to feel his hair as well. Nerves tangled with needs and she kept her hands to herself.

As her hair tumbled down to her waist and swung softly behind her, he caught a handful and brought it to his cheek. He rubbed against it softly, as if it was the finest of silks. Breathless, she could only watch him helplessly. He felt her gaze and smiled slowly. "I take pleasure in everything about you. I thought you realized."

"Realizing it, knowing it, and understanding it," she said, her voice slightly huskier than usual, "are three entirely different things." She drew a long breath and moved away slightly. "Can we talk about something else?"

"Of course." He reluctantly released her hair and watched it slide through his fingers. He could hardly wait until he could see it fanned across his pillow back home. "What do you want to talk about?"

"Teach me majiks." She smiled suddenly. "I want to try and turn into a Dragon."

He grinned. "You do, huh?"

"Absolutely!" She scooted closer to him once more. "So . . . what do I have to do? How do I do it?"

"I'll help you. You won't know how to bend the majiks otherwise." He moved closer until their knees bumped together. Instead of wrapping his power around hers as he often did, this time he blended them together. It was quite easy when the power between them flowed back and forth as an endless loop. "Just watch what I do, and do it yourself."

She closed her eyes and watched how he was bending his majiks. She drew the majiks into herself and began to bend them as she had seen him do. Her body began to feel cool like water and she felt her skin throbbing as it responded to how she was changing her power.

She was concentrating so fiercely that when the change occurred it startled her. With a little gasp, she opened her eyes. Two things dawned on her belatedly. One, she was in Dominic's hands. Two, she was only barely half a foot big. Her eyes widened as she looked up at him. "I think I did something wrong."

He bit his lip. Then he bit his tongue. As her indignation grew, he bit his cheek. Finally he gave up and began laughing as he held her up to eye level. She was, easily, the cutest little Dragon he had ever seen. She was barely half a foot long and covered with soft auburn scales the same color as her hair. Little streaks of blue along the scales rippled like waves and marked her Water power.

"I think," he said, his voice warm, "that you just need practice. You're a cute little whelp, though. You'll be quite beautiful as a full Dragon. Little, probably, but beautiful." He rubbed his cheek against her gently. "Want to try flying?"

"Of course!" She was still in his mind, and she followed the knowledge inside him as to how to make her wings work. It warmed her to know he had crashed more than once while learning to fly. She wanted to do much better, especially because she wasn't born a Dragon. She concentrated hard, flapped her wings lightly, and rose up over his hands. "I did it!"

"Show off." Pride filled him. "Even full Dragons don't always hover first try."

"I know." Her voice was smug as she cautiously began to fly around him in circles. She landed on his shoulder and balanced delicately. "This is *really* wonderful, Dominic. Thank you." She tickled his ear with her tongue in the Dragon's form of a kiss.

"No tickling." He rubbed his cheek against her. "Take your time," he told her.

Much as she would have liked to, she had sensed his hunger before he could block it. She shook her head slightly and flew off his shoulder. It was even easier to unbend the majiks and return to her normal form. She shook her hair back then moved closer and wound her arms around his shoulders. "Teaching me drained you. I can feel it."

"Only because it was the first time you'd tried. It'll eventually be easy enough that it doesn't affect me at all." He watched a drop of water run down her neck and shoulder from her damp hair and told himself not to sink his teeth in as if she was a dessert.

Her eyes widened. She had always assumed biting someone was meant to hurt. But if the flutter of her heart and blood was anything to go by, the ideas tumbling in his mind were certainly starting to appeal. She was beginning to understand them, and to recognize inside herself the beginnings of that third emotion that was so volatile in her Fury. The feeling that Dragons called *ishke*.

She was also beginning to believe that even that word wasn't enough to encompass her feelings, or his, and it was an oddly comforting belief. She smiled. "Let's see about feeding you now, and dessert can be planned for the future."

He gave a laugh then caught her close against him in a fierce hug. He was absolutely and completely over his tail and madly in love with his beautiful Chronicle. A part of him was even beginning to pity the Magi. They would never know this feeling. "Their loss," he said as he eased back. "Now, about that dinner."

75

Chapter Ten

Tariah awoke the following morning to discover herself sleeping on top of Dominic. It was more comfortable than she would have thought and the feel of his heart beating under her ear was deeply soothing. With a soft sigh, she curled closer. There were times it really was nice to be small.

There were also times it wasn't nice to be an early riser. She stifled a yawn and slid off his chest. She sat up with a languid stretch just as a misty rain began to fall. The storm overhead was typical of the desert: small, lightweight, and welcome respite from the heat. The rain felt wonderful as it fell on her skin.

She lifted her hands and studied them. Her skin was still hypersensitive, but she was beginning to enjoy it. Somehow it turned everything into a small thrill. It felt a bit like being born again.

Dominic was still asleep. She moved to the edge of the pool and sat on the side with her feet in the water. She felt oddly suspended. Something inside her heart and soul seemed to be waiting. She couldn't put her finger on what it was but decided it didn't matter. She just smiled and closed her eyes. She tilted her face up to enjoy the rain just as Dominic had taught her to enjoy so much else.

When he woke, he automatically reached for her only to realize she wasn't there. He sat up quickly and looked around. His initial grumpiness faded immediately when he spotted her sitting on the side of the pool with her face lifted to the rain like a desert flower. Desire fisted inside his body with gleeful force. It was getting harder and harder to keep his hands to himself.

She had known when he woke, and she suddenly felt the intensity of his emotions. It sent off little shivers of delight through her body that grew steadily stronger as she probed the force of his feelings and saw how deep they went. "Dominic?" she asked without turning around.

"What is it?" He walked over to sit beside her. For the first time, he wasn't sure what she was thinking. Her emotions seemed like an enigma suddenly and they swirled with brilliant colors he could not decipher.

She turned to look at him. Her silver eyes were dark like the lining of the clouds over their heads. "I want you to kiss me."

Lightning cracked to the ground near them. It could have been coincidence or the storm responding to the surge of his power. He held his breath as he stared into Tariah's eyes. They looked like the eyes of a grown woman, and they were dark with mysteries he was desperate to unlock. "Are you sure?" he asked huskily, lifting a hand to cup her cheek.

She smiled and rubbed her cheek against his hand. "I wouldn't ask if I wasn't. You told me I would know. And I do." With an instinct that was stamped into her very cells, she moved closer and wound her arms around his shoulders. He was strong and powerful and the feel of his body was thrilling. "I know how I feel when you aren't touching me. Now I want to know how I feel when you are."

"I'm going to lay down some rules first." His voice was thick with his emotions. It felt as though he was being given a gift beyond measure. "You have to hold my hands."

Her brow lifted ever so slightly. "Why?"

"To keep me in line," he said in frustration. "Do you know how long I've wanted to kiss you? To *really* kiss you? If you don't hold my hands I might start putting them places that would terrify you right now."

She had a feeling he was right. As badly as she wanted his kiss, something inside seemed to shy back at the idea of someone touching her intimately, even her Fury. A part of it was trepidation. She *knew* that how she felt could only grow stronger. She just wasn't ready for that yet. "I trust you." Despite saying it and feeling it, she took his hands with hers and laced their fingers together.

Since it meant he could not hold her, he curled his power around her instead. Her power met and merged with his in a return embrace and it was once more flowing between them like an endless loop. "Do you want to kiss me, or should I kiss you?" he asked her softly.

She thought about it then smiled. "I want to kiss you."

"Then I'm all yours, *ishke*."

She eased closer, her eyes moving over his face with a hunger she had never felt before. Just like the rest of the world, it seemed as if she might be seeing him for the first time too. She had always believed him to be handsome but it was different now. Now the lines of his face brought up an urge to touch rather than merely admire. Curious how that worked.

She softly touched her lips to his and a little shiver of delight went down her back. His lips were the same as they had always been, yet now the shape and feel of them made her body tingle with pleasure. She sighed and let herself savor the feeling as she memorized the shape of his lips with her own.

He was *very* glad she was holding his hands. His eyes smoldered with desire as he watched her face. The feel of her lips was seductive, and the look on her face as she began to learn what was between them was doubly potent. He wanted to snatch her up in his arms and take the kiss from her. He wanted to cover her body with more kisses and satisfy her every curiosity and claim her for his own. It was nearly pain inside him, the hunger for her, and he couldn't have hidden his feelings if he had tried.

His feelings swept over her but she did not fear them this time. She *wanted* to know he needed her. The fierceness of his feelings unlocked that strange feminine feeling inside and she felt an odd urge to put her mark on him. She wanted other women to look at him and know that he was hers. A little confused because she didn't know how to obtain what she wanted, she eased back. Her eyes met his smoky gray gaze and he murmured thickly, "Don't worry about that right now. It's just a kiss." He freed his hands and buried his fingers in her hair to draw her closer. "Let me kiss you this time."

His breath was hot and made her shiver again with delight. He had promised to claim her first kiss. She wanted him to have it. "Be my guest," she whispered. "I'm still not sure how to do it properly."

He pulled her onto his lap and surrounded her with his body heat as thoroughly as she was surrounded by his power. The scent of her seemed sharper now, the rich and drugging scent of water in a desert. "If I scare you, tell me immediately."

She ran her hands up over his arms, loving the feel of his skin and muscle beneath her palms. Had he always felt this way? She wished she had noticed sooner. "I will," she promised. She tilted her face up instinctively, asking for his kiss like a flower asked for the sun.

He stopped breathing for a moment. He gently framed her face in his hands and leaned down to kiss her. Her power flowed up between them like an endless spring and covered them both with a soft blue aura. She could no more control the response of her power than he could. They were made to be this way.

He tenderly tilted her head back and teased the edges of her lips with his tongue. He wanted to taste her, truly taste her, but he didn't know just how ready she was. The answer came when she sighed softly and parted her lips for him. A shudder rippled through his body and he groaned as he deepened the kiss, his tongue gliding into her mouth to taste.

Her breath lodged in her chest as little waves of heat began to roll through her body. She had never felt anything as wonderful as his kiss. Her hands slid up to curl around the back of his neck and hold him closer. Wanting to know more, wanting to make him feel the same way she did, she followed his lead and curled her tongue around his eagerly. He tasted like what smoke smelled like. Rich and drugging.

He felt the wash of her emotions and it shook his control. He slanted his head and hungrily deepened the kiss even further, letting go of the edge of his desire for her. It seamlessly merged with his hunger for her power and he found himself feeding on the blue aura that was begging for his attention. It was richer now, stronger, as if the act was finally being done properly.

She couldn't breathe anymore but didn't care. The sensation of him drinking her power was making her entire body feel as if it had been caressed. It was nearly frightening how powerful the pleasure was. Shivers rippled along her skin and she was helpless to do anything but return the ravenous kiss.

Her body went weak in his arms and swayed toward him. Her breasts flattened against his chest, and a sharp lash of desire came through strong enough to frighten her. She jerked back, her eyes wide with distress. Her arms shot down to cross over her chest defensively and a frown marred her brows as she realized her bust seemed a little . . . bigger. "What did you do to me?" she asked warily.

He held up a hand to hold off the question. Carefully he went through all one thousand characters in the Draconic language. The mental act gave him just enough time to find some control and resist the urge to snatch her back into his arms. His arousal was literal pain in that moment. He would have considered a cold shower but the only water he wanted to be immersed in was the water of his Chronicle.

"Dominic?" she asked carefully. Her heart flipped up into her throat as he looked at her with his eyes nearly black. He was trying to withhold his emotions from her, but as she reached out a mental hand and brushed against them, she realized how turbulent they really were. It was a little frightening, but she was beginning to feel the stirrings of the same inside. She wanted to kiss him again.

"Don't you dare," he growled. "Otherwise I really will scare you." He drew a deep breath. "And all I did to you was arouse you. Don't ask me why your body responds the way it does; I'm not a female, I haven't a clue. But I can tell you that it's just your body saying that it likes how you feel. Male bodies do the same but react a little differently."

"Oh." Her eyes lowered and she spotted very clearly the evidence of his body's response. Her cheeks slowly turned pink. "Oh," she said again.

He had to grin. "Is that the best you can manage?"

"I'm not sure what else to say." She glowered at him. "I'm still new at this." She averted her eyes. "How did I do? For a kiss I mean."

He leaned over and softly touched her lips with his, careful to keep it light and tender. "When you want more practice, just let me know." He looked around as he realized that the rain was beginning to stop and the sun was starting to shine brightly. Steam lifted from his skin far more visibly now and he looked at it in amusement. "Well, there's the evidence of your effect on me, *ishke*."

She looked, and she began to smile. The smug and feminine curve to her lips was more evidence of her growing maturity, and he fought the urge to kiss her again. Instead, he ran his hands lightly down her arms where there was a matching steam lifting lightly. "And here's some evidence of my effect on you," he said huskily.

She lifted her hands and looked at the steam curling from her fingers. In consternation, she said, "I hope this doesn't stay for long. People will begin to think I was hit by lightning."

He threw back his head with a rich laugh and caught her up in his arms to hold her fiercely. "You're an amazing woman, Tariah Chronis. And I'm very proud you're mine."

She smiled and curled closer. "I'll remind you of that next time you get mad at me." Needing a distraction, she got to her feet and looked around. "I'm hungry. There's probably some cactear around here."

He watched her curiously. "Cactear?"

"It's a fruit that grows in the desert." She was hunting very cautiously through bushes around the pool. "If you can manage to get the shell off, the fruit inside is very sweet and very soft. But the shell is covered in really nasty thorns. And then there's the problem of . . ." There was a rustle and a prickly little creature shot out of the bush and attached to a tree. "Catching it."

He looked at the sharp little spikes all over the cactear and grimaced. "Don't touch it, Tariah. I don't want you to get hurt."

She rolled her eyes. "Oh you big baby! I've been hunting these for a long time." She began to ease closer to the cactear and water began to flow around her ankle. Little shards of ice began to condense within the water but they were invisible to all but Dominic.

She suddenly shot a stream of water at one side of the cactear. It lunged off the tree in the opposite direction and was instantly encased in ice. It dropped to the ground with a thud.

Dominic began to applaud. "I stand corrected."

She grinned at him and went over to the frozen fruit. She drew the dagger out of the sheath he wore on his hip to get to work on the ice. It cracked open and fell apart around the cactear. The spikes fell off moments later and left only the fruit behind. She held it up triumphantly. "And that's how it's done. Once the spikes are gone it's no longer able to draw power in."

He eyed the green and blue polka dotted yellow fruit. "Is it a fruit or an animal?"

"Well, that's a good question." She broke the fruit in half and offered him some. "But it has no body like an animal, so we call it a fruit." She began to eat her share with great delight, discovering that it tasted better than it ever had before. It seemed that everything was far more pleasurable to her now, just as Dominic had said it would be.

As she was licking some of the stray juice from her fingers, she saw him watching her with fire in his eyes. Literal fire. His power was as hungry for her as the rest of him was. The sight of it took her breath away, and she leaned toward him without thought to kiss him. His lips were sweet from the fruit and it seemed to taste far more delightful on him.

He firmly set her away from him. "Stop torturing me."

She averted her eyes with a blush. "Sorry." She was beginning to seriously feel bad for her Fury. If her sudden desire to touch and taste him was anything like what he had been feeling all along, he must have been miserable.

"Let's just say," he said ruefully, "that when I do finally have you in my bed for more than sleep, I won't let you out for a week." He watched her eyes widen and couldn't hold back a laugh. "When we get there, *ishke*, you won't look nearly so alarmed." He wrapped an arm around her shoulders and tugged her back against him just so he could snuggle her. "Ready for more walking?"

She stifled a sigh. Prismatic was more than a couple weeks away by walking. She was tired of walking. She loved the desert, and she loved Dominic, but a part of her wanted to rail

and scream against the law of the land and the law of the Magi that had caused her to be stranded in the first place.

He buried his face in her hair comfortingly and an idea occurred to him. "You want to ride? If I'm in Dragon form, I can walk far faster than in this form. We might even be able to get up to a running speed that rivals my flight. If we're touching the land, it might not cause any ripples."

She rested back against him, enjoying how his arms felt around her. "I'm willing to try if you are. I admit it. I don't want to walk any more. I just want to get to the king, get the meeting over with, and get on with going to the Isle. I don't belong here," she said fiercely. "I belong with the Dragons."

"You belong with me." He eased her head back and kissed her. He made sure it was quick and tender, but he couldn't resist taking it deeper than just the pecks he had been getting. He loved her taste.

She shivered softly in reaction and it was beautiful to him. Her lashes lowered partially over her eyes and they looked like pools of melted silver. His breath hitched and she smiled, loving his reaction to her. "I belong with you," she concurred, "but at least the Dragons won't try to kill me."

He chuckled. "I suspect you'll be running the place by the end of the first month." Keeping her close, he picked up his backpack and they began to walk toward the exit of the oasis. There were too many trees around them for him to go into his natural form safely. Either he or the oasis would be injured, and they didn't want either to happen. Once they were out on the desert sands again, she took his backpack and slipped it on over her back so that her hands were free. Then she rolled her eyes and waited while he tightened the straps since it was too big for her. "Not a word," she warned him.

"I wouldn't dream of it." He moved a few feet away from her to have space, then closed his eyes and let his power well up. He unbent his majiks and the power reverted him once more to his Dragon form. As he was blinking his eyes to clear them, he felt Tariah softly scratching him on the back of his neck. His just-cleared eyes nearly rolled back in his head and he laid down on the sand with a sound that was almost like a purr.

She began to giggle. "Dragons purr?" Delighted with the sound, she scratched him some more. She wasn't surprised he liked it. In this form it would be hard for him to reach his neck for anything.

He reached around and scooped her up gently with one of his claws. He brought her up to eye level then nuzzled her gently. "When you can manage to take a proper Dragon form, I'll
return the favor." He brought her around toward his back and she climbed gracefully onto his shoulders.

She had barely gotten settled when he suddenly took off running across the desert sands. With a shriek of laughter, she grabbed onto him for dear life and ducked down so that the wind wasn't slapping her in the face. It still pulled at her hair and she realized belatedly that she had never put it back up. She was going to have tangles in her tangles at this rate.

The desert sped past them in a blur of brown and white. He could nearly run as fast as he flew, especially once she found a water stream under the land that he could run along the top of. She could draw power from the water, and by linking to her, he was able to lean on her power. It didn't stop his majiks from draining, but it allowed him to run as fast as water could flow.

By the time afternoon was beginning to turn into evening, they could see Prismatic ahead of them. As evening was becoming twilight and the moons were rising, they were less than a few miles outside the city limits. He had been walking instead of running but when he realized how close they were, he stopped altogether. "Let's wait out the night, then go in tomorrow morning. We don't want to alarm them."

She rubbed her eyes. "Good idea," she agreed on a sleepy yawn. She had been tempted to nap but she had been enjoying the ride far too much. She slid down off his back then staggered and fell to her knees when her legs wouldn't support her. "Oops."

He turned into Magi form and knelt beside her to gently lift her up into his arms. "Magi and Chronicles are rather flimsy little things," he teased her gently. "Your legs get weak when you don't use them."

She glowered at him. "And you don't fall asleep when you're not moving something for a while?" She promptly forgot the conversation moments later as she felt his heated breath on her shoulder. A shiver rippled through her body even as her power flowed instantly to the surface.

He shuddered lightly as her power teased his lips. "I can't tell anymore," he said huskily, "whether it's my need to feed that calls your power, or your power that calls my need." Eagerly he drank in her power at the curve of her shoulder but this time he actually touched her skin with his lips. He hungrily tasted her flesh and realized that the

81

combination of her Water power and slightly salty skin made him feel as if he was drinking from the ocean. "I love desert girls."

She shivered again and held him closer as his lips trailed over her jaw and toward her lips. She wanted his kiss with a vengeance. If he didn't kiss her soon she thought she would die. His lips covered hers, and the desperation was replaced by pure pleasure. With a little sound of delight, she pressed closer and deepened the kiss, craving his taste as deeply as he craved hers.

His arms slid around her more firmly and he pressed her even closer against his body. Her breasts pressed against his chest but it didn't frighten her this time. The feel of him hard and close made her breasts ache deliciously, and she slowly rubbed against him to savor the feeling.

It was only when she felt his knuckles skim the outside curve of her breast that she became afraid again. The sharp sting of pleasure was like a whiplash, and she jerked back instinctively.

Immediately he was gathering her close in a comforting hug. He released her tenderly from the kiss then nuzzled her softly. "I can't keep my hands to myself," he said, his voice rich with masculine laughter. "You're too beautiful."

It wasn't an apology because one wasn't needed. The compliment was precisely what she required to find her footing, and her body relaxed once more. "Every time I think it can't get stronger, I get proven I'm wrong," she said with a touch of rueful amusement.

"You're not the only one." He reluctantly released her then took the backpack from her to retrieve the blankets that were inside. Like anything else made by the Kin, the blankets were the size of bandanas for travel. Once he was holding it, the blanket recognized his race and grew immediately to full size.

In a burst of playful energy, he pounced Tariah and tackled her down to the sand. He got them both tangled up in the blanket, which had gotten bigger to accommodate them both, then he began to tickle her without mercy.

She had no compunction about plucking knowledge out of his mind, and she zeroed in on his ribs. Within moments they were both laughing too hard to do anything except collapse on the sand. She snuggled closer against him and he tucked the blanket around them tightly. Their combined power created a protective barrier around their small camp and before long both were able to sleep.

In the middle of the night, however, something awoke Tariah. Dominic realized she was awake only when he felt her leaving his arms. He sat up beside her quickly. "Tariah?" he asked softly. The two moons that were visible overhead gave just enough light for him to see her face. It was calm and serene like the deepest of pools. It was an odd sight because he could feel the wild surge and snap of her power like the seas.

At first he was unsure what was wrong. Then he realized that he could feel someone else through her. His senses went on full alert and feral anger darkened his eyes. He didn't know who this mysterious person was that was able to connect to his Chronicle, but he was going to kill them for even brushing her power.

He curled his power and presence around Tariah warningly even as he pulled her into his arms. Her connection to the other person was severed, and she gave a sleepy yawn as she

cuddled more firmly against Dominic. "Is something wrong?" she asked sleepily.

"No, *ishke*. You were having a dream." He laid down and tucked her protectively under him. He didn't want to share her with even the moons.

"It seemed like a nice dream," she murmured as she snuggled closer. "It felt like I had found a friend."

She was asleep again moments later, and he was left very puzzled and very wary. He didn't like the idea that someone, anyone, could connect to his Chronicle in anyway. And, even deeper, was niggling fear for her. Prismatic was the home of the Black Magi. If they somehow were able to call to her then there could be far bigger problems on the horizon than just the king. It was a long time before he was able to go back to sleep.

He woke the next morning to discover that Tariah was still tucked in his arms. Locks of hair were falling in her face and he ran his eyes over her eagerly. It was as if every time he looked at her she became more beautiful. He bent his head and kissed her softly. It was wonderful that he could kiss her as he had wanted to for so long.

She awoke to pure pleasure. He was kissing her and she could feel his power caressing hers at the same time. She pressed upward to return the kiss and reached for him with her power. She could really grow addicted to him, she thought as they slowly parted. She licked her lips, tasted him there, and very nearly kissed him again.

"If you do," he warned huskily, "I might not have enough control to stop." With visible reluctance, he released her and rolled to the side to sit up. As she sat up beside him, he reached out and tangled his fingers in her hair. "When we get to the inn," he said softly, "I'll brush this for you."

She looked at him in surprise. "You want to?"

His smile was slow and devastating and made her pulse flutter wildly. "I suspect it will be much like when you were scratching my neck. Besides, I'll take any excuse to pamper you outrageously." His hands slid down to rest over her stomach. "It'll be practice for when you're pregnant with our children."

Her eyes grew round. "We can have children together?" When he lifted a brow, she said, "But . . . you're a Dragon! You lay eggs!" Horror filled her eyes. "I am *not* laying eggs!"

He began to laugh. "No, no!" He gave her a swift kiss. "Furies and Chronicles are perfectly capable of crossbreeding. Usually, the race of the child is determined by the race of the mother. I'm not going to lie and say you will never potentially carry a Dragon egg. But our doctors are just as equipped to deal with that as they are to handle a Fury who finds herself carrying a Magi."

"They better be," she muttered. She smiled and covered his hands with her own. "I really don't mind whichever it turns out to be. I'm just happy to think I could have children. Like everything else, I believed for a long time that I would never get to experience it."

He grinned. "Dragons are notorious for big families. You'll have plenty of children to experience." He stole a hard kiss. "Just make sure to give me a daughter precisely like you."

"I'll do my best," was the dry response.

Two hours later, as the morning sun was growing stronger, they found themselves approaching the farmlands that marked the outside edges of Prismatic. The workers out in the fields who saw them either didn't care or didn't realize what they were because not a single one said a thing.

Before long the farms were becoming merely houses. Then the houses began to be grouped much more tightly together. And by mid-morning, Dominic and Tariah were entering into the city proper. Tariah was awed. It was built like all other desert cities, but it was *enormous*.

Some buildings were indeed as high as six stories, and the streets were made of stone. People rode all sorts of different mounts to get to where they needed to go, but there were wide sidewalks for pedestrians as well.

Her skin began to crawl as she felt all the eyes that fastened on her. She defensively moved closer to Dominic and held onto his hand. He drew her closer still, more protective than possessive, and swept his gaze over the crowd. Most who felt his gaze immediately stopped staring though whispers still flowed swiftly.

A stone landed in the street directly in front of her feet and shattered. It sprayed sharp pieces everywhere. Several nicked her flesh and drew blood. Dominic snarled softly and looked around. "Who threw that?" he demanded in a growl. "If you fear anyone, it ought to be me." He bared his teeth. "I'll gut the next person who harms her."

The Magi said nothing and hastily went back to their business. The few Kin who were observing were pleased with what they saw. They had been about to step in themselves but it looked as if Dominic had things well in hand. Or claw, as it were.

Tariah's trepidation grew as she spotted one or two members of the Black Magi among the crowd. There were not as many of them as she had expected to see, however. Like the Elite, the regular Black Magi wore heavy white cloaks that covered them from head to toe and on the back was a black chalice. Unlike the Elite, there was no dagger. Oddly, that little difference made her feel a little better.

Prismatic was split into various sections. Most of the residential was grouped together and most of the commercial was grouped together. The various districts were built in a circular shape around the large palace at the very center. It was the largest building of all and some towers stood at an impressive ten stories.

It was through the commercial district that the two Dragoons walked. There were several inns in that district and they wanted to get a room to rest and get washed up before they were called in to meet the king.

The inns metaphorically, if not literally, shut their doors in their faces. They had plenty of excuses for their actions because they feared the wrath of the Kin, but it was blindingly obvious that they despised Tariah for being a Chronicle, and Dominic for being her Fury.

While Dominic argued with one of the innkeepers, Tariah walked away to where there was a bench at the edge of a shady park. She felt tired from the soul outward. As she looked around, she had to wonder to herself how long it would be before the mindsets of a thousand years were finally changed.

"May I join you?"

Startled, she looked up. Her surprise didn't fade as she studied the young man standing beside the bench. In fact, it grew stronger. The man could have been her brother. He was of shorter height, around five-six, and he had thick dark auburn hair that clung to the back of his neck. His eyes were silver as well and held a slight twinkle that indicated he would be quick to laugh when he was amused. She could see his shoulders were strong, but she couldn't guess at the rest of his build because the thick cloak he wore obscured him from view.

He was a Black Magi.

As if sensing her trepidation, he said, "I'm not going to hurt you. Please don't think that. There is a vast difference between the Black Magi and the Elite. May I join you?"

She nodded slowly. "Of course." She scooted over on the bench to give him room and watched him intently from under her lashes. She didn't trust him no matter how familiar he seemed to feel to her. She didn't trust any of the Black Magi at all.

"What is your name?" he asked her.

"Tariah Chronis."

His eyes shot to hers in surprise. "Well. That's a surprise." He smiled. "We might be cousins. My name is Morgan Chronis. I'm an Air Magi." He offered a gloved hand but she didn't take it. She simply watched him with eyes that were far too old. His heart wept for her. "Please, Tariah, don't hate me."

"I don't hate you," she said carefully. "I just don't trust you." She turned her gaze toward where Dominic was still arguing with the innkeeper. "When I was trying to escape Choral, I encountered the Elite. They tried to recruit me. In an effort to find out what I was and who I was really, the leader ripped the wings off a SunKin Faerie who had no crime other than being in love with my Kin partner."

Morgan's face tightened and he cursed softly under his breath. "Son-of-a-bitch, Soh," he muttered. "Is there no length you won't stoop to?" He turned back to her and his eyes were intense. "The Elite are their own band. They have no affiliation with my Black Magi. They were once a part of us but their . . . ideals changed. What they want goes against everything I have tried so hard to bring to the Black Magi."

"You're the leader?" She looked him over quickly. "But you seem so young."

"I'm twenty-five," he told her. "I started the Black Magi about five years ago." He stood and held a hand out to her. "Please. Come stay with the Black Magi. We will happily give you a place to rest. You and your Fury both. Once you see what the Black Magi stand for, I am sure you will understand everything."

She hesitated then took his hand to let him draw her to her feet. The minute their fingers connected, she felt a raw surge of power up her arm. He was holding her right hand so he was holding her hand that had her lines. All the way through her lines she felt a surge of power that was neither hers nor Dominic's. It was Morgan's.

Her eyes shot to his in shock. "You're a Chronicle," she whispered.

Chapter Eleven

Morgan's hand tightened on hers for a moment and Tariah fell quiet. She was stunned. She was stunned and she was shaken to her core. She wasn't the only Chronicle that had survived? But *how*?

Dominic, sensing her distress, was quick to hurry over to them. He saw her holding Morgan's hand and gave a soft snarl. He snatched her into his arms and removed her from the other man's reach entirely. "Don't touch her," he ordered in a dangerous growl. A split second later, his nose flared as he realized Morgan didn't smell like a Magi. "What the . . ." Tariah pulled him into her mind to share what she had felt and learned and his eyes shot to Morgan's in shock. "I'll be damned," he murmured.

Morgan smiled. "You're not going to eat me then?"

"Not at the immediate moment."

He gave a quick laugh. "How did I know that would be the answer?" He smiled at Tariah. "Please, come to the sanctuary of the Black Magi. There is so much I would like to talk to you about. And we can easily offer you a room to rest in before you meet the king."

Dominic said nothing. It was Tariah's decision. She was still confused but her trepidation had faded. Somehow, knowing Morgan was also a Chronicle made her trust him. "Alright. Thank you, Morgan." She gave Dominic a dry look and wiggled her feet where they were dangling over the ground. "Are you going to carry me, or am I walking?"

He sighed and put her on her feet but kept her close beside him. He was no less startled than she was. If Morgan was a Chronicle and he was alive, then that meant that his Fury had to be out there. But Dominic was sure that if the Fury was on the isle, the Dragons would have known another had survived. Where was Morgan's Fury?

The sanctuary of the Black Magi was a three-story building in the corner of the commercial district. A couple of other Black Magi were tending to the landscape in front of the building, and they called friendly greetings to Morgan and Tariah alike. Tariah glanced at Dominic but he shook his head. Neither Black Magi was a Chronicle.

They had barely walked in the door when a girl with bright red hair came running toward them. She was no higher than Tariah's collar and looked no older than ten. She launched herself from several feet away and attached herself to Morgan's arm. "Morgan!" she wailed. "Roman took my doll!"

"I did not!" came a voice from a boy as Morgan hugged the girl. "Jayda did it!"

"I did not neither!" A girl with sea green hair in a tangle of curls around her face was standing in the doorway to an inner room with a look of indignation on her face. "Kelsey left her doll at the park." She diverted as she saw Tariah and Dominic. "Hi!"

Kelsey peered around Morgan at the newcomers. "You're pretty," she told

Tariah. "You have lines on your body. Why? What do they do?" She held her arms out to Tariah demandingly. "You hug me too."

Tariah automatically bent and hugged the child when she hurried over. Ten-year-olds were notorious for their blend of clinging to childhood and beginning the first steps to first puberty and maturity. A feeling not unlike when she had taken Morgan's hand seemed to ripple through her lines, though, as she hugged Kelsey. Her eyes widened slowly with shock as she stared at the child she was holding. "She's . . ."

"A Chronicle child." Morgan nodded. "As are the other three terrors." He turned with a smile and called, "C.J.! Roman! Come in here!" He scooped up Jayda as she came over to hug his hip. "You're holding Kelsey. We call her Soot because she's always getting into it. This is Jayda."

Tariah spotted a smudge of soot on Kelsey's face and had to smile. "So I see." She rubbed it away gently. "Bet you'll be a Fire element, huh?"

"It's pretty." Kelsey was eyeing Dominic. "You're a Dragon."

"I am." He blew a ring of smoke at her and made her giggle.

Two boys came hurrying into the room and skidded to stops in front of Morgan. One was a blond with clear blue eyes. The other had ash brown hair and black eyes. Both were amongst the most adorable kids Tariah had ever seen. The blond was, however, her instant favorite. On one look at how he was dressed she knew he was from the desert.

"This is Roman," Morgan said, ruffling Roman's blond hair. He rubbed his hand over the other boy's ashy hair. "And this is C.J. He has expressly forbidden his parents to tell us what the C and J stand for."

C.J. wrinkled up his nose. "It's silly."

Tariah smiled. "Well, I won't ask then." She drew her thumb over her cheek and nose as a sign of greeting. "I'm Tariah Chronis."

"Are you Morgan's sister?" Jayda asked. "You look a lot alike and you have the same name."

"We might be cousins. We don't know." Morgan tossed Jayda in the air, then set her down. "But she's like a big sister to you just as I'm like your brother."

Kelsey leaned back to look at Morgan. "That's because she has lines like yours, right?"

"That's right."

Roman walked over to look up at Dominic. "You're a Dragon?"

"Yes I am." Dominic crouched down until they were closer in height. "My name is Dominic Whisperer. Tariah and I are Dragoons." He gently ruffled Roman's hair. "An easier way to explain for now is to say that we're Linked."

"Oh!" Roman grinned and showed he was missing a front tooth. "That's really neat!" His ears perked up suddenly as he heard a bell ringing. "Lunch is ready!"

Tariah hastily let Kelsey go as all four children went tearing out of the room, shouting over one another to be heard. She didn't need to touch the other three to know they would be the same as Kelsey. "They're Chronicle children," she whispered.

"Yes." Morgan gestured down another hall and the two Dragoons followed him. "They are the whole reason the Black Magi exist. Kelsey was the first I found. It was an accident. It stunned me, to be truthful. I got to know her parents and realized they would love her more than they feared her."

"So you decided to form a place where she could grow safely," Dominic said quietly as he sat down on one of the chairs in the study. When Tariah sat beside him, he took her hand and held it to his heart to comfort her. "Under the guise of being Master Magi."

"Yes." Morgan removed his gloves and his cloak. The light from the lamps in the room washed over his arms, bared by his short-sleeved tunic. The golden lines flowed over the entirety of his arms and hands and then disappeared somewhere beneath his tunic. The design and pattern was completely unique and looked nothing like Tariah's.

He sat down heavily with a sigh and raked his hands through his hair. "Only four. I've met at least ten over the last five years." A haunted look filled his eyes. "The other six . . . their parents could never accept them. I had to walk away else I risk those I had already saved."

"Your parents?" Tariah asked softly.

"I don't know." Morgan closed his eyes. "I had to leave my town . . . rather swiftly." He looked at her and his eyes darkened. "I'm so sorry, Tariah. I heard about your parents and the MoonKin. I wish I had gone to Symphony and found you. I just didn't have the time to get to Choral."

"Maybe it's better this way," Dominic said. "Maybe the king will actually listen to us and see that Tariah is not the monster of every Magi's nightmares. If he can accept her, then maybe eventually the people can as well." He looked at Tariah. "I'll let you stay here with Morgan and I'll go speak with the Militia to let them know we're here."

"They probably know," she countered dryly. She smiled and leaned up to kiss him softly. "Go. I'll be safe here."

"I know." He skimmed his thumb down the lines on her face then got to his feet and walked out of the room.

Morgan watched him go then cleared his throat. He recognized the signs of a very frustrated male. "So. Still in second puberty?"

Tariah glared at him. "Shut up, Morgan." He grinned at her and she relented with a sigh. "It's been a learning experience in more ways than one. Assure me that it will get easier, please. I'm going through this whole ordeal in a matter of weeks rather than a year!"

He thought about that. "Well, I don't know that it gets *easier*, but you'll be better able to deal with it. You have Dominic." Sadness clouded his face as he got to his feet and walked over to look out the window. From this height, no one on the street could see them. "My Fury . . . I feel her." He lifted a hand and pressed his fist to his heart. "It hurts so badly," he managed to say. "But my lines won't tell me where to go. I can only stay here."

She got to her feet and walked over to stand beside him. "She's out there," she said softly. "From what Dominic told me, Furies always know when their Chronicle is alive or dead. She must know you're alive, Morgan. Surely she is seeking you too."

"What's it like?" he murmured. "To be with your Fury?"

She thought about it then said simply, "It's the greatest thing in the world."

"I thought it might be." He drew a long breath. "Well. Let's find you a room to rest in." He smiled. "When Jayda heard that there was another Chronicle alive, she said that we ought to have a room ready for you because you'd come here."

"Why'd she think that?"

He laughed. "Her words were 'Because no one else will let her stay anywhere. Adults are jerks.' She's quite astute, that child."

She smiled. "She's not the first child I've heard make a statement similar. Perhaps there is something about being a child that allows you to see clearly. Or maybe they simply haven't had a chance to be instilled with all the rules that grown-ups abide by."

"I like to think of it as the hope for the Magi race. Now, come along with me." He put his cloak and gloves back on then led the way down the hall toward the stairs to the next floor. "How old are you, Tariah?"

"Twenty. I'll be twenty-one in a few months." She linked her hands behind her back as they walked. "Where are you from, Morgan? You seem quite comfortable in a thick cloak in a desert. I'd be smothering. Or wanting to rip the cloak off."

He laughed. "I'm from Glacia. You'd likely freeze up there, desert girl. Take the coldest temperature of the desert at night and make it twice as cold. That's the warmest day where I'm from." He saw the horrified look on her face and began laughing harder. "Just snuggle your Fury and you'll be just fine."

She shuddered. "No disrespect, Morgan, but I'd just as soon never go there." Her ears and nose both perked up as she heard and smelled the sound and scent of hot water. It was coming from the room Morgan had stopped in front of. "I can have a bath?" she asked eagerly.

"I thought of it!" Kelsey was sitting on the stairs up to the third floor and happily eating a bowl of mashed fruit and syrup. "Morgan's a *boy*. And boys don't know anything about girls!"

Morgan quirked a brow. "I pity her Fury," he murmured under his breath.

Tariah elbowed him. "Be nice," she scolded. She walked over and knelt down to be eye level with Kelsey. "Are you going to boss your Fury around, Kelsey?" When the little girl nodded enthusiastically, Tariah stole the spoon and scooped up a bite of fruit. "You'll have to teach me some pointers. I don't boss my Fury around enough."

"Probably," Morgan said dryly, "because you're at a disadvantage right now. Once you finish puberty you'll have all sorts of ways of keeping him at your mercy."

Tariah fluttered her lashes at him as she sashayed past him into the room. "You'll get yours, wait and see." She turned around and smiled. "Morgan . . . thank you." She held her right hand out to him and he took it tightly with his own. "After Dominic returns, will you tell us about the Elite? I have so many questions."

"I will tell you whatever I can." He squeezed her hand tightly then stepped back as she shut the door. With a sigh, he walked over to where Kelsey was sitting. Years of practice made it easy to hide the fierce and painful longing that seemed to well up inside him endlessly. He wasn't the only Chronicle anymore . . . but he was still alone.

Tariah shut the door firmly and looked to where there was a large tub filled with hot water. There were blankets and towels stacked beside it along with an assortment of soaps and perfumes. She had never before understood the urge people had for primping or pampering themselves but as she stood there and contemplated Dominic's reaction, she found the idea irresistible.

She hurried over to the tub and tested the water. It wasn't quite hot enough to suit her so she used her powers and increased the temperature. She swiftly stripped off her clothes then stepped into the tub. She winced as the hot water stung the cuts on her legs from the flying rock but she determinedly ignored it as she sat down.

With a contented sigh, she closed her eyes and rested her head against the rim of the tub. Once she had rested a little, she was going to wash her hair and skin thoroughly for the first time in a few days. Without intending to, however, she slipped asleep.

When Dominic returned to the sanctuary, he was not entirely happy. The Militia had been very rude in their opinions of Tariah. It seemed they held a grudge for her killing one of their soldiers even though she had acted in self-defense. Dominic hadn't known about the incident. If it came from the wild jumble of memories inside her mind, he suspected that she didn't remember it herself.

Moreover, according to the Militia, the king was not ready to see them today. He wanted them to come back tomorrow around mid-morning so that he had enough time to decide what he wanted to say. Dominic thought that was fair enough but had to wonder what the king was going to be saying that took that much thought.

"Do you fly?" The question came from C.J. as he attached himself to Dominic's ankle. "How fast?"

Dominic kept on walking though the boy was wrapped around his ankle. "Yes I do, and when I have Tariah, I can cross Spectrum in a day."

C.J.'s eyes widened. "Wow," he breathed.

Dominic spotted Morgan coming down the stairs. "Morgan. Get your ankle biter off me." He held up his leg. "It's doing an impression of a leech."

Morgan smiled and plucked C.J. off Dominic's leg. He tossed the little boy over his shoulder and made him give a shriek of laughter. "Tariah is upstairs," Morgan told Dominic. "Kelsey's mother had a bath waiting for her, and I have no doubt she's probably bathing right now." He covered a grin as Dominic went for the stairs far faster than was polite. "Have fun," he called cheerfully. "And you, ankle biter," he added to C.J. as he flipped him right-side up, "need to finish your dinner."

"Rar!"

Dominic took the stairs two at a time, eagerly looking forward to catching Tariah naked and wet. But even steps before he reached the door, he knew she was asleep. Her power was still and quiet inside him. His eyes softened and his heart filled with tenderness. He gently eased the door open and slipped inside.

She was in the tub, yes, but she was sound asleep with her head resting against the edge. With a sigh, he shut and locked the door then walked over to crouch beside her. He tenderly brushed her bangs out of her eyes. She seemed heartbreakingly young. So much was riding on her shoulders, and she was barreling through second puberty faster than a Dragon could fly. It was as if she had never once been granted a childhood.

He straightened and removed his cloak and vest. He knelt beside her again and leaned over to kiss her softly. She began to wake slowly, and her soft sigh was as sweet as her power when it was breathed into his kiss. "I'm back," he murmured huskily.

Her eyes opened slightly. "I was going to get cleaned up and surprise you," she said softly. His hand cupped her cheek and she rubbed against his fingers. "I was going to wear perfume."

"You don't need it." He lifted her wrist to his lips. "I like how you smell all the time." He was counting his lucky stars, though. Finding her clean and perfumed just for him might have been more than his control could handle.

She contemplated the imagery in his mind. "A wolf falling on a bone? That's not flattering."

"But accurate." He smiled as she straightened up. "Besides, I promised to pamper you. Hand over the soap and I'll scrub your hair for you." He waited while she poured water over her hair to wet it, then took the soap she offered and began to lather up her hair. He firmly rubbed away the knots of tension he found. They were manifestations of her emotional stress, and he refused to let them linger.

She nearly whimpered. As it was, she had to brace her feet against the other end of the tub to keep from sliding down in a boneless heap. She had never felt anything as wonderful as the feel of his hands rubbing her head and the back of her neck when he found more knots. "If this is how it feels to scratch your neck," she said faintly, "then you're welcome." It only mildly startled her to realize it felt almost as good as his kiss.

He chuckled softly. "I told you. I find everything about you pleasurable. It's no surprise that it is the same for you toward me." He waited until she had rinsed her hair free of soap before beginning to scrub her back. At the same time, he rubbed away all the knots he found. "Where were these hiding?"

She muttered something wordless and arched into his touch like a cat asking to be stroked. His body hardened in a wild rush of desire. Carefully he kept his hands neutral. It was the hardest thing he'd ever done. For the moment, she was not connecting this feeling with the ones that were inspired by the passion between them. He could hardly wait to teach her the two could be combined.

She was feeling like a puddle of water herself as he rinsed her off and lifted her out of the tub. She felt like all her muscles in her back and neck had turned to mush. As she was set gently on her feet, she picked up a towel and wrapped her hair in it snugly. She swathed a blanket around her body, then made a startled sound as he scooped her up. "What're you doing?"

He carried her over to the bed and set her down on her stomach. "Getting rid of the rest of those knots. But I expect you to return the favor eventually."

The idea intrigued her. She rested her head on her arms and relaxed as she felt him tug aside the blanket so he could reach her legs. At first, the knots he rubbed away were painful. She endured it. She knew full well that it wouldn't get better unless she did. "What did the Militia say?" she asked.

He found the nicks on her legs and stopped rubbing long enough to apply some salve and bandages. "The king will see us tomorrow. It seems that he has to decide what to say."

She grumbled something uncomplimentary under her breath. "You'd think he would have had enough time to decide that already."

He smiled. "My thoughts exactly." Pleased because he could now feel the relaxation in her body, he sat on the bed and lifted her up onto his lap to cuddle. He nuzzled his nose into her hair softly. "You like Morgan?"

She snuggled closer and rested a hand over his heart. "I do. It's like suddenly finding a member of my family. I just wish I could find his Fury for him. He hid it well, but I could see how terribly it hurts him." Suddenly she straightened. "Wait! Daylar!"

Dominic dodged quickly before her head hit him in the chin and lifted a brow as she scooted off his lap. "Daylar? Are you going to try to write to him?"

She was studying her power internally. "I'm going to definitely try. Maybe he can put word out through the other Kin and they can find Morgan's Fury like they found you." She found the information on how to write the letter inside her as if it had been placed there, and she suspected it had come with her Kinship. "You don't think she's on the Isle."

"She couldn't be." He watched curiously as she began to write in the air. It was in the language of the Magi and easy to read. What fascinated him was that he could see that she wasn't writing with her power. She was writing with Daylar's energy. It made Dominic smile. Her handwriting was as unique as her lines, and nearly just as beautiful. "If she was on the Isle, we'd have known Morgan was alive."

She added that information to her letter then asked, "Maybe she left the Isle. In your memory, how many Furies left the isle that never returned? Specifically the females of a Soil element."

He thought about that. "I can think of three in my memory. I've seen one of them in recent years though. Another . . . well, we lost her two years ago. The last . . . it might be her. Tell Daylar to try and locate the Fury known as Jazz Eaglewind."

"How do you write that?" she asked.

He leaned over and caught her hand. He traced the characters in the air before bringing her hand to his lips and kissing her palm. The symbol there seemed to tickle his lips. "Did you ask if Morgan has this on his hand?"

"No, I didn't think to." She pulled her hand free and finished the letter. "But if he does, then I suppose we really are cousins in some way." She smiled. "It's a nice feeling to have family again. I mean, I only really need you, but anything extra is like . . . like a good dessert on top of a really good dinner."

"You humble me." He pulled her back onto his lap and buried his nose against her shoulder. "You don't need perfume," he murmured huskily. "I already love how you smell. Like water in the desert. There's nothing more seductive." He turned and lowered her to the bed and trapped her against the pale green blankets. "*Ishke.*" His voice had grown thick with emotion. "I think the word was made for you."

She wrapped her arms around his shoulders and held onto him fiercely. She had no words to describe how she felt. She could only show it. She could only wrap her power and mind around him and let him feel how terribly she loved him and needed him.

He trembled as he felt the searing wave of her emotions. That third part, the desire she had never felt before, was growing stronger. It was nearly as strong as the emotions he felt inside himself. He knew that soon there would be no more barriers between them. Soon he would be able to know her as intimately as he craved.

Someone knocked lightly on the door. "Tariah? Dominic?" The voice was unfamiliar and belonged to a woman. "Morgan asks that you join him when you're ready."

As the footsteps faded away, Dominic very reluctantly released Tariah. "I wish I could begrudge him that. But I can't." He sat up and watched as she got to her feet and crossed over to where her clothes had been tossed. He smiled. "I'll have to get you into some clothes of the valley. You might like them."

"Really?" She pulled on her bikini and looked at him curiously. "What are they like?"

"Slightly covering, but they tend to be loose and light to accommodate the winds around there." He stood and pulled his vest on once again. Since they were indoors, he didn't bother with the cloak.

When she was dressed as well, he pulled her close to escort her out of the room. C.J. and Jayda were chasing each other up and down the halls and nearly ran both Dragoons over. "Watch where you're running," Tariah scolded.

"Yes'm!" Giggling, the kids kept on running.

Downstairs, Morgan was reading a letter when they walked in. He looked up with a smile and set the letter aside. "You look like you're feeling better, Tariah." He gestured to the couch across from where he was seated. "Please sit down. I would like to tell you about the Elite."

Dominic sat down and pulled Tariah down onto his lap. He knew she needed the anchor to keep herself grounded. Her memories of what had happened to Daylar were still very vivid in her mind, and they were more horrifying than ever now that he was her brother. "I assume they were part of the Black Magi at some time," he said.

"Yes." Morgan's hands clenched into fists. "Soh's son was a Chronicle and was killed for it. He wanted to join me to stop it from happening to others . . . or so I believed." He closed his eyes. "I found out shortly that Soh wanted revenge."

Tariah took a quick breath as everything made sense. "He wants to erase the Magi from the world. But . . . that could *destroy* the world!"

He looked at her sadly. "Soh firmly believes that Chronicles will take the place of Magi. Nothing I said would convince him otherwise. He drew other fanatics to his side and they left the Black Magi entirely to form their own group of Elite. I honestly don't think half the Magi that are in the Elite understand what Soh's true intent is."

"Is that why he wanted Tariah?" Dominic asked quietly. "Because he thinks she should hate the Magi as much as he does?"

"I think so." Morgan's knuckles were nearly white. "I have to be careful," he said faintly. "Soh . . . if he could come back and take these children away, he would. They're so young . . . he might actually be able to brainwash them over to his side. Especially if he arranged for their parents to die at Magi hands."

"I want to think he wouldn't do that," Tariah whispered, "but I know he would. After what he did to Daylar . . ." She drew a long breath and her intense silver eyes met Morgan's identical ones. "I'll do whatever I can to help you, Morgan. I won't let these children be harmed. When I get to the Isle, I'll tell them all about the children and where they are. The Furies can come find them and take them to safety." She found a smile. "Even if they do have to go through what Dominic is right now."

"It's certainly been an . . . interesting test of my self-control," her Fury muttered.

Morgan pulled off his glove and held out his right hand to Tariah. Sure enough, there, etched into the center of his palm, was the symbol 'chron.' She took his hand with hers and their fingers laced together tightly. "I wouldn't join the Elite," she said, "but you could consider me an honorary member of the Black Magi, if you like."

"Only honorary," he said softly, "because neither of us wants any connection to be made between you and these children. But, Tariah, I want you to know something. If anything should ever happen to me, you are the only person I trust to protect these children."

"You have my word," she said just as softly. "I'll do whatever I can."

Chapter Twelve

Tariah awoke to conflicting signals through her body. On one hand, her body was sending out messages of pure pleasure. Her skin felt more sensitive than ever and her breasts ached and throbbed. On the other hand, her body was as confused as her mind and unsure of where the messages were coming from.

"Now you're awake," Dominic's voice murmured huskily in her ear. He was propped up on an elbow behind her, his body heat curling around her even as his free arm did. He bent his head and trailed soft little kisses over her ear. "I was beginning to think you would oversleep."

She shivered softly. Ears were sensitive? "I don't think that's a worry now." The confusion had faded. His hand was resting just under her breasts and her every breath caused his knuckles to skim against her resilient flesh. She was still wearing her bikini, but for a moment she wished that she wasn't wearing it at all.

His breath hitched as he caught the thought. He gently turned her onto her back and leaned in close. "Do you trust me?" he asked thickly. His fingers trembled lightly as he drew them up over the outside curve of her breast.

"How can you ask me that?" She lifted her hands and smoothed her palms over the skin of his chest. The lines etched there tingled her skin. "I always trust you." She knew what he was really asking and looked inside herself for the answer. Her lashes lowered slightly. "Touch me. I want to know what it's like."

He held his breath as he slowly covered her breast with his hand. She was soft and fragrant, and her body was perfectly formed for his hands. He gently kneaded her flesh while watching her eyes and tangling his emotions to hers. He felt her first flicker of shock and then he felt the wave of pleasure that followed. As he felt her nipple tighten against his palm, his breath was released in a soft sigh of relief. "Tell me if I scare you," he murmured.

She trembled and arched to press herself more firmly against his touch. Fear was the last thing on her mind. Her lips were tingling, begging for his kiss. He sensed it and lowered his head to kiss her deeply. His tongue curled around hers with the familiarity of a lover.

With a little purr of delight, she slid her hands up into his hair to hold him closer. She loved the way he kissed her and the way it made her feel. Her entire body was aching, and she pressed closer instinctively. She knew, somehow, that he could make it stop.

He released her lips and lifted himself enough to watch her face. He began to slowly untie the little knot at the front of her bikini top that held the cups together. Because she had been wearing it to sleep in, the knot was larger and not as tight because she didn't need the support. It opened easily for him.

As he tugged the cups apart to leave her half-naked in his arms, she felt a moment of nerves. They faded immediately as she saw the look in his eyes. It was a look she had always seen in his eyes when he looked at her, but for the first time she recognized it and understood it. She thrilled to it. "You want to touch me?"

"How can you ask that?" he said thickly, returning her words to her. "I've wanted to touch you since I laid eyes on you. Since I felt you were born. Since I was hatched and felt that there was something inside me missing."

His fingers slid up and cupped her naked breast warmly. Her entire body jerked slightly and her eyes widened. A faint blush stained her cheeks. He was still touching her emotions and felt savage triumph as he realized the reactions stemmed from pure desire. He hadn't thought his own emotions could possibly get stronger, but as he caressed her satin skin, he realized he was wrong.

Unable to resist the lure, he skimmed his thumb over her taut nipple. She took a sharp breath and her silver eyes darkened to the color of storm clouds. Encouraged, he slowly caressed her, memorizing the weight and feel of her. The temptation was too powerful to resist, and he lowered his head to press his lips to her rapid heartbeat.

She shivered and held onto him tighter. She felt his lips suddenly close over her nipple, and the pleasure was shockingly more powerful. It streaked through her body and made a strange ache bloom between her legs. Suddenly afraid again, she jerked away and rolled onto her side. She wrapped her arms around herself protectively.

He immediately gathered her close and cuddled her tightly. His hand rested on her stomach softly. "I'm sorry." His voice was tender. "I couldn't help myself." He ran his hands soothingly over her beautiful lines, careful to keep his touch neutral and not alarming.

"I wish I could talk to Sparkle," she said on a sigh. "She's been through second puberty. She could hopefully explain what is going to happen next so it doesn't frighten me so much!" She looked at him over her shoulder. "I'm not afraid of *you*, Dominic. I promise. It's my body that frightens me. It's like I don't know it anymore."

"I know, *ishko*." He nuzzled her shoulder softly. "It's no less scary for men." His lips curved. "You might even say it's a little scarier. We can't always hide our bodies' reactions."

Since she could feel him pressed entirely along her back, she could clearly feel the proof of his desire pressed against her bottom. It made her feel better and she smiled. "I've often thought I was glad to be a girl. I don't grow hair on my face that I need to trim away."

He skimmed a finger down her cheek. "I will concur that I am quite glad you are a girl as well." Less girl and more woman now, though. An inner certainty told him it would not be long before she was ready to take the final step to adulthood. Knowing that he would be the one to help her was one of the more incredible feelings he had ever had. He had always thought it was a beautiful development, but in her it was even more so.

He reluctantly let her go as she slipped out of his arms. With a sigh, he sat up and got out of bed to find his vest and boots. He had to smile. He supposed the desert dwellers had it much easier for changing clothes since they wore so few. He eyed Tariah as she pulled her shorts on. There were some distinct benefits for non-dwellers too.

Once they were both dressed, they headed downstairs to the first floor. Jayda spotted them from the doorway to what looked like a kitchen and ran over to take their hands with hers. "Good morning!" she said cheerfully. "We made breakfast!"

"We as in . . .?"

"Jayda and I," a man said from the doorway. His hair was the same rich sea green as Jayda's, and he wore the familiar heavy cloak of the Black Magi. "My name is Eli Lakemore. Jayda is my daughter." He drew his thumb over his cheek and nose. "I am an Air Magi. I'm honored to meet you, Dragoons."

Tariah returned the gesture and Dominic gave a slight bow. With a smile, Tariah smoothed a hand down Jayda's hair. How odd that she had to be far from her birthplace to find a place that felt like home. "What's for breakfast?"

Breakfast was fresh fruit and a bread and rice pudding covered in cream. It reminded Tariah of her childhood and of the days when things had been much easier. It still hurt to even think of her parents and Maxim. Their only flaw had been loving her, and they had died for it.

Dominic gently cupped the back of her neck and drew her close for a soft kiss. "If I had found you sooner," he said softly, "I'd have taken you away before any of this ever happened."

"I know." She sighed and pushed her bowl away. She was more than full. Because she didn't know how hot it was going to get that day, she began to expertly twist and tuck her hair up into a neat coil on top of her head. Her stomach fluttered with desire as she saw the look in her lover's eyes and remembered how it had felt to take her hair down for him. "Don't stare at me," she whispered. "It makes it hard to breathe."

"Get used to it, dear," Jayda's mother said as she went past. "It will never stop. Eli still takes my breath and we've known each other since before second puberty. We've been Linked together for nearly fifteen years."

"They're *always* kissing," Jayda said.

"That's because it's fun." Dominic caught her up and gave her a smacking kiss on the cheek. "See?"

She giggled and hugged him tightly. "You're silly." As she was put back down on her feet, she heard a knock on the front door. "I'll get it!"

"No, I will!" Kelsey shouted. "I'll get there first!"

A few moments later, Jayda was back in the doorway, her face solemn. "Tariah, the Militia is here. They want to take you to the king." Her lower lip trembled. "Are you going to get in trouble?"

"I'm hoping to get out of it." Tariah held onto Dominic's hand tightly as they left the kitchen and headed toward the front door. Several Militia soldiers were indeed standing there, and one of them was the captain who had gone to Symphony. Her stomach churned.

None of the soldiers said anything as they stepped back to let the two Dragoons out of the building. The silence remained as they walked down the road to where there was a cart waiting to carry them to the castle.

There was barely enough room on the cart for all of them but neither Tariah nor Dominic complained. They just sat as close together as they could, and Dominic kept an arm around Tariah's waist to keep her from bouncing out of the cart as they went down the road.

The morning sun was very vivid on Tariah's lines and revealed the wing mark on her shoulder plainly. Because of it, there was no one who wanted to risk saying a word. There were enough Kin in the city that things could become very dicey. Pacifists or not, the Kin protected their own.

The castle was in the center of the city and nearly the size of a district all on its own. Tariah was astonished by the sheer depth of the building because she had never seen anything like it. Even Dominic was impressed and he had seen many large and beautiful buildings on the Isle.

The captain and two other soldiers took over the escort as they led the Dragoons into the castle proper. The courtyard was busy at that time of morning as Militia soldiers trained and servants maintained the land. All of them eyed Tariah with intense scrutiny, and Dominic bristled as he saw more than one derogatory look. Warningly, he bared his teeth.

The throne room looked like the definition of decadence. Everything was made of ivory and bronze, and there were even several silver statues sitting around. The floor was covered with tile so polished that it showed the perfect reflection of all who walked across it. The ceiling was well over their heads and chandeliers dripped toward the ground with plenty of light.

At the end of the throne room sat an ivory and bronze throne, and on it sat the king of the Magi. Tariah compared the pomp and haughtiness of the king to the relaxed and open manner of the Kin and found the Magi to be lacking. Dominic compared the king to the loud and argumentative, but always willing to listen, Dragon Elders, and came to a similar conclusion.

When they were several feet before the king, Tariah drew her thumb across her cheek and nose, and Dominic bowed. The gestures of respect were more automatic than deeply felt. After a moment where the king didn't speak, Tariah realized he was waiting for her to say something. "I am Tariah Chronis," she said. With more ease than she had imagined, she continued, "I am a Water Chronicle. I am also a Dragoon. This is my Fury, Dominic Whisperer."

"A Fire Fury," Dominic concurred. "Dragon Lord, fourth tier." He squeezed her hand in a promise to explain later more about the tiers among the Dragons.

The king leaned forward on his throne and studied them intently. His eyes lingered on Tariah's lines, as if trying to assure himself that they were real. "Is it true?" he asked. "Is there gold in your lines and this is why the metal is so rare?"

She stared at him. "Of course not. My lines are made of my Fury's power, but what flows in them is my own. There are no . . . stones or metals in my body. I am the same as anyone else in that."

The king nodded slightly. "And what about the rumor that having sex with a Chronicle will give you power?"

Dominic's face darkened. "I suggest you not mention that again. Several of your *upstanding* citizens tried to assault my mate over that ridiculous story. If that rumor were true, you Magi wouldn't have been so quick to kill off Chronicles."

Tariah's stomach was beginning to churn. "Your majesty," she said, "I have been running for my life. I have been forced to watch someone I loved be killed. And all of it was because I was born a Chronicle. I was able to walk among the Magi disguised as a Master Magi. No one knew the difference. Surely that should tell you something."

97

"Chronicles are said to seek the destruction of the world," the king said curtly.

"I seek only to be able to live as I wish," she retorted. "I am bound to follow the map within my lines. At the end of my map will be the Isle of Dragons. I would sooner stay there or visit Kindred where my honorary family is. The Magi wouldn't have to worry about me if they would simply leave me alone."

"I am through with talking to a pet!" the king snapped. He looked at Dominic. "Why do you not curb her tongue, as you should?" When his response was a narrow-eyed look, the king scoffed. "Do not play the fool. Everyone knows that Furies are little more than owners of Chronicles. Chronicles only exist to feed Furies. What does she feed you? Blood?"

"Tariah is my partner," Dominic said carefully. His temper was on shaky ground and only the knowledge that they could be killed kept him in line. "She is, to use a Magi term, my Linked mate. We are equals. The world made us as two halves of a whole." He glanced down at Tariah. "I've heard enough. We're leaving."

She kept her trembling inside where it could not show. "Gladly." She did not worry about insulting the king. He didn't dare harm her for fear that he would bring down the wrath of the Kin and Dragons alike.

"I did not say you could leave!" the king snapped. "Bar the doors!" he ordered the Militia. As they leapt to do his bidding, he narrowed his eyes toward Tariah. "I have no desire to have you wandering across the landscape. You will remain here until I can have the Kin fetch you. Chronicles will destroy the world."

Though Dominic was the one with the hot temper, it was Tariah that lost hers first. Her hands clenched into fists at her sides as she shouted, "I don't want to destroy anything! If anyone is guilty of destroying anything, it's the Magi! You destroyed the Chronicles! You tried to destroy the Kin, and in the process you destroyed a lot of the world! Now you're trying to destroy whatever freedom I've managed to fight for! If you'd get to know Chronicles, you wouldn't have to fear them! You're nothing but jealous bigots!"

"Watch your mouth!" the captain snapped as he came toward them swiftly.

Dominic's eyes flashed red and he hurled the captain away with Telekinesis. That same power caused a force that prevented anyone from drawing near. He felt Tariah opening herself to him and willingly gave her his majiks though he didn't know what she was about to do. He got his answer as he saw her eyes turn blue and her mind seemed to sharpen.

The king's eyes slowly turned a matching blue and his expression stilled. "Release them," he said, and his voice was monotone. "Let them leave."

The Militia stared in disbelief at him, then one soldier saw the matching eye colors of the king and Tariah. "She's controlling him!"

"And if you do not let us go," Tariah said quietly, her voice as cool as a midnight ocean, "I will shatter his mind."

No one dared call her bluff when they did not know just what a Chronicle was capable of doing. The soldiers backed away from the doors and left plenty of room for them to leave. Dominic lifted Tariah into his arms as he backed toward the door. As soon as they were there, she released the king from her hold and he turned and ran out of the palace.

There was silence for a moment then the Militia lunged for the door to stop them. "Stop!" the king commanded shakily. When they all turned to stare at him, he lowered his head into his hands. "Let them be," he said quietly. "When she took control . . . I touched her mind. She is not a monster." He lifted his head and stared at his hands, stricken. "Dear god," he whispered. "What have we Magi done?" He got to his feet. "I must think on this. In the meantime, do not harm Tariah Chronis or Dominic Whisperer! They have not earned it."

Outside the palace, Dominic didn't put Tariah down as he hurried toward the street. To his surprise, Morgan was standing on the side next to a cart. Dominic put Tariah down as they approached and Morgan said, "It didn't go well."

"No, not really." Tariah shivered even though it was a normal desert day. "I can't stay here," she said fretfully. "I feel like everyone is staring at me!"

"I didn't think you could." He gestured to the cart. "This is for you. There's a pack of supplies in the back. It should be enough for a few days if you want to avoid cities altogether. If not, you might consider Crystalia to the northwest. It's an oasis town and not very big. If you leave now, you could make it there by this evening."

She impulsively reached out and hugged him tightly. "Thank you, Morgan," she said. "I hope you find your Fury soon," she whispered. It was the greatest thing she could wish for him and they all knew it.

He returned the hug then let her go. "Be safe, Tariah."

Dominic helped her up into the cart then climbed up beside her. "Good luck, Morgan," he said, then he flicked the reigns and the finned beast tied to the cart began to walk and pull them down the road.

Tariah studied the beast. She knew of them, naturally, but she had never seen one up close. They were called findrals and they were used for riding and pulling carts because they were fast and strong and they could both walk on land and also swim in water. They looked like a very big dog but with a face like a bird and instead of wings they had fins.

This one seemed especially spry and she suspected Morgan had gotten it specifically for them. The idea made her eyes burn with tears. In such a short time, he had become very dear to her. Cousins? Inside her heart, she felt like she had found a missing brother.

"I'm sorry, Tariah," Dominic said quietly as they continued down the road. When she glanced at him, he explained, "For not defending you better. I should have known it was a bad idea."

She shook her head. "No, don't be sorry." She turned on the seat to look into the cart behind them and spotted a heavy cloak. Though she knew it would make her warm, she pulled it on with the hood tugged down over her head. Right then she didn't want to deal with the stares or the rumors.

He kept his eyes on their surroundings until they were beyond the city. It wasn't until they were past the farmlands and there were no more Magi around that he actually relaxed. He immediately lifted his free hand and tugged her hood down. "We're safe now, *ishke*."

"I know." She leaned against his shoulder with a sigh. "I need to be distracted. Tell me about the tiers. Is it a hierarchy of sorts?"

"So to speak. The tiers are how we define the strength of a Dragon Lord. A fourth tier is technically only a Fury, but there have been other Lords who are that strong. It's defined by how well and how long you can hold a form other than your own." He smiled. "First tier Dragon Lords have a horrible time with things. They could be in the middle of a city and suddenly turn back to normal."

She frowned thoughtfully. "Elder Juniper said Dragon Lords can take a Kin form."

"Sure. I once ran around as a SunKin Faerie."

She thought of her big Fury as a small Faerie and found it amusing. "I'd like to see that some time." She tilted her head. "So . . . do you think it might be possible for us to disguise ourselves as Kin? Then we wouldn't need to worry about anyone refusing us service."

"It's a good idea," he decided. "It'll take a drain on my majiks though." He shot her a quick grin of anticipation. "But I don't see a problem with replenishing it. It's been too long since I kissed you last."

She smiled. "It's more addicting than I thought it might be. I keep catching myself staring at you and hoping you'll kiss me."

"Hope louder," was the murmur in response. "I hadn't noticed. If I had, you would have gotten your kisses as wished." He felt the warm caress of her power thoughts, and he sent her a heated look. "Not while I'm driving. The findral might run away with us."

She smiled and cuddled closer against his arm. She was contented with the knowledge that he wanted her. His power flowed around her and merged with hers to make once more that wonderful feeling of something that would never end. A sudden thought occurred to her and she sat upright. "Wait! Dragons are immortal!" She looked at him in horror. "Does that mean that someday I'll die and leave you?"

"No." He held the reigns with one hand and curled the other around her neck to pull her closer. "We're both immortal, Tariah. Our power is endless and infinite because it is shared. As long as no one kills us, we will live forever."

After a moment of thought, she said, "I don't think I'd want to be immortal if I wasn't with you. It would be boring. But because I'm going to be with you, it sounds really wonderful."

He pulled the findral to a stop and put the reigns down. He turned and pulled her into his arms as his lips came down to cover hers. He didn't bother to be gentle this time, knowing that she would enjoy the rough kiss as much as he did. Hungrily he devoured her lips, his tongue inviting her to return the favor.

She shuddered and wound her arms around his neck. She eagerly kissed him back and used everything he had been teaching her. It always felt wonderful to kiss him, but she was beginning to feel like there was something more her body wanted. His hand gently cupped her breast through the cloak and though it sent a wave of heat through her body, it wasn't enough either. "Dominic . . ."

He forced himself to release her. "We'll see what happens tonight," he said huskily. "For now, I just wanted to kiss you."

"Why?" she asked.

He picked up the reigns again and started the findral walking once more. "Mostly for you being you, but because I never seem to get enough of your taste." He sent her a quick grin. "You're the perfect definition of water in the desert. It's probably the most wanted thing in the world."

She *felt* like the most wanted thing in the world and found it to be very enjoyable. With a little sigh, she rested against him once more and closed her eyes. She much preferred riding on his back as they ran or flew, but this was nice too.

Crystalia was in their sights as afternoon was beginning to turn into evening. They were less than a mile outside the limits when he stopped the findral and the cart. "Well, this would be a good time to try out our disguise," he told her.

She closed her eyes to concentrate and began to draw on his majiks to change herself. He could handle changing himself just fine. He showed her how to bend her power and the way it needed to bend to become a Kin. It was a complete blind shot for her. She had no way of determining what sort of Kin she might become by bending her power.

She got her answer as she felt the wind rustling the ears now perched on top of her head. She was a Kin Elf, apparently. She opened her eyes and looked down to see that her skin was now the color of dark gold, and her lines had shifted to turn into the familiar silver tattoos of the MoonKin. She lifted her hands to her ears and discovered they were the sharp and angular ears of a feline of some kind. She decided it was apt since she liked it when Dominic was petting her.

He was also a MoonKin Elf now, and his ears looked like they could belong to a canine. He gave a mock growl and scooped her up into his arms to nuzzle her throat. She smelled the same as ever even if she looked quite a bit different. "Be careful I don't go chasing you."

"I wouldn't run." She ran her fingers over the tattoos on his arms. She liked them, but she much preferred seeing his lines and knowing it was her power that made them. Testing, she probed at his majiks and saw that he was weakened. "Once we get to the inn," she promised, "then I'll feed you. Inside the inn room, we should be able to drop the disguise."

"And it won't be as draining next time because you'll know what to do." He started the findral again and they continued down the road toward Crystalia.

Crystalia was an oasis town because it was built in a large oasis. It was no bigger than a mile in diameter but it had a high traffic flow because it was between Prismatic and the port town of Scopic to the north. The inn was located directly in the middle of the main street which itself ran through the middle of town.

Not a single Magi suspected a thing. They looked at Tariah and Dominic and saw two MoonKin traveling together. There were one or two Kin in the town, but they just smiled and said nothing even though they knew full well what the two really were.

The innkeeper was very happy to rent them a room for the night so Dominic tethered the findral and the cart outside. He was feeling very tired, but the anticipation of tasting his Chronicle's power again was more than enough to keep him moving. He still had no idea how he had gotten along without her.

As the door to the room shut behind them, she asked, "How *did* you get along? I mean . . . I wasn't there to replenish your majiks."

He bent his majiks back the other way and went back into his Magi form. As she also unbent the majiks to return to normal, he reached out to draw her into his arms. "We Furies can put ourselves into hibernation for long periods of time to replenish our majiks ourselves. But, to give you an idea of how long that could be, even this minor drain I'm feeling right now would have required a year of hibernation."

She slid her arms around his waist and held onto him tightly. "That's horrible." Her breath caught as he lifted her into his arms and carried her toward the bed. "Is the door locked?" she asked.

"Locked and sealed." He lowered her to the top of the bed before removing her boots for her. He eased down beside her and began to unfasten the cloak, his fingers trembling lightly with desire as he uncovered more and more of her body. "I'm going to indulge myself," he murmured huskily.

She wasn't sure what he meant but she shortly found herself naked in his arms. It didn't bother her in the slightest. As he gathered her close and bent his head toward hers, her power welled up and flowed over her like a blue veil.

He didn't bother to work his way to her lips. He kissed her immediately, craving her taste as deeply as her power. It flowed into him like wine and he slid his arms around her to hold her even closer. Lazily he slid his tongue into her mouth, and his heart and body tightened equally as she returned the soft caress.

When his hunger for her lips was appeased for the moment, he released her and slowly began to trail kisses along the side of her neck. Her pulse was pounding rapidly and he brushed against her emotions to be sure she was not afraid.

She wasn't afraid of anything. She felt as if she were drowning in pleasure. Her body was hot and aching but nothing he did seemed to make it better. It *felt* better but it didn't seem to be enough. She felt his hot mouth moving over the curves of her breasts and it sent those same tugs of before through her blood. It didn't seem nearly as frightening anymore.

Instinctively she twisted toward him, offering herself to him. He was hardly one to deny her, and he closed his lips hungrily over the tightened nipple begging for his attention. Her back arched and he held her closer as he eagerly tugged at her with lips and teeth, savoring her power as it flowed into him. It tasted slightly sweeter at her breast and certainly stronger.

A low moan vibrated out of her throat as he switched to her other breast. The ache was spreading and demanding more. Without thinking about it, she reached for him, wanting to touch him and make him feel the same. Her fingers found the material of his vest and she tugged at it in frustration.

His lips curved against her breast. "You want me naked?" He straightened and shrugged out of the vest. As he was reaching for her again, she flattened her hands against his chest to stop him. With a smile, he laid down on the bed beside her and tucked his hands behind his head. "I'm yours to explore, *ishke*."

She hadn't even realized that was what she had wanted until he had said it. Her curiosity had grown. She wanted to know his body. She wanted to see if he would respond the same if she touched him the same as he touched her.

She rose to her knees beside him and the lack of feeling her hair over her skin made her realize it was still coiled on top of her head. She reached up and began to untuck the little twists to let them fall down around her shoulders and waist. Dominic was still touching her emotions and she was feeling his in return. Her breath hitched as she felt his utter absorption and delight in watching her hair come down.

Once her hair was freed, she ran her hands through it to completely untwist it. She moved closer to him and lightly put a hand on his chest. She had touched his chest a lot, but now she was noticing how hot he was, and how strong the muscle beneath his skin was. The lines flowing over his chest tingled her palms and she loved knowing it was her power that made them.

Delighted with her freedom, she slowly ran her hands over him, memorizing everything. He watched her through lowered lashes, his eyes nearly black with emotion. It was exceptionally hard to keep from snatching her up and pulling her over him to teach her how to ride him properly. His arousal couldn't have been hidden if he tried.

She didn't notice, lost in her study of him. Her questing fingers found one flat male nipple and she gave in to temptation to lean down and taste him as he had tasted her. His body jerked and a soft growl rumbled in his chest. Nothing could have delighted her more. "You like that too?"

He caught her hand and pulled it down so that it was pressed against his erection straining against his pants. "What do you think?" he asked in a soft growl.

Her eyes widened and she hastily snatched her hand back. Though she would have liked to have petted him more, she was nervous of going any further than that, and she didn't find it fair to him to make him so frustrated. Unsure what to do, she lowered her hands to her sides.

He sat up and softly ran his hands down her arms. "It's alright, Tariah. One day at a time. Look how far you've gotten already."

"I'm just so tired of being nervous." She sighed as he pulled her into his arms. She let herself relax against him and closed her eyes. "I want to belong to you. But something is nervous."

"That's the part of you that is still growing." He ran his fingers through her hair. "It knows that there is no going back and it doesn't want to grow up. Growing up means complicated feelings and emotions and living. Everyone feels that way. It's perfectly natural." He lowered her to the bed and covered her gently, wrapping her in his arms and his power all at the same time. "Rest now," he murmured.

She snuggled closer and slid her arms around him. "Dominic?" she asked. "Hmm?"

"Thank you."

"For what?" He nuzzled her gently.

"For being you." She smiled and sighed softly. "The rest of the world could never change and I'd be happy just with you." She gave a little yawn. "I'm sorry I'm such trouble for you."

He smiled. "You're well worth all the trouble." He gathered her even closer and buried his nose in her hair so that her scent would follow him into his sleep.

Content, she closed her eyes and let the sound and feel of his heartbeat lull her toward sleep. She was beginning to feel like her puberty was taking too *long* rather than being too fast. A part of her couldn't wait to find out what happened next. Growing up meant that she would be with Dominic forever.

Childhood stood no chance against that desire.

Chapter Thirteen

They decided to eat breakfast at the restaurant in town instead of leaving and hunting their own meal. Tariah was tired of always being on the run, and Dominic was worried because she had lost weight.

Hearing that, she walked over to the mirror and frowned. "Have I really lost weight?" She peered at her figure for signs of skinniness. Sure enough, she *did* seem a little more slender in places. Her muscles were a little more pronounced in her legs and arms. No ribs were showing, though. "I guess I hadn't noticed."

He walked up behind her and wrapped his arms around her waist. "You don't spend as much time staring at yourself as I spend staring at you." He nuzzled her shoulder softly. "You've been on the run for so long, and there's been so much trouble, and we haven't had full meals consistently . . . it's amazing you haven't lost *more* weight."

"I don't want to lose weight." She crossed her arms. "I'd rather be happy, fat, and lazy." She waited a moment then began to snicker softly. "Okay, maybe not. Sparkle's on the pudgy side and I love teasing her. I can't gain too much weight or she can take revenge."

He chuckled and turned her around in his arms. His hands slid warmly over her back. "Eventually you're going to get fat, you know." He kissed her softly and lingered over her flavor. "Pregnancy does that to a woman, no matter her species." One of his hands rested tenderly over her belly. "You'll be beautiful."

She cuddled closer. Her Fury always knew precisely what to say to make her feel better. She lingered for a moment then reluctantly released him and went to get dressed. "Someday I'll cook breakfast for us."

His brows lifted as he pulled on his vest. "You can cook?"

"Don't sound surprised," she scolded. "I'm a *very* good cook." She smiled. "Mountain boy. I assume you've never had pitcher crab cakes with cactear syrup."

His mouth watered at the very idea. "No, but it sounds decadent." He scooped her up for a quick kiss. "Something tells me I might be the one in danger of getting pudgy if you start cooking for me."

She snickered. "I'll make you chase me across the dunes and you'll burn it off. I've yet to meet someone not of the desert who can outrun a desert dweller across dunes."

"We might try that even if it's not needed for exercise." He set her down and began to bend his majiks to change him to a Kin form. As he had thought, her use of his majiks this time had barely any effect. She learned *very* quickly.

She also made a beautiful Kin. He ran his fingers lightly over her ears and grinned. Because there was a smaller discrepancy between the heights of male and female Kin, she was actually only two or three inches shorter than his height. Her delight in that small thing warmed his heart. "But I like you when you're cuddle size."

"Me too, but this is nice too." She eased up the scant few inches between their heights and kissed him softly. "See?"

He hugged her tightly, then released her. He kept her close as they left the inn room and went downstairs to checkout. They wanted to leave right after breakfast and head to the north. They hadn't received any new direction to travel; they could only continue along what they had already been told.

The restaurant was only slightly busy this time of morning. It was very easy to find a place to sit where they wouldn't have to be too close to other people. Both ordered large breakfasts and had only started to eat them when a Magi walked up to the table. "Excuse me?" she asked.

"Yes?" Tariah's heart was pounding as hard as Dominic's was. Were they found?

"I just wanted to remark on your tattoos. They're quite lovely. I've never seen another MoonKin with the like." The Magi smiled. "I hope that isn't too rude."

"No, not at all!" a SunKin Elf said as he came up to the table. He put a hand on Tariah's shoulder companionably. "To us, it's the same as complimenting a Magi on their hair or their eyes. Of course, our Tiarrah has beauty in all three."

"She does indeed." The Magi drew her thumb over her cheek and nose. "Well, it was nice speaking to you, Tiarrah."

Tariah, remembering Rumidia, touched her ears and bowed slightly. "Likewise." As the Magi walked away, she turned her head and looked at the Kin gratefully. "Thank you. I wouldn't have known how to react."

The Elf smiled and tapped her nose. "We Kin watch out for one another. Good luck, little Chronicle." He bowed gracefully then headed back over to his own table.

She glanced at Dominic who was chuckling. "What?" she asked warily.

"What he called you." He smiled. "I believe in the language of the Kin, it means something like 'little creature.' I've heard it used as a term of endearment among family." He grinned when her nose wrinkled. "I also notice that it's a variation on the characters of your name. The Kin must have been waiting for a chance to remark on it."

"Shut up, Dominic," she mumbled as she dug into her breakfast. So she was short, even by Kin standards. What crime was that? Still, she had to smile. She liked knowing that her name was nearly the same as one in the Kin. They had become more of a fellow race to her than the Magi, and she was more closely connected to the Magi in her species.

Once they had finished breakfast and had paid for their meal, they went outside to where their findral and cart were waiting. Tariah was feeling better than she had in a long time. It had felt good to be able to eat to her fill. She was mildly impressed by Dominic's appetite though. "I never imagined anyone could eat that much."

"I *am* considerably bigger," he reminded her, "even if I currently don't look it." He helped her up onto the seat before climbing up beside her. Moments later they were heading down the road. "Will it bother you to live with the Dragons, Tariah? Even the Dragon Lords tend to stay in their normal shape unless they leave. You'll be slightly overwhelmed."

"As long as they watch where they're walking," was her impish response, "I don't mind. I don't want to get stepped on."

He laughed. "I'll carry you on my shoulder, how's that?" He held the reigns with one hand and wrapped his other arm around her shoulders to draw her closer. A part of him missed the Isle, but he wouldn't have changed a single minute with his Chronicle. His only regret was that because they were cut off from the Isle, she was being forced to suffer the Magi's prejudices. She needed to be home.

The findral suddenly balked and reared in the air, and it nearly dumped the cart over. Tariah went flying right over the side, and she shrieked as she landed unceremoniously in the sand. "Ouch!"

"Tariah!" Dominic released the reins and leapt clear of the thrashing beast to rush to his lover's side. "Are you alright?"

She spit sand out of her mouth and pushed herself up. "I'm okay, I think," she said shakily. "A little scared. Maybe a lot scared." She grabbed his vest tightly as she saw the way the findral was reacting. "Dominic . . ."

He looked and immediately recognized what was occurring. His stomach churned. "Stay here." He moved a few steps away and returned to his natural form. He wasn't risking her life on power alone. He planted himself in front of her defensively.

Her stomach quivered. "It's the power in the land, isn't it?" she whispered. "The findral is being mutated into a monster. But I didn't feel any fluctuations in the land!"

"It must be something in Prismatic," he said grimly. "The findral was born there. Something is happening to the power balance in Prismatic. You don't have to be in the city of your birth to be affected by it if it's big enough."

The findral gave a screech like nails across glass that shortly turned into a guttural roar. Sharp spikes burst out of its back and ripped the fins cleanly away. Its fur fell off to leave nothing but bare skin beneath, and Dominic covered Tariah's face with a wing as he saw the chunks of skin falling off the creature's face to leave nothing but a skeleton behind. "Close your eyes," he ordered her.

She very nearly hid behind a sand dune but changed her mind at the last moment. She was *not* letting him handle this alone. Her stomach rolled when she saw how the findral looked, but she braced her shoulders and gathered her power to wait for an opening. She was new to combat just as she was new to so much else, and she was damned well going to get through this too.

The findral lunged for Dominic, but the Dragon was bigger and stronger. One swipe of his massive claw sent the findral tumbling away. It recovered and came after him again on his blind side. He couldn't turn in time and the monster's sharp beak stabbed into his flank. With a roar, he flung the findral away once more.

It noticed Tariah and went lunging after her, sensing she was the smaller and easier target. She released a steady stream of ice projectiles at the monster, her quivering fingers the only hint of her nerves. Most of the ice shards pierced flesh, and the findral was forced to back away. Dominic struck like a blur and his teeth tore through what remained of the monster's flesh. He hurled it violently aside, and a spear of ice cracked down through the air. It encased the beast entirely, and he destroyed it with a solid swipe of his tail. Both monster and ice shattered in hundreds of pieces and dissolved in the hot sun.

His side aching worse than the fires of the Underrealm, Dominic laid down on the sand and scolded Tariah, "I told you to stay back!"

"I wasn't about to let you fight alone." She went over to his side and began to gently examine his wound. It was two sharp puncture wounds, and they were sullenly bleeding green blood. "This would be easier to tend if you were in Kin or Magi form," she told him. "I can rip my cloak for enough cloth to wrap your side that way."

He closed his eyes and focused his concentration on bending his majiks. His body shifted and glowed, and he turned into his MoonKin form. He also nearly fell flat on his face. The wound had transferred to his side and thigh both because this body was much smaller, and the wounds were much more disabling because of it.

She managed to catch him and break his fall, and she carefully helped him sit down on the sand. She pulled her cloak off and began to quickly and efficiently tear it into strips. He watched her with a wry smile. "You seem to be good at that."

She began to bind his leg first. "I used to climb cliffs, remember? There wasn't a day when I didn't get some sort of cut or scrape. It was easier to mend it myself rather than going home and coming back. We'll have to find a Soil element who can mend this better."

He grimaced as she bound his side tightly. "Easy on that. It hurts."

"I imagine so, you big baby!" She put the knot right over the wound to attempt to stem the bleeding. He sat up and she hastily braced him. "Take it easy," she warned. "Don't pull open the bandages."

An explosion in the far distance rocked the land around them and knocked them both off balance. He had to catch himself before he accidentally squashed her, and he covered her bodily as the sand erupted around them. The power in the land had gone haywire. From where they were, they could even hear the screams of the people in Crystalia as they were knocked off their feet.

The land stopped shaking and Dominic got carefully to his feet. He pulled Tariah up and held onto her tightly. "Are you okay?" He ran his hands over her swiftly.

"I am." She was shaking though unharmed. "What was that? That . . . that wasn't a normal quake! It felt like the power in the land was just . . . exploded!"

He stared over her head at the distance. Grimly, he said, "It was definitely Prismatic. I can see it from here. There's smoke pluming from the buildings. Something is happening there."

Terror closed her throat. "Morgan! We have to go back," she pleaded. "We need to make sure he's okay! If something happens to him and those children . . ." She paled as she remembered Symphony and how her sudden disappearance had disrupted the land. If the land had adjusted to the presence of five Chronicles, even if four of them were not yet developed, and they were suddenly removed . . .

Dominic cursed softly and stepped back from her. Once more, he turned back to his natural form. The bandages ripped away in the process, but the wounds were almost gone. The spewed elements from the eruption had acted as a natural healer. "Get on my back!" he ordered. "We can fly to the limits and then go inside!"

She climbed up onto his back and held on tightly as he took to the sky and began flying swiftly. Neither worried about disrupting the flow of power in the land. It was already so riotous that it would never notice the effects of Dragoons. A wave already in motion wouldn't notice more waves if they went in the same direction.

It was only half an hour before they were landing in the farmlands outside Prismatic, but it felt like forever. The farmers didn't notice a Dragon landing in their field. They were too busy scrambling to secure their animals and crops. Everything was being shaken up by the tremors in the land.

Dominic changed to his MoonKin form and spotted a findral running loose. He caught it and swung up onto its back. He reached down to pull Tariah up with him and they took off down the road as quickly as possible.

The city was a sea of chaos. Buildings had fallen, and some animals and Magi alike had been mutated into monsters. The Militia was everywhere and running mad as they struggled to protect and save everyone. Random bursts of power in the land spewed fire and water into the air. Storm clouds were rushing in over the city and lightning was arcing to the ground even without them.

Smoke was billowing out of the district where the sanctuary was located. Tariah's heart seemed to freeze in her chest as she saw that the building had been nearly decimated. Fires still burned and leapt hungrily toward the sky. Through it, she caught the smell of Air and recognized Morgan's power. It was clashing with another familiar scent.

Soh had been here.

Dominic stopped the findral outside the sanctuary and Tariah leapt down to run over and join the Water Magi who were trying to put out the flames. Her power was far more potent, and with her assistance, the flames were shortly smothered. "What happened?" she demanded of the nearest Magi.

Shakily, the man said, "The Black Magi Elite. They . . . they came in and went to see the Black Magi. The next thing we knew, the sanctuary was exploding. Moments later the land went wild. We can't even get inside to see if there are any survivors." He gestured at the door. "It's too strong for Magi." He looked at her. "You're Kin. Can you get in?"

Even a Kin might have had trouble, to be honest. If she got in, it would be only because she was a Chronicle. Without waiting for Dominic, and she ran toward the sanctuary doors. The barrier around the place didn't offer even a token resistance to her as she dashed inside. "Morgan!" she shouted. "Kelsey! Eli! Anyone!"

There was no response, and she could feel no power that indicated someone, if they were there, still lived. The entire place was charred and scorched. It got worse and worse as she went deeper down the hall toward Morgan's study. The detonation had occurred there, she was sure of it.

Dominic came up behind her. "I don't smell anyone here," he told her. "Either they got out or they're dead."

She flinched and opened the study door. The entire room was decimated. Not a single thing had escaped the explosion. There were no bodies, however, so no one had been in there to die. Oddly, Morgan's Black Magi cloak was still present, and it was lying thrown across the floor haphazardly.

She walked over to pick it up and discovered, to her shock, a piece of paper with her name on it. It had no legible writing on it, but as she picked it up, the characters formed and became clearer.

"He must have written that before the attack," Dominic said quietly. "He knew it was coming."

She looked down at the letter and felt her stomach quiver. "He did," she whispered.

Tariah, my sister;

Well, not really my sister, but it feels as if you are. As I write this letter, I can feel Soh coming toward the sanctuary. He is after the children. His power . . . it has gotten stronger. I don't know how, but I know that whatever he has planned will be terrible. My only hope for protecting these children is to send them away.

I have erased the memories of the children and their parents alike. They will remember nothing of the Black Magi or what was done here. To further ensure their protection, I have locked their powers with my own. They will develop normally, but their Chronicle powers will not become visible until they are in the presence of another Chronicle or a Fury.

I will be sending the children away shortly via my Air powers. I do not know where they will land. It is better this way. If Soh gets his hands on me, and I lose the fight, then he cannot get their locations from me. I'm counting on you, Tariah. Find the children and lead them to the Dragons.

May the moons watch over you, Morgan

Tears welled and flowed down her face. "He's not dead," she whispered. "I'm sure I would have known! I can't feel as if he died here. I can feel that he fought here, but not that he died."

Dominic looked around the room intently. "It may be that he had just sent the children away when the attack struck. He was a smart man. If he had sensed or seen that Soh was too much for him, he would have used his power to get himself away as well. That would be why the land went wild as it did, in two waves. The first was the children being sent away. The second was Soh's attack and Morgan's disappearance."

"So where are the Elite then?" she asked. She rolled up the letter and put it in the sack she still wore on her hip. She wiped her tears away fiercely. "No one saw them leave, right?" Suddenly she froze. "If the Elite want to destroy the Magi . . ."

"The king!" He cursed softly and got to his feet. He grabbed her hand and hurried with her away from the scene. Rather than go out the front, they made their way to the back exit. A quick look around assured them that the Militia was likely too busy chasing monsters to notice anyone going into the palace.

They made their way through the city as quickly as they could by cutting corners and hanging to back alleys. The chaos was even worse as they got closer to the castle. The people with stronger power lived around the castle and the disruption had been greater.

The Militia didn't once notice Dominic and Tariah as they ran behind the buildings toward the gates. Tariah was quick and agile enough from all her years of cliff climbing to make her way up over the wall and into the courtyard. Dominic was forced to climb a tree to get over the wall, but he was shortly beside her once more.

The area was a tomb. The people who had been mutated into monsters prowled the edges. Those who had not been changed were either dead on the floor or had already fled the scene. The castle itself seemed to be un-breached, and two Militia guards stood outside the throne room doors.

Dominic, however, could smell something odd. "They're dead," he said flatly. "They're just propped up to look like they're alive."

Tariah nearly was sick to her stomach. She fought it back and hurried toward the throne room doors. When she opened them, the doors swung inward and the two Militia soldiers fell to the floor in a heap. Their heads rolled away from their bodies, and she gagged.

Dominic hustled her past the scene and through the throne room. "Your majesty!" he shouted as he saw the king standing down the carpet from them. Abruptly he stopped and pulled Tariah to a stop with him. "Something's wrong."

The king toppled to the floor and Tariah gave a cry as she rushed forward. She slid to her knees beside him and rolled him over onto his back. She immediately flinched. His chest had been torn open. Not even a MoonKin could have mended this. His power was draining away too fast to be stopped. When it was gone, his body would be gone. Without power, no body of any species could live. Their bodies were power.

His eyes opened and he stared up at her in confusion. "Kin?"

She shook her head and unbent the majiks to return to normal. "No."

He sighed as he recognized her. Blood stained his lips in the process. "I am sorry," he said brokenly. "Sorry for what I did to you. What the Magi have done. What we've done for so long. I touched your mind. I saw inside you. You're no monster."

She held onto his hand tightly. "Who did this? Was it the Elite?"

"Yes." Bloody tears slid down his face. "He called me a murderer. He was right."

"No, he wasn't! You're not guilty of the sins of others," Dominic told him sharply.

"No, but I am guilty of my own sins." He met Tariah's eyes. "If my daughter had lived . . . she would be your age."

She took a sharp breath. "Your daughter was a Chronicle."

"I was so afraid of a rumor that I had my own child killed." His eyes closed. "She never got mad at me. She just . . . looked at me and asked me why. I couldn't tell her." He coughed, and blood gurgled from his chest around the wound. "Dragoons . . . please. Stop the Elite. They want to destroy the Magi. If they do . . . then they destroy the world."

Tariah closed her eyes. "I'll try," she said softly.

Dominic's lips thinned. He was beginning to hate how everything had to come down on her shoulders. Why was she the one who had to carry the burdens of a race that had brought their own destruction upon them?

"The world needs Magi," she told him. "Without them, there would be no seas. The world would shrivel away. Someone has to do something. It might as well be me."

"I'm sorry, Tariah." The king gave a faint sigh. "I hope your children are Chronicles as well. Our world needs them again."

There were no further words, and Tariah and Dominic both felt as his power stopped entirely. His skin slowly turned gray, and his blood disappeared entirely. Without his power, his body was nothing more than a shell.

The doors burst open and the Militia surged into the room. They stopped in shock as they saw Tariah and Dominic beside the dead body of the king. Tariah could read their thoughts on their faces even without her Telepathy. "No!" she said. "We didn't do it!"

Before the soldiers could retort, the captain walked forward and knelt beside the king's body. After a moment of scrutiny, he said, "She tells the truth. The king was killed by the Elite. I recognize their power. Those bastards!" he cursed softly. He looked at Tariah. "You need to get away from here. The people are in an uproar. They won't be able to define friend from enemy. A Chronicle would be a good scapegoat."

Dominic pulled Tariah up to her feet when it was apparent she was frozen with shock. "But why are you helping me?" she asked the captain. "You hated me!"

"For a time." The captain studied her. "But I've seen the Elite, and I've seen you. I may fear you more, but I trust them less. Get away from here. And I might suggest staying away from Magi cities entirely."

Dominic evaluated the power in the land and saw it was still rocking like waves. He backed up several feet and turned to his natural form. Tariah climbed up onto his back, and he looked at captain. "Tell me something. Are you finally seeing that it was the fault of the Magi for the existence of the Elite?"

The captain's face tightened. "Get out of here," he said harshly.

He didn't need to be told twice. He flew straight up into the air and through the broken ceiling toward the sky. Once they were well over the city, he began flying to the west. The entire continent of Spectrum was being affected. The only way he or Tariah would rest was if they were not on its land.

She said nothing as they flew. Her emotions felt like the land. They were shaking and turbulent. Nothing seemed to be secure in her world. At the whims of any person who crossed her path, her life could change. She just wanted to make it all go away.

Dominic felt grim and a little terrified. Only his presence was anchoring her to this world. He needed to get her somewhere safe and dedicate his full attention to her. The abundance of her inner strength had continued to astound him, yet he could see how terribly close she was to the end of her rope. Without him, she might very well attempt to detonate her own power.

A few miles into the ocean past Spectrum, he spotted a tiny island. It was hardly bigger than an oasis itself, but it was not part of the main landmass. He swiftly angled down and landed on the strip of sand that made a beach. He turned into his Magi form and caught Tariah safely in his arms as she tumbled toward him.

A brief scan of the island told him that they were alone. He put up a shield to keep it that way then began to walk into the trees to find a place that would be good for camping. Tariah was silent in his arms, her head resting tiredly on his shoulder. His worry increased as he brushed against her emotions and found them to be completely numb.

There was a small clearing among the trees, and he gently put her down on the thick grass. She didn't move as he gathered small logs to make a fire. It was still daytime but it was dark among the trees and she was beginning to shiver. He used his powers to make the fire smokeless, then went to her side and wrapped her in a blanket from his backpack. "*Ishke.*"

Her eyes closed. "I don't know how much more I can take, Dominic," she whispered. "All I want is to have some peace. But Morgan needs me to find the children. The king needs me to stop the Elite." Tears slid down her cheeks. "I don't even know what *I* need anymore."

He pulled her into his arms and held her tightly. "Whatever it is you need," he said fiercely, "I'll get it for you. Just don't leave me. I feel like you're slipping away from me. I'm so sorry, but I need you too. I need you to be with me. Stay with me, Tariah."

She leaned back and studied his face. "You're hungry." Her arms wound around his neck. "I'm sorry I didn't notice." She eased up and teased his lips with hers. "I need *you*, Dominic. I feel like you're the only reason I have left to live."

His hands framed her face and her power welled up in silent pleading. He kissed her long and tenderly, drinking her power as it flowed generously into him. He deepened the kiss as she sighed, and his heart clenched with emotion as she returned every caress with one of her own.

They eased apart and she felt something inside her heart suddenly still. A calm certainty swept through her and banished all her lingering doubts and fears. Her eyes lifted to meet his. The words were there and unexpectedly easy to say. "Make love to me."

He stopped breathing. He searched her eyes and probed at her emotions with his own. Even when he curled his power around her, he could find nothing but certainty. She knew what she wanted even if she didn't wholly understand yet what she needed. A low groan caught in his chest and he kissed her hungrily as he lowered her to the ground.

The blanket was the perfect bed. She felt nothing but eagerness as she ran her hands slowly over his arms. When he began to slowly undress her, she didn't hesitate to reach for his vest and return the favor.

When he felt her fingers at the fastenings to his pants, he laughed and caught her hands. "No, you don't." He gently caged her hands at her sides then eased back to look at her naked body in delight. "If you get me naked, you'll start exploring, and if you start exploring, I'll go crazy."

"Isn't that the idea?" She rubbed her power against his for the sheer delight of seeing his eyes darken. When he returned the invisible touch, her eyes closed helplessly at the feeling. "I want to know everything."

"Then let me show you." He lowered his head and brushed his lips over the curves of her breasts. Her power still flowed over her body, and he drank it slowly, savoring it like one would savor a rare drink. "You won't think of anything but me," he promised.

As his mouth closed over her nipple and sucked so strongly that her back arched, she had the feeling that thinking was going to be impossible. Heat surged through her body and the ache of pleasure spread swiftly. Just the feel of his hair on her skin was maddening and wonderful.

He released her hands and began to run his own over her body slowly. He trailed soft fingers over the length of her long legs and over the flat curve of her stomach. Her power followed him, and he was helpless but to feed on it wherever he found it. It sparked a feeling not unlike how it felt to be drunk. This drunkenness consumed his entire essence, from his power outward. "Tariah," he murmured thickly against the skin of her stomach, his lips tracing the lines that were there.

She shuddered as his hand closed over her breast and kneaded gently. "What are you doing?" she managed to whisper as she felt his lips skimming over her thigh. He didn't seem to be making the ache better. He was making it worse and she could feel a throbbing between her legs. "My body feels odd."

He grinned with savage delight as he felt just how odd through his connection to her emotions. He wanted her to be completely mindless with desire. He wanted her to crave his possession of her so deeply that she would never doubt they belonged together. "Good," he said. "Take a breath."

She open her mouth then sucked in a sharp breath as she felt his hand slip between her legs. Little shockwaves rolled through her body of raw pleasure and she curled her fingers into the blanket beneath her. She moaned brokenly as she felt him stroking her gently. She had never imagined it might feel like this.

He caught her hand and drew it down her body until she was touching herself.

"You see?" he murmured huskily. "This is how your body shows its pleasure."

She slid her hand free and instead held his closer. "I like your touch more," she whispered. Her voice broke on a soft cry as she felt his hot breath where her fingers had just been. "You're not going to kiss me there."

"Of course I am." He shuddered as her power beckoned to him. Almost desperately, he closed his lips over her and caressed with his tongue the little knot of flesh he had awakened. She tasted like nothing he had ever known before.

She grabbed onto his shoulders for dear life as her muscles began to draw tighter and tighter. He was still making it worse! She couldn't breathe, couldn't think, for the pleasure that consumed her. But it still wasn't enough. It felt as if her whole body was going to shatter. "Dominic," she pleaded. "Fix it!"

Her hips twisted helplessly as she felt his fingers slowly stretching her. One strong finger slid inside her body even as his power consumed hers, and her entire body convulsed as ecstasy shuddered through her. As the pleasure swept over her, she realized it was almost exactly what she had felt missing. But there was something still lacking. "Dominic?" she asked huskily as she felt him gathering her closer.

He tilted her chin up and kissed her desperately, his tongue surging into her mouth to torment them both. His hands were shaking as he ran them slowly over her body, tracing every curve damp with sweat. "We're not done yet," he said thickly. "I'm just trying not to lose control."

The idea of an out-of-control Dominic was deeply appealing to that feminine place in her heart. She had been out of control in his arms. She wanted him to be the same. She pushed at his shoulders, and when he rolled onto his back, she rose to her knees beside him. "My turn." Her husky voice was a promise of delight.

He covered his face with an arm. "Be gentle," he warned her. "I'm already pushing the limit. I want to be inside you so badly I can taste it."

She glanced at the front of his pants and her eyes widened slightly. Curiously, she reached out a hand and covered the interesting bulge under the fabric. He groaned and, encouraged, she began to unfasten his pants.

He watched her with gray eyes stormier than any cloud and lifted his hips slightly to help her in removing the offending material. When he was completely naked, he gave a quick stretch. He hated clothing, truthfully. He had always assumed it was a quirk of Dragon nature.

"Not just Dragons," she said. Her mouth was dry. Her Fury was *beautiful.* Unclothed, he was even more so. She felt as she had the first time she had seen him as a Dragon. She was shocked and awed that such a magnificent creature was hers. "I hate clothes too." Testing, she reached out a hand and ran it over his stomach and steadily lower. "I'd run around naked if I could."

"I repeat." He stifled a moan as her soft fingers skimmed over his erection. He was so hard for her that it hurt. "I repeat," he tried again, "that I love desert girls." His breath hissed in as her hand curled around him. "Careful with that."

"Why?" She smiled and memorized the feel and look of him. She hadn't realized how beautiful a man's body could be. Or maybe it was just Dominic. She didn't think anyone else would compare.

His hand slid between her legs before she could stop him. A soft moan slipped past her lips as he stroked her. "Because it belongs here," he said thickly. "Let me show you everything." Her hands lifted and he pulled her on top of him before rolling over to tuck her safely underneath him.

Their lips met in a long kiss and she trembled as she felt his hands slowly stroking over her body. He lifted her legs to curl them around his hips, and she realized how strangely vulnerable the position seemed. Oddly, it didn't frighten her. Only hunger stirred deep inside. She *needed* him. "Dominic." She drew him down to kiss him again. "Hurry up," she whispered, and nipped at his lip with her teeth.

"Tease." He positioned himself then slowly began to push inside her body. His eyes locked with hers, and he saw them widen with utter shock. He shuddered at the feel of her. She was snug and hot, fitting him as perfectly as he had known she would. Only when he was fully inside her did he stop to savor the fierce triumph in his soul. She was *his*.

She twisted slowly underneath him, her breathing shallow. She felt stretched and full of him, nearly on the verge of pain. But it wasn't pain. It was raw pleasure. Deeper still was the delight of knowing he was hers. Her Fury. She'd finally claimed him.

He hissed softly as her muscles clenched around him even as her power rubbed sensuously against his. "Stop it," he said hoarsely. She did it a second time, her eyes like pools of melted silver and a little smile on her lips. She knew precisely what she was doing, and the knowledge broke his control.

His hands fisted in her hair and he dragged her up for a kiss as he pulled out and drove back in. Quicker he began to thrust, driving himself as deeply into her welcoming warmth as he could. He tangled their emotions together just for the sheer delight of knowing how he made her feel, and ecstasy boiled up without warning and consumed him. He could only dive himself to the hilt and pour himself deep inside.

She barely noticed. The instant she had felt his emotions tangling with hers, allowing her to share his emotions, the pleasure had detonated inside her body with the force of a firebomb, sweeping through her in waves of delight that overshadowed everything before. With a faint cry, she clung onto him tightly as an anchor against melting away.

Blessed peace fell in their secret camp. When Dominic was finally able to breathe more normally, he found the strength to lift himself onto an elbow. Tenderness filled him as he studied Tariah's face. She looked content, satiated, and very happy. Her lips were still swollen from his, and a beautiful flush clung to her skin even as lingering tendrils of steam did. He could feel the answer to his question, but asked it anyway. "Was it worth the wait, *ishke*?"

She opened her eyes and smiled at him. More than ever she felt as if she was finally where she belonged. "It was well worth it," she said huskily. Her arms tightened around his shoulders as she leaned up to kiss him lingeringly. "What about you? Was it worth waiting for?"

The corner of his mouth kicked up. He doubted she could miss his joy since it was overtaking most of his heart. "What do you think?" He skimmed his fingers down her arm and realized in surprise that her lines felt hotter.

He lifted himself further away and noticed that her lines from her face down to her breasts and partway down her right arm were darker than before. But it was a darkness that faded and grew like light rippling over waves. He could *see* her power flowing through the lines. "I wonder why," he said softly.

She looked at her shoulder. After a moment of thought, she said, "Perhaps it is telling us that part of my journey is done. I've finished that part of the map." She smiled up at him. "I guess that makes it the most important part." She skimmed her hand over his chest where some of the lines were also darker now in response to her change. "I don't seem to be as worried about the rest anymore."

"Tariah," he breathed. He gathered her close and hugged her tightly. He knew how she felt. It was as if the rest of the world no longer seemed to be so much trouble now that they were together as they belonged.

And yet, beyond their feelings, he felt inside both of them a lingering worry for another Chronicle somewhere else in the world.

Where was Morgan?

Part Two

Morgan

Chapter Fourteen

Dear readers,

My name is Morgan Chronis. I was born in a normal city, at the edges of a normal country, on the normal world of Lucksphere. I was a normal boy, with normal Magi powers, and I had a normal life. My parents were normal, both Fire Magi. They had grown up normal, in normal cities, inside normal countries, on this normal world.

Unfortunately, that normality changed during my fourteenth year of life. As I was preparing to go to sleep one night, something changed. In the space of two breaths, my body entered first puberty . . . and I developed lines.

These were not normal lines. They were dark gold against my skin, and they seemed to be made of loops and straight lines as they traveled down the outside of my arms and hands and across my chest. Their pattern seemed to be no pattern at all but something inside me knew they had meaning.

I was a Chronicle. I was a member of the most hated race on the world. I don't know why. The rumors were outrageous, talking of parasites and feeding, and Dragons that owned a Chronicle's soul. Oddly, the Dragons were not hated for this. Just the Chronicles. It was little wonder the Dragons disliked Magi so much.

It was law. Any child that developed Chronicle lines was to be instantly put to death. I was terrified. I did not want to die. I was going to hide my lines entirely and not tell anyone. But my father came into my room and saw me. I thought my parents would hate me but . . . they didn't. They loved me. They let me live.

No one in my village knew. I wore gloves and long sleeves and professed to having a sudden sensitivity to the cold. As I developed into an Air element at this same time, no one found it to be a surprise. When I began to develop Thunder power at the same time, it was accepted by all that I was a Master Magi.

I and my parents never corrected them. It was just so frustrating for me! I was often too hot because of my clothes, and yet I could never once complain or remove my shirt. More still was the worry for when I would enter second puberty. I was bound to end up naked and any girl in her right mind would panic if she saw my lines.

It was a frustrating way to be living your life, but at least I was living. Day after day, year after year, my life continued. Silently I was snubbing all those Magi who believed I ought to be dead.

Then in the summer of my twentieth year, it all changed. And that is the summer where my place in this story begins.

Morgan T. Chronis

Chapter Fifteen

(Five years ago)

The snow that covered the ground crunched lightly beneath boots wherever people walked. Here, in Glacia, it was always cold. Even in the summer it was cold. Snow would fall at any time of day, any time of the year. It was the whim of the power in the land. And here, the whim was to make it cold.

Few Fire Magi called Glacia home. It was mostly made up of Air and Water Magi. But, then again, Morgan thought to himself as he dug in the snow for roots, his parents were hardly normal Fire Magi. They were . . . quirkier, he supposed was the term. After all, they had let him live. Him, an abomination.

His lips thinned as he wiped away dirt from the root and put it in the basket next to his feet. For a moment he looked at his hands. They were covered with thick leather gloves to keep the snow from freezing his fingers. But even when he wasn't digging in the snow, he was wearing gloves. They were as common a part of his attire as shoes were.

The gloves, and the long sleeves of his tunic, kept his secret from being shown to the world. He was a Chronicle. Across his arms and chest and down his arms there were golden lines that flowed with Dragon power. Those lines were his death sentence if anyone ever found them out.

With a sigh, he got to his feet and slung the loops of the basket over his shoulder. It was much harder now to keep his secret than he'd ever imagined. He was going through second puberty. There was, in fact, a particular girl in town that he had his eye on. He wouldn't have minded exploring his curiosities with her in the slightest. But he didn't know how she had react.

Ah, well. It wasn't a concern since she hadn't given any clue that she was equally interested. Smiling wryly, he headed back for his town. Such were the odd quirks of life.

He lived in Stalagmite, the town that served as the main port for the entire continent. Because it was cold, all the buildings were made of thick stone and hard packed mud to keep out the bitter winds. Snow covered every rooftop and created white blankets in front of every wall.

The streets were almost always being swept to keep the snow from getting into the tracks that carts rolled on. There wasn't a single door that didn't have a shovel sitting next to it to forge a path toward the street after a heavy fall.

It was mid-morning and the port was busy. People passing through and stopping over were enough to make the crowds thick along the sidewalks where there were canopies stretched overhead to protect pedestrians.

The sounds of bells blowing on ships were loud in the crisp air. Flags with the symbol of the Magi flew high in the air. Looking around, Morgan found it hard to imagine living anywhere else on this world.

A MoonKin Faerie that was flying by paused for a moment to study him then flew on with a hidden smile. It did not surprise him. There were one or two Kin living in the town and they knew he was a Chronicle. They never spoke of it, but he was sure they knew. He was also sure that any of the few Kin who passed through were sworn to secrecy. There was never any knowing who might overhear and suspect.

His parents ran a restaurant. He went in the back door and scraped the snow off his shoes at the door. Once they were clean, he headed directly into the kitchen and put down the basket of roots. "As ordered," he said with a smile.

"Your nose is red," his mother scolded as she hurried over. "Go upstairs and get warm." Her hands were quick and competent as she began to chop up the roots. Her hair, the same auburn as her son's, was pinned up on top of her head to keep it out of her way. "Go on now."

He grinned at her. "When will you remember that I'm twenty, Mom?"

Iria Chronis wrinkled her nose at him. She didn't like remembering that her baby boy was no longer a baby. She liked even less thinking that he would soon be a man and likely move out on his own. She had seen the way his eye was lingering on Merideth Caradina. It made her heart ache. "Don't remind me," she grumbled.

"All children grow up," her mate said dryly as he walked into the kitchen with a tray of empty dishes. "I'm sure he won't move away and abandon his poor, old parents to their miserable and lonely lives." London Chronis' silver eyes twinkled as they met Morgan's identical ones. "Will you?"

"Depends on the incentive offered to me." He stuck his tongue out at them and ducked out of the kitchen before the towel his mother threw at him smacked him in the face.

As he walked through the restaurant toward the stairs to the next floor where the Chronis family lived, every female eye followed him. Morgan was not as tall as most Magi men since he only stood around five-six, but he was by far the most attractive male in town. Half the females in the city had been waiting for him to enter second puberty. The other half were almost regretful that they were not single.

His auburn hair glowed with faint red highlights under the lamps and it clung to the back of his neck. His silver eyes were quick to smile but could darken with intensity. He was intelligent, and he was powerful. He was also strong in the shoulder, and his face was handsome. Every available female in the restaurant felt as if they were in a race to catch his eye first.

When Morgan got upstairs, he locked the door and made sure the window was shut tight. He also pulled the curtains and tied them in place so they couldn't even accidentally move and let anyone see inside. Only when he was sure that it was safe did he remove his gloves. His thick cloak was next and then his tunic.

With a grateful sigh, he fell on his back on his bed and stared at the ceiling overhead. He tucked his hands under his head and studied the pattern in the ceiling almost morosely. He *hated* to be confined by clothes, despite the city in which he had been raised. He would have made a better desert dweller, he thought in amusement. They rarely wore much at all.

Someone knocked lightly on the window, and his heart gave a dull thud. He yanked on his tunic and gloves and checked the mirror to be sure everything was hidden. Only then did he creep over to the window and pull the curtain back. The Faerie of before was hovering outside his window. He opened it warily. "Is something wrong?"

"Not at all." The MoonKin had dark sapphire skin and green eyes. Silver tattoos marked her body and shimmered as evidence of her bloodline. "May I enter, Morgan? I wish to speak to you about . . . something."

His eyes widened slightly. After a moment, he held the window open to let her fly in. Once she had joined him, he shut the window and retied the curtains in place. "Is this . . . is this about me being a Chronicle?" He had never before admitted the words out loud. It felt odd.

"It is." She flew over and landed on his desk. "You see, I know some things about Chronicles. My grandfather was there at the final battle between the Chronicles and Magi. He told my mother the tales, and then they both told me. We Kin have always tried to remember everything about Chronicles so that we could tell someone someday."

He was immediately interested. He sat down on the side of his bed. "Tell me what, precisely?"

"I thought you might want to know about Furies."

His heart gave a dull thud in his chest. A sharp and painful longing rose up inside him so fiercely that it stole his breath and made his eyes sting with tears. "Fury?" he whispered softly.

"Fury." She watched with compassionate eyes. "You see, Chronicles are one half of a whole. Their other half is a Fury. A Fury is a Dragon. To be precise, a Dragon Lord. I've heard that the bonds between Chronicle and Fury are even more powerful than those who are Linked or Bonded. It's imprinted in you before you're born."

He pressed his hands against his eyes. Even the idea of there being someone out there, someone who would understand him, took his breath away. He'd always been a loner. He'd never had any close friends. But his Fury . . . they would automatically trust each other, would be able to share everything. It was a tempting thought.

The Kin flew over to touch his cheek. "Morgan," she said softly, "stamped in your lines is a map. This map will lead you to the Isle of Dragons and your Fury. Follow this map no matter where it leads. Your lines . . . they are made of your Fury's power. They connect you to her."

"Her?" His head came up. "Furies are female?"

The Kin smiled. "No, not all. But Chronicles and Furies are always opposite gender because they are nearly almost always lovers. Since you are a male, your Fury is a female." She leaned over and kissed his nose. "Hold this knowledge close. Someone out there needs you like you need them. Her power is not infinite like other Dragons. She will need to feed on your power. In return, you will be able to use her majiks."

He opened the curtain and window so she could leave and secured them again after she was gone. His mind was swimming with what he had learned. His Magi upbringing told him that he should be horrified and appalled at the idea of anyone feeding on another's power. Yet his heart and his soul ached with longing to give his power to his Fury. How did one love someone they had never met? He wasn't even sure 'love' was a strong enough word.

There was a knock on his door. "Morgan!" Iria called. "Go fetch the bread from the baker! It should be ready by now!"

He sighed. "Yes, Mother." He put his cloak back on before leaving his room and heading downstairs. The baker was a few blocks over but he didn't mind the walk. It was growing later in the day and the sun was beginning to sink in the west. Even then the town didn't seem to be winding down. It wouldn't do that until at least the second moon had risen.

The baker was waiting with the loaves in a basket for him. He picked it up and turned around only to bump into someone. He swiftly reached out and caught their arm to keep them from falling. "I'm so sorry," he said on a laugh.

Sparkling blue eyes met his. "It was my fault," Merideth Caradina said with a laugh in her voice. "I wasn't watching my step."

Morgan's young heart skipped a beat even as his body tightened with desire. Merideth was the loveliest girl in Stalagmite and possibly even Glacia. She was only an inch shorter than he was and she had thick black hair. Her young figure was graceful and generous all at once. "Hi, Merideth." It was all he could manage.

"Hi, Morgan." She eased closer, smiling from under her lashes. She and Morgan were the same age. She had started second puberty first and had been hoping he would eventually catch up. She knew she could very easily fall for him if she let herself. He was so wonderfully easy to like! And, of course, he was downright gorgeous.

Somewhere inside him, the motion of her body was recognized. He barely remembered how to breathe. "Are you, in a subtle manner, asking me to write you a letter when I'm available?" he asked softly.

She giggled and took his free hand with hers. The fact that he wore gloves was all the more sexy to her. Imagining what his hands would be like under the gloves was a wonderful, and frustrating, pastime. "I could be." Her cloak had fallen open, and she moved closer to give him a better view of her figure.

His mouth almost watered. "If you let me drop off this at home, I'm free tonight," he told her, his eyes moving over her heatedly. He could hardly believe she was interested in him in return. All he could think about was finally getting his hands on her.

Her heart skipped a beat. "My parents are out for the evening," she whispered. "We could go back to my home."

"Done." He held onto her hand with one of his and hefted the basket with the other. Swiftly they headed back to the restaurant to drop off the bread. Even in his distraction, he was amused. A cook never ate her own bread. His mother was such a contradiction.

Once the delivery was made, Morgan and Merideth set out through the town toward the second district where she lived. Her parents were indeed out for the night and the place was dark. She lit only two lamps and carried one with her down the hall toward her room. "I kept hoping," she said softly, "that you'd catch up with me."

He smiled. "I was afraid you didn't want me."

"Oh no!" Her eyes widened with horror. "How could you *think* that?" She set the lamp down in her room and filled the area with soft light. "Morgan, most of the women in this town are attracted to you. The rest haven't started second puberty yet."

Flustered, but pleased, he reached out to tug her into his arms. Somewhere inside him, something under his hormones seemed to protest. It was as if it was saying she was the wrong woman. He ignored the voice in favor of enjoying how she felt in his arms. She was so beautiful!

Their mouths met without hurry. After waiting for so long, they wanted to enjoy every second. Her arms wound around his neck and she pressed her body against his. "Take off your gloves," she said. "I've dreamed of feeling your hands."

He wasn't about to argue with that, and he tugged his gloves off. His hands splayed over her back then slid under the edge of her tunic. She gasped. "Your hands are so hot! It's like I can feel your power."

He grinned. "Maybe it's just your effect on me." He kissed her again and tugged her even closer. Eagerly he began to trace kisses over her face. Before she could stop him, he had stripped her tunic over her head and left her in her bikini top. "I knew you would be worth waiting for," he murmured thickly, his eyes devouring her curves.

"Oh yeah?" She grabbed the edge of his tunic. "Well, let's be fair here." She stripped his tunic off him then stopped in shock as she saw the golden lines that flowed over his body. A part of her saw them as being absolutely beautiful against his strong chest. The rest of her was horrified. "Morgan . . ."

He only then realized his folly. He stiffly took his tunic from her and stepped back to give her room. "Yes," he said. "I'm a Chronicle."

She wrapped her arms around herself. "I don't know what to think," she whispered. "Most of me is thinking 'this is Morgan. He's no monster.' But a part of me is scared of you." She looked at him sadly and with longing. "You're still Morgan. I would still want you for my first lover. But . . . there's a rumor that . . . that mating with a Chronicle will give you power. If I got power from you . . ."

He pulled his tunic on. "It would put us both at risk." He looked at her longingly. "I completely forgot my lines, you know. Thank you, for that."

She managed a wan smile. Her heart felt like it was breaking. "You're welcome." She walked over to look out the window. What she had to do was somehow easier now, and also harder. "You know," she said. "Maybe you ought to leave Stalagmite."

He looked at her in shock. "What?"

Her fingers curled into the windowsill. "It would be hard on both of us. We wanted to be lovers, but we can't. People would be suspicious as to why we didn't give in. And when you never had anyone for a lover . . . it might make someone begin to snoop around."

There was a very cold sort of logic in what she said. He picked up his gloves and pulled them on. "You're probably right." His frown darkened. "And I really shouldn't tell my parents. If they know why I leave, then if someone finds out, they could be blamed. Bad enough they have allowed me to live. They could be murdered as traitors."

She fought to keep her voice from quivering. "Then you're leaving?"

He hesitated. "Yes," he finally said. He reached out and softly touched her hair. "Merideth . . . you'll make a man very happy someday. I'm sorry it can't be me."

"Thank you." She closed her eyes as she heard him leave the room. Only when the door shut behind him did tears well up and flow down her cheeks. "Tell me," she whispered brokenly. "Tell me that the Fury in his life will love him more than I do."

The MoonKin Faerie flew over to hug her around the neck comfortingly. "She will," she said softly. "I swear it on my wings."

Morgan left the house and pulled the hood of his cloak over his head. Snow was falling lightly now. He kept the hood pulled low over his head to keep the few people still milling around from recognizing him. He thought there might be one last ship leaving for Spectrum that night, and he was hoping to get onboard.

He was in luck. The last ship to Prismatic was just preparing to leave. There was room for one more, and he used the last of the money he had on hand to pay for the ticket. His cabin was on the lowest passenger deck near the back but he didn't mind. He felt slightly numb. It was hard to believe he was running away from home to protect his parents and Merideth.

As he was locking his door for the night, he felt a sudden fierce throbbing in his chest. It spread through his entire body and brought with it an ache that was physical pain. *North.* His lines burned and throbbed. He needed to go *north*.

Spectrum was technically both north and south, but boats only sailed north around Glacia; the currents were too strong to sail south. Because of it, Spectrum was considered very, very, very far north. It was nearly a month's journey away by boat.

He walked over to look out the window. Maybe in that month's time he would be able to accept how his life had just changed. The really absolutely worst part was probably the frustration. Frustration for the restrictions of the world. Frustration for not being able to live his own life.

Frustration, he thought grouchily, for not getting his hands on Merideth. He might as well get used to it though. Odds were that he would never get to satisfy his final curiosity until he someday met his Fury.

Whenever that may be.

Chapter Sixteen

For the first two weeks of the journey, Morgan didn't emerge from his cabin unless he was going to get food. Word quickly began to spread among the passengers. All of them were *positive* that he was a Master Magi. He was young and attractive yet single. He was powerful enough that you could sense it, but he was a loner. He had all the trademarks of a Master.

As he was standing on the deck for fresh air, he felt someone coming up behind him. He turned sharply, his senses very acute and growing sharper by the day. He didn't trust anyone. He knew what people were suspecting and he let them. It didn't mean he would let his guard down.

Behind him he found an attractive young woman with thick ebony hair and sparkling blue eyes. He didn't need to see the bracelet around her wrist to know she was Linked to someone; it could be felt on her power. She was dressed like a forest dweller, and he had to assume she would be disembarking at Carnelian when they stopped there briefly in a day or two. "Yes?" he asked warily.

"I just thought I'd do what no one else seems to have the nerve to do and actually approach you." She walked over to lean on the railing. "My mate and I were visiting Glacia with our daughter. We're on our way home to Carnelian now." She drew her thumb over her cheek and nose. "Mildred Renaire, Soil Magi, at your service."

He returned the gesture. "Morgan Chronis, Air Magi. Likewise, ma'am." He leaned on the railing as well, and the wind ruffled his hair. "Are you on a family trip?"

"We wanted Kelsey to see other lands." She chuckled. "That girl. She's barely five but she's a handful." She glanced toward the afternoon sun in the distance. "She's well before first puberty, but . . . we suspect she may be a Master Magi."

He lifted a brow. "Stronger than average lightning?" It was a mark of Masters and Chronicles alike because he had been the same way himself. "Don't tell me she set a house on fire."

"Guilty of that, are you?" she murmured drolly. He had to smile. "No comment."

She laughed. "As I thought. Well, no houses on fire, but her lightning is as strong as an Air/Thunder Magi's. Most people I've ever talked to indicated that was usually the first sign of a Master Magi."

He tilted his head slightly. "Are you asking me if I can confirm this for you?" He smiled wryly. "I'm not sure whether I can or not. I've never met another Master Magi. I have no idea if we, er, resonate to one another."

"Well, could you try? It's an imposition," she apologized, "but if she is, I want to know as soon as I can so that her father and I can make her transition as easy as possible. I've heard rumor that Master Magi develop their secondary element at the same time as their primary."

"They do," he said. He grimaced as he remembered first puberty. It hadn't been easy to learn to control his Air power when his Thunder power had been trying to start storms over Stalagmite. People had walked around with hoods on their cloaks for months, even in the dead of summer when storms were almost non existent.

He thought about not getting involved. Then he thought about the image he needed to uphold. With a sigh, he said, "Alright. I'll meet her. I can't promise anything, though."

She smiled gratefully. "Thank you, Morgan." She began to look around. "Luke and Kelsey should be around here. I swear they were right over by the stairs."

He glanced around but he didn't see any children in the vicinity. Carefully he sensed the air, trying to find a power that was not developed. He caught the feeling of one, but it seemed to be coming from over his head. Puzzled, he wandered closer to one of the walls that supported the deck's game cabin; it had all manner of games inside and was used for entertainment by the passengers.

A young man not much older than Mildred came running up to her, his brown eyes dark with worry. "Mildred, I can't find Kelsey. She up and vanished on me!"

She groaned and put her head in her hands. "That girl!" She began to look around in unlikely places. "Kelsey! You come out here this instant!" She pointed down the deck. "Luke, check over there."

Luke Renaire didn't object and hurried that direction. Morgan studied the wall he was in front of, then called on his power. Air swept around his feet and lifted him up into the air and over the roof. He landed gently and knelt down to keep his balance. He immediately spotted a small figure crouched near the pipe that was spewing smoke into the air from the heaters below.

She was no higher than his knee in size, despite his own shorter height, and she had a cap of bright red hair. Her eyes were crystalline blue and reflected the sunlight like gems. Her face and arms were both liberally covered with soot. "Hi there," he said softly.

Her lower lip trembled. "Hi," she whispered. "Am I in trouble?"

"Afraid so. Can you crawl over here so I can get you down?" He eased closer, worried that if she got startled she might lose her balance and go tumbling off the roof.

"But you're a stranger." She watched his outstretched hand warily. "You might kidnap me or something."

He grinned at her. She seemed like a spunky little thing. "Well, of course I would. I kidnap children and make them clean my house."

Her eyes grew saucer round then suddenly she shot him a dirty look. "You're fibbing! Meany!" The fib, however, had made her more inclined to trust him because now she could recognize what his power felt like when he was telling the truth and when he was lying. "My name's Kelsey."

"I'm Morgan." He edged closer to her. "Come here, Soot."

"Soot?" She tilted her head as she began to carefully creep toward him. She was wary of falling too.

"Your face is covered in it." She was in reach, and he swiftly reached out and scooped her up in his arms. His lines immediately pulsed and a tingling sensation swept through them. It was a shock of recognition that resonated through his entire body. Stunned, he stared at the little girl in his arms. She wasn't a Master Magi. She was a

Chronicle. He was sure of it. "By the moons," he breathed softly.

She seemed to have sensed something too because she was staring at his chest. "You're warm," she said. "And you make my skin itch. How come I feel your power?" She wrinkled up her nose. "You're a Master Magi, aren't you?"

"After a fashion." He held tight to her as he used his power to carry them back down to the deck and safety. "Found her," he told Mildred with a cheer he didn't truly feel. His mind was racing a mile an hour. A part of it was shock. A part of it was terror for Kelsey. Even the most loving parents could turn on their child.

Luke got to him first and snatched Kelsey up into his arms. "Kelsey!" he said sharply. "Don't scare us like that again!" He clutched his daughter tight for a moment and looked at Morgan gratefully. "Thank you." He handed Kelsey to Mildred as she came running up so he could run his thumb over his cheek and nose. "I am Luke Renaire, a Water Magi."

Morgan started to return the gesture but saw there was soot on his hands from holding Kelsey. He smiled ruefully. "I would return the gesture, but I would look like your daughter if I tried. Morgan Chronis, an Air Magi."

Mildred gasped as she saw his pale brown gloves were covered in soot. "Oh no! Kelsey!" she scolded. "Apologize to Morgan."

Kelsey lowered her gaze. "I'm sorry, Morgan." She held her arms out to him. "You carry me again. You're warm."

Morgan obligingly took her and settled her on his hip. Seeing the two parents' surprised faces, he explained, "It seems Master Magi do indeed recognize each other. Like always does recognize like, I suppose."

"Oh dear." Mildred studied her daughter. "She was trouble enough before. The moons help us if she turns out to be a Fire element!"

Morgan thought of Kelsey's natural gravitation toward heat and smoke and had to think Fire sounded like a good guess. He flipped her over and tossed her over his shoulder. She shrieked with laughter. "You are a Water Magi," he reminded Luke. "If anything that should give you a means to extinguish blazes."

Kelsey wiggled around till she could see her parents. "Can Morgan have dinner with us?" she asked.

"Well, that is up to Morgan," Luke reminded her. He smiled at the younger man. "We would be honored if you joined us, though."

Morgan hesitated. "Well . . ."

"Please?" Kelsey's lower lip trembled and her eyes swam with tears. "Please? Please, please? I'll eat my vegetables and everything."

Morgan discovered something then. He discovered that he had absolutely no willpower to resist the little blue-eyed, soot-covered scamp. It wasn't just the sense of like meeting like. It was Kelsey herself. It would have taken a hardhearted man to resist her. She would break a few hearts in her life, of that he was sure. "Alright," he sighed. "Thank you for asking me."

As he was preparing to go to dinner that night, he discovered that his cloak and his gloves were both covered in soot and neither was washing clean with what he had on hand. His options were to go without, and reveal his lines, or to not go at all.

He scrubbed a hand over his eyes. Why couldn't his lines have been on his legs? It would have made everything even easier. Or at least not his hands. He studied his right palm where the symbol 'chron' was etched. He had often wondered if it was a fluke or there for a reason.

Someone knocked on the door and he hastily yanked his gloves and cloak on. "Just a minute!" he called. A look in the mirror assured him that everything was covered, and he walked over to open the door. "Yes?"

"Morgan!" Kelsey attached herself to his leg. Thankfully, she was clean this time. "Mama made you a present! And I got to bring it because it was my fault you got all dirty!"

Without dislodging the child attached to him, he picked up the box sitting by the door. He set it on the table and curiously opened it. Inside, he found a new cloak and gloves. Since they were white, there was a matching pair of slacks and a tunic to go with them. "Well, thank you," he said to Kelsey. "I was beginning to worry I wouldn't be able to attend dinner."

"Why do you wear them anyway?" She climbed onto a chair to watch him. "Are you burned?"

"I'm sensitive to the sun," he told her.

She regarded him solemnly. "You're fibbing again."

He said nothing. Only Magi before first puberty had the ability to tell the difference in someone's power when they were telling the truth or lying. Linked mates also had that ability, but only between one another. "Yes," he finally said. "I am."

"Why?"

"Because I can't tell you the real reason." He ruffled her hair gently. "Go back to your parents. I'll see you at dinner."

She hopped down and ran to the door. "You better not forget!" she scolded. Quick as a blink she was out the door and gone.

He just sighed. He was stuck now. With a wry smile he traded his dirty clothes for the clean ones. He was very grateful to Mildred for providing them. He had been getting tired of the same old thing over and over again anyway.

When he walked into the dining room, it was mostly full. The Renaires were sitting at a table to the side near a window, and Kelsey was standing on her seat waving at him. With a smile, he walked over to them. "Know what?" he told Kelsey. He scooped her up for a hug. "I'm going to start calling you Soot." He swiped his thumb over her cheek to remove a lingering trace. "Because you seem to be always in it."

"Believe me," Luke said dryly, "that's more accurate than you know." He smiled. "Thank you for joining us."

"Thank you for inviting me." Morgan set Kelsey down and took his seat. He was well aware of the inviting gazes of several females around the room but he ignored them. Not only did he not trust anyone, he felt again that feeling inside that was telling him none of them were right. He wanted his Fury.

Mildred caught sight of the gazes and hardly blamed them. If she hadn't been madly in love with Luke, she might have made an invitation herself. Still, Morgan's disinterest caused her to ask, "Not through second puberty?"

"No, I am." He smiled wryly. "It's just . . . difficult to find someone I trust enough to share my power with." In more ways than one, he thought.

For a while, there was silence as they ate dinner. Morgan and Luke, each on a different side of Kelsey, took turns picking up the things that she managed to drop. In the process of straightening after picking up Kelsey's napkin for the fifth time, Morgan heard someone at the next table over say, "They killed another Chronicle in Crystalia."

"How old was it?" a male at the table asked. "Twelve."

"Good riddance to bad rubbish."

It took considerable willpower not to let his hands shake. He had entirely lost his appetite and couldn't find a way to pretend he wasn't upset by the news. He didn't have to. Mildred was equally disgusted and pushed her plate away. "What filth," she said softly but scathingly. "Any parent who could do that to their child ought to be the one killed!"

Morgan looked at her in surprise. Luke nodded. "I agree. I've heard so many outlandish tales that I've stopped believing any of them." He smoothed a hand down Kelsey's hair. "The idea of any parent capable of killing their child . . ."

Morgan glanced out the window at the rolling sea. "People believe something for so long that it becomes truth," he murmured. "And they're so willing to accept that truth that they don't recognize it for a lie when it walks by."

"Aptly put." Mildred sighed. "Well, I have effectively lost my appetite. I need fresh air. This room is suddenly stuffy."

Since they were all in agreement, they left the dining room. Kelsey rode on Morgan's shoulders and held onto his hair for balance. He held her legs securely so she wouldn't tumble off his shoulders. He was beginning to feel more comfortable about Mildred and Luke because of their statements during dinner. Something told him that maybe, just maybe, there was a chance for Kelsey.

"Are you from Glacia, Morgan?" Luke asked. "I am."

"Were your parents sad to see you go?" Mildred sat down on one of the benches near the railing and stretched her legs out. She was beginning to get tired of being on a boat.

Morgan lowered his gaze. His parents were probably worried sick about him. He was fairly sure they would understand why he left, but that wouldn't change the fact that they loved him and would worry. "Yes," he said quietly.

Luke studied him closely. He was beginning to feel a suspicion inside that he couldn't quite put his finger on. There was something about Morgan that wasn't adding up. "Why do you wear gloves and a cloak all the time?" he asked. "Is it because you're from Glacia?"

"I'm just sensitive to the light."

Luke looked at Kelsey and could see by the look on her face that he was fibbing. Though he didn't want to make assumptions, Luke could only think of one reason anyone would wear such confining clothing when they weren't truly sensitive to sun or cold. He had heard that the lines that marked a Chronicle could appear anywhere on the body. They were also reputed to be exactly like Master Magi in many ways. They were the only two rumors he had ever believed.

His heart stopped. If Morgan *was* a Chronicle, and he was responding to Kelsey . . . Terror for his daughter closed his throat. He reached out and grabbed Morgan's arm. "Tell me!" he said urgently, but quietly. "If Kelsey is in danger, I want to know!"

Mildred got to her feet. She had been following his line of thought and was in complete agreement. "Morgan," she pleaded. "Please. We won't look down on you.

Kelsey is our child. We need to know as soon as we can so we can be prepared to protect her!"

Morgan lifted Kelsey off his shoulders and set her down gently. "Not tonight," he said quietly. "Too many people might hear. But if you come visit me tomorrow . . . I'll tell you whatever I can." There was no other choice. He had to take the risk for Kelsey's sake and his own.

He didn't sleep that night. Anxiety would either keep him awake or torment him with nightmares. By the time dawn came, he had given up on any sort of rest. He simply sat by his window and watched the sea roll by.

The knock came on his door right after breakfast. He took a deep breath and walked over to open it. "Come in," he said to the family standing just outside. On one look he knew they had not slept well either. Only Kelsey seemed to be full of energy, as usual.

As he shut the door behind them, Mildred and Luke walked over to sit at the small table in the cabin. Kelsey climbed up to sit on the edge of the bed. She didn't know why everyone was afraid suddenly. She liked Morgan. He was like a big brother, and she had always wanted one of those.

Morgan didn't know where to start. Finally, at a loss, he simply removed his gloves and held up his hands. The golden lines flowing over them were plainly visible. There truly was no mistaking them, especially because his skin was fair from lack of exposure to the sun.

Mildred took a sharp breath. "You really are a Chronicle," she breathed.

"Yes, I am." He removed his cloak and the short sleeves of his tunic revealed the lines flowed up his arms and disappeared under his sleeves. "They're also across my chest," he said as calmly as he could. "They developed when I entered first puberty."

"Pretty . . ." Kelsey reached out to touch his arm when he walked closer. The lines were warm and tingled her hand when she placed it on his arm. "What are they?"

"Near as I can tell," he told her, "they're lines made from Dragon power." He looked at the two astonished adults. "They're a map that will lead me to my Fury." He smoothed a hand down Kelsey's hair. "But you can't tell *anyone* about these lines, Soot."

"I promise," she said solemnly.

Mildred found her voice first. "Then Chronicles do have a pact with Dragons?"

"Not exactly." He shrugged one shoulder. "I don't know very much. The Kin could tell us more. But from what I was told already, Chronicles and Furies are two halves of a whole. They are complete together. I'm not sure what it means."

A sharp stab of longing rose inside him and he pressed a fist against his heart. *North.* Always north. He felt her. He felt his Fury calling to him. "I want to find her," he said softly. "So terribly. I've never wanted anything more."

Luke drew a long breath. "Then Kelsey . . ."

"Is a Chronicle child." Morgan glanced at the little girl. "I'm not sure how I know. Maybe it is because the Dragon power meant to make her lines is present even now, just as her Fire element is. Neither can manifest till she develops. But because I am fully developed I can feel it."

"And maybe," Mildred whispered, "it is something new in Chronicles. Maybe it is nature's way of trying to save Chronicles. Perhaps this world needs you." She straightened her shoulders. "It changes nothing," she said fiercely. "Kelsey is our daughter. I will not . . . not kill her for being another race." Even the idea was sickening. "We'll just have to move with her somewhere that we can keep her under wraps till her lines appear."

"If rumor is right," Morgan said, "then her lines could appear anywhere. She might end up with them on a place that's hard to hide, like her face. And when she enters second puberty . . ."

Luke winced as he suddenly understood. "I'm sorry, Morgan."

Morgan smiled wryly. "Well, the girl I wanted didn't report me to the Militia. She helped me escape actually. But Kelsey might not be so lucky. If only we could find her Fury," he murmured. "He could protect her. He'd also be the one perfect to help her through second puberty."

Mildred's eyes widened. "A Fury is . . ."

"A Chronicle's lover? Apparently. Someone that will understand us and belong only with us." He struggled to keep his voice neutral and not give away all his fierce desperation to find his own. "The Kin who told me said it was a bond stronger than even Linked Magi felt. Somewhere in this world there is a man who is meant to love Kelsey. There is a Fury for every Chronicle."

A chill went down Luke's back. "By the moons," he whispered. "If we've been killing Chronicles . . ."

"Then the Furies are dying of broken hearts," Mildred finished softly. "How it must hurt to look for your other half and discover they were killed!" She covered her face with her hands. "What have the Magi done? There must be something we can do to try and stop it!"

Luke shook his head. "Like what? We can't change the opinions of the world overnight, Mil. And even if we somehow managed to find other Chronicle children, their parents might not be as open as us and Morgan's parents."

"But . . . there should be *some* way to disguise them! If it weren't for his lines, no one would ever know Morgan wasn't Magi. We all thought he was a Master Magi."

Morgan suddenly had an idea. It was risky, and slightly crazy, but it might just work. "What if we formed a . . . group of sorts? Like a haven for Master Magi? We could look for other children. If their parents were amiable, we could have them join. And maybe someday we could help them live long enough to find their own Fury."

Mildred frowned thoughtfully. "That might work. We'd have to get approval from the king in Prismatic, of course. But I don't see it being a problem. The rest of the world will be kept in the dark as to our real motives." She looked at Luke. "What do you think? If we can, I want to do this. For Kelsey's sake, and for Morgan's."

"Mine!" He stared at her.

She smiled. "To help you find your Fury as well."

Luke nodded. "I am in agreement as well. What do you say, Morgan? Will you lead us? You're the Chronicle." He smiled. "You're the one who would recognize the children if we found them."

Morgan slowly sat down. He felt more than a little dazed. But a part of him felt that this was right. It was the same feeling that told him his Fury was waiting for him. It was a feeling he couldn't help but trust. "Okay," he said on a long breath. "So what do we call ourselves?"

"Good question."

"I know, I know!" Kelsey began jumping up and down on the bed.

Morgan hastily caught her before she fell. He firmly sat her down again. "What do you think, Soot?"

"Well," she said, "because we're gonna keep the world in the dark, how 'bout Black Magi?"

"Her level of astuteness frightens me," Luke muttered.

"I think it's perfect," Morgan said. "For one thing, she's definitely right. For another, it gives up a very easily recognized symbol we can use. We'll just take the chalice symbol that represents the Magi and make it black. If we stick it on the back of some long white cloaks, then no one will be the wiser. It will also cover all but the most troublesome of lines for any Chronicle."

Mildred, as a Soil Magi, always carried a bag of sand with her to make cloth items from. She opened the bag and poured some of the sand into her hand. It swirled up and around her palm as her power flowed into it. There was a flash of green colored light and suddenly the sand condensed into the shape of a white cloak. On the back was the black chalice.

It was just the right size for Morgan and he pulled it on. The sleeves went slightly past his wrists and the ends of the cloak just touched the tops of his boots. It fastened down the front in such a way that it could not be seen through. On the back was a hood he could pull over his head as needed. It was also much lighter than his prior cloak and therefore more comfortable. "How do I look?" he asked.

"This might work," Luke said. "Mil, let's go with Morgan right to Spectrum. We can cross the land by findral and stop at every city. That way we can get word started."

"And maybe we can find more children to save," Morgan said quietly. He looked down at his hands where the lines were etched so vividly. He had never known if there was a reason for his existence. He had never known if he had a purpose, or if it truly was a quirk of destiny that his parents had been so unusual.

For all he knew, this wasn't his purpose either. But he was going to do his best. He was going to make a place where Chronicles could be nurtured in safety even if in secret. And while he was doing that, he was going to find a Kin who could tell him more about Chronicles. It was slightly awkward to realize he knew nothing about his own race.

Chapter Seventeen

The ship put to dock in Mirah on the southern edge of Spectrum two weeks later. When Morgan and the Renaire family disembarked, all of them were wearing the white cloaks that they had chosen to mark them as the Black Magi.

Poor Morgan wasn't ready for the weather. He had known that the primary lands of the Magi were deserts, but he hadn't realized how hot they really were. His acclimation to the snow, and his heavy cloak, immediately made him feel as if he were smothering. He had to quickly use his Air power to bring his temperature down before he passed out. "Ugh."

Mildred chuckled softly at him. "Too warm for you, snow boy?"

"Just a little!" He glowered at her but couldn't hold the expression for long. Mildred and Luke had become as close to him as family. Kelsey, well, he had no objections to admitting that she'd had him wrapped around her finger from day one.

She was currently riding on his back. She was sleepy and ready for a nap because it was mid-morning, but she was also energized from the new places and new people she was seeing.

The four of them went directly to the inn to get rooms to rest. Many curious gazes followed them as they went, but no one said anything. The innkeeper seemed equally surprised but he just smiled and said, "Welcome. Two rooms or three?"

"Two." Morgan smiled. "Kelsey can share a room with me. That way Mildred and Luke can have some personal time."

Mildred's cheeks turned pink. "Morgan!" Kelsey giggled. "Mommy's blushing!"

"Because your daddy's gonna kiss her silly," Morgan said cheerfully, bouncing her on his back. "You get to be my roommate, Soot. But no hogging the blankets, and no snoring." "Kay."

The innkeeper chuckled. "She reminds me of my daughter, so my sympathies." He drew his thumb over his cheek and nose. "Eli Lakemore, Water Magi."

"Morgan Chronis, Air Magi, leader of the Black Magi," Morgan said calmly. He had been waiting for an opportunity to say it.

They had decided on the boat that it was best not to go crying their name from the rooftops. Better to mention it casually in introductions and explain only when asked. Master Magi were known for being loners, and they had to keep up that illusion at all times.

"Mildred Renaire, Soil Magi, also of Black Magi. This is Luke, my mate. He is a Water Magi." Both mates drew their thumbs over their cheek and nose. Mildred gestured to Kelsey with a smile. "Our daughter, Kelsey."

"Hi!" Kelsey gave an ear-splitting yawn and rubbed at her eyes. "I'm sleepy, Morgan," she complained. "I want a nap."

"Okay, Soot. You can have a nap." He plucked her off his back and carried her in his arms. She tucked her head on his shoulder tiredly. "Which rooms?" he asked Eli.

"Five and six." Eli studied them curiously. "I have never heard of Black Magi."

"We just formed," Luke said. "Morgan is a Master Magi, as is Kelsey. We're hoping to gather more Master Magi, particularly children, to aide them in the difficulties of first puberty. Morgan set roofs on fire."

"Sure," the younger man mumbled, "tell everyone, why don't you?"

Eli's eyes widened then narrowed slightly with immense curiosity. "You recognize children who are future Master Magi then?" When Morgan nodded, Eli leaned on the counter. "In that case, if you wouldn't mind, I'd like you to meet my daughter. She is about Kelsey's age I think, and she is certainly not using normal lightning."

"I would be glad to meet her," Morgan said with a smile. "Perhaps around dinnertime? For now, we need to get this one to sleep before she falls over."

"Gladly." Eli smiled. "I will speak with her mother in the meantime."

Luke and Mildred followed Morgan as he left the room and headed down the stairs to the next level lower. Most desert inns had three stories, but one was under the sand to keep it cooler. "What if she is not a Chronicle?" Mildred murmured.

"I'll think of that when I get there," Morgan murmured back. "If anything, we might be able to check Eli and his mate out and see how they feel. If they're still open-minded, we might as well ask them to join. Odds are that his daughter, if not Chronicle, really is Master Magi. She'll have a tough time of it anyway."

At dinner later that evening, the small restaurant attached to the inn was busy. But because inn patrons had priority, there was a table just big enough for the Black Magi to sit at with Kelsey. There was even a large pillow for her to sit on to reach the table better.

A buzz of confusion and speculation ran through the room as people studied them. People had asked Eli about the odd strangers, and he had given them what he had been told. Because of it, the Magi were more curious than ever.

One of the patrons there that night was a Militia soldier. He walked over to the table where the Black Magi were sitting and saluted crisply. "Good evening. Is it true you are forming a faction?"

"We'd like to," Morgan said as calmly as he could. Nerves he couldn't help fluttered in his stomach. He fought an urge to check and make sure his hands and arms were still covered. "But we need permission from the king, of course."

"Perhaps I can assist." The soldier smiled. "I am returning to Prismatic on the morrow. I can take word with me to the king. By the time you reach the city, he should be ready to make a decision and meet you."

"We would be very grateful," Mildred told him with a smile. "It is kind of you to go out of your way."

There was sadness for a moment on the soldier's face. "My sister was a Master Magi. She couldn't handle regular society. She disappeared into the forests and never returned. Maybe if there'd been a group like you, she'd have had a better chance of adapting."

"That's what we're hoping for our daughter," Luke said. "Provided she doesn't burn down cities."

The soldier laughed. "We'd appreciate it if she didn't. Good luck." He turned and headed back to his own table to let them finish their dinner in peace.

"That is lucky," Luke murmured softly. "It may save us a lot of time in the end." "Thank goodness," Morgan said with heartfelt feeling. "I have to admit, I was having trouble figuring out what I wanted to say to the king, and how. A couple votes of confidence from others will go a long way."

After dinner, they went to lay Kelsey down to sleep. She was already yawning again. Once she was settled, the three adults went back upstairs to meet with Eli. He was in the lobby of the inn and sweeping out sand that had been tracked in.

An attractive young woman with pale blond hair was straightening figurines on shelves. The bracelet she wore matched the one Eli wore. She was obviously Eli's mate, and the mother of the aforementioned daughter. "Good evening," Morgan said to her pleasantly.

"Good evening." She turned with a smile and drew her thumb over her cheek and nose. "I am Serenity Lakemore. Most call me Ren for short. I am a Fire Magi." She studied Morgan and the two Renaires curiously. "Are all of you Master Magi?"

"No, just Morgan and Kelsey." Mildred smiled. "If Morgan wasn't barely eight years younger than Luke and I, we'd have adopted him."

"It doesn't stop you from bossing me around," Morgan mumbled. "Naturally."

Ren and Eli exchanged a smile. While he went to fetch their daughter, she sat down on the edge of the counter. "We truly do appreciate you at least meeting our daughter," she said. "Jayda is . . . a handful. Her lightning rivals that of Magi with Air/Thunder power. She also seems to develop far faster than normal Magi. Most Magi stay as children mentally till first puberty but she has these moments of insight that are almost frightening."

"That certainly sounds like our Kelsey," Luke said. "Morgan?"

Morgan grimaced. "Don't ask. Please, I beg you. You already blabbed about me setting roofs on fire."

Eli walked into the room with a little girl in his arms. Her eyes were black in color and very sleepy as she rubbed at them. Her hair was a riot of sea green colored curls inherited from her father. "This is Jayda," Eli said as he set her down gently on her feet. "She will be turning five in a few months." He nudged his daughter gently. "Greet them properly, Jay."

Jayda yawned again then obligingly drew her thumb over her cheek and nose. "I'm Jayda." She focused on Morgan fully and was immediately intrigued. He looked . . . different. Somehow he seemed completely different from all the other Magi she had met. "Who're you?"

He crouched down closer to her height. She was a striking young child and he had no doubt that she would only grow lovelier as time passed. What he liked most, though, was the spark of humor in her eyes. This one had a playful streak to rival Kelsey. "My name is Morgan."

She walked closer to him, studying his face. "You're pretty."

He felt his cheeks heat. "Shut up, Luke," he muttered at the softly snickering male behind him. He ignored his friends and focused on Jayda again. "You're pretty too," he told her. He offered a hand. "I don't bite, promise."

She took his hand and he instantly felt the same tingling sensation sweeping

136

through his lines. His heart began to beat harder. Another one. This was another Chronicle child. "Yes," he said softly, "she's like me."

"Oh thank goodness," Ren breathed softly.

Luke lifted a brow then smiled sympathetically. "Were you worried she might be a Chronicle? I have heard they are very similar to Master Magi."

"Very much so." Eli let out a breath. "Not that we would have killed Jayda." Disgust crossed his face. "Any parent who could do such a thing should be flayed alive. It's more of an abomination than any Chronicle could be."

"You're in the minority with that view," Mildred noted. "The rest of the world is firmly set in their beliefs. And the saddest part is that they don't even have a good reason why."

"I must agree." Ren lowered her gaze. "There was a boy in town five years or so ago. He . . . well, when he hit first puberty, he grew lines. He was a Chronicle, and he was put immediately to death. He was a good boy. He liked sweetbread. And yet, suddenly, to everyone he was a monster."

"You knew him." Morgan lifted Jayda into his arms as he stood. She looped an arm around his shoulders and yawned sleepily. He had to smile, some things were universal.

"He was my little brother." She ran her hands over her arms to fight a chill. When Eli wrapped his arms around her, she leaned against him gratefully. "My parents . . . I haven't spoken to them since."

Morgan glanced at Mildred and Luke. Both nodded slightly. Turning back to the Lakemores, Morgan said, "Is there somewhere we can talk privately? The Black Magi prefer to keep their secrets from outside ears."

"Understandably." Eli gestured toward the door behind the counter. "My study is there. We can speak in there privately. We've already closed the inn for the night." He smiled wryly. "We have no more room."

Following Eli, they all headed behind the counter and into the room he had indicated. There was only just enough room for all of them, and Morgan and Luke opted to stand because there weren't enough chairs. Jayda sat on her mom's lap and was asleep within moments.

"I suppose you wish to discuss Jayda joining you," Eli said as he sat on the edge of his desk. "It would mean Ren and I joining you as well, of course. We would need at least a month to take care of the inn and such."

"Before we discuss that," Morgan said, "first, I need to tell you something." "What is that?" Ren asked.

Because there was no way to say it that they would believe, he simply removed his gloves and held up his hands. Lamplight flowed over his lines and they were stark in the golden light.

Both Eli and Ren took sharp breaths of shock. "You're . . ." Ren's hands flew up to cover her cheeks as she looked down at her daughter. "Oh no! By the moons . . . no!" She clutched Jayda tight against her heart. "No one is touching my daughter!" she said fiercely.

"It is that very thing that makes us willing to tell you the truth," Mildred said softly. "Kelsey is also a Chronicle child. We too could not bear the idea. Morgan had the idea that we make a haven for Chronicle children to protect them till we can find their

Furies or a Dragon to take them to safety."

Eli slowly raked a hand through his hair. He didn't know what to think or how to feel. The only thing he could be absolutely certain of was that they could not stay in Mirah. There were too many people who knew Jayda. If her lines were in a visible place, that would be bad enough. But even if they weren't, when she began second puberty . . . "We can't stay here."

"You are welcome to join us," Luke said. "The Black Magi exist for this very reason. We are heading to Prismatic. It is such a big city that we can blend in. We can operate a base from there and travel as needed to find others. Perhaps after a while they will come to us."

"Then we will go with you." Ren looked at Eli. "We might not change the world, but we can change a part of it. And . . . who knows? Maybe someday things will get better." She looked back at Morgan, then at Luke and Mildred. "Thank you for trusting us. We are glad to join you."

Before Eli and Ren could leave Mirah, there was a lot they had to do. They needed to arrange the sale of their inn, and they needed to get rid of most of their belongings. Morgan and the Renaires helped however they could by promoting and arranging sales. Although, much to Morgan's amusement, he more often found himself babysitting the two children.

Not quite three weeks later, they were in possession of a sturdy cart, a couple tents, and a pair of strong findrals. Eli and Ren donned the cloak of the Black Magi, and they all set out into the desert just after dawn one morning.

Jayda and Kelsey had become the best of friends. They would take turns climbing all over Morgan, much to the amusement of everyone else. He took it all in stride. He loved both girls very deeply.

The trip across the desert was two weeks long. It could have been shorter but they needed to rest often. It was hotter than average during this time of summer, and it tired out the little girls. It also sapped Morgan's strength.

"You'll adapt," Eli assured him. "I promise."

Lying on the bottom of the cart with a blanket over his head to block the sun and trap his power to keep him cool, Morgan could only say, "I get to zap you with lightning if you're wrong."

The lightning was unneeded. Eli was proven right just before they reached Prismatic. The 'trial by fire' exposure to the desert sun had forced Morgan to adapt very swiftly. By the afternoon that they were riding into the city limits, he was barely using his powers at all. He couldn't wait, however, to have his own room where he could strip down and relax for a few minutes.

As they were riding through the main street, a Militia soldier came running up to them and made them stop. Morgan recognized him immediately from Mirah. He smiled. "Good morning. I hope you have been well."

The soldier smiled and saluted. "I have been. I hope you have been the same." He tugged gently on the pigtails of both girls as they peered out of the cart at them. "I see you have gotten more Master Magi."

"We have. We hope more will soon follow suit."

The soldier nodded. "As to that, the king would like to speak with you, Morgan. When I spoke to my captain, and he spoke to the king, the king professed an interest in your Black Magi. I have every confidence that you will soon have your official sanction as a faction."

Morgan ignored his nerves. A part of him didn't want to meet the king. "When will he wish to see me?"

"He asked that you come to see him upon your arrival. I can escort you there now if you wish."

"Please do." He firmly stomped on his jittery stomach and told himself to get a grip. The king, unless by some miracle was a Chronicle too, would not know what Morgan and the children were. He would be as easy to fool as the rest of the Magi were. They were so willing to believe what they were told that it made Morgan sad for the future of the world.

"Wow," Jayda whispered as she saw the palace looming in front of them a short while later. "It's so big!"

"Why does a king need a big place like that?" Kelsey demanded of her mother. "Why can't he live like normal people?"

The soldier coughed to hide a laugh and the other adults covered smiles. As 'commoners,' they couldn't help but hold a similar feeling. Only children were allowed to get away with speaking such thoughts out loud though.

Morgan was the only one who was allowed into the palace. The captain of the Militia escorted him personally into the throne room. Morgan wasn't sure what to expect but the utter decadence of the place was slightly disturbing. Why did anyone need ivory and bronze statues? It seemed an absolute waste to him.

The king was an older man who sat on a throne of ivory and bronze. Morgan couldn't help but wonder if the lack of comfort in the chair was what made the king's posture so rigid, or if it was because he was so deeply entrenched in his status that he had forgotten how to feel anything.

He stopped several feet before the throne and drew his thumb over his cheek and nose. "I am Morgan Chronis, a Master Air Magi, of the Black Magi." He linked his hands under his cloak to keep their trembling from showing. "You asked to see me, my king?"

"Yes." The king studied him intently. He had heard Morgan was young but he had not expected to meet a young man barely past second puberty. And yet Morgan's power was potent enough it could be felt. The king sensed it as a feathery feeling along his neck, a sensation warning him that there was a stronger power present. "Your Black Magi . . . what is their purpose?"

Morgan smiled. "To make a haven for Master Magi, particularly children. It is hard to grow up different. The differences are visible even before first puberty. What I went through . . .

I only made it because my parents supported me." There's an understatement, he thought. "I wish to help other children make it through."

The king was silent for a few moments. Then, "I can feel it in you. What you wish is not against the ways of the Magi. There is something very strong in you. I will give your Black Magi my official approval. You may establish a main base wherever you wish."

"We would like to be located here in Prismatic. It is easier to hide in a crowd," he said wryly.

The king laughed. "So I have heard. Very well, Morgan. Good luck."

Taking it for the dismissal it was, Morgan touched his cheek in farewell then left the throne room. The others were still waiting outside, and he climbed up onto the front seat of the cart again. "He approves," he said.

"I thought he might," the soldier said. "Because I was so sure, I arranged for a house to be ready for you." He offered the keys to an astonished Morgan. "If you ever need assistance, do not hesitate to ask the Militia. We have seen many Magi lost to society because they could not fit in with their power."

"You have no idea," Ren murmured so softly only Eli and Luke heard her.

The keys and the locks they would fit were made with Soil power. The thin ties of power between the two allowed Morgan to follow the trail into another district. The end of the trail was a simple two-story house with a third underground. It was rather large overall. More than large enough for however many children they could find. It was also, unfortunately, in somewhat neglected condition.

Mildred took one look at the house and said, "I can fix this."

Ren considered things. "Curtains first. And we'll make Luke and Eli remodel."

"Why us?" Luke complained.

"Because we said so."

Morgan grinned as he hopped down from the cart. He reached up to help the two children down. They were officially a faction now, but he couldn't help but feel as if they were a large family as well. A part of him still missed his parents and always would, but the Renaires and the Lakemores were helping to fill in the gaps inside his heart.

A sudden sharp stab of longing went through him. It was so fierce that it nearly drove him to his knees. Only sheer willpower kept him standing. It hurt. More than ever, it hurt. He wanted to find his Fury. He *needed* to find her.

The longing hadn't brought a direction for him to follow. It could have meant he couldn't track his Fury anymore. It could have meant that he needed to stay put. Either way, he knew he would be in Prismatic a long time.

He only sighed and scooped up each girl under an arm. "Let's find you two a room to share. And no pillow fights this time." He was *never* letting them near feather pillows again.

Chapter Eighteen

(One year later . . .)

The small town of Umber on the continent of Carnelian was located between two forests. One forest led eventually to a series of mountain cliffs. The other led eventually to the closest ocean.

Overall, Umber was not much bigger than an average sized city. It was only ten miles in diameter and had a population of only ten thousand. These people, like the rest of Carnelian's population, were forest dwellers. Their manner of dress was more acclimated for the cool weather and the stinging bugs that lived in and around trees.

For the first time in a year, Morgan no longer felt as if he stood out. By the standards of some people, he was actually underdressed. The cooler weather was also a welcome balm after the heat of Prismatic. He had adjusted, but he still liked to be cool and comfortable. Maybe he wasn't better suited to be a desert boy after all.

The Black Magi had grown in size. Not by much, but it had grown. They now had another child. A little boy by the name of Roman Arequo who was a year younger than Jayda. He and his parents had been living in a small town on the edge of Spectrum. Now they resided in Prismatic with the rest of the Black Magi.

A letter had arrived recently that had asked him to meet a child who might be a Master Magi. Because the child had sounded suspiciously like a Chronicle, he had been quick to make the journey to Umber.

The father of the boy was a man named Soh Emik. He and his son ran a small shop that sold wooden statues and figurines. Soh was a Soil/Wood Magi and very strong. His son, Phedo, was borderline first puberty and most presumed he would inherit his father's element since he already had a natural inclination for it.

Morgan walked into the shop and looked around. The figurines truly were exquisite. His attention was diverted as he saw a man walking out of the back of the shop. The man seemed normal enough with his slightly grizzled face and salt and pepper colored hair and beard, but for some odd reason, Morgan felt his power stinging his skin as if sensing there could be danger.

The man spotted him and smiled. "Welcome."

"Thank you." Morgan walked closer and drew his thumb over his cheek and nose. "Morgan Chronis, Air Magi, of the Black Magi."

The man returned the gesture. "Soh Emik, Soil Magi." He studied Morgan intently. "You're much younger than I assumed."

"Most say that," Morgan agreed wryly. He tilted his head slightly. "You sent me a letter asking me to meet your son?"

"Yes." Soh's face tightened. "He is displaying traits vastly unusual for a child. He is nearing first puberty and I'm worried he may be a Chronicle. If he is . . ."

"You don't want him killed?" Morgan asked softly.

"Of course not!" Soh was outraged at the idea. "He is my child! His mother died in a quake a few years ago. Phedo is all I have left. Him being a Chronicle would change nothing for me."

"Well, let me first meet him and we'll find out what he is," Morgan suggested. Inside, he was smiling. His odd sense of danger or not, he knew Soh and Phedo would be welcome among the Black Magi.

"Dad!" The door swung wildly as a slender boy with black hair came running into the store. He looked no more than eleven or twelve, but he was already beginning to develop into a handsome young man. He sat down the sack of sand he was carrying, then regarded Morgan curiously. "Who are you?" he asked.

"Morgan, an Air Magi." Morgan made the sign of respect. "You must be Phedo. It's nice to meet you."

"Likewise." Phedo studied him curiously. He had never met someone like Morgan before. Something about the older man made him feel safe suddenly, as if he had found a friend he could trust. His shoulders unconsciously relaxed and he smiled. "What brings you to Umber?"

"I came to meet you." Morgan had learned to recognize the feeling he got near Chronicle children. He was nearly positive that Phedo was one as well. "To see if you are a Master Magi. I seem to have a tracking system for others."

"Oh." Phedo smiled. "Am I one?" When Morgan offered a hand, he automatically reached out to take it. An odd feeling tingled along his power in recognition of something different. Something powerful. It was oddly soothing.

Morgan smiled, his suspicions confirmed. "Yes," he said. "You're like me."

Soh's shoulders relaxed. "Phedo, run and fetch the bread before the baker forgets us. Morgan and I need to talk."

"Okay!" Phedo released Morgan's hand and ran off with a wave.

As the door banged shut behind him, Morgan turned to Soh. "He is not a Master Magi," he said very quietly.

"But you . . ." The color drained from Soh's face as he looked at Morgan's gloved hands. "Oh. Oh no. By the moons . . ." He braced his hands on the counter as fear churned in his stomach. Mixed with it came a fury for the Magi who had brought them to this point. "Is your whole group . . .?"

"Me and the children. I made the Black Magi as a haven. You and Phedo are welcome to join us as well," Morgan offered.

"Gladly!" Soh straightened. "The sooner we leave, the better. He could start first puberty any day now."

"In that case, I suggest restricting him to indoors until we can leave. Once we know where his lines are, we can take the steps to hide them." Morgan looked at his hands and grimaced. "As uncomfortable as they may be at times."

There was, quite abruptly, a loud scream on the air. Morgan and Soh whirled toward the door instinctively just as they heard an outraged and disgusted voice exclaim, "It's a *Chronicle*."

"Phedo!" Soh was gray as he rushed around the counter and out into the street, Morgan hot on his heels. The scene they saw made them stop in horror.

Halfway to the baker's place, Phedo had begun first puberty. Under normal circumstances, no one would have known until he began to demonstrate maturity and elemental powers. But he was a Chronicle. His shift into the next stage of his life had brought with it the most vivid part of a Chronicle's existence: lines.

His lines crisscrossed over his face and down his neck. They disappeared under his clothes, but Morgan could spot bits of them on the skin of his knee where his pants had ripped.

He was crouched on the ground and staring at his lined hands in shock and disbelief. He knew what they were but at the same time he didn't know why they were so bad. The crowd gathered around him was like a seething wave of anger. Several of the people were armed with a multitude of weapons.

"Stop it!" Soh lunged forward.

One of the men looked at him in pity. "Soh, it's a monster. We have to kill it."

"It's Phedo! He wasn't a monster until a minute ago! What makes him different?!" Soh whirled toward Morgan. "Do something!"

"I can't." It was the hardest thing Morgan had ever done to simply stand there. "If I do something, I might give myself away. If I do that, the other children will be found. I'm sorry, Soh."

Soh lunged for the crowd but he was too late. One of the men carrying a sword lifted it and shoved it deep into Phedo's back. Blood flew and there was a small shockwave in the land as the power was disrupted. A second later, Phedo's power was no longer subconsciously felt by anyone present.

As his body fell to the ground, the crowd let Soh pass. He rushed to his son's side and lifted him into his arms. He rocked back and forth with grief. Rage was becoming hatred. How dare the Magi do this? They deserved to suffer. To suffer the way so many others had suffered.

Morgan walked over to kneel beside him. "I'm sorry," he said softly.

"It's not your fault." Soh's eyes glittered with a madness held barely in check. "Why don't you hate the Magi?"

"It's a waste of time." Morgan got to his feet. "I will return to Prismatic in the morning." He didn't say he had wished he had gotten there sooner though he felt it inside. He had learned not to wish for things that could not be changed.

As he was walking away, his lines pulsed invisibly under his concealing clothes. He felt her. He felt his Fury. For just a moment, he could feel her. Shocked, he could only stand still as a painful longing rose inside him. Tears stung his eyes and closed his throat. Wherever she was, she was so close he could feel her emotions. She was feeling his and wishing to comfort him.

He waited, wished fiercely for a clue, but the map in his lines remained stubbornly silent. Impotent anger welled inside him and tangled with his grief and longing. A strong gust of wind shook the town but no one really paid heed. He certainly didn't.

As he was waiting on the boat the following morning, he was surprised to see Soh approaching him, a bag slung over his shoulder. "Soh," he said, startled. "What brings you here?"

"I want to join you anyway," Soh said in response. "I can't stand being in this town any longer." He lowered his voice to add, "And I don't want to see what just

143

occurred ever happen again."

Morgan hesitated. Somehow he felt as if Soh was walking a thin line between sanity and insanity. But Soh knew their secret. If he told . . . at least if he was with them, Morgan could keep an eye on him. If he was around him long enough, he might be able to even isolate and remove his memories.

All Air Elements could do tricks with the minds of other people, but on a small scale. It also took constant and steady exposure. On the other hand, Morgan possessed many strong and unusual mental gifts that he could only assume came from him being a Chronicle. He had heard Chronicles could use high-level mind skills *without* constant exposure, yet he had been too wary to try. If it was needed on Soh, however, he would do it. "Very well," he said. "You are welcome to join us." He could only hope he didn't live to regret it.

~*~

(One year later . . .)

The Black Magi had grown no larger in size. Soh was still the only other member of the Black Magi, but Morgan was beginning to think that he was going to have to make him leave. He had already taken the steps to ensure that Soh could not speak of the Chronicles to anyone outside the sanctuary, but it saddened him to know he'd had to do it.

As he sat behind his desk and studied the older man standing across from him, he felt a chill. Soh's eyes had always been borderline mad but Morgan had dismissed it because of what he had endured. He could no longer dismiss it, not when Soh's eyes were bright with full madness. Always tangled in it was his dangerous intellect. Morgan's danger sense was high and his power was stinging his skin.

"Morgan, you think too small!" Soh accused his leader. "Why not find other powerful Magi and have them join us?"

"The risk is too great. And why do we need them? The purpose of the Black Magi is to shelter the Chronicle children." Morgan got to his feet, feeling shorter than he ever had before. "Soh, this not the first time you've given me this tirade. What in the name of the Underrealm is going through your mind?"

"I've come up with the solution, Morgan!" Soh's smile widened as he threw his arms wide. "The best way to protect the Chronicles is to destroy the Magi!"

It took Morgan a few seconds. He was sure he had heard wrong. But the look on the older man's face didn't change. "Destroy the Magi?" he repeated. "Absolutely not. It would destroy the world!"

"Chronicles will take their place. We will gather the most powerful Magi, and if they have Chronicles, then we'll have more. Why don't you hate the Magi, Morgan? Look what they've driven you to!" Soh gestured to the door behind him. "Those children are merely the first step for us."

The air trembled around Soh warningly as Morgan's face tightened with anger all the more potent because it was rare. "You will never lay a hand on those children," he warned softly. "I won't let you use them. You've lost your mind, Soh."

"Then I will leave." Soh sneered at him. "I will find my allies and we will be an elite Black Magi. Don't worry," he added snidely. "I won't speak of your precious sanctuary. You didn't need to weave such a complicated block in my mind."

Morgan's eyes closed partway, the silver color beneath like chips from glass. "Don't expect me to remove it," he said in a hard voice. "I'm not the naïve fool you believe me to be. Kindly remove yourself from these premises."

"Gladly." Soh stalked toward the door and shot back over his shoulder, "but I will return for those children, Morgan! Mark my words!"

The door slammed loudly behind him and Morgan slowly sank down to sit in his chair. He pressed the heels of his hands against his eyes and tried to think of what he could do. He didn't doubt Soh would be back. And he didn't doubt that Soh would find his followers. There were many crazy people in the world, and there were just as many foolish ones who would believe whatever story Soh fed them.

The study door opened slightly and the three children peered around the edge. Kelsey was seven now, and the tallest. Jayda was months shy of seven herself, and she was the same height as Roman who was five. All three were trembling with fear. They had never liked Soh but they had tried. And now Morgan looked sad, and it broke their hearts. He was their hero. He wasn't supposed to be sad.

"He needs a hug," Jayda whispered.

"Yeah." Kelsey was the first across the room and she climbed up onto Morgan's lap to wind her arms around his neck. "You need a hug," she told him imperiously.

Jayda and Roman were not to be outdone. Roman climbed up so that he was dangling off Morgan's back and Jayda wrapped her arms around Morgan's leg. Morgan's heart clenched tightly for a moment as he held them all closer. These children were more precious to him than anything.

A light hand knocked on the door, and Liza Arequo, Roman's mother, looked around the edge. She was a rather ordinary young woman with brown hair and blue eyes, but she had a lively energy that made her appealing. Her mate, Tomas, laughingly admitted to being enchanted by her plain appearance despite it. "Morgan?" she asked softly. "Is everything alright?"

"Not really." He found a smile for her. "Soh left."

"Good riddance." She crossed her arms. "We tried, Morgan. That's more than most would have. What was his problem?"

He was hesitant to tell her and worry both her and the children. And he knew if he lied that the kids would know it and give him away. "He hates the Magi," he finally said simply. It was, after all, the utter truth.

"Why hate what you can't change?" She shook her head. "It doesn't matter. Morgan, there's someone here to see you. A couple and a little boy. They heard of you across the world. They're from somewhere on Choral. They want to see if the boy is a Master Magi."

He gently set the kids aside then got to his feet. "Alright." In the last two years he had gotten adept at recognizing real Master Magi for their differences from Chronicles. The few he had met had been lucky to have parents willing to help them grow. They hadn't needed to join the Black Magi though the parents would infrequently write to Morgan for help. He was always prepared in case a Master Magi did need to stay.

As he walked into the lobby area and saw the little boy with ash colored hair and

145

oddly iridescent black eyes, he knew this was not going to be a time it was needed. The boy was strong enough to be sensed across a room. "Hello," Morgan said. He made the Magi sign of respect. "I am Morgan Chronis, Air Magi."

The young woman holding the boy's hand used her free hand to return the gesture. Her brown eyes were the same interesting iridescent as her son's. "Ferris Daragon, Air Magi as well."

The man beside her also made the sign of respect. "Alline Daragon, Fire Magi. This is our son, C.J."

Morgan smiled. "What does it stand for?"

C.J. wrinkled up his nose. "Not telling."

"We're under orders not to tattle," Ferris said dryly. "We gave him what we thought was a wonderful name, but he hates it. We ended up compromising." She lowered her gaze. "C.J. is quite strong, Morgan. His lightning is exceptional, and he has such an unnerving maturity at times. Rumor stated that those sort of children became Master Magi."

"Most of the time, they do." Morgan smiled at C.J. as he said it because he knew it wasn't a lie. He knelt down and offered a hand to the little boy. "Of course, some become Chronicles." He glanced at the two parents. "I assume that is what you fear most?"

Alline nodded tightly. "Our town is small. The people are . . . strict. If they even got whiff of the possibility that C.J. was not Magi, they would kill him to eliminate even the chance. Chronicle or Magi, C.J. is our son."

"Anyone who touches my child will find themselves flying," Ferris said flatly. "And I assure you, they won't enjoy the landing."

C.J. wasn't listening. He was watching Morgan. He was kind of short for a Magi, but his eyes were kind. There was something really familiar about him. C.J. knew he was absolutely safe here in this place. Without hesitation, he took Morgan's hand.

The familiar tingling sensation of power recognizing power swept through Morgan's lines. He smiled. "Yes, he's definitely like me and the other children here." He got to his feet again and looked at the Daragons. "However, he is not a Master Magi."

It took a few moments before either Ferris or Alline realized what he was saying. Both looked immediately at his gloves, and he removed one to reveal his lives. "Let me reintroduce myself," he said. "I am Morgan Chronis. An Air Chronicle."

"Oh my." Ferris looked down at C.J. in fear. "Then he is a Chronicle." She turned and took her mate's arm. "Alline, we can't go back. The minute C.J. enters first puberty, everyone would know! I won't let them take our son!"

"Nor will I." Alline smiled wryly at Morgan. "I don't suppose the Black Magi have room for more, do they?"

"There's always room," Mildred said as she went past. "Eli has an incurable building bug. We'll get you your own room, and C.J. can bunk with Roman if he likes."

The two boys eyed each other then both shrugged and went running off to play. Kelsey and Jayda, not to be left behind, were quick to follow them down the hall. Morgan just shook his head slightly. "I can only pray they don't all start first puberty at once," he said wryly.

Eli laughed at him from the railing of the second floor over their heads. "You'll make a good father someday, Morgan, mark my words."

Chapter Nineteen

(Present . . .)

Tariah and Dominic were on their way out of the city.

Morgan was still feeling shaken. He had never, not once, in the last five years thought he would ever meet another Chronicle who had made it past first puberty. He still wasn't sure what to think or what to do. He felt helpless to do anything except stand on the sides and watch his sister suffer.

His sister. He wasn't sure why she felt so strongly like one when they were cousins at best, but there was something inside his power that resonated to hers strongly. He liked her. More than that, he was comfortable with her. It had been a long time since he had felt like he had a friend close to his own age. The other Black Magi were his friends but . . . they couldn't truly understand him.

A sudden sensation of trouble slid down his back. His power began to sting his skin. *Run,* a small voice inside him urged. *Something dangerous is coming. Something that threatens your life.*

He could only grab his head in pain as the voice inside brought with it a fierce and powerful longing for his Fury that literally brought him to his knees. Shaken, he could only kneel there in his study. His Fury . . . she had to be close. He *felt* her. His lines throbbed with her power.

"Morgan?" Mildred and Luke were in the doorway and Kelsey was riding on Luke's back. All three looked concerned as they saw him. "Is something wrong? You called for us."

"Yes." He pushed down the feelings as he always had. The danger . . . he knew the source. Soh was coming, and he was coming with the intent of trying to take the children. Morgan knew Soh had gotten more powerful, though he did not know how. The Elite had vastly grown in number as well.

There was no way they could fight Soh alone the way they were. He had too many people on his side. Too many people who could sacrifice themselves. Morgan was powerful, but he didn't think he could take on a crowd without giving himself away. Doing that would ensure the deaths of the four children he loved so deeply.

He walked over to stand in front of the Renaires. His silver eyes were grave. The seriousness in his mood had Luke putting Kelsey down on the ground. She too knew there was something wrong and her lower lip trembled. On a deep breath, Morgan said, "I must ask something of you. Something very, very important."

"Name it," Mildred said simply.

"Soh is coming. I feel him. My lines tell me there is danger." He looked at his ungloved hands. "I can't fight him alone. Perhaps Tariah and I could together but . . . to do that would reveal me for what I am. It would endanger the children."

Luke closed his eyes. "You want to send us away."

"No!" Kelsey lunged forward on a sob and grabbed onto Morgan. "No! No! You promised you'd always be there for us!"

Morgan hugged her tightly, his heart aching. "Soot, this is the only way I can protect you. You know what the Magi have been doing to Tariah, don't you? They will do it to me too, and they will suspect you unless I do something."

"What do you think to do?" Mildred asked quietly.

"I want to use my powers to lock the children's. I've been working on it ever since Soh left, just in case." He released Kelsey and walked toward the window. It was shielded to keep anyone outside from looking in. "If I seal her powers, they will not trigger until she is in the presence of a full-grown Chronicle or a Fury."

"Can you do that?" Luke asked carefully.

"I believe I can. I am an Air Chronicle. I have some very powerful gifts I have not used yet." He sighed. "And . . . I want to erase all of your memories. Of this place. Of me." He turned around. "If I erase your memories and replace them, and send you away, no one will know the difference."

Tears slid down Mildred's cheeks. "But what about you?" she whispered. "What will you do when Soh gets here?"

"Fight. If I survive, I will come find you when I have found my Fury. Then we can take all of you to the Isle just like we always wished. If I don't survive the fight . . . well, it will be Tariah who comes for you." He looked at the couple, then at Kelsey. "Will you go?"

"You'll come for us again, right?" she whispered in a small voice. "I will do my best, Soot."

"You have to promise!" Her face crumpled as tears ran down her cheeks. "Because you *promised* to always be there! So you have to come back!"

"All right. I promise." He hugged her tightly, then slowly released her. He was going to miss her, and miss watching her grow into a young woman. Something told him that she was going to be one hell of a lady someday. No matter what he promised, he was sure it would be a long time before he saw her again.

Mildred and Luke exchanged a look, communicating without words, then both looked at Morgan. "All right," Mildred said. "It is the least we can do. You've done so much for us, Morgan."

"I'm the grateful one," he protested. He found a smile. "I'd have been awfully bored these last five years without all of you."

Thought was power. Power was instant. He had been around the Renaire family for so long that it was easy to slip past their guards and touch their minds. It was even easier to simply dissolve their memories of him. He erased all traces of his presence from their minds.

Then, in Kelsey, he instead placed a thin layer of his power along all surfaces of her skin. Her lines would never show through. As she grew, his power would eventually be replaced by hers and would serve the same purpose until someone removed it. Only Chronicles past second puberty and Furies would ever know. And the Kin, of course.

Before any of them could say anything, he used his Air powers to translocate them from the city. Translocation was an ability of Air elements. It took them or their target to any random location on the world. It took nearly all the strength of a Magi, and even Morgan felt strongly drained despite his limitless power.

It was evening before the Lakemores came to see him. He had needed the time to rest. He had no doubt that the entire sanctuary knew now what he was doing. Ferris and Tomas were Air Magi. They would have felt the translocation and all would have noticed the Renaires were gone.

"Soh is coming, isn't he?" Ren asked quietly as she closed the door behind herself and her family.

"Yes." Morgan lowered his gaze. "I'm sure you've noticed. I sent the Renaires away via translocation so I don't know where they are. Before I did . . . I took their memories of me and their time here. I locked Kelsey's power so her lines won't show until she is near another Chronicle or Fury."

Eli let out a rough breath. "And you want to do the same to us and to Roman and C.J." He gently rested a hand on Jayda's head as she clung onto his waist. "Morgan," he said softly, "You've done more than you know for us. If sending us away will help you, then we'll go."

"It's the only way I can protect you until I find my Fury. Without her, I am only half a whole. There's so much I need to be able to do to stop Soh and his insane Elite." He crouched down to look at Jayda. "But I promise. Either Tariah or I will come for you someday. We'll take you somewhere safe."

Tears welled in Jayda's eyes. "But I want to stay with you."

"I know. But it's not safe. Will you trust me?"

"I will." She scrubbed at her eyes and straightened her shoulders. "I'm gonna grow up," she warned him. "And when I'm a grown up I'm going to come find you if you don't find me first."

He smiled even though he knew she would not remember him when they met again. "Okay. I'll hold you to that."

Less than five minutes later, he once more found himself alone in his study. His heart was breaking. Both physically and emotionally he was exhausted. Sending the Arequos and the Daragons would have to wait until the morrow.

Dinner was very solemn. C.J. and Roman had sensed that something was very odd and didn't ask questions. Alline and Ferris were thoughtful in their silence. They had not known Morgan as long, only about two years, but they thought that they knew him as well as the other Black Magi. They were fairly sure he was doing the only thing he could.

Liza and Tomas felt much the same but they also knew that Morgan would stop at nothing to protect the children. Whether he sent them away or not, he would come for them again, or send Tariah if he could not make it. Just thinking about the reasons why it would be left to Tariah made them both lose their appetite. Morgan was a part of their family more than he was their leader.

Right after dawn the following morning, Morgan sent the Arequo family away with their memories gone and Roman's powers locked down. He only gave himself enough time to recover before sending away the Daragons. He knew it would shake up the power in the land to clump the boys close together, but his danger sense was screaming. Soh was in Prismatic. He was sure of it.

The sanctuary was quiet and lonely without the other Black Magi. He stayed in his study and wrote a letter to Tariah. He used paper made by the Kin that would not reveal its lettering until the intended recipient handled it. It was also strong enough to withstand even a detonation of power, just in case.

As he was tucking the letter into the pocket inside his cloak, he felt the hair on the back of his neck quiver. He dodged and whirled around at the same time, and a shield of Air power protected him a second before the blast struck. It streaked around and instead blasted into and through the bookcases.

From where he was standing in the doorway, Soh said caustically, "Always running, Morgan? Seems such a pity."

A chill went down Morgan's back. He had believed Tariah when she had said that Soh had gone beyond mad. But when he looked into Soh's eyes now, he saw just how deeply he had been corrupted. Even his power was tainted with madness. Madness . . . and death. "It was more of a dodge than a run," he said as evenly as he could.

"Same difference." Soh walked into the room. "Memory lane, isn't it? But where are the children, great leader? This place seems awfully empty now."

Morgan's lashes lowered and his silver eyes glittered with satisfaction. "I sealed their powers and sent them away by translocation."

Soh could only gape at him for a long moment. He had not realized just how far Morgan's skills could go. The shock was replaced by hate and rage, and his face turned slightly purple. "You bastard!" he roared. "How did you know I was coming?!"

"Two reasons. One, I believe I felt my Fury warning me." He unfastened his cloak calmly and removed it to leave himself in plain slacks and a tunic. "And for two, well, your power is really starting to reek. Sort of like dead flowers, or dog urine. Take your pick."

Soh gave a high-pitched scream of rage and lunged toward him. The Chronicle hurled his cloak at Soh and caught him in the face, to obscure his view. Before Soh could recover, a shot of Air power had slammed into his chest. It hurled him violently backward and he crashed entirely through a wall and into the hall.

He yanked the cloak off as he got to his feet and threw it into the study. He immediately spotted Morgan beginning to glow. He was using translocation again. Evil power began to gather around Soh. "You won't escape me. You think you'll land somewhere safe?"

"It's got to be safer than here," Morgan said with a cheer he didn't feel. The spell wasn't casting as fast as it should because he was so tired.

A split second before Soh's attack hit, Morgan disappeared. In the giant explosion that followed and the sudden quake that shook the entire continent, no one heard the scream of raw rage that pierced the sky.

~*~

Morgan landed in the middle of the mountains of Carnelian. It had to be Carnelian. Choral and Spectrum didn't have mountains, and Glacia's were covered in snow. These mountains were cool and dry and snow free.

There was no strength left in his body. He fell to his knees on the ground and stared blindly at the distance. The sun beating down on his bare skin was a foreign feeling. He couldn't focus his eyes or his mind. The horizon was a blur of green that was probably trees grown closely together.

It was some time before he realized that his arm hurt. He looked down and saw a long cut along his left arm that was slowly bleeding. His torn tunic was already quite stained. He vaguely remembered feeling a bit of Soh's attack getting through the translocation, but he hadn't actually noticed getting hit.

With some effort, he managed to rip a piece of material from his tunic and tie it around the wound. He had to use his teeth to make a knot, and just that small effort wore him out. He knew his odds of survival were low. He would have to find food and water or try to get out of the mountains and find a city. The city was the worse of the two options since his lines were now visible.

He sat down on a sigh and then fell over onto his back. He would rest for a while before figuring out what his options really were. He had absolutely no intentions of actually sleeping out there in the open, but the option was taken away from him. Even as he was trying to think of some way to contact Tariah, he slipped unconscious. He had been pushed too hard for too long.

~*~

(Isle of Dragons)

The Elders were fighting again. It wasn't anything new, not really, but this time they were arguing over something they agreed on. They all agreed that it was time they did something about the world, but they couldn't agree on how to do it!

Their voices could be heard through the large doors, and the slender young woman standing outside muttered, "Cantankerous idiots." She blew a streak of violet out of her face and it settled into her pale blonde hair. She walked a few steps from the door, and power swirled around her to change her back to her natural form.

She was a larger sized Dragon though not as large as most of the males. No one had ever picked on her for her height. She was a Fury, and there were many who treated her gently because they knew she would die someday soon. Her Chronicle had been born somewhere.

"Grecia!" One of the younger Dragons flew over and landed beside her. "We've got big news!"

"What now?" she asked.

"There are more Chronicles!"

She stared at him in disbelief then demanded, "How old?"

"According to what we heard from the Kin who are sheltering Dominic and his Chronicle, they're children! The other adult Chronicle was sheltering them!" A trace of hope was inside his eyes that matched hers. He was also a Fury. "Maybe . . ."

Grecia whirled and flew over to the meeting room doors. She banged on them with her tail. "Open up!" she ordered. "Grandpa! Open the damned door!"

The door flew open and the Elder Air Dragon rose to his full height. He towered over her seventeen-foot length with ease. "How dare you speak to me in that tone!"

The Soil Fury didn't back down. "Dominic and his Tariah sent word through the Kin. There are several Chronicle children."

"What!"

The bellow from inside the room would have been heard a few hundred miles across the ocean where the Magi were if the island hadn't been shielded. Grecia rolled her eyes expressively. "You heard me!"

Her grandfather nodded slowly. "We must find these children, and this other Chronicle you mentioned before. We may not be able to bring them to this isle, but we can protect them!" He studied her. "Where are they?"

"That's the problem," the Fury who had brought the news said as he walked up. He was a younger Dragon, only two hundred or so, but he was swift and smart for his age. "Nobody knows. They were all translocated from Prismatic."

"That explains the explosion," the Fire Dragon Elder said. "It's time we left the island. Or more specifically, it's time *you* left the island." He pointed a claw at the two Furies. "You and the rest of the Furies are to go live among the Magi from this day forward. Find the Chronicle children! Find any others you can!"

"What!" Grecia looked at the other Dragon. "Solis, talk sense into your uncle!"

"You credit me with more talent than I have," the Water Fury muttered. "Uncle," he said patiently, "what if our Chronicle is killed in the meantime?"

Silence fell. It was something no one liked thinking about, let alone speaking. Only the Furies, ironically, seemed capable of mentioning it out loud. Perhaps because they lived with the knowledge of how likely it would happen. Finally, the Water Elder said, "If that happens, return to the Isle."

"Have we had any luck locating Jazz?" Grecia asked the Elders. "Daylar of the Kin was fairly sure that Dominic was certain that she was the Fury that belongs to the other Chronicle that isn't Tariah."

There was a brief silence before Solis finally said, "You fascinate me."

"I have that effect on a lot of people."

The Elders collectively shook their heads. "No," the Soil Elder said. "She has gone deeply into hiding in the mountains and has not responded to any of the messages we have tried to send her." He beetled his large brows together. "Both of you go to the lands of the Magi. Find the children. Find Dominic and Tariah. And for the sake of the moons, find out what in the hell is going on with the Magi!"

Grecia and Solis winced as the doors were slammed shut in their faces. "They don't ask for much," Grecia said wryly, "do they?"

Chapter Twenty

Jazz Eaglewind was a Soil Fury and over four hundred years in age. For the last twenty- five years, she had been living by herself in the mountains of Carnelian, in the most remote corner of the highest peak that she could find. Her life was simple there. All she had to do was simple. She only had to wait to die. When that time came, she wanted to handle the deed herself and not burden her family.

She was being kept up-to-date on the events of the world by turning herself into a Kin form and walking among the Magi in their villages on Carnelian. She knew of Tariah Chronis and Dominic Whisperer. She knew of the Black Magi and the Black Magi Elite. She also knew about the horrendous events in Prismatic. She just couldn't bring herself to care.

She had felt her Chronicle's birth twenty-five years, ten months, and six days ago. Somehow, she wasn't sure how, he had managed to escape death. There was no way he hadn't gone through first puberty. In fact, he had to be past second puberty by now and the knowledge was unpleasant. As terribly as she wished him to be happy, she *loathed* the very idea of anyone else touching her Chronicle.

She wanted to find him. With every fiber of her being, she wanted to find him. She had always been alone inside with a part of her soul missing. There had been times over the years where she had been sure she felt him. She had tried to touch him, but she hadn't been sure she had made it. It had always brought her to tears.

She had been tempted to leave her shelter and go to find him, but every time she begun to make plans, something stopped her. It was frustrating enough without learning that Tariah had successfully hid herself for seven years.

Stifling a sigh, Jazz left her house. It was hidden in a cliff face and could not be found accidentally. She needed fresh water from the stream nearby, and the idea of a long shower under the waterfall appealed deeply. She climbed the first set of cliffs with lithe strength, then went up the pathway to the second.

The jug she had been carrying fell out of her hand and landed on the ground with a thud. Shocked, she could only stare at the sight of the young man lying near the edge of the cliffs. Her first reaction was sheer disbelief that he had gotten that far. Her second reaction was terror as she saw the golden lines flowing over his bare arms and hands. *A Chronicle!*

She rushed toward his side only to stop sharply as she felt his power. It curled around her like a cool and tender breeze and swept into her heart and body where it belonged. She slowly sank to her knees beside him, and her heart was pounding madly. Her eyes memorized him longingly. Hers. This one man was hers alone. *Her* Chronicle.

Her entire body trembled with a sudden hunger. Hunger for his power, something that she could nearly taste. Hunger for his starkly beautiful face and body.

She softly reached out and put a hand on his chest. His lines were hot against her skin even through his tunic. Sharp possessiveness filled her as she realized what it meant. It was *her* power creating his lines.

She stood and backed away several steps. Green light flowed over her as the ground trembled lightly beneath her feet. When the light faded, she had returned to her natural Dragon form. At eight feet long, she was on the smaller side, but she found herself taking great delight in it for once because her Chronicle was short himself.

She gingerly picked him up in her claws and flew back toward her house. It was capable of accommodating her Dragon size, and she walked in the front door without any trouble. She very carefully put her Chronicle on the bed and changed back to her Magi form. She sat down beside him and brushed at his auburn hair. She couldn't bear the idea of leaving his side.

She spotted the wound on his arm and her eyes narrowed. She untied the knot and unwrapped the bandage expertly, and her breath hissed in sharply. The jagged wound marred his lines, and it insulted her that anyone would dare mark her Chronicle.

Soil power welled around her, and she formed a needle and thread from it. Healing had always been her specialty. She carefully stitched the wound closed and applied a thin layer of power that would numb pain. The needle dissolved when she was done, and the thread would heal into the wound within an hour. It wouldn't even leave a scar. Such was the gift of powerful healers.

She picked up one of his hands and studied it intently. His were hands accustomed to hard work. Despite the gloves she knew he must have worn—his skin was very fair—his hands still bore calluses and possessed remarkable strength. Heat fluttered through her body at the idea of having these wonderful hands touch her.

A brief dizziness was perplexing until she realized her majiks were draining without her doing anything. It wasn't moving at a rate that alarmed her, but she was definitely beginning to feel exhausted without cause. It was countered by an increase in her Chronicle's power, and she looked at him longingly.

His power was like the purest of air. Like a brisk snowy morning on the top of a mountain. But there was some sort of spark to it, like a delicious tingle from tasting something minty. She had to force herself not to kiss him and see if he tasted the way his power hinted he might.

She moved closer and held tight to his hand. She would wait as long as it took until he awoke. She wanted to look in his eyes and know that they belonged together. She had waited centuries for him. "Please wake up," she whispered. She lifted his hand to her cheek and closed her eyes. "Don't you want to be with me?"

~*~

Morgan awoke slowly to a raging headache. His entire body hurt from head to heels. He felt out of control. He was being blown away on his own power. It was so powerful and fierce inside him that he wanted to sweep across the land like a tornado, raging until there was nothing left.

He instinctively shifted to escape the feeling, and his muscles violently protested the movement. Terror began to well inside him as he realized he was no longer on the cliff. He didn't know where he was, but he was lying on a soft bed and the lingering scent of flowers clung to the air. He tried again to move, and again a torrent of pain ripped through his body. "Shh," a soft female voice said. "Don't move. You're safe, I promise."

The voice reverberated through him. As he focused on the voice and not his own pain, he became aware of a Soil power beside him. The power and the voice were achingly familiar. Tears burned his eyes as something inside awoke and reached out eagerly. *His.* This woman was his. His . . . Fury?

Hope and shock mingling inside him, he forced his eyes open. He instantly found himself staring in a pair of green eyes as deep and rich as a spring meadow. They were set into a face too beautiful to be real. Her long hair was golden brown and streaked with green the same color as her eyes.

She seemed much shorter than average for any species, let alone a Magi or Dragon. She was probably only an inch taller than Tariah, but she possessed a lushly curved figure that would catch the attention of any member of any race. She was impossibly beautiful to Morgan, and far too perfect to be real.

Desire awoke and gleefully ripped through every nerve in his body with the force of a hurricane. He had felt desire on occasion since second puberty. He had been able to quite easily control it and ignore it. There was no controlling the hunger he felt for his Fury, and there was sure as hell no ignoring it. It consumed him from his power and soul out. "Good morning," he said huskily. "Where have you been all this time?"

Jazz's eyes closed and she rubbed her cheek against his hand. "Waiting," she whispered. "Waiting all my life." She leaned over him and her hair fell forward to curtain them. The soft strands glided over Morgan's skin teasingly. "You smell like the snow," she whispered. "It's driving me mad."

He threaded his free hand into her hair. She smelled, to him, like the rich scent of a summer meadow. Of lazy days where you could lay in the grass and stare at the blue sky overhead. Such places were rare on Lucksphere. It was why they were so deeply hoarded.

She sensed his pain even before he winced. "We need to complete the bond," she said softly. "It's natural. My majiks drain and your power grows so that we can bond." Her mouth was nearly watering with the desperation to taste his power and his skin. "I'm going to try to behave myself."

"Behave yourself?"

Her head lifted and she looked at him in surprise. It was such an innocent question coming from a man over twenty. "Haven't you . . . aren't you past second puberty?"

"Technically." He smiled. "But I never got around to actually graduating, as it were. These," he held up his free hand to show his lines, "sort of stunted that effort. They cover my hands, my arms, and my chest."

Triumph filled her as jealousy lost its green-eyed grip. He would be hers alone. "Good," she said succinctly. She lowered her head again and nuzzled her nose against his shoulder. His power immediately flowed up and covered him like a soft white aura begging for her attention. "I'll be delighted to help you 'graduate.' It'll be my pleasure."

"I think it'll be both ours." His eyes closed as her soft lips teased his skin. The sensation was electrifying. "Tell me your name before I forget how to think. It's the only thing I don't know about you."

"Jazz Eaglewind." She was smiling when she lifted her head, and it was strangely foreign to her. It had been decades since she had last smiled, yet it was suddenly easy again. She wasn't alone. There was someone to walk beside her. Someone to protect and be protected by. "What about you?"

"Morgan Chronis."

Delight filled her. "*Morignan* is a Draconic word much like your name. It means rainfall in the mountains. It was always one of my favorite words." Unable to resist the lure any longer, she pressed her lips to his shoulder and slowly breathed in as if drinking. His power flowed into her, the taste the same as the scent, and her hunger for him grew.

He didn't bother to fight a shiver as her lips teased his neck while she fed on his power. In fact, he was so enthralled with what she was doing that he was startled when he felt his tunic suddenly disappear. His eyes opened. "Well."

"It was in my way," his Fury defended herself with a pout that had his pulse hammering with lust. "I wanted to see your lines." She ran her hands slowly over his chest, loving the feel of his power tingling her skin. She was still feeding on his power, and she traced his lines with her lips and little touches of her tongue.

He endured it as long as he could. It was wonderful torture but he was losing his mind. He wanted to kiss her, to learn her taste as well. He wanted to merge her so completely to him that they would never be apart. "Jazz," he said huskily.

She shuddered. She had never thought hearing her name could be seductive. She would give everything she owned if only to hear him calling her name. "What?" she asked. There was a fascinating dip along his collarbone and she tasted it lightly. She felt slightly drunk and reveled in it.

"Are you ever going to kiss me, or do I have to pin you down and claim it?"

She lifted her head with a grin. "You're a sassy little boy. Are you daring a Dragon, *ishke*?"

He grinned back, and his arms shot around her waist. He rolled quickly, dragging her across his body and pinning her to the bed beneath him. He laughed as he saw her astonished expression. In that moment he realized he had never felt happier in his life. For the first time he was no longer alone. "You forgot I'm an Air element, didn't you?"

"I did. I'll remember it from now on." She buried her fingers in his hair and drew him down eagerly. She wanted his kiss with a vengeance. His weight over her was wonderful, and it made her feel small and cherished. Maybe her size wasn't that bad after all. "I like this," she decided.

"Good." He cupped the back of her neck and lifted her until their lips met in a hungry kiss. He shuddered. She tasted like springtime and summer and sunshine all rolled into one. He couldn't wait to completely explore her and learn everything he had never gotten to learn before.

She returned the ravenous kiss and could only moan helplessly at the combination of his power flowing into her and his kiss devouring her. Her fingers slid down to his shoulders and ran over his skin slowly, memorizing how he felt. He was wonderfully hot to the touch. She would never need a blanket again.

The ebb in his power was felt by both of them. They slowly parted and their eyes locked. Between one breath and the next, they were breathing inside each other. A soft flickering light rippled over her body and identical lines appeared. They flowed around her neck, then in a wide ribbon around her body that wrapped twice before ending just past her hip.

Most of the lines were hidden beneath her leggings and strapless top, but he could feel them tingling wherever their bodies touched. He could feel *her*. Her age and her power. He reached out with his mind and power and found her there. He curled both around her in wonder, and her memories slipped into his mind. His throat tightened as he read her determination to die alone. She was much stronger than anyone had ever thought.

Her eyes closed on a wave of emotion at feeling him inside. She reached for him in return and held on just as tight. His memories swept into her mind, and she saw his determination to protect the children. His struggle to use his dedication to the Black Magi to cover his loneliness. "I'm so sorry, Morgan," she whispered achingly.

"For what?" He swept her hair out of her face. "You couldn't track me. My lines kept me there. I'm sure there was a reason. Maybe it was to meet Tariah and Dominic." He searched her eyes. "So . . . how do we get to the Isle?"

"We . . ." Her voice trailed off as her eyes widened. She couldn't remember. In fact, she couldn't even put a finger on the energy output of anyone of her race to contact them. She frowned. "I don't remember. Dominic was the same?"

"He was. I think the running theory was because of Tariah. That means your problem is likely because of me." He released her and rolled to the side to sit up. He felt fine now that his power was back to normal. Okay, maybe not *fine*. He had a raging arousal that wasn't exactly comfortable. But he would be damned if their first time was there in that house. There were too many echoes of loneliness in the walls.

Jazz scooted closer and pressed against his back. Her arms wrapped around his chest and her hand stealthily crept lower on his body. Her stomach quivered with sheer lust. His tunic had hidden a lot of muscle. He was short, but every inch was used to perfection. "I bet I can change your mind." Her voice was teasing and husky as her fingers rested above the fastening to his slacks.

"I bet you could," was his slightly strained response. He quickly caught her hands and held them against his chest. "But it's not right here. Can't you feel it?"

"I can but . . ." Frustration filled her voice. "You're mine. You're my Chronicle. I have every right to claim you as mine. Making me wait when I've been waiting for this long is cruel, Morgan."

He turned to grin at her. "At least you won't be waiting for *weeks*."

She lifted a brow. "Weeks?" She saw the knowledge in his mind of Dominic's plight, and she bit her lip to muffle a laugh. "Oh dear. Poor Dominic." She sighed and rested her cheek on his back as she nuzzled him softly. "I guess we follow your lines," she said simply "We'll find your cousin and reassure her that you're alive. And then we'll *all* do something about the Elite." Her eyes narrowed with menace. "I claim Fury Right to kill Soh."

"Fury Right?" He turned and held her closer. She nuzzled against his shoulder and he returned the gesture before burying his nose in her hair. He had a feeling he was going to enjoy the Dragon form of affection.

"The right as a Fury to destroy anyone or anything that has threatened my Chronicle." She met his eyes. "It is a right that we Furies have been very careful to control."

157

Suddenly he understood something that had always bothered him. "No wonder the Dragons left. It wasn't just anger and grief. It was to remove the temptation of killing Magi for breaching those rights."

"It was certainly among the reasons." She slowly released him and ran her eyes over his half-naked body. Her entire body throbbed with the need to claim him. "You sure about waiting?" Her voice was a velvet invitation, and she didn't bother to hide her thoughts or feelings.

His eyes darkened to gray. He could no more resist her than the sun could resist rising in the morning. "Sure enough," he murmured thickly, "but I think you know you could change my mind in thirty seconds if you tried."

"Thirty?"

"Erring on the side of caution. It'd likely take you less."

She drew a deep breath. "Alright. If Dominic can find self-control as a Fire element, I can find some as a Soil element. Damn." She shook her head wryly. "If I discover that I have a bad temper, I blame you. I'm normally very even-tempered."

"The land may rest most of the time, but when it shakes, it shakes with enough force to alarm everyone," he noted.

"Very philosophical. Much like the air that is calm and serene, but can whip into a torrent at the right provocation?" she slid off the bed and got to her feet. "We'll need some new clothes for you," she said briskly. She walked over to where she kept a bag of sand. "We don't want the Magi to know you are a Chronicle until it can't be avoided."

"For the sake of the children?" He shook his head. "Don't worry. I've already thought of a reason. Because I was a Chronicle, I wished to prove I was not a monster by living among the Master Magi where I had a chance of blending in. The rest of the reasons for forming the Black Magi still stand."

"I suppose they do." She tugged him to his feet and smiled. She was only three inches shorter. "You're very short."

"Look who's talking." He skimmed a knuckle down her bare shoulder. She wore a pair of form fitting leggings and a strapless form-fitting top. She had sleeves, but they were only fastened around her upper arm before falling in folds to her wrists. "It looks like you took a little bit of each land."

"It gets warm in the mountains during summer, so I need lighter clothing. But it gets cold in winter, so I needed more coverage. And the winds are strong, so I didn't want a lot of loose material." She smiled. "This also makes it easier for me to hunt if needed."

He lifted a brow slowly. "You fight bare-handed?"

"Most Dragons do." She glowered at the look on his face. "Quit looking at me like I'm some sort of little Magi."

"Right now you are."

She opened her mouth then closed it. "I hate it when I'm wrong." Ignoring his grin, she focused instead on the sand. Her skill was quite high at her age, and it took only a matter of moments to weave new clothes for her lover. She made him a new tunic and cloak, but the cloak was only waist length. She also didn't make any gloves.

As he was dressing, he asked, "Dare I ask why?"

"I like your hands." Her eyes were dark green jewels warm with invitation. "You're welcome to put them on me at any time and in any place you wish."

He tired to ignore that but it was impossible. His breath hissed out as her power temptingly flowed around him. "I'm going to get you for that," he warned her.

She threw her arms around him happily. "Good!" She buried her face against his shoulder and couldn't fight a tremor through her body as his arms went around her just as snugly. She had been craving the feel of his arms her entire life without knowing it. "I don't want to leave here."

"Me neither." He held her even closer. He finally understood what Tariah had meant when she had said being with her Fury was the most incredible feeling in the world. He knew he would sooner die than give up Jazz.

They reluctantly eased apart and, hands linked, they went outside. Jazz released his hand and walked several steps away. "I'm also a small Fury," she confessed. "But you should still be able to ride on my back."

He shielded his eyes from the light as it consumed her and lowered his hand when she sat before him in full Fury form. There was nothing gentle or tame about her. She was fierce and almost frightening with the hard lines to her face. Yet, to him, she was still the most beautiful thing he had ever seen.

He walked over and reached up to frame her face. Even as a small Fury, she was slightly more than twice his size over all. Her scales, he realized in delight, felt as soft as feathers. Her body was golden brown and there was a patch of green over her back like a grassy field growing from the ground. "I think you're amazing," he said softly.

She lowered her head and nuzzled him, her heart tightening with emotion. Mixed with it was a heady dose of excitement. She had never had anyone ride on her back while she flew. It was impossible. But Morgan was a part of her. This flight would be the true evidence of their bonds. "Let's go."

He climbed up onto her back gracefully and with no fear. He knew he would never fall. "Go where?" he asked.

"There is a Kin outpost not far from here. We can go there for any news. It's safer than Carnelian." She flapped her wings and they shot up into the air. She laughed as she felt him grab her tighter. "You won't fall!"

"It was a little unnerving," he defended himself. Delight spread as they began to fly swiftly across the sky. The feeling was indescribable. Deeply linked to Jazz as he was, it almost felt as though he was the one doing the flying. "Don't go too fast. I want to take forever."

"I do too." She dipped down toward the ocean and skimmed the surface before flying up higher in the air. She loved carrying him like this. She barely felt his weight, and his power was deep inside her. Their power cycled between them like an endless loop.

The outpost was, by boat, three hours away from the nearest beach where her mountain had been. By flight, even without pushing herself, she made the journey in less than a single hour. It was with some regret that she angled down toward the beach of the outpost and landed gently in the sand.

Morgan slid down off her back and staggered as his legs didn't want to quite work. She quickly turned back and tried to catch him, but he was now bigger than she was and they went tumbling down to the sand.

He blinked up at her sprawled over him. He slowly smiled. "Hi there."

"Hi yourself." She braced herself up on her arms and sighed contentedly as she looked at him. "You're so handsome, Morgan." She lowered her head with the intent of taking the kiss she craved when she heard someone clear their throat. "Spoil a good moment," she muttered as she rolled off her Chronicle and gained her feet.

The MoonKin Elf who had gotten their attention could only grin as he watched Jazz help Morgan stand. "My apologies, but if you'd like more privacy, we do have an inn."

Morgan put his hands on Jazz's shoulders then reached down and caught her hands to keep them away from any particularly sensitive portion of his body. The unfortunate part was that where she was concerned, it happened to be his entire body. "We'll take you up on that later."

The Kin's eyes lowered to his hands and the lines vividly displayed. "Ah," he said. "So you're the one Daylar mentioned."

"Daylar?" Morgan asked curiously.

"He is the honorary brother-Kin to Tariah Chronis. She let all Kin know you were out there, Morgan." The Kin bowed. "Though it seems some of us already knew but were careful to keep you a secret. You, and your Fury, are always welcome among the Kin."

"Thank you." Jazz leaned against Morgan. "Please, tell us, what is going on with the Magi? I had ignored the explosions and quakes, but now that Morgan is at the heart of it . . ."

"The Elite." The Kin gestured for them to follow and they fell into step beside him. "The Black Magi Elite have retreated to Glacia and made a worldwide proclamation. They are taking full credit for the death of the king of the Magi, and they are declaring their intent to destroy all Magi."

"Soh, you idiot," Morgan said softly.

Jazz's eyes widened. "But doing that will destroy the world!"

"Soh thinks Chronicles will replace the Magi," Morgan said on a sigh. "But the simple fact is that Chronicles and Magi need to work together. Magi overpopulate the world. The power is unbalanced. Only Chronicles are able to make the balance. That was Tariah's theory at least."

"She has a sound theory." Jazz crossed her arms. "Are there any Chronicles in the Elite?"

"No. Tariah and I are the only ones past first puberty, let alone second. But Soh has a few Master Magi, and many fanatical normal Magi. He needs Chronicles in order to really have any chance of taking out the Magi. He blew it with Tariah, and he never had a chance with me. He wants the children."

"He won't get them, Morgan." She turned and wrapped her arms around his waist, trying to comfort him. "We'll find them, and we'll take them somewhere safe. If we can't take them to the Isle, we'll bring them here to the Kin. We'll do whatever it takes."

"We need to kill Soh." His eyes were as flat as his voice. "We need to destroy the Elite." He looked at the Kin. "Please. Please contact your Daylar and have him tell Tariah that I am well, and that I have found my Fury."

"Consider it done," the Kin said quietly. "Will you go to meet Tariah and Dominic then?"

North. The sudden throbbing of his lines took Morgan by surprise. He hadn't felt them urging him in any direction for years. "Yes," he said slowly. "I think we will. I have to go north," he said to Jazz. "Somewhere north."

"*We* have to go," she corrected. "We're in this together, Morgan." She lifted one of his hands to her cheek so she could nuzzle against his fingers. "We'll leave as soon as we know where Tariah and Dominic are." She looked up into his soft silver eyes and felt her stomach flutter. She was completely unaware of the Kin's smile as he walked away.

Morgan was equally oblivious as he slowly drew her closer toward him. "Teach me," he murmured as he lowered his head. When his lips were a breath from hers, he amended, "Teach me majiks."

Her eyes flew wide. "What? Why you . . ." She sputtered but couldn't stop herself from laughing. "You're going to be a terror to live with, aren't you?"

He grinned at her. "Very likely." He lowered his head to brush his lips over hers. "Teach me everything."

"Everything?" she repeated, her voice warm with love and desire.

"Everything," he confirmed, his voice just as warm. "You'll find I'm a quick study. But I need lots of hands-on practice, you understand. And repeating a lesson is not discouraged."

She just smiled. "Consider school to be in session."

Chapter Twenty-One

Jazz and Morgan kept their hands linked tightly as they walked together through the Kin outpost. Morgan had never been happier. He glanced down at their linked fingers and thought to himself about the long years he had been waiting. He knew they were a drop in the bucket compared to how long she had been waiting but it had still seemed an eternity.

She suddenly scowled. "You're thinking about another girl."

He lifted a brow then smiled. "So to speak. I was just thinking that if it had been you I'd been around when I was twenty, I wouldn't have hesitated in going after you." He tugged her closer, enjoying how she was smaller than he was. There were so few that were; Kin didn't really count.

She brought his hand to her cheek and nuzzled it softly. "If I'd been there," she said softly, "I'd have carried you away and made damn sure I was the only female in your line of sight. Your Merideth was an idiot."

"No," he said softly. "I've thought about it over the years, and I think she was right. She did what she did because she cared about me." He bent his head and kissed her quickly. "Quit being jealous. Your skin will turn as green as your eyes."

"It will not!" she grumbled. She didn't like being jealous. She knew it was entirely unreasonable. She knew that he was hers and that he would always be there within reach as she would be for him. But the very idea of any other being laying a hand on his gorgeous form . . . it made her mad.

"You don't see me getting worked up over your past," he told her.

"You're more even-tempered than I am," she said with a sigh. "That or you're more open-minded. I'm not sure which."

"Well, I'm certainly not less possessive. A part of me wants to get enraged at the idea of any man touching you," he said thoughtfully, "but the practical part of me keeps pointing out that you were an adult long before my great-great-grandparents were born. However," he continued, his silver eyes darkening, "if any man tries to take you away from me now, I'll kill him where he stands. Fair enough?"

Strangely comforted by that, she cuddled close against his arm again. "You'll like it on the Isle," she told him. "There's a little bit of every sort of landscape. We could live in the mountains, or in the valley. Or in the desert, or along the ocean."

"I love the mountains," he said softly. "Probably because the air is always so clear on them. You'll have to pick us out a perfect spot and make our house there."

"Me?" Her brows shot up.

"Of course. I can see into your thoughts, Jazz. You've always wanted to build your own home. The home of your dreams. So you're going to."

She felt tears spring to her eyes. Blinking them away, she turned and threw her arms around him and almost knock them both over. "It's your dream home too!" she said into his neck. "You'll have to help me."

"How can I help?" He held her even closer just for the delight of feeling her warm body pressed to his.

"You can stand there shirtless." She eased back with a grin as she felt his embarrassment rise. "You're blushing!" she said in delight as she saw his slightly reddened cheeks. "Morgan Chronis, never tell me no one has ever mentioned how utterly and absolutely *gorgeous* you are!"

He cleared his throat. "There's a difference between knowing it, having it mentioned, and having someone blatantly take full and utter advantage of it." Under the embarrassment was delight. He wanted her to find him irresistible. He wanted her to want him as terribly as he wanted her. It was hard to tell anymore whether his curiosity was purely because he hadn't made love before, or because of Jazz herself.

"It's probably me," she said huskily. "Because sure as rain in the valley, I've never been this desperate to know everything about a man before."

He felt her fingers skimming over the nape of his neck and quickly caught her hands. The sly little Fury had plucked the knowledge from his mind about the most sensitive parts of his body. But that was okay. He had gotten the same information from her. He just needed her mostly naked to get to where she was sensitive.

She almost stopped breathing. For whatever reason, innocents were always the most seductive and imaginative. She was fairly sure half of what he was thinking was physically impossible, but she was quite willing to try. "Inn," she said firmly. "Now."

He just smiled and let her drag him in her wake as she headed for the inn ahead of them. The Kin were fast when it came to news, and the innkeeper was waiting for them. She offered a set of keys then pointed to the stairs heading up. "Second floor, last on right," she said cheerfully.

"Thank you," he said. It was all he could say before his Fury was dragging him toward the stairs. He was no longer in doubt about her fighting capabilities. She was short, and she was slender, but she was almost fascinatingly strong. "Do Dragons retain their strength in any form they take?"

She shot him a grin over her shoulder. "Yes. Which means, *ishke*, that if you pin me down, it's because I let you."

"Just for future reference," he said, "that just makes you even more appealing to me. I like knowing you're willing to let me be stronger." He shut the door behind them then took the keys from her to turn and lock it.

Her arms suddenly slid around his waist and he stopped breathing. The impact her mere presence had on him was devastating. It was made all the more powerful because she was softly curling her power around his, rubbing slowly, like a cat asking to be touched. His mouth went dry. "I get the feeling you're always going to win any argument we enter," he managed to say.

She nuzzled his shoulder softly. "Is that a way of saying you can't resist me, *ishke*?" Her hands spread warmly across his stomach and her own stomach fluttered as she felt the strength in his muscles. In her long life she had had both Magi and Dragon, and a few Kin, for lovers. Only in Dragon form around other Dragons had she ever felt smaller than someone. In Magi form she was too conscious of her true strength. "How is it you make me forget?" she whispered.

He turned and pulled her close, savoring the feel of her curves molding to his body. "Well, I can't speak from experience, but I'd think that the stronger the feeling, the weaker it makes you."

"Do I make you feel weak, Morgan?" She slid her hands up under his tunic and thrilled at how his lines tingled her palms.

"So weak that I can't get away. You'll be stuck with me forever, Jazz." He lowered his head and took her lips slowly. He wanted to memorize their shape and feel and taste. He had half expected to feel rushed after waiting so long, but he felt instead as if they had all the time in the world. He could learn everything. Feel everything. Even things that he would never have learned without her there.

Her head fell back as his lips pressed to her throat. Her hands fell to her sides and curled into fists. It was the hardest thing in the world to let him set the pace when her very soul cried out that she possess him now. But there was an incredible sense of power in giving him free reign. And when she brushed his emotions and felt the overwhelming surge of his love for her, tears ran slowly down her cheeks.

"Don't you dare," he breathed. He began to kiss away her tears. "You'll make me tear up and then we'll spend all night crying about how much we've wanted to be together instead of actually being together."

She gave a hiccupping laugh. "You're so odd to me, Morgan, and yet so wonderful. I see why you led the Black Magi so well." She leaned forward and nuzzled his shoulder, loving how his scent seemed to burn her lungs.

Just as he was seriously considering the merits of tossing her on the bed and having his way with her (something she had no issues with), there was a loud and thunderous explosion that rocked the entire building.

The roof shook and a piece came down toward them. Jazz knocked Morgan to the floor and half shifted back to Dragon. Only her wings shifted forward and she used them to protect them both. Morgan could only stare. "I didn't know that was possible."

"Fourth tier Dragon Lords are the only ones who can, and even then, it takes at least two centuries of practice." She kept him safely covered until the land was done shaking and the ceiling was in no more danger of falling. "We wanted a room with a view, right?" She peered up at the holes over their heads.

He contemplated how she was sprawled over him and how the angle gave him a very enticing view of her supple breasts hidden behind her sleeveless top. "The view isn't half bad," he agreed.

"Morgan!" She wanted to be indignant but her sense of humor wouldn't let her. Everything about him was utterly perfect for her. With a sigh, she rested her head on his shoulder and shifted her wings away. "I'm crazy about you."

"It's mutual." He carefully sat up as she slid off him. "As much as I'd like to ignore that event and return to something far more important, we'd better find out what happened."

She could only sigh. His sense of honor and responsibility were going to be a pain in the ass. Still . . . it made the idea of making him forget everything all the more appealing. She slid closer and leaned up slightly to nibble on the edge of his ear. "Don't forget where we were."

"Trust me," his voice was thick with desire, "that's not likely to occur." He got to his feet then offered her a hand and pulled her up as well. Together they walked to the door then headed down the hall.

The innkeeper spotted them and said, "The Militia caught a member of the Elite. She ruptured her own power rather than tell them anything."

Morgan and Jazz both flinched. Among all the ways it was possible to kill yourself, rupturing your power was the most lethal—to you and everyone around you. It literally tore your power apart and detonated it like a firebomb. In killing those around you so quickly, you disrupted the flow in the land. A quake was one hundred percent assured in that situation.

"How many were killed?" Jazz asked quietly.

"Ten. Two Militia and eight bystanders." The innkeeper shook her head sadly. "I'm sure the Elite considers it a justified loss. After all, they lost one member, but ten Magi died."

"I'm not saying I want to see anyone else die," Morgan noted, "but if the Elite keeps up that attitude, they'll be gone soon. There's how many of them, and how many Magi?" He tucked his hands in his pockets. "I'd like to say that they're stupid enough to do it, but Soh is brilliant."

Jazz wrapped her arms around him and softly nuzzled his shoulder. "You want to fight them."

"Want to?" He shook his head. "No. Not really. Need to? Yes. If only for the sake of the children. As long as the Elite exists, they're in danger. The Magi won't recognize them, but Soh will."

The Kin nodded. "That's the opinion of the Kin and Dragons alike. We Kin are beginning to retreat back to our islands. Under normal circumstances we would ally with the Magi against the Elite. But the Magi are angry with us for siding with Chronicles. They would not accept our help."

Jazz snorted. "Hang themselves with their own rope!" she said derisively.

"Did you know your kind are spreading out across the lands?" the Kin asked her.

She stared. "No, I didn't. My kind as in Dragons, or Furies?"

"Furies. Seems that your Elders ordered the Furies to go out and look for any Chronicle they can possibly locate. Word reached them of the children. There is hope among the few who have felt their Chronicle's birth but not death."

She lowered her gaze. "It's such a shot in the dark. We don't know a Chronicle until we're directly in front of them. We can't track them, not even our own. It's why we stayed hidden away. It always felt so futile."

"If you do nothing, then you ensure nothing gets done," Morgan told her softly. He gathered her closer and buried his face in her hair. "Even if it's a one in a million chance, staying on the Isle made it a zero chance."

Her smile was wry. "Tell me you're going to confront the Elders with that. Please tell me. I want to bring the other Furies to watch."

He grinned. "I'll leave it to my cousin. She has had a much harder time of things than I, and she can be much more eloquent." His smile slowly faded, though, as he thought about things. "We need to find Tariah, and quickly." This time it was his smile that turned wry. "The sooner the better."

She very nearly growled but bit it back. She knew he was right, no matter how much she hated it. Damn it, she wanted him. She wanted to claim him as her own as the world had intended. If she didn't get a chance to taste every one of his lines, she thought she was going to go mad.

Suddenly grateful that his cloak was on the long side, he cleared his throat. She wasn't the only one going out of their mind. His hunger to touch and taste her was closer to a craving than ever before. But something inside . . . it told him that if they could resist it, then it wasn't time yet.

She knew he was probably right but still didn't like it. "Alright," she finally said. "Let's fly to Spectrum. We'll scope out a port city for information on the Elite and get a better idea of what they're up to. Then we'll try and track down Tariah."

He bent the few inches between their heights and kissed her lingeringly, curling his power around her in an equal caress. Her power curled around him in return and flowed between them endlessly.

They went down to the beach where there was room for her to change back into her Dragon form. Once she had, he climbed up onto her back and held on tightly as she took off across the sky. As he watched the ground rushing below them, he said thoughtfully, "I wonder how I'd look as a Dragon."

She chuckled. "I think you'd make a very handsome Dragon. Once you managed to transform properly, of course." She did a loop in the sky and thrilled to the sound of his laughter. He didn't laugh nearly often enough to suit her. His life had been too lonely, and too hard, for someone so young.

"But now I have you," he said softly. He pressed his lips gently to her neck as he leaned down to hold her tightly. It was as if the rest of his life no longer existed. He could barely remember how it had felt to not have her there. She filled the corners in his heart he hadn't known were empty.

"Keep up thoughts like that and I'll crash us." She flew a little faster, unafraid to push her limits when she had her Chronicle to feed from. It was such a wonderful experience that she knew she'd have to watch herself lest she become addicted. Then again . . . there were much worse addictions in life.

By the time they landed on the beach on the outskirts of Mirah, she knew she would definitely have to feed soon. Just turning back into Magi form tired her enough that she stumbled when she tried to take a step forward. She landed in Morgan's arms and smiled sheepishly. "Sorry."

"Don't be." He smiled. "I can carry you on my back if you want."

"I'll be fine." She leaned up to kiss him but stopped with her lips a breath away from his as she saw the Magi watching them. Several were armed with weapons. She instantly moved and put herself in front of Morgan defensively. Her entire body braced for battle. "Harm a hair on his head and I'll make you into a midnight snack."

The Magi were very hesitant to do or say anything. Truth be told, they had far bigger problems on their hands than the shock of a second Chronicle being alive. There was no mistaking that he was one. His lines were vivid in the setting sun, and they were matched by the lines on his partner. Because that meant she was a Fury and not just a Dragon, they knew she could level the town in a single swoop.

"We're not asking for shelter," Morgan said calmly. He put a hand on Jazz's shoulder in restraint. He didn't argue with her protecting him. He argued with her temper, which, he knew, she did indeed possess. Given the slightest provocation, she would flatten the Magi. "We just want to get some supplies."

"I guess we can let you do that," one man finally said. "Lately no one is sure what to think or do."

"Try living your whole life that way," Jazz muttered. Her narrowed eyes were nearly serpentine in their intensity.

The Magi were smarter than to provoke a creature that was bigger, faster, and stronger than them. They put their weapons away and went back to their village.

Morgan slid his arms around Jazz and rested his chin on her shoulder. "You're something amazing."

She hooked her arms back around his neck with a smile. "I don't like people threatening the man I love." With a sigh, she slowly released him. "Let's get some information. I presume that was what you really meant when you said supplies."

"It was. If they're too confused to do anything, I want to keep it that way." He started to say more when he felt the skin along the back of his neck crawling. Instinctively, his mind swept the area for the source of his unease. Almost instantly he picked up on the mind of another Magi.

Jazz sensed his unease and lifted her head to sniff the air lightly. Her nose flared as she caught the scent of someone near them. Normally she wouldn't have been concerned, but the scent carried the bite of corrupted power. It was a scent impossible to mistake. It came across as bitter, infested, and disgusting.

Both Dragoons turned in the same instant. Their powers merged seamlessly into a single pulsing blast of Air and Soil that streaked across the beach and into the shadowy area behind a large stack of crates and barrels. The blast lit up the area briefly as it struck a shield but the Magi stood no chance against a Dragoon team. He toppled over.

Morgan nearly gagged as the fully rotten scent of corrupted power filled the air. He shoved aside the disgust and went around the edge of the crates to find the source. Somehow it didn't shock him to find a Black Magi Elite lying on the floor in a heap with blood seeping from the wound on his chest.

What was shocking was the blood itself. It was a sickly shade of yellow. Morgan was very careful not to touch the man as he stepped closer. "What are you after?" he asked quietly. "How can you think to stand against so many when you are so few?"

The Elite looked at him from dull eyes and gave a gurgling laugh that made blood stain his lips. "You don't know? The Dragons aren't the only ones with a hidden isle."

Jazz took a swift breath. "You're mad!" she said sharply. "The power hidden there . . . it will destroy you before you can use it! It's not for Magi to tangle with!" There was no response, and the sense of power died entirely. She could only curse.

Morgan grabbed her arm quickly. "Jazz! What are you both talking about?" he demanded.

She looked at him sadly. "The lost land of the Chronicles. The Chronicles had their own isle once. It was where they and the Furies retreated to when the Magi came after them. It was there that the massacre took place."

He took a sharp breath. The power that would be imbedded in the very land of such a place would be immense. Likely powerful enough to rip apart the very world. If Soh found the land and claimed it . . . "No," he said fiercely. "We won't let it happen!"

She went into his arms and held on tight. "It could tear you and Tariah apart if you tried to claim the power for your own. I refuse to let you even try!" But even as she said it, she saw the answer inside him. There was no other choice. If they didn't find it first, then they would be destroyed anyway. "Why does it have to be you?" she asked achingly.

"Maybe it's the destiny of the name Chronis." He smiled a little wryly. "Seems Tariah and I are both burdened by it."

She held him tighter and buried her nose against his neck. "No matter the burdens you carry, I will be right there beside you." She lifted a hand to touch his chest and savored the throb of his lines beneath her hand. "Where do we go?" she asked simply. "I will follow wherever you lead."

He closed his eyes. Almost immediately he felt the burn in his lines. *Northwest.* "Northwest," he murmured, his eyes unfocused as they opened. "It's almost like I can see the map in my mind now. Somewhere to the northwest is where we'll find Tariah. We need to find her before we do anything else."

"Then let's rest tonight and set out tomorrow." She held tight to his hand as they began walking down the beach slowly. The sun was setting around them and the moons were steadily beginning to rise. Neither wanted to be near the town, not when it still smelled like the taint of the Elite.

They selected a place to camp almost an hour away from the town. Morgan watched in fascination as Jazz used her powers to craft the sand into a sturdy tent structure for them. "I can tell you're a master of your craft," he said.

She shot him a grin. "I've had time to practice." Her smile faded as she saw him sitting down and staring across the ocean. She walked over to sit beside him, and she leaned against his shoulder. "How did you know he was there?" she asked softly.

"I felt a warning in my lines and used my mind to find his." He fell over onto his back on the sand and tucked his hands under his head. "I've always had stronger than average mental skills, but that was new. I assume it's my Dragoon ability."

"Telepathy, yes." She smiled. "Mine must be Ultravision. I tried Telepathy and Telekinesis both as we were leaving the village but had no success."

"What's Ultravision?" he asked curiously.

"I can touch objects and see their history." She closed her eyes. "It's not the easiest of skills from what I've heard, but I can handle it." Her eyes opened again and her heart skipped a beat as she saw the intensity on his face as he looked up at her. Hunger prowled through her body with the suddenness of a storm. Hunger for his power. Hunger for his skin and his heat.

He slowly sat up and pulled her closer. Her hands flattened against his chest, and his power rose instantly to the surface as a soft white aura. "This time," he said huskily, "don't stop." His fingers threaded through her hair. "Never stop."

Trembling with the force of the need inside, she began to remove his cloak for him. "You won't be needing this." As she tossed it aside, she gave a stifled yelp as she found herself lifted into his arms as he stood. Unnerved, she clutched his shoulders. "Put me down."

He grinned wickedly. "You don't weigh much in this form. I won't drop you."

She gave a shaky laugh. "I've discovered a fear of heights." She grabbed him tighter as he ducked into the tent. "In case you didn't notice, I've never been carried before." As deep as her trust was in him, her heart didn't stop fluttering until he had set her on her feet once more.

His amusement was clear, and she gave a little growl. Her foot hooked his ankles and dumped him onto the blankets she had made for a bed. He only lifted a brow at her, and she dropped to her knees to start removing his tunic. When she discovered it would take too long, her power swept out in a green wave that dissolved the material back to sand.

He could only shudder and hold her closer as her mouth fastened hotly to his shoulder. He couldn't even tell the difference in the emotions inside him. It was all tied up and tangled together. All he could be certain of was that he was going to go mad if he didn't get to have her soon.

She eagerly fed on his power, her lips trailing hot forays across the lines on his chest. They tingled wherever she touched them, and knowing it was her power that made them was thrilling. She felt drunk on him. She slowly slid up his body to kiss him, her fingers burying in his hair to hold him closer.

His fingers burrowed in her hair as he returned the ravenous kiss. He could not seem to get enough of her taste. Her body moved temptingly against his and he groaned. His body twisted and he rolled to pin her beneath him. He cuffed her hands beside her head and nipped at her lower lip. "Gotcha," he said thickly.

She tugged lightly at her hands but his grip was firm. She knew she could get free with raw strength but . . . she didn't want to. It was a heady power to know she was his first. To know she was the one who would teach him what it meant to be an adult. With a very feminine smile curving her lips, she let her power dissolve her clothes entirely to leave her naked in his arms. "Need a map?" Her voice was both husky and teasing.

His mouth went dry. "I have one." To prove it, he bent his head and ran his lips softly over the lines curving across her collarbone and down over her chest like a ribbon or a river. Little touches of his tongue soothed his need for her taste and made them both shudder. "I'm still learning," he murmured against the curve of her breast. "Tell me if I get it wrong."

She could only moan softly as his lips claimed the tip of her breast and tugged so strongly that her back arched in raw pleasure. "I'm not seeing that being a problem," she managed to say. Belatedly, it dawned on her that he was keeping his emotions tangled with hers; he knew *precisely* how she felt and could track down the places that gave the most pleasure. As his lips found a particularly sensitive place near her stomach, she whimpered, "Cheater."

"Cheater? How so?" He released her hands to have the freedom of his own. He slowly ran them over her supple skin, memorizing her every curve. Deliberately tempting her, he skimmed his knuckles across the skin of her stomach then slowly lower.

She opened her mouth to respond but could only suck in a sharp breath as his hand slipped between her legs. She clutched desperately at his shoulders for balance in a world that was melting around her. "I'm going to get you for this," she gasped out as he continued to stroke her teasingly.

He had no doubt about that, but right then he was too consumed with the delight of learning her body. He didn't need to be experienced to know that what they had was special. That this was something he would have never found with Merideth. This was his Fury. She was everything he would ever want. "Jazz," he said thickly, his body trembling with need as he felt how hot and wet she was. "Is there a word for this?" he asked. "It's not love. It can't be."

She framed his face in her hands and drew him down. "Dragons call it *ishke*," she murmured against his lips. She kissed him deeply until it was nothing but a tangle of tongues and lips. "What're you waiting for?" she asked when she released him. "Hurry before I go out of my mind."

"I'm still . . ." He gave a husky laugh as he felt the rest of his clothes dissolve, ". . . dressed. Never mind then."

She nipped at his jaw lightly. "You should have mentioned them sooner." If she had ever seen anything more beautiful than Morgan's unclothed figure, she didn't remember it. She wanted to pet and kiss him from head to heels and back again. And why shouldn't she?

She twisted quickly and tumbled him over. Her hands pinned his to the ground in a sensual payback. With a hunger she was becoming familiar with, she raced her lips over his face and shoulders. He trembled underneath her and made her feel powerful in a way she had never felt before. She lifted her head. "How did I go four hundred years without knowing this?" she whispered.

His eyes were like silver coins as he looked up at her. "I wasn't there." Her grip loosened, and he wrapped his arms around her as he rolled again. He couldn't wait any longer. He needed to be inside her and finally erase the loneliness that had haunted him for years.

She curled her legs around his hips, anchoring him from leaving her even if he had wanted to try. Her breath caught and lodged in her chest as she felt his hard arousal slowly pressing into her body. Ripples of pleasure radiated from the contact, and it felt as if he was sinking into her very soul as well. Desperately she twisted under him, tangling her emotions to his, wanting to share everything.

He shuddered but didn't move any faster. He wanted to savor every second, to memorize everything about her. Only when he was buried to the hilt inside her did the tension ease from his heart. Finally. Here, at last. He lowered his head to kiss her deeply. His Fury. Finally they were together.

She wound her arms around his shoulders and held him as tightly as she could. She couldn't separate her feelings. Desperation for an end to the ceaseless pleasure. Hunger to feel him as close as she could. Savage possessiveness in knowing that he was hers at last. Her Chronicle. Finally she had claimed him.

Their powers flowed together and between them in an endless loop as he began to drive in and out of her welcoming heat with instinct and desire fueling him. Ecstasy hovered, promised, and lured. And, as he felt her emotions swirling around him, sharing her deepest feelings, it swept over him hotly unlike anything he had dared imagine.

She felt his emotions even as he felt hers and the sensation was too much. Ecstasy swept over her, each wave rippling hotter and more powerful than the next. She would have cried out with it but his mouth sealed hers and she could only sink into the kiss helplessly, replete at last.

He didn't know how much time passed before he felt her stir beneath him. Their emotions were still tangled together and so were their powers. He softly curled his mind around hers in another caress. "Am I too heavy?" he asked into her hair.

She sighed softly and slid her hands over his damp shoulders. It was all she had the energy to do. "Don't move," she murmured, her voice still huskier than usual. "I've never had a blanket this wonderful."

His arms tightened around her for a moment then he rolled to the side and onto the blanket. Before she could voice a protest, he tugged her closer and enfolded her in his arms. "That's better. I think even a Dragon might have trouble breathing with something bigger than her sleeping on top of her."

"I'm resilient." She caught the edge of a blanket and tugged it over them. Contented, she sighed and snuggled closer against his body. Her hand automatically lifted to cover his heart, and she realized in surprise that some of the lines were hotter than normal.

She looked closer and discovered that almost a third of the lines from his left side and across his chest were darker than before. Yet it wasn't a solid darkening. The darkness flowed and changed like light rippling over water. She could literally see his power flowing through his lines. "It must mean that you've completed a part of your journey."

"You sound surprised." He tugged her closer once more. His eyes closed as he smiled. "I would think claiming your Fury is the most important part of a Chronicle's journey."

Unexpectedly, he felt a mental hand reaching out toward him. He reached for it in return, deeply curious. It reminded him of a night some time back. He had been dreaming, and had felt someone reach out to him. He had been *sure* that he had found someone that he hadn't seen in a painfully long time. The tie had broken before he could complete it, and he had just chalked it up to an odd dream.

This was no dream. He touched the other hand, and their fingers meshed. Their minds and their powers meshed in turn, and his eyes widened slightly as he recognized at last who he was touching. *Tariah?*

Morgan! Tariah was no less stunned. *But . . . how?*

"Telepaths," Jazz muttered as she buried her nose against Morgan's shoulder. She felt disgruntled. She didn't like someone else able to touch Morgan's power even if it was his 'cousin.' She couldn't stop the possessive feelings anymore than she could stop breathing.

You're a Telepath too, aren't you? Morgan asked Tariah.

I am. Her mental voice warmed. *I see her inside you. It's nice, isn't it?*

It's wonderful. He could see Dominic just as thoroughly inside her and see his disgruntlement matching Jazz's. *Welcome to being an adult*, he thought warmly, knowing that only the completion of their bond would result in such a merger between Tariah and Dominic.

I beat you into adulthood, actually.

By a few hours.

Who's counting a few hours? There was a long silence then she asked softly, *What do we do, Morgan? I can sense it inside you, that there's something more going on.*

It's bad, Tariah. Where are you right now?

On an island outside of Spectrum. You?

Near Mirah. Can Dominic safely bring you here tomorrow? It's a port so he can fly around the ocean edge.

He can. We'll get there tomorrow. Together we can do something, I'm sure of it.

I'm sorry to drag you into my battle.

Her voice softened but was no less firm. *Soh has hurt two men that I am honored to call my brother. It is as much my battle now as yours. I'll fight beside you.*

Sleep well, little sister.

Sleep well, my brother.

Their mental fingers slid apart but he could still see and sense the path that would lead him back to her mind again, no matter how far apart they were. He couldn't understand how the connection even existed. It couldn't be merely because they were both Telepaths. "I can't understand it," he said quietly.

Jazz regarded him quietly. "Perhaps," she said softly, "it is not merely coincidence that you share the same name. You suspected you were related, but I think it is more than speculation. There is blood shared between you, somehow strong enough to make you connect like twins."

"I wouldn't argue with that." He smoothed a hand slowly over her arm before gathering her closer and burying his face in her hair. "She hid it, but I think something happened to her that shook her down to her soul."

"Dominic will be her strength, as I will be yours." She leaned up to kiss him softly. "Tomorrow we will meet up with them and we will decide what to do. Tonight is just you and I. There is no Soh, there are no Magi. Just us." Her hands framed his face tenderly. "Tomorrow will come soon enough."

He held her closer, more than willing to let her help him forget. Forget his enemy, forget a world that hated what he was. Forget that, somewhere inside, her words were stirring up something he felt he had to understand. There was a promise he needed to keep. He was sure of it.

Part Three

Chronis

Chapter Twenty-Two

Tariah was still feeling slightly confused even after she and Morgan had stopped communicating. In her mind, she could see the line that would lead back to him. She hadn't even known she could reach out to him in the first place. She had been lying in Dominic's arms, wishing for some evidence that Morgan was fine, and then suddenly she had felt as if she could see him.

"I don't understand it," she said softly. She curled more firmly against Dominic's side, her hand resting over his heart. "I thought only Linked mates could touch one another's power like that."

He tucked his hands under his head and contemplated the stars in the sky overhead. He still felt slightly disgruntled. He didn't like it that someone else could touch his Chronicle's power. The only consolation he could find was in the knowledge that it had likely been Morgan who had touched Tariah on the night before they had entered Prismatic. "I think it's because you are related," he said thoughtfully after a moment. He turned onto his side and draped an arm across her waist to hold her close. "It was just assumption before but now it seems to be more than that. Do you know the legend of the first Chronicles?"

She smiled. "Elder Juniper told me. I always found it comforting to think I shared their name." Her heart gave a dull thud as she felt what was inside him. "You think I and Morgan are . . . are descended of the twins?"

"I'm almost certain." He rolled and tucked her underneath him. He lowered his head and began to sniff along her shoulder. "Stop wiggling," he muttered. "I'm checking something."

"It tickles!"

"And you're distracting me." He closed his eyes and breathed in deeply, taking her scent into his lungs. This time it wasn't just because he loved the way her skin always seemed to smell like the elusive fragrance of water in the desert. This time he was looking for the trace of Dragon that would be in her blood if she was a descendant.

Because it was so faint, it took him a minute before he was able to pinpoint the slightly sharp tone of Dragon blood. "There you are," he murmured. He softly nuzzled against her, his tongue tasting the curve of her shoulder. "There's some Dragon in you. *Very* faint so it's at least a few thousand years removed."

She shivered as his lips trailed up to her ear. She had stopped marveling at how swiftly her body and power responded to him. She was simply enjoying it. There was an ache in her muscles that she couldn't help but savor. "So it's possible?" she asked softly.

"I'd have to check Morgan's scent to see if it is the same." He grimaced wryly. "Somehow the idea of sniffing at him doesn't appeal as much. I'll leave it to Jazz." He smiled suddenly. "I'm glad they found each other. Do you suppose the translocation dropped him at her feet?"

"If it did, we'll have to thank Soh." Her silver eyes hardened suddenly. "Before we kill him, of course."

He slowly smoothed a hand up and down her arm. "So fierce." He bent his head and kissed her softly, savoring the freedom to touch and caress her at his will. All the frustration he had endured since meeting her had been worth it. Everything was worth it, if only to look into her eyes and touch her power and know she was his. "Will you let me claim Fury Right?" he asked softly.

She tilted her head slightly. "Fury Right?"

"The right of a Fury to kill anyone who threatens their Chronicle. I'm sure Jazz has claimed this right herself, and I seek to claim it as well." He nuzzled her gently then rolled onto his back and tugged her over until she was lying on top of him. "We can fight over who eats him later."

She buried her face against his shoulder and giggled helplessly. "Oh, will you stop it! You wouldn't eat him!" She couldn't quite stop the comical image, however, of Dominic in Dragon form and roasting Soh on a spit like a wild hog.

He began to laugh. "Where do you get these ideas?" He buried his hands in her tangled hair and tugged her down for a long kiss. When he finally released her, he instead rolled them up within a blanket and kept her tucked snuggly against him. "Time for sleep, *ishke*. Tomorrow will be a long day."

She gave a contented sigh and nestled closer. "I really shouldn't get used to being babied like this. I'll get lazy and spoiled. Remind me when this is all over that I owe you some spoiling in return."

He smiled and buried his nose in her hair. "Deal." With a sigh of his own, he closed his eyes and let go, his mind instinctively seeking hers and weaving them together so that even in their dreams they weren't parted.

The sun was creeping over the horizon when Tariah awoke. With a long stretch, she sat up and looked down at her sleeping lover. The fierceness that was so innately a part of him as a Dragon, even in Magi form, was softer when he was asleep. He had been through a lot for her, and the idea of spoiling him rotten was deeply appealing. She couldn't carry him around and threaten to eat people who were mean to him, but she could do something no one else could.

She carefully slipped out of his arms and fetched her clothes. Once dressed, she began to silently slip through the foliage of the island. Some kind of fruit or food was bound to grow or live there; there were few things in the world that weren't edible with a little effort. She lucked out and found a bush laden with dark purple berries ripe enough to bend the branches under their weight.

She picked a few handfuls and carried them back to camp. Dominic was still asleep, and she smiled. She couldn't wait to tease him. He took such delight in teasing her about being a 'weaker being' that she wanted to savor knowing she had outlasted him at *something*.

The berries weren't ready as they were. She left them to simmer in some water over the campfire then headed back through the trees toward the closest beach. They weren't actually far from it. Dominic had been in a hurry to camp and hadn't taken them very far inland.

She thought about things as she hunted through the sand for crustaceans or clams. Yesterday morning, she had been ready to fall apart. She was fairly sure that Dominic was the only reason she hadn't detonated her own power. But now . . . she wasn't so worried.

She had her Fury. That was worth fighting everything to keep. She wasn't a child anymore. She was an adult in every way. And she was a Chronicle. The world had made her. Why did she have to argue her right to existence? Why did the children?

Of course, it would have been easier if the Dragons had been looking for all of them all along. She understood their feelings, but she was beginning to be annoyed with everyone's 'we're doomed' mentality. She was going to give the Elders a piece of her mind.

She returned to the campsite with the clams she had dug up and shelled them easily; they weren't much different from desert crabs, really. She added the meat to the berries and let it continue to cook. She ground the shell down to fine powder and mixed it with ice to make a cold drink. Crustacean shells made some of the tastiest drinks on the world if mixed with ice. She took the cup with her and went over to kneel beside Dominic.

She touched his shoulder softly with her free hand and lightly curled her power around his to coax him awake. "Dominic?" she said softly. "It's morning."

"Mrmph." He rolled over onto his stomach. "I'd rather sleep." His nose twitched and he lifted his head curiously. "What's that scent?" His mouth was watering from the decadent smell alone.

She smiled and waved the cup she was holding. "This. I made breakfast."

It took his sleepy brain a few moments to register what she had said. When it did, the sweetness of the gesture overwhelmed him. It was such a simple thing, and really not important compared with everything else she gave him, but the fact that she had done something just for him moved him deeper than anything. "You didn't have to."

"I wanted to." She put the cup aside as he sat up. When he reached for her, she went into his arms eagerly and lifted her own to wind around his neck. "You act as if I brought you jewels."

"You brought me you. That's worth much more than jewels." He lowered his head and kissed her lingeringly. A tremor went through his powerful body as he heard her contented sigh. How in the name of the Underrealm had he deserved this? He couldn't think of anything he'd done that was great enough to earn his Chronicle.

"You were just lucky," she teased.

He laughed and hugged her fiercely. "You're a brat." He released her and held her comfortably on his lap as he reached for the drink she had set aside. He sniffed at it but couldn't quite make out what she had put in it.

She hid a smile. "Chicken."

Incensed, he took a drink. The flavor seemed to explode on his tongue with so many nuances he couldn't catch them all. It was potentially one of the most delicious things he had ever had other than Tariah herself. "By the moons, woman, how'd you do that?" He peered at the cup.

She grinned happily. "I told you I was a good cook. It's made from ground crater clam shells and ice."

"*Shell?*" His eyes widened.

"Most people don't know the shell is that good since you normally can't eat it. But if you grind it down with ice until it's a fine dust, it's perfect as a drink." She stretched then slid off his lap to go check the simmering soup. "The meat from the clams is over here, mixed with some fruit."

He scooted closer to sniff at the reed pot she had made and the smell was even better than before. On a groan, he fell onto his back. "Yes, I foresee myself getting fat and lazy within a year or two. That and I'll never get rid of my family and neighbors. You'll need to open a restaurant or something."

Her flash of longing was almost hidden before he truly felt it, but he still saw it as it rippled through her heart. He sat up in surprise and stared at her. "Where did you hide that?" he murmured. When he went looking, it took up an amazing amount of her deepest heart. She had locked away such a fierce desire in a way that even he hadn't spotted. Her years of hiding her emotions had produced habits she couldn't break overnight.

She turned her face away. Her cheeks were slightly pink. "It's just a daydream."

He cupped her cheek tenderly and turned her face back. He kissed her gently. "And you're going to have it." He smiled. "You can have your restaurant on the Isle, and then someday you can have one in Prismatic, also known as Magi central."

"But Magi would never buy from a Chronicle!" she protested.

He grinned. "*Ishke*, we're immortal. We can wait them out. In a thousand years, they might have collectively gotten over it."

Her mind whirled. She was twenty years old. It felt like a long time already. She could barely fathom living for a thousand years or forever. But the idea of being with Dominic for all of those years was something even more tempting than her dreams. "Okay," she said. "Deal."

After breakfast, Dominic could only sigh contentedly. His Chronicle was one hell of a cook. In a playful burst of energy, he caught her around the waist and tumbled her down onto the grass. He grinned as he heard her laughing. She laughed more freely than when they had met, but there was still something solemn in her eyes. "You're too melancholy. It breaks my heart."

She lifted a hand and smoothed her fingers over his face. She couldn't get enough of touching him. "I don't mean to be. It's just frustrating to be kept from having what I want. All I ever wanted was a place to live freely. And now I have to fight for it when others get it without asking."

He nuzzled her hand then lowered his head and kissed her softly, lingering over her flavor and rubbing his power over hers to comfort and soothe. "We'll make it, *ishke*. I promise."

He got to his feet and pulled her up as well. They had already tided up the camp area and they were free to leave whenever they wanted. He walked a few steps away then turned into his Dragon form. They would fly along the coast until they were outside Mirah. At that time they would land and disguise themselves once more.

Tariah, as she climbed up onto his back, remarked musingly, "Maybe I'll try a Kin Faerie form this time. At least then I'd have a *reason* to be short."

He gave a crack of laughter and flew straight up into the air just to enjoy hearing her delighted shriek. "Look at it as more evidence you and Morgan must be related. He's short too."

178

She beamed. "That's true." Content with that, she wrapped her arms around his neck and held on as they flew swiftly across the sky.

Though the flight would have normally taken the better portion of a day, if not a whole day, Dominic pushed himself to go faster. Anticipation hummed inside his body. Now that his Chronicle was an adult, there was no need to hold himself back when he fed on her power. "I think I'm beginning to enjoy this Dragoon thing."

"Beginning to!" She lightly pinched his ear in retaliation and listened in satisfaction to his yelp. "That implies you weren't happy with me until you made love to me."

"That is not true," he scolded her. "You know damned well that I've been happy with you no matter what. But my patience was wearing thin. Do you have any idea how badly I wanted you?"

"I do." She smoothed a hand over his neck. She had always seen his emotions and how volatile they were for her. She could see the same inside herself and she loved it. She could barely remember the long years of restraining her emotions now that she had so thoroughly reveled in them. "Now you can have me whenever you want."

"You do know how to tempt a man." He began to angle down toward the shore as he saw the town in the distance.

"Just you." She waited until he had landed before sliding off his back. She caught her balance easily and shot him a smug look as he turned to Magi form. "Now who is a weaker being, mighty Dragon?"

He scooped her up in his arms and swung her in a giddy circle. "No one I know." He caught her close for a long and drugging kiss then slowly released her lips. "I love you, Tariah," he murmured. "It's such a paltry word Magi use, but it's the only one I can seem to find."

"We'll have to make up our own word." She rested her head on his shoulder for long moments then reluctantly released him as he put her down on her feet.

It was amazingly easy this time to reach for his majiks and bend them to a Kin form. This time, instead of bending them the way she always had for Kin Elves, she bent them the other way, instinctively assuming that would result in Kin Faerie.

She shortly proved herself right as she felt her body suddenly become exceptionally smaller. Dominic suddenly looked a whole lot bigger since he had opted for SunKin Elf. He was also grinning, something that made her wary. "What?" she asked carefully.

He gently plucked her out of the air and carried her over to the edge of the ocean where she could be able to see her reflection. Delight spread through her when she noticed her wings. She really did look like Daylar's sister now; her wings were the same cloudy that his original wings had been. Instead of being white, however, they were closer to a silver shade that matched her eyes.

Her figure also, oddly, seemed lusher. She considered her bust size. "You know, proportionately, Kin have better figures. But I refuse to tell Sparkle. She'll *never* let me live it down."

Dominic chuckled and placed her gently on his shoulder. She sat down comfortably and crossed her ankles to keep her balance as he began heading for the city.

Mirah was smaller as a port town than Refraction was but it was still of considerable size. Neither Dragoon felt uncomfortable as they entered the town because they now knew their disguise was good enough to fool all but the Kin. Or other Dragons, Dominic noticed with surprise, as he spotted a Fury having lunch at a restaurant.

Tariah was no less surprised. "I wonder why he's here," she murmured. "Can we ask safely without giving ourselves away?"

"We can try." He walked over to the table where the Fury was and touched his ears as he bowed. "Sorry we're late," he said by way of greeting.

The Fury quirked one brow slightly in surprise then amusement filled his eyes. "Well, I wasn't in a hurry," he said as he got to his feet. "Let's get out of the sun. Your partner looks a little faint. MoonKin don't like the sun as much as their cousins after all."

Tariah said nothing but inside she was a little awed. She didn't need to see inside Dominic's mind to know she was in the presence of a Dragon Elder. The man walking beside them was so powerful that it couldn't be muffled. She felt it as a ripple of Fire along her skin and knew he was another Fire Fury.

Once they were out of sight and hearing of the Magi, the Fury said dryly, "Dominic, you make a fine SunKin, but I have to say that any attempt you make at being a pacifist would fail."

Dominic restrained an urge to stick out his tongue. No matter how old he was, Xander always managed to make him feel like a whelp again. "You're one to talk." With a smile, he gestured to Tariah. "This is my Chronicle."

Tariah stood and folded her wings around herself as she bowed gracefully, naturally adopting the Fae form of greeting without thinking about it. "Tariah Chronis, Water Chronicle." She smiled. "Naturally, of course."

"Naturally." The other man bowed just as gracefully. "Xander Journe, Fire Fury." His lips quirked. "An Elder, as I'm sure you've felt." Sadness suddenly darkened his eyes. "Well . . . for the time being."

Dominic went very still. "You felt her?" he asked quietly.

"Almost ten years ago. I just didn't speak of it." Xander turned his gaze toward the sun in the distance. "I wasn't going to speak of it until too late. I didn't want to make others suffer. I've lived so long after all, and I'm the only Fury Elder we have. But when I heard of the children . . ."

Tariah suddenly thought of little Jayda and her distinctly Water presence. She said nothing. She didn't want to get Xander's hopes up if she was wrong. "Why are you off the Isle? Because of the children?"

"Yes. Word reached us." He smiled. "You're making some serious waves, little Dragon. We heard of the children from the Kin who have been helping you. The Elder Council decided it was time to send us Furies out to hopefully locate them, or any others."

"It took them long enough to figure that out!" Tariah complained. "Any idiot can see that doing nothing means nothing gets done!"

Xander's eyes widened. Then, slowly, a grin began to curve his lips. "Dominic," he said, "when she takes on the council, I want a word-for-word description of the event. I'd happily be witness to it if I could."

Dominic laughed as he felt Tariah's sudden chagrin for speaking in such a way to an Elder. "Gladly." He offered a hand that Xander took and held tightly. "Swift winds to you, Xander. I hope you find her soon." He too had thought of Jayda, but was keeping his silence for the same reason.

Xander headed back to his meal, and the two Dragoons headed toward the inn down the road. It wasn't hard to tell that Morgan had been by at some point; Magi were still whispering about seeing a second Chronicle. The general opinion was one of high confusion. The good guys had become the enemy, and the enemy had become an ally.

After getting a room, the Dragoons headed downstairs to where it was located. Dominic shut the door and locked it with a Dragon seal only another Dragon could undo. Only Jazz would actually do so since she was the only one who would have reason.

Tariah wasn't stupid. She landed on the floor before unbending the majiks to return herself and Dominic to their natural forms. If she had gone back to normal while flying, she might have crashed onto the floor. She really didn't trust her sense of scale or depth perception.

She had just given a long stretch when he swooped her up into his arms and tumbled her down onto the bed. She laughed happily and threw her arms around him fiercely. "No matter what has happened, having you makes it all worthwhile!"

He froze for a moment then his eyes closed as emotion welled inside. His eyes glittered with unshed tears as he opened them and met her gaze. He lowered his head until their lips were barely touching and held his breath as her power surged to the front and covered her with its soft blue aura. There was nothing more beautiful than water in a desert.

He pressed his lips to her shoulder and fed from her power there. It was even stronger now and hit his system like a shot of rich wine. Hungrily he trailed his lips up her neck and nibbled on the edge of her ear, listening in delight as her breath hitched. Deliberately, he tangled their emotions together and rubbed his power along hers.

Happily seduced, she returned the caress and lifted her hands to thread her fingers through his hair. She lightly rubbed his scalp in a way she knew drove him crazy and he shuddered. Her delighted laugh was cut short as his mouth covered hers demandingly, and his tongue surged past her parted lips to drink her flavor and power all at one time.

She whimpered as pleasure surged through her body. She eagerly ran her hands over his chest and felt a thrill as his lines tingled her palms. "I love how you feel," she murmured when he released her lips. "It's my power that makes your lines. I hadn't imagined how possessive it would make me feel."

His eyes glittered with male satisfaction. "Good." He bent his head and took her lips again, his need for her power appeased but his hunger for the rest of her was as strong as ever.

The door opened behind them. "Whoops," a woman's voice said, humor in her tone. "We're interrupting."

"Considering what he went through," was Morgan's dry response, "I'm inclined to feel even more guilty than normal."

Tariah immediately began to wiggle to get free, and Dominic released her reluctantly. Despite being disgruntled at the interruption, he smiled when he saw Morgan standing in the doorway with the familiar form of Jazz. He was very glad to be right. "Swift journeys, Jazz."

181

She smiled. "And the same to you, Dominic."

Tariah leapt off the bed and rushed across the room. She threw her arms around Morgan and held on with a strength that was almost surprising. He caught her just as close, something inside his heart and soul finally relaxing now that he knew she was alive and well. Her relief was no less deep, and their Furies shared a speculative look over their heads.

"I was so scared!" Tariah said into Morgan's shoulder. "When I saw the sanctuary . . ." She shuddered.

"It wasn't exactly fun for me either." He held her tighter then released her slowly. He searched her eyes. "I saw it when I touched your mind, and I can see it now. What happened? Something weighs on you."

Jazz shut the door behind them and sealed it in the same way Dominic had. "If it has to do with Soh, I claim seniority for killing him." She met Dominic's eyes. "But you are more than welcome to break his neck as long as you don't actually kill him."

"Gladly." He held out his arms and gathered Tariah close as she crossed back over to him. He gently smoothed a hand down her hair. "Essentially," he said as calmly as he could, "we witnessed the death of the Magi's king. He asked Tariah to stop the Elite and save the world." Morgan cursed softly. "That's a nice thing to ask the person you've been trying to kill!"

He sighed and held Jazz tighter when she wrapped her arms around him to comfort. "Well, it connects with what we've discovered. The Elite *have* to be stopped."

Jazz looked at Dominic. "They want the hidden isle."

He shook his head quickly. "They're insane. No Magi could control that." His heart gave a dull thud as he realized what would need to be done. "No," he said. "I don't like it. It could kill them both."

"As I said but . . ." She looked up at Morgan sadly. "He was right about one thing. If the Elite aren't stopped, we're all dead anyway."

Tariah frowned. "Someone tell me what we're talking about."

"There's an isle," Morgan said quietly. "Where the Chronicles used to live with their Furies. It was where the final massacre took place."

Her eyes widened. "The power in the land there would be immense and highly unstable! Any Magi would be torn apart if they tried to take command." She took a sharp breath. "That's why Soh wants the children. To let a Chronicle take the power and use it for him." Her hands curled into fists at her sides. "We'll get it first."

Morgan held out a hand and she laced their fingers together. "Are you sure?" he said quietly. "I was already intending to try but I wouldn't ask it of you. You've been through enough."

"And so have you." She shook her head. "I'm not going to run away. We should go after the Elite at their source and try to take them out. If we don't succeed there, then we can go after the children and the isle. Whichever we find first will keep the isle out of Soh's reach."

"That was my thought as well."

"So the Elite are gathering in the north," Dominic said quietly. "Do either of you know where in the north?"

"Well, there's only one other land in the north," Tariah said.

Morgan's eyes flickered. "Glacia. I haven't been back in five years. I'm sure they've heard of my leading the original Black Magi but . . . I'm not sure how to face them. Especially not my parents."

"They knew you were a Chronicle, right?" she asked softly. When he nodded, she smiled. "Then, if anything, they'll be glad that you have your Fury now. It sounds like they were like my parents were." Her voice broke then steadied. "They would have been happy just to know I was happy finally."

Dominic slid his arms around her waist and rested his chin on top of her head. "It sounds like we will be heading for Glacia. We can fly around the coast then across the ocean when it is safe. Let's not cause Spectrum any more trouble than it can handle."

"Agreed." Jazz pulled Morgan along with her as she headed for the door. "Let them be now. I'm hungry."

Tariah fluttered her lashes at her brother. "You'll get used to it," she told him cheerfully. "I've decided it's a Fury thing."

"I do have one advantage over mine though," he noted. He caught Jazz around the waist and tossed her over his shoulder. "See?"

Tariah considered that. "You're right," she decided. "I can't do that."

Dominic was laughing too hard to say anything. Jazz just sighed and propped her elbow on her Chronicle's back. "Dominic," she said, "I envy you."

As the door shut behind them, Dominic walked over to seal it once more. He was still chuckling. "I think there's always balance in a good relationship," he said. "After all, I can out power you and . . ." He turned around as he spoke and his voice trailed off as he saw Tariah had already begun to remove her clothes. His mouth went dry. "And you," he managed to say, "can have me at your mercy with a smile."

She was indeed smiling. Feeling wonderfully smug and feminine and desired, she walked over to her Fury and leaned up against him to wind her arms around his neck. "I can?" she asked teasingly. "I can have anything I want?"

"Anything at all." He lifted her and carried her toward their bed. His pulse was pounding. The ideas in her mind were interesting to say the least. "Where do you come up with these things?"

Her smile turned into a grin. "Morgan."

"Morgan!" He stared at her in shock.

She couldn't help but laugh. "Well, that's what you get for having a Chronicle who can touch the mind of her brother." She leaned up and nibbled on his ear. "You'll have to deal with it now."

He had no objections to that, but he had to wonder if she realized she had stopped calling Morgan her cousin. Something was very odd about these two Chronicles, and he couldn't help but wonder if it was related to the name both carried. Ah, well. It wasn't worth thinking about right then. The answers would come with time.

Chapter Twenty-Three

It was almost evening when the two Dragoon pairs met up again in the lobby. Morgan took one look at his sister and burst into laughter. She wrinkled up her nose and waved a fist threateningly. "What're you laughing at?"

He plucked her out of the air and studied her with dancing eyes. She made an adorable little SunKin Faerie. "I wasn't expecting this. How did you do it?"

"I used Dominic's majiks." She smiled. "You could do it too, using Jazz's."

He was instantly interested. "Really?"

Jazz smiled. "We'll practice when we get a chance. After a while you'll be able to do it easily." She smirked as she looked at Dominic. "Not quite brave enough to become a Fae, whelp?"

His ears twitched in annoyance. "You're only two hundred years older than me. Don't call me a whelp." He took Tariah back from Morgan and settled her on his shoulder. "We've been disguising ourselves while in town even though the Magi have been ordered not to attack us. It's just . . . uncomfortable."

Morgan looked to where some Magi were whispering behind their hands when they saw his lines. "Tell me about it."

Tariah's gaze lowered for a moment then she flew off Dominic's shoulder and landed on the floor. It took only a moment to return to normal. Her appearance made the whispers burst out in furious force. Her lines were even more obvious; they covered more of her body and her clothes revealed them clearer. She reached out for her brother's hand. "I'm not hiding anymore. If you walk freely, then so do I."

Dominic also returned to normal and smoothed a hand gently down her hair. Jazz contemplated both of them, then opened the bag of sand she was wearing on her hip. She removed a handful and poured it into the air. Her power welled up and the sand began to swirl together and take form.

A few moments later she had created three cloaks. In color and symbol, they were the same as the one Morgan wore. Hers and Tariah's, however, fastened around their upper arms and left their shoulders bare. The hood would cover their shoulders if they pulled it up, though. It was the more modern variant on the cloak, and she knew she had gotten it right when Tariah's eyes lit happily.

Morgan's heart tightened as he looked at them. "You don't have to wear the cloak of the Black Magi," he said quietly. "We don't exist anymore."

"Sure we do." Tariah fastened her cloak and began to tuck her hair up out of the way. "We need to keep the Black Magi. Once people get over their initial shock of you being a Chronicle, we may be able to use the same cover again. Looking for Master Magi who want a place to grow safely . . . *and to be kept from becoming like the Elite.*"

Jazz's eyes widened slightly then she looked at Dominic. "Damn. Why isn't she a scholar?"

"She's the daughter of scholars." His pride couldn't be hidden from his voice as he fastened his cloak around his shoulders. "She's very intelligent."

Tariah smiled as Morgan gave her a light cuff across the chin affectionately. "I read too much as a kid. It was the only way I really felt like I was living." She walked over to the window and looked out across the street. She defiantly stared down an old woman who was gawking at her. "I never got to go to the festivals," she said wistfully. "I was always inside reading about them."

Morgan looked at the Furies. "Do Dragons have festivals for the seasons too?"

"We have festivals whenever we feel a need, but most assuredly on season changes as well." Dominic was watching Tariah. He was willing to bet she would be one hell of a dancer. There was incredible grace and strength in her slender body, and she enchanted him with the simplest of movements. If she wanted a festival, she would damned well go to one.

Jazz had a feeling they were thinking the same thing; the look on his face felt like the one on hers. She could see inside Morgan that he had also missed out on a great deal because he was different. "Let's stock up on supplies and start making our way north," she said only. "We can walk until we need to camp, then we can fly tomorrow."

All were in agreement and they left the inn. The shopkeepers were wary of having three Dragons in their town (they had spotted Xander), so they didn't refuse service to the Dragoon pairs no matter how much they might have wanted to shut their doors. Because of this, the teams were shortly leaving the city and following the coastline north.

"I'm still a little stunned that the Dragons are finally doing something," Morgan commented after a long silence had passed comfortably.

"Hey," Jazz said in disgruntlement.

"It's true!" Tariah muttered. "Okay, so you can't track us. There aren't so few Furies that you couldn't stick one in each town of the world and watch for Chronicles. Okay, Prismatic would need more than one, but you know what I'm saying."

Dominic shook his head when Jazz opened her mouth. "She's right, Jazz. We both know it. Isn't that why we both left the Isle? Even if it was only subconsciously?"

Jazz was silent for a moment then she nodded. "Yes, you're probably right." She smiled. "Can I watch when you take on the Elders?" she asked Tariah.

Tariah's cheeks turned pink. "Why does everyone seem to believe I'm going to rake them over the coals?"

"Because you have an intense dislike for blind ignorance and have something of a temper?" Morgan asked dryly. He dodged with a laugh when she tried to hit him. "It's true! You're surprisingly impassioned for a Water element. I guess your affinity is for the ocean, it being deep and uncontrolled and all. Maybe it's your bottled emotions." He ducked again, and his grin gave away that he was deliberately harassing his sister. "I've seen broken dams on rivers. It takes a while for the initial flood to taper down."

She swung her pack and clipped him in the shoulder with a thump. She was grinning, too. She knew he was only ruffling her feathers. She felt somehow starved for the companionship of her brother. How had she missed him without knowing him? Turnabout was fair play, though, and she took an instinctive guess. "At least *I* never set a roof on fire."

185

"Damn it!" He glared at her. "Who told you that?"

She started laughing. "I *guessed*!" She muffled a shriek as he made a grab for her, and she shot away across the sand. She spun around and pulled down her eyelid as she stuck out her tongue. "Missed me!" The gesture and tone invoked the childhood she had never gotten.

He returned the gesture though he was laughing almost too hard to try. As they chased each other around the beach, their Furies just grinned and kept on walking. Like any other emotion, bottling up childhood fun and playfulness could also break down a dam. Morgan and Tariah had been cheated out of a lot in their lives. They deserved their chance to play.

The sun was setting when a carrier bird flew overhead. It wore a flag marking it as a Militia bird. The Dragoons exchanged a look before running down the beach after the bird. Tariah was by far the fastest, and she got close enough to fire an ice projectile that numbed the bird's wings without hurting it. It tumbled into her arms and she smoothed a hand over its feathers comfortingly. "It's okay. You're safe."

Jazz plucked the message out the bottle tied to the bird's leg and opened it. Her eyes promptly darkened with anger. "They're out of their league."

"Now what?" Dominic asked.

"According to this, the main Militia is calling for all troops to gather at the northern port on Spectrum. They want to storm Glacia and take on the Elite. Doing that could destroy the world anyway! All the cities will be unprotected, and I'm not sure Glacia can hold up under the strain." She broke off as Morgan's horror stabbed into her heart. "*Ishke*." She wrapped her arms around his waist. "I'm sorry, I spoke without thinking."

He held onto her, his eyes stricken. He felt terrified and sick to his stomach. No matter how long it had been, Glacia was still his home. His parents still lived there. The idea of everyone and everything being destroyed was horrifying.

"What if we took out just Soh?" Tariah asked quietly. She was thinking out loud to include Jazz and Morgan. "The Elite would fall apart without their leader then the Militia could come in and deal with them."

Morgan nodded. "I would concur with that."

Dominic grabbed the letter and erased the writing. He began to write on it himself, and he made a credible job of copying the Militia's style. "We're changing our letter to say that. The main Militia is telling the troops that the Chronicles will remove Soh to prevent disruption to the land. After he is gone, the Militia will move in."

"Ah, I see." Jazz smiled. "Because we can get to Glacia before the Militia ever makes it to the port, we can remove the problem before he arrives to contradict the false order."

"Exactly." He returned the message to the bottle and watched as Tariah released the bird so it could continue on its way. Thoughtfully, he looked around. The sun had wholly set and the moons were rising. From their position, they could see a moon to the west and a moon to the north. "I think we better camp for the night."

They moved inland away from the tides and found a flat place to set up. Jazz started showing off when she made two fancy tents and elaborate blankets for everyone. Dominic was compelled to compete and made a smokeless fire without wood—it was no mean feat to make a continuous fire without fuel. Morgan and Tariah sat to the side and just smiled.

Calling it a draw, Jazz sat down beside Morgan. She lifted a hand and sand swirled over her palm. Leaves and bark mixed with the sand as she called on her Wood powers, and in a few moments she was holding an oddly shaped wooden instrument. It looked like a pipe but had keys for her fingers.

"What is that?" Tariah asked curiously.

"A *ler*." She smiled. "Well, that's what we Dragons call it." She began to play and a haunting melody lifted on the air. "We're having our own festival," she told them. "Tariah, work on Dominic. He has an incredible singing voice."

Dominic's cheeks turned dull red as the two Chronicles stared at him. He cleared his throat. "Supposedly." He eyed his lover warily when she scooted closer. "Don't you *dare*."

She rested her hands lightly on his leg, and her silver eyes were deep and liquid in the firelight. "You don't have to sing right now." Her voice was both gentle and soothing. She knew exactly what buttons to push. She could see them inside him. "But you will probably want to practice in the future. You know, for when we have children." She kissed the corner of his lips. "You'll want to sing them lullabies, won't you? I can hold them, and you can sing."

The mental image made his throat close with fierce longing. How he wanted to have a family with her! He knew she was deliberately provoking him, but he just couldn't get past the idea of needing to sing their son or daughter—or both!—to sleep. He cleared his throat. "I guess I might as well practice now."

Morgan grinned. "Nicely done, Tariah." He settled back comfortably and propped himself on his elbows beside Jazz. He had no desire to tease Dominic about going weak-kneed. Truth told, the thought had already crossed his mind about children with Jazz, and he had gotten weak-kneed too. It was also terrifying in a way because he knew kids turned him to mush, but the longing was far stronger. He sent Jazz a warm look. They would have to start trying for a family as soon as the Elite was gone.

She nearly missed a note but kept playing. She smiled at him from under her lashes. She lowered the *ler* and blew him a soft kiss. As Dominic got to his feet, she said, "*Festa heq doj.*"

Tariah tried to repeat the words, but her tongue couldn't wrap around the syllables. The hiss on the S was easy enough, but it needed to be rolled somehow at the exact same time. "Draconic is hard."

"You'll get the hang of it." Dominic smiled at her. "It's the name of the song she was telling me to sing. It means 'Glory of the Festival.' It's basically a song sung at *every* festival we have. Whelps learn it as their first song in school."

She pulled up her knees and rested her chin on top of them as she watched him begin to move. He was an unexpectedly good dancer, and it made her smile. She wasn't the only one who had hidden a longing successfully. Her big, bad, tough Fire Fury wanted to be a bard. Who would have thought?

At a certain point in the music, he started to sing. The words were in Draconic, but neither Morgan nor Tariah needed to understand the words to realize that Jazz had been understating the situation. Dominic had a voice that most bards would kill to possess. "We'll make him sing lullabies to our kids too," Morgan murmured for Jazz's ears only.

187

Tariah was only enjoying the melody at first but the words began to slowly unravel inside her mind and take meaning. She recognized Dominic's presence and it dawned on her that he was providing a translation while singing. The fact that he could underscored his skill overall. She focused on the words and realized how beautiful they were. Blessings and thanks to the sun and world for supporting and sustaining all that lived. Unable to resist, she got to her feet and moved to his side.

He smiled and drew her closer to share the steps to the dance. He flicked a look at Jazz and she obligingly started the song from the beginning when it ended. It took little for Tariah to pick up the dance though there was some laughter when she nearly stepped on his toes once or twice. The Magi lyrics were in her mind, and Dominic's heart tugged at hers until she gave in and sang with him.

It surprised and pleased all of them to hear her voice. Perhaps not as talented as Dominic, there was something else in her voice that made it memorable. It meshed seamlessly with his and somehow enhanced his natural gifts. Like everything else, their voices were meant to blend together as one.

Thinking it, Morgan smiled at Jazz. He played one or two instruments. He would have to get one so that he could play with her. He had picked it up as a hobby to stave off loneliness. Now he could share it with the woman who had brought him everything. "Just don't ask me to sing," he said ruefully. "I make dogs howl."

She just laughed at him.

~*~

By the afternoon the following day, the Dragoons were approaching the port of Glacia. As Morgan watched Stalagmite growing larger in the distance, he felt his stomach quiver with nerves. It immediately drew Tariah's gaze. The longer they were around each other, the stronger their connection grew. Their minds were nearly always touching, and their hearts and souls weren't far removed.

It was a very curious thing that puzzled their Furies. If it had been merely a product of Telepathy, then Dominic and Jazz would have been privy to the link. They weren't. Morgan and Tariah could actually shut them out of the communication if they desired. It was something wholly unique to the Chronis 'cousins'.

"Morgan, are you worried about your parents?" Tariah asked softly.

"Yes." He looked at her wryly. "I'm getting close to twenty-six years old. I'm an adult. And yet I worry what they think of me."

"You'll never outgrow that." Jazz's voice was warm. "I'm over four hundred and I still worry about my parents' opinions. Just remember: they love you. If they didn't, they'd have killed you."

"This is true."

They landed on the beach of the actual port, and the two Furies took their Magi form again. Tariah began to shiver violently and wrapped her arms around herself as her teeth chattered. "M-morgan," she managed to say, "your town is beautiful. But it's too damned cold!"

The other three burst into laughter. Dominic caught Tariah in his arms and wrapped her inside his cloak with him. "I'll keep you warm, *ishke*, promise." He smiled at Jazz. "Do you have enough power left to make her some new clothes?"

"This is very easy." Jazz smiled as she opened her bag of sand. "Besides, there's nice incentive for using my power now." She sent a wink at Morgan who returned the gesture. Working quickly because she too was cold, she formed new clothes from the sand for both Tariah and herself. "Here, bundle up," she told the other woman.

Tariah wasted no time in pulling on the long sleeved tunic and leggings over her regular clothes. They, combined with her cloak, served to keep the cold out very well. They covered most of her lines too, but the ones on her face were still very stark. Oddly, only a sense of pride came this time at the knowledge. She was beginning to be *honored* that she was a Chronicle. When had that happened?

As they were entering the town, there came a happy cry and a crowd of people rushed toward them. "Morgan!" one man said. "Welcome home! This is such a surprise! Who knew that with all the terrible things going on that we'd get such a . . ." His voice trailed off as he saw Tariah and Dominic and recognized them.

The happy clamor of the crowd slowly died as they too saw Tariah and Dominic. Jazz's lines were effectively hidden by her tunic and hair, and no one realized what she was. Likewise, Morgan's hands were at his sides and also not visible yet. One older woman managed to find her voice and demanded, "Morgan, how could you? How dare you bring those . . . abominations here?"

"Tariah is my sister." He held up his hands and revealed his lines. Jazz pulled her hair back and the lines at the edge of her neck appeared. Morgan swept his gaze over the crowd. "I am an Air Chronicle. I have been my whole life. I never told, and you never knew. Am I suddenly a monster?" he challenged.

As the crowd was quiet, a woman suddenly snapped, "Oh, get your heads out of the snow! Of course Morgan isn't a monster! He's our Morgan and nothing changes that!" She shoved her way through the people and stopped in front of the Dragoons with her hands on her hips. "They look perfectly fine to me, though I'd kill for her figure," she said after a study of Jazz.

Morgan felt a smile curving his lips. "Merideth."

Merideth Caradina was as beautiful as ever though her ebony hair was now cropped closer to her face. Her blue eyes still danced merrily, and she was still the loveliest woman in the city. "As always," she said warmly as the crowd behind her slowly dissipated. She walked over and leaned up to kiss his cheek softly. A part of her would always care for this man who had been her first love. "You're happy now," she said quietly. "I'm glad."

Jazz discovered she could hold no resentment for Merideth. Not when the girl was so clearly different from the rest of the Magi with her open-minded nature. "I'm doing my best to make sure he stays that way." When Merideth glanced at her, she bowed gracefully. "Jazz Eaglewind, Soil Fury."

Merideth drew her thumb over her cheek and nose. "It's an honor, Jazz. I am Merideth Caradina, Water Magi." She looked at Tariah and Dominic with a smile that was no less warm. "And it's also an honor to meet you as well." She looked twice at Tariah, and her eyes widened. "I see why Morgan called you his sister. You're a dead ringer for him."

Tariah smiled and drew her thumb over her cheek and nose. "Tariah Chronis, Water Chronicle."

Dominic bowed. "Dominic Whisperer, Fire Fury."

Merideth tucked her hands in her pockets. "Well, why don't you come home with me?" She smiled. "I live on my own now. There's plenty of room."

Morgan hesitated. "Merideth . . . about my parents . . ."

Her eyes darkened. "Morgan . . . there's something you need to know. But I don't want to talk here. Please come back with me."

"Alright."

She turned and began walking into the city. As he fell into step beside her, she glanced at him with a smile. "Leader of the original Black Magi. Respected by the Militia and king alike. And, gasp, suddenly a Chronicle. Magi are so fickle sometimes." She slid a smile at Jazz. "You're welcome, by the way."

Liking her all the more, Jazz grinned. "Thank you, indeed."

"Dare I ask?" Morgan grumbled.

Tariah grinned. The look on Dominic's face told her that only the women understood the byplay. Since it would be fun to keep it that way, she blocked him from getting the information from her mind. It would be their secret that Merideth had deliberately not gone through with being Morgan's first lover so that Jazz had the honor.

Morgan just rolled his eyes at the women in his life. They could keep their secrets. He had a feeling he didn't want to know. He managed to keep his silence on everything else until they reached Merideth's home, but as soon as he shut the door behind everyone, he said, "Meri, please. What's this about my parents?"

Merideth sighed and lit a lamp as she sat on the overstuffed couch she owned. "When the Elite arrived here a few days ago," she said quietly, "they came in looking for more members to join their ranks. They zeroed right in on your parents. We all assumed it was because you were the leader of the real Black Magi but now . . ."

"It was because they were the parents of a Chronicle," Jazz murmured.

"And because it's personal." Morgan's hands curled into fists at his sides. "Soh has always blamed me, even if not consciously, for not saving his son. I stood by and did nothing, remember?" His silver eyes were dark with anger. "It's personal for me, too."

Dominic glanced at Merideth. "Where have they gone? Glacia isn't that big. It's also lightly populated. Mostly farmland, correct?"

"Correct." She looked down at her hands. "There are three main cities on Glacia. This one, another on the coast to the very north, and the capitol in the very middle. The rest of the land is covered in farms and mining communities. We're one of the biggest agricultural places, very spread out . . . and so easy to control." She got to her feet and paced away. "Morgan . . . I hate to ask you this."

He found a smile for her. "What's his name?"

She turned in surprise. "How'd you know that?"

"Male intuition."

She was more willing to bet it was *his* intuition alone. She crossed her arms around herself tightly. "His name is Caleb. He's a good man. We were . . . we were supposed to have a ceremony and become Linked mates. But the Elite came and convinced Caleb that because I had been exposed to a Chronicle, I might be in danger. They told him if he joined them, they would protect me."

"We'll get him out," he promised. He glanced at the window as snow and wind slammed into it, and he grimaced. The clouds had turned into a good, old-fashioned blizzard. "We can't go anywhere in this. As soon as it clears, we'll leave. No matter what time of day or night."

"In the meantime, please, stay here and rest. There are spare rooms." Merideth got to her feet and went over to the door to put on her hat and gloves. "I have to go to work. Morgan . . . thank you."

"You're welcome." He sighed only after the door was shut. He also turned and caught Jazz in his arms before even she realized how weak she was feeling. His eyes narrowed slightly. "Next time don't play at being fine when you're not. You should have said you were that tired!"

She smiled wryly as Tariah started shoving Dominic toward a spare room. "I'm not *that* badly drained, *ishke*. I just lost my balance, that's all. Now, if we'd been flying all day . . . well, then you'd likely be carrying me and Tariah would be rolling Dominic across the floor."

"She would not!" Dominic muttered as he caught the last of the conversation just before the door shut behind him and Tariah. He wasn't exceptionally tired either thanks to the constant and steady flow of power between him and his Chronicle. It was a subconscious replenish of his power at nearly all times.

Tariah smiled. "Yes, I would. It's not like I can carry you." She wound her arms around his neck as he lifted her and sat on the side of the bed with her on his lap. She sighed contentedly and let her head fall back as her power welled up and covered her with a soft blue aura. His lips pressed softly to her shoulder and she held him closer. Times like this made her feel as if the world had stopped and there was nothing to worry about in the world.

It was only as they were lying in bed together watching the blizzard slowly taper off outside that he noticed something different about her lines. He propped himself up on his elbow to study her intently.

More of her lines had darkened. Now they were dark gold down to the top of her hip and entirely down her arm. Her power was growing more potent. It was starting to manifest physically now and not just through her lines. Her hair seemed to ripple like water whenever light touched it.

It was affecting him, too. His lines had darkened and his hair burned like fire under the light. Thoughtfully, he smoothed a hand over her hip and traced her lines. "We're close," he said softly. "We're close to the end, *ishke*. In a month . . . well, I'd hazard that we'll likely be on the Isle and living however we want."

Tears burned her eyes. "Good," she whispered.

"What's the first thing you want to do?" he asked her softly. "Name it and it's yours."

"I want a Linking ceremony with you." She smiled when she felt his surprise. "I know it's a formality, but I want it. I never thought I'd get one so . . ." She tilted her head. "Or are there special ceremonies Dragons have?"

"There are. We call them Unification ceremonies. But . . ." He searched his memory. "I seem to have memory from the Fury before me that there was a ceremony for Dragoons. It was basically a Linking ceremony but it also named them full Dragoons. I can't be sure. We'd have to ask Xander."

"How old is he?" Tariah asked.

"Over twenty-five hundred."

She took a swift breath. "Then he was there. He might know where the lost isle is."

"No, unfortunately." He sighed. "All memories were erased of the location of the lost isle. I think the world feared this very situation. That someone would seek to find the isle and use the power. Lucksphere wants to survive above all else. That's why it made all of us."

"That's why there will always be Magi. Soh's a fool." She closed her eyes and cuddled closer against him as he lay down again. She wanted some sleep. They were going to need all their strength for the coming battle.

In the middle of the night, Tariah and Morgan were both awakened by the silence outside. It had stopped storming. Inside both Chronicles, they could feel the throbbing of their lines and the sudden sharp compulsion that was guiding them on. But unlike so many times when their lines had urged them north, this time the feeling was more definite, and more precise.

Go north and fight. Fight to live.

It was time to finish their journey.

Chapter Twenty-Four

The capitol city of Glacia was known as Bergia. It boasted a population of twenty thousand and had a large manor in the very center where the city leader lived while he was in office. Like most city leaders, he was an elected official.

But as the Dragoons approached the city two days later in the early morning, they were fairly sure that the city leader was no longer in residence. Hovering over the large building was a dark cloud of ominous proportions. It was a thick and malevolent mass of power, as if the Flutterlies that made the clouds had been corrupted as well.

The cloud was expanding and covering the entire city. The people were either ignoring the cloud—and if they were, they were wearing Elite cloaks—or they were loading up wagons as fast as they could to escape. More were leaving than staying, but there were still enough left that it was like a sea of white cloaks.

Because they would have stood out, Jazz had turned all their cloaks brown and they were wearing hoods to cover their distinctive hair and lines. Their power could still be sensed, but no Magi recognized it as being anything other than above average. There were enough Master Magi to provide an effective cover. The disguises allowed the Dragoons to walk among the crowds and listen to conversations. There weren't many. It was as if the entire city had fallen silent.

The closer they drew to the center of town, the thicker the crowds grew. The Magi were gathered together around the leader's manor where there was a large balcony for him to use for speeches. This time it was Soh who stood on the balcony.

"What's he doing?" Tariah whispered. She was too short to see over the crowd.

Jazz and Morgan had the same problem, and Dominic skimmed his gaze over the area. He focused on Soh's lips and concentrated on reading what he was saying; it was too far away to actually hear. "Seems like he's just touting a lot of nonsense about purifying the world," he said quietly.

"Purifying . . . ?" Morgan began to push his way through the crowd to get closer. What was going on now?

They found a spot to see and hear from, and they were able to remain behind several large pine trees to keep themselves from being seen in return. It wasn't the best place, but it was the best they could hope to have.

"My fellow Magi!" Soh was saying. "The time is now for us to wrest this world from the people who don't understand! We must purify this world of the foolish ones! Those that would destroy the powerful because they fear them! Those that would destroy this world by removing our one saving grace! We will make a world for those saviors to live in! We will make a world where Chronicle and Magi live together!"

Jazz nearly gagged. "Hypocrite," she muttered.

"He's completely lost his mind," Tariah whispered. "Didn't the events two thousand years ago prove that genocide won't create peace?" She suddenly took a sharp breath and the color drained from her face. Her agony was so sharp and acute that not only did Dominic feel it, but Morgan also felt it as a psychic backlash. "No . . ." she whispered.

Dominic followed her gaze and felt his heart turn to ice. He knew who they were from her memories. Even if he hadn't, he would have been able to guess. The man had Tariah's silver eyes and the woman had her auburn hair. "How is it possible?" he said softly. "We were told they were killed."

Morgan suddenly sucked in a sharp breath as well. He had just recognized the two figures standing beside Tariah's parents. They were *his* parents, and all four were wearing the cloaks of the Black Magi Elite. "We have to get them out of there," he said urgently.

Knowing the two Chronicles were likely to follow their hearts and potentially get themselves killed, Dominic grabbed Morgan and Jazz grabbed Tariah. The two Furies hurried away from the scene as fast as they could, each carrying a Chronicle under their arm. It was only when they were well beyond the city limits that they put down their burdens.

"Ouch!" Tariah rubbed her hip. "You dropped me!" she accused Jazz.

"I was in a hurry, honey. I'm sorry." Jazz skimmed a hand down her hair in apology then went over to where Morgan was standing. She wrapped her arms around his waist and held on tightly. "We'll get to them eventually. For now there are far too many of them for us to take on by ourselves."

Dominic lifted Tariah up off the ground and enfolded her tightly in his arms. For all her sass to Jazz, she was in shock. Her entire soul seemed to have shaken down to its foundations. She had believed her parents were dead. But here they were, and they were her enemy.

"How do we handle this?" Jazz asked Dominic. "We need more help. But we can't contact our clanmates right now." She looked at Tariah. "Can you contact your Kin brother? Perhaps the Kin will assist us. After all, what Soh proposes to do to the Magi is as abhorrent as what the Magi did to Chronicles."

"They said that the Magi won't accept their help," Morgan noted.

"It's not the Magi asking. It's us." Tariah straightened her shoulders and eased back from Dominic. "I'm sure they will assist us. And they can notify the Dragons and the Furies as well."

Unexpectedly, all four felt a very strong and *very* distinct presence, and they turned to see a Dragon flying across the sky. His body was black with red swirls throughout the scales. He was, easily, the largest Dragon either Chronicle had ever seen. At their best guess, they thought he had to be fifty feet in length.

"Xander!" Jazz gasped. "What's he doing here?"

"We saw him in Mirah," Dominic managed to say. "You didn't?"

"Not at all!" She held an arm in front of Morgan to give him a brace as Xander flew in for a landing and his wings began to kick up snow all around them. Belatedly, she noticed that Xander had his claws very gently folded around two beings. "He brought someone."

Tariah peeked around Dominic's arm and gave a delighted gasp as she saw the two Xander was carrying. She rushed forward with a cry. "Sparkle! Daylar!"

"Tariah!" The two Faeries shot forward and attached themselves to her neck in fierce hugs. "I missed you!" Sparkle wailed. "It wasn't the same without you there! I kept hearing all these things and I was so scared!"

Tariah hugged both of them as tightly as she could and tears filled her eyes. "I missed both of you so much!" She released them and held one on each hand. "But why are you here?"

"We're here to help fight," Daylar told her. He looked at Dominic and the other pair of Dragoons. "We Kin are glad to fight alongside the Dragoons. We won't let another tragedy occur, especially not when it will destroy the world."

"The Dragons also feel this way," Xander noted. Light engulfed him and he went into Magi form. He pulled his hair back and tied it out of his way at the nape of his neck. "The minute I saw you in Mirah, I knew what your intent was. I sent word to the Elders and to the Kin. Both races are marching this way as we speak."

"We're already here," came Elder Juniper's voice from the air. "We Kin march vastly differently than you Dragons do."

Everyone looked around but couldn't see anything. Daylar and Sparkle giggled. Then, suddenly, the snow began to billow up into the air and formed swirls upon swirls of light and dark. From every swirl appeared a Kin, Moon and Sun alike, both Faerie and Elf, and all of them were armed for battle. Within moments, the land was filled with Kin.

A thousand . . . two thousand . . . Tariah couldn't guess at the amount of Kin standing there. Every Kin, for the strength of their power, was worth at least two regular Magi. In half the size, they had twice the army.

Before anyone could say or do anything, the land seemed to go dark as a shadow passed across the sun. It wasn't from the gathering storm clouds. It was from the thick mass of Dragons that were flying across the sky. There were fewer of them than the Kin, but they were far bigger and far more deadly.

The air was filled with the flapping of their wings and the snow was kicked up in the air as they found places to land. Most were Furies. Some were merely Dragon Lords. And more still were normal Dragons. Each seemed bigger than the last, though none were as big as Xander. Tariah and Morgan felt vastly overwhelmed and both ducked behind their lovers.

Juniper and Xander walked forward as the representatives of their races. "Dragoons," Juniper said formally, "we are here to assist you in your battle against the Elite. We will hold the field for you while you take out the leader. When the leader falls, so will the army. If you're ready, we will begin the assault."

Tariah and Morgan exchanged a look then looked at Dominic and Jazz who both smiled. With matching looks on their faces, the siblings turned to Juniper and said, "We're ready."

Dominic and Jazz turned into their Dragon forms, and Tariah and Morgan got onto their backs. Dominic carried Daylar in his claws and Jazz carried Sparkle. The two Kin were going along to add supplemental magic that even the Dragoons couldn't use.

As they took to the sky, Juniper murmured to Xander, "I must know. Did you recognize them?"

Xander's hair ruffled in the wind. "Yeah," he murmured equally. "More than that, I could smell it in their blood. We're going to see something spectacular today, Juniper.

Something I thought I'd only see once in my lifetime. This time though . . . this time I suspect a much better outcome."

Inside the city, silence was falling. The Elite and Magi couldn't see outside the city walls because of the sudden snowstorms covering the town, but they could definitely feel that there was something going on.

Soh was afraid. He paced restlessly in the main hall of the leader's manor. He had thought that everything would go perfectly according to plan, but he was beginning to think he had erred somewhere. He knew that the two Chronis cousins had joined forces, and something about it told him he was in over his head.

The silence of the city was broken sharply as Kin suddenly appeared from out of thin air and Dragons rushed up over the sides of the city walls and began to fly in to land. The land shuddered and rippled with the force of such sudden power but quickly calmed.

Elite leapt into battle and threw everything they had against their invaders. In the violent battle that raged, no one noticed the two Dragoon teams flying to the leader's manor. They landed in the back courtyard, and Sparkle and Daylar attacked the guards leaping for them. The combined Light blast repelled all enemies around them long enough for Dominic and Jazz to take Magi form again.

They fought their way past the guards and Elite that surged at them from all sides. Tariah and Morgan were full Chronicles; their powers were far more potent than any Magi could hope to achieve. More than one guard was either frozen solid or sent flying through a wall. Those that made it past their powers couldn't hope to make it past the Furies and their deadly fighting skills.

Halfway down the hall toward the main meeting room, the team was brought up short by the sight of Persia and Dublin Chronis standing in the hall waiting for them. Tariah's throat closed. "Mom . . . Dad . . . it's me!" She ripped off her cloak and tossed it aside. "See?"

Dominic's nose flared slightly as he caught the scent of the two Magi. His gut clenched as he smelled the unmistakable scent of power that had been tainted beyond repair. Alive or not, neither Magi would have any sort of life even if Tariah could reach through to them. They would be sick until they died.

Tariah closed her eyes as she understood his thoughts. "Soh's trying to stop you," Sparkle whispered from where she was riding on her shoulder. "He knew this would make you hesitate. But Tariah . . . they're already dead."

The others looked at her in shock. "It's true," Daylar said sadly. "The power you sense flowing in them is a false power. Their true power stopped long ago."

Water began to well up around Tariah's feet as shards of ice formed. Her hair unraveled and fell down around her body in auburn waves as her lines glowed and rippled. No one said anything, and not even Dominic offered to help. This was something she needed to do herself, and they all knew it.

Without hesitation, she released the ice at her former parents and the shards impaled them both with enough force to send their bodies flying to the floor. Whatever was fueling them was cut off, and both bodies turned to skeletons. The flesh melted away and the yellow blood filling them stained the floor. The smell made all of them gag.

They hurried past the scene and down the hall. Tariah stripped off her leggings and tunic as she went and left herself in her regular desert clothes. Something told her that she wouldn't want her lines muffled in the slightest. Morgan clearly felt the same for he was also removing his cloak and shirt.

"Bet that made for interesting fights," Sparkle said to Daylar. "Half-naked Chronicles everywhere."

None of them got a chance to laugh, though they all wanted to. They were stopped short by the sight of Iria and London Chronis standing in front of the doors to the main hall. Neither smelled of tainted power, and both turned white as they saw their son. "Morgan!" Iria managed to say. "We were told . . ."

"I know what you were told." Morgan kept his voice even and calm. "But it's okay. Quickly, get over here." The urgency nearly choked him. "There's something in that room. Something evil. Hurry. Please."

"Of course!" The couple moved forward, and they unknowingly triggered a hidden trap. Air blades formed in the air and shot forward to strike them in the back. They were sent flying to the floor and across it several feet before sliding to stops where blood pooled under their bodies.

"Mom! Dad!" Morgan rushed to their sides and realized both were still alive. "We need to heal this!"

"Leave it to us!" Daylar said. He flew over to Iria and began to dissolve the blade protruding from her back. "We Kin are better at healing than even the most adept Magi. We'll keep them alive until backup comes." He inclined his head toward where Sparkle was already summoning several more Kin, especially MoonKin to assist them. "We'll make sure they survive," he promised.

Jazz helped Morgan stand once more and the four Dragoons moved alone toward the doors. Dominic kicked them down, then covered Tariah protectively as a surge of power flooded out at them in a razor sharp wave.

Tariah felt Dominic's pain and realized that he had been wounded. A quick look at Jazz told her that she too had been wounded in the wash as she protected Morgan. "What was that?" she demanded. "I've never seen the like!"

Dominic and Jazz shared a grim look. "Dragon power," the male Fury said quietly. "There's a Dragon working with Soh."

They carefully edged into the throne room. There were no people present but for Soh and a woman sitting on the edge of a table. It wasn't hard to see that the woman was a Dragon for her hair was blue with white streaks, but her very appearance also noted that she was a Dragon Lord.

And, as they actually got close enough to feel her power, they all sensed it. "You're a Fury!" Morgan said in shock. "Why?" he demanded. "Why are you helping this sick bastard?" He gestured at Soh furiously.

The Fury looked at him and her green eyes glittered with hatred and grief in equal doses. It was as if everything she felt was dead. Everything except hate and pain. Something inside the two Chronicles wanted to weep for her. "Because," she hissed softly. "Because the Magi killed my Chronicle . . . *and you did nothing!*"

Jazz realized it first. "You were Phedo's Fury!" She shook her head violently. "Don't you think he would hate that you are doing this?" she demanded. "I would never let my Chronicle be alone, even if meant I took my own life to be with him! Sistra, where is your loyalty to your Chronicle!?"

Sistra lifted her hand and blasted her halfway across the room. As Morgan rushed to her side, the other Fury said in a stifled tone, "I waited. I waited for five hundred years only to watch the Chronicles be massacred. Still I waited. I waited for a thousand years! And then I felt him! I felt his birth! . . . Barely eleven years later, I felt his death! And you know where I was? I was on the Isle!"

"It's your own fault!" Tariah shouted at her. "No one *made* you stay there! There's no one person at fault for everything! Everyone has been stupid!"

Sistra moved as if to blast her, and Dominic quickly moved her out of harm's way. Soh began to laugh maniacally. "When I met Sistra, I knew we could work together perfectly. She will help us find the Chronicle children."

"Furies can't track Chronicles," Jazz said as she painfully got to her feet. She was bleeding, but Morgan was binding the wounds as fast as he could. "If she told you they could, she was lying."

Soh looked at Sistra in shock. "You said . . ."

"Ignore her!" Sistra ordered.

"But . . ."

Dominic and Jazz exchanged a glance then both turned into their Dragon forms. The hall was so big it could have held Xander let alone the two of them. Sistra saw what they had done and swiftly changed back as well. She was no bigger than Dominic in size but there was something about her form that seemed less beautiful and more . . . terrifying.

Jazz and Dominic both lunged for her and the building shook as she countered and sank her teeth into Jazz's wing. Soh turned to go assist Sistra when suddenly Morgan and Tariah both stepped in front of him. He stopped short. He couldn't say why but something about the two of them together terrified him. "If you'd just joined me," he told Tariah, "then this wouldn't have happened."

"True," she countered icily. "But then I would have suffered not knowing my Fury. I would have become my brother's enemy." Her eyes narrowed. "I'm going to kill you, you sick bastard. For what you're trying to do, but more for what you did to Daylar!"

"Who? Oh." He scoffed. "The Kin." He sneered at Morgan. "So you translocated right into your Fury's arms, did you? Where's my thanks?"

Morgan lifted a hand and a blast of air knocked Soh halfway across the room. "There's your thanks," he bit out. "Don't think you can play mind games with us. We're not going to be swayed." His eyes sharpened as he saw the blast Soh was gathering. "Move!" he snapped at Tariah.

They both dove out of the way, and the immense blast blew a hole in the floor. The two Chronicles rolled up to their feet and shot raw bolts of power at Soh from opposing directions. To their immense shock, the two powers merged together halfway and transformed into the shape of a Dragon as it rushed at Soh.

Soh opened his mouth to scream in terror but it was too late. The beast was upon him and it swallowed him whole. The power faded away and left nothing behind except Soh's cloak. It fluttered to the floor and melted into sand. It could not hold its form without the power of its owner.

Tariah swallowed hard. "Morgan?"

He was no less shaken. "I don't have a single clue." He turned sharply as the room shook, and he saw that Jazz had just been thrown into one of the walls. He sucked in a sharp breath and rushed to her side. One of her wings was visibly broken, and she was bleeding even worse than before. Her body was marked with bites and claw marks.

A moment later, Dominic hit the wall as well. He was in no better condition. Tariah hurried to him and began using ice to cover the wounds and stop the bleeding as best she could. A quick look told her that Sistra was wounded but still strong. "How is it possible?" she whispered. "Shouldn't a Dragoon be stronger?"

"Should but . . ." Dominic drew a labored breath. He hurt from head to tail. "It's like she's linked to someone and they're giving her power. So you could say that she's a Fury with infinite power without her Chronicle."

"That can't be right." Morgan pushed Jazz back when she tried to get up. "You're too wounded! Stay put!"

Sistra laughed dangerously. "And if they don't fight, who will stop me from erasing this entire city? Magi, Kin, Dragons . . . they're all the same!" She flew straight up into the air and burst through the ceiling. Pieces rained down onto the ground in her wake.

Tariah and Morgan looked at one another silently, and Dominic sensed their intent first. "She'll kill you," he told them. "You can take the form, certainly, but how will you know how to use it?"

"We can't just sit here," Tariah told him. She framed his face in her hands and kissed his forehead gently. "Let us protect you for once." She released him and walked over to her brother.

Both Chronicles began to draw on the majiks of their Furies, and the mental link between them allowed Tariah to show Morgan how to bend the majiks to the shape they needed. Air and Water power filled the air and engulfed both of them, stretching and reforming them as they bent their own power as well.

When the power faded, it left behind two fully-grown Dragons. Morgan was barely bigger than Jazz, and Tariah was slightly smaller. Both were auburn in color, the same as their hair, but while Tariah was marked with blue streaks, Morgan was marked with spots of white. Their silver eyes were eerily identical.

It took a few attempts, and reading of their Furies' minds, but Tariah and Morgan were able to fly up into the air and through the hole in the ceiling to follow Sistra. Their passage opened the hole more, and the entire ceiling gave way. Despite the debris that landed on them, Dominic and Jazz were grateful for the view of the fight. If there was anything they could do, they wanted to do it.

Sistra saw the two Dragons flying after her and began to laugh uproariously. "What nonsense! Whelps think they can take on an Elder?" She flew directly at them and forced them to dodge and scrambled to stay aloft at the same time. "You can't fly and fight, you fools! How does this help you?"

Tariah flew closer. "We can try," she said fiercely. She shot a blast of power at the other Dragon.

Sistra dodged hastily then flew even further up into the air. She flew so high that the manor became a speck on the ground, but she wasn't very surprised when the siblings followed her. She even had to be reluctantly impressed with their ability to learn quickly. Both were flying more steadily. Still . . . they were out of their league.

"Enough toying around!" She began to gather her strongest attack. "I commend you for your bravery, but you never stood a chance. Goodbye, little Chronicles." She released the blast at them both, and it struck Tariah first. It sent her flying into Morgan, and they were both hurtled back toward the land far below.

Dominic and Jazz struggled to get themselves into the air and toward their Chronicles to save them. They barely missed them. The two siblings shot past their grip and slammed into the ground with such force that they blew out a hundred-foot crater. The shockwave caused everyone who was fighting to stop wherever they were. The silence was absolute.

Dominic and Jazz hurried toward the scene. Both knew that, somehow, oddly, their Chronicles had survived. "Tariah!" Dominic shouted. "Morgan!"

There was no response, yet something suddenly moved within the darkness of the crater. A massive claw lifted and grabbed the edge of the hole. Another followed suit and the beast within the hole began to pull itself out. It was the most shocking thing anyone had ever seen. No one had ever seen anything like it . . . except for Xander and Sistra.

The Dragon was a hundred feet long from nose to tail. It had four wings on its mighty back, and it was covered in silver scales that glowed brightly in the sun. Each claw was as big as a Magi. Its head was sharp and angular with two great fins extending from its head near where its ears would be.

"C-Chronis," Sistra managed to whisper. Even from her position high in the sky, she could see the Dragon clearly. "The Chronis Dragon." She had been sure she would never see such a thing ever again. A vivid memory cut across her mind of watching the Chronis Dragon fly across the field and cut down enemy Magi sent to destroy them.

Chronis looked up at Sistra then suddenly flew straight into the air with a speed and grace only found in Elders. Sistra was still frozen with shock. It was only at the last moment that she was able to dodge, but she didn't get out of the way in time. The greater Dragon ripped her arm and wing off as easily as picking the petals of a flower.

Sistra screamed and began to plummet toward the ground. Out of desperation, she sought her Air power and cast a translocation spell. She, and the Elite still standing, disappeared from the field all at once. The Kin and Dragons were left standing as the winners.

Dominic and Jazz landed on the field and turned back to Magi form. Kin swiftly descended on them to heal their wounds, but all eyes were fixed on the silver Dragon that was circling overhead as it slowly came in for a landing. Chronis landed at the edge of the hole it had come from and let out a roar. The sound was a promise and threat all at once. It chilled those hearing it.

Light engulfed the Dragon, and it suddenly split into the two Dragon forms belonging to Tariah and Morgan. They too glowed and shifted back to their natural Chronicle form. Both collapsed where they were standing, and their Furies rushed to their sides.

Though both Furies had been drained dangerously low, they were replenished the moment they touched their Chronicle. Their majiks came back in an instant as if they hadn't been drained at all. Morgan and Tariah were glowing brilliantly, emanating enough power that the land quivered in the wake. Finally, slowly, the land stilled. The power ebbed. The twins stopped glowing.

Silence overtook the field. Neither Kin nor Dragon said a word. There was nothing any of them could think to say. The snow fell softly around them as they wondered what they were supposed to do next.

Chapter Twenty-Five

Tariah awoke to the feel of sunshine across her face. She was lying snuggled in Dominic's arms, and she wasn't wearing a bit of clothing. Neither fact surprised her. For a moment, she simply savored how it felt to be in his arms. Memory returned in a rush and she sat up swiftly. "Sistra!"

He sat up and pulled her into his arms again. He smoothed his hand through her hair gently. "Easy," he said softly. "We're safe. We have no idea where Sistra is though. Or the Elite. Her translocation scattered them. The good news is that the Elite is down to a handful of members. They were being slaughtered by our allies."

A chill rippled down her back and she moved closer to his comforting warmth. "If that is the good news . . . what's the bad news?"

He took a long breath. "Well . . . it's as if the Elite never existed. Like the lost isle, the memories of the world have been erased. The Magi remember the Elite, but not who they are. Even I can't seem to bring to mind the faces belonging to them. So now they walk among us and we're blind to their presence."

"It will take a long time for Sistra to heal," she reminded him. "Perhaps long enough for us to find the children."

"It's possible." He eased her back. "Would you like to tell me what you and Morgan did? I've never seen the like!"

"I have," Xander said from the doorway.

Tariah shrieked and yanked the blankets over her naked form. Her free hand lobbed a pillow in his direction, and the Fury was so surprised that it popped him in the face. He looked at Dominic. "I *really* want to know about that meeting."

Dominic grinned. "It's one of the many reasons I love her." He peeked under the covers. "You can show your face at the least."

"I just hit an Elder!" she wailed in response.

Xander laughed. "I deserved it. I am sorry for startling you, Tariah." He smiled when she pulled the blankets down to her shoulders. "No harm done." He walked over to sit on the side of the bed. "I already spoke with Morgan about things this morning. I wished to speak with you as well. To tell you of the Chronis twins."

"Dominic suspects Morgan and I are descendants," she said.

"It's no suspicion. I recognized your scent, and his, instantly. I knew the Chronis twins. They and their Furies still lived at the time of the first battles between Magi and Chronicle." He took a long breath. "They were . . . fascinating to know. And powerful. In the first great war, they took the field to fight. Their Furies became mortally wounded. The twins then did something no one had ever dared imagine possible. They didn't just turn into Dragon form . . . they merged."

Dominic's eyes widened. "Like Morgan and Tariah did."

"Yes. They obliterated the field of Magi. Nothing could stop the Chronis Dragon. But . . . their Furies died shortly thereafter. The twins just . . . slowly began to fade away." Xander looked down. "It was painful. Finally, other Chronicles offered to put them out of their misery. They agreed. But before they were struck down, and I remember this clearly, they looked at all of us and promised to come back and finish what they had started."

Dominic looked at Tariah. She was silent for a few minutes. Then, slowly, she said, "Morgan and I . . . we didn't know what was wrong with us. When we were falling we just . . . we just knew what to do. But we have both felt it. That there was a promise to keep." She looked at Xander. "And we will."

"I'm sure you will." Xander stood. "Just to let you know, the Militia has put out word that you and Morgan are sanctioned by them. The Magi are heralding you as heroes."

"But . . .?" Dominic asked.

"The law stands. Chronicle children are to be killed upon discovery." Xander crossed his arms. "I think they're of the 'if they don't exist, the Elite can't get their hands on them' mindset. So we're not quite at square one, but pretty damned close. Still . . . we Furies are going to do our best." As he was heading out the door, he added, "Remember to invite me to the ceremony."

The Dragoons smiled. "We will," Tariah promised. As the door shut, she fell over onto her back. "Are Morgan's parents alright?"

"They are." Dominic leaned over her and tugged the sheet out of the way to admire her beauty. She seemed impossibly perfect no matter what form she took. "They wanted to meet you, but Morgan made them return to Stalagmite. Even the Kin couldn't fully heal London. He will always use a cane from now on."

"I can meet them later." She closed her eyes for long moments. "It's not quite over yet but . . . I feel as if we might have some peace for a little while. Even looking for the children would never be as bad as what we just went through."

Her eyes suddenly flew wide, and shock filled her face. The door flew open and Morgan rushed in. He was fully dressed again, but his tunic was sleeveless to show his lines. Jazz was right behind him, but she was as puzzled as Dominic. "Did you feel it?" Morgan asked his sister urgently.

"I did!" Tariah held the sheet to her chest as she sat up. Excitement was humming through her body. She could barely breathe as she looked at Dominic. Inside her body, she could feel the throbbing of her lines and the direction they were urging her. "We know where the Isle of Dragons is."

Go west.

"What? How?" Jazz asked Morgan.

Go west.

"I don't know. I just feel that this time we're heading to the Isle. The feeling is so precise it's like someone is whispering in my ear." He caught her in his arms and swung her around before kissing her soundly. "We're almost home. Finally."

Go west and you will find the Isle.

Tariah wasted no time in getting dressed. Once all of them were prepared, they left the inn they had been staying at. They had been in Arctica, the city on the western coast of Glacia. Bergia was in the midst of massive repairs. The land was still a little unsteady at times but was returning to normal slowly but surely.

They stocked up on supplies, and Dominic and Jazz turned into their Dragon forms. With their Chronicles on their backs, they took off across the ocean. They flew at a slower rate than usual to preserve their strength, but they still moved faster than any boat.

They stopped only once over the next week, at one of the Kin outposts along the western coast of Carnelian. They restocked their supplies and obtained a strong boat for the rest of the journey that would take them into open ocean waters. They were still following the Chronicles' lines, and every day their lines seemed to steadily grow darker further and further along their bodies as they charted the last of their maps.

It was another week at sea before they knew they were approaching the Deepest Ocean. The waters were growing turbulent and steadily darker. The air was much more active and wind blew ceaselessly. Even the sky seemed darker than usual though there were no clouds. Oddly, Tariah no longer felt the trepidation she always had when contemplating the Deepest Ocean. It was oddly comforting.

They were awakened the following morning by the sudden calm of the sea. The ocean had stopped seething around the boat. When they emerged from the cabin onto the deck, the entire ocean was shrouded with fog. It was quiet all around them as if the world was holding its breath.

Dominic took command of the boat and sailed them silently into the fog. It was not yet dawn, and there was only one moon in the sky. The only light came from lanterns on the boat. It felt a little as if time had lost all meaning, yet the slowly rising sun proved it still passed. Steadily, the morning rays stretched across the sea and began to erase the fog.

When the fog lifted entirely, it was not gradual. It evaporated so suddenly that the sunlight on the ocean blinded everyone and forced them to look away. The glare faded just as quickly, and they slowly lowered their hands. Sitting across the ocean, less than a mile away, was an island. It had emerged from the mists as if it had been there all along.

"The Isle of Dragons," Jazz breathed. "I had forgotten how beautiful it is."

Beautiful was not the word for the Isle. It was exquisite. It was what Lucksphere had looked like before war and malice had destroyed the land. Mountains rose high in the sky, and the top peaks of several were snow-capped. The lower lands on this side of the mountains were filled with brilliant green grass and pockets of trees. Both Chronicles knew from their Furies that the other side of the mountains held lush deserts and oases. This one isle had the best the world could offer. It was blessed.

Dragons flew through the air, and occasionally a plume of fire or soil could be seen. Something inside Tariah's chest finally loosened, and she reached for Morgan's hand. Their fingers linked tightly together. "We did it," she whispered. "We found it. Somewhere we belong."

The Dragons were already gathering as they were pulling in to dock. Those who were Lords were in Magi form. Those who were not shrank themselves down as small as they could to try to prevent themselves from overwhelming the newcomers. Excitement was high in the air. Everyone wanted to be the first to see the Chronicles.

Dominic got off the boat first and helped Tariah down. In delight, one Dragon exclaimed, "She's so tiny! And so pretty!"

Morgan hopped down off the boat and said to Tariah teasingly, "You must have an appeal to transcend race."

"Don't tease her too much!" someone at the back of the crowd called. "You're cute to us too!"

His cheeks went pink, and Tariah smirked at him. Jazz and Dominic just laughed. Dragons were always drawn to objects of beauty, and their Chronicles fit the bill both inside and out.

The crowd drew closer and everyone was beginning to talk excitedly. "They need to go meet the Elders!" someone said. "They said to bring the Dragoons immediately, remember?"

"Alright, everyone!" a female voice said from the air. "Calm down before you scare them off!" The cream-colored Fury was circling overhead, and there were white spots scattered across her scales like freckles. She was Dominic's size but was vastly more slender. She turned into Magi form just as she was landing and became a tall woman with blonde hair and cream-colored eyes. She walked forward with a smile and hugged Jazz.

Jazz smiled and hugged her equally. "It's been a long while, Dahlia." She gestured to Morgan. "This is my Chronicle. Morgan, this is Dahlia Stalker, an Air Fury. We've been friends since we were whelps."

Dahlia bowed gracefully. "An honor, Morgan."

He drew his thumb over his cheek and nose with a smile. "Likewise."

The crowd began to disperse as Dahlia had asked, and she led the Dragons away from the port and toward the dirt road leading deeper into the Isle. "We Dragons," she told the Chronicles, "don't have cities like yours. We live wherever we please and build homes wherever we want. When we gather, we gather in the cliffs where the majority of buildings are. That's where our shops are and where the Elders meet. It's the closest thing to a city we have, really."

Dominic tucked Tariah close against his side. "My home was in the mountains, but we can live wherever you like." He smiled. "You can never really take a girl out of a desert, or so I've heard."

"Something like that," she said wryly. "But I'd like to try living in the valley you once mentioned. I've never seen one before."

"Hurry up!" a Dragon called from overhead. "They're getting impatient!"

With sighs, the three Furies turned into their Dragon forms. Tariah climbed onto Dominic's back, and Morgan onto Jazz's, then both pairs took to the sky with Dahlia following. As the other Dragons saw the sight, a cheer rose in the air. It was the most vivid sign in existence that could tell them all that Dragoons had returned again.

At the entrance to the meeting room, Grecia and Solis were both waiting. They waved their wings happily in greeting before changing into Magi form as the others landed. Grecia walked over to peer at Tariah as she slid off Dominic's back. "They weren't kidding when they said you were little!"

Tariah could only sigh. Dominic turned into Magi form and offered, "They say great things come in small packages, and they were right."

Solis grinned. "I certainly think she's fine as she is." He winced as there came a loud thud from inside the meeting room. "Better hurry before they knock down a mountain." Under his breath he added, "Again."

Dominic and Jazz wasted no time in hurrying to the doors and opening them. Urging Morgan and Tariah ahead of them, they went inside. The doors did not, however, shut behind them. Grecia caught them with her foot and peered inside. Solis and Dahlia quickly joined her. In fact, within a matter of moments, half the Furies left on the Isle were hovering close to see and hear. Word traveled fast among Dragons. No one wanted to miss this!

The meeting room was bigger than the king's palace, Tariah and Morgan both realized. The practicality was obvious since Dragons were much bigger. Yet there was something so simple about the room that, despite its size, it didn't feel overwhelming. Unlike the Magi king's throne room, there were no decadent statues displayed to flaunt wealth. The only statues were carved of wood and stone.

The four elder Dragons were as big as Xander, and each wore a colored sash to represent their clan. The Soil Elder studied Tariah and Morgan, then nodded in satisfaction. "Welcome, young Dragoons, to the Isle. We have searched for you for many centuries."

"Technically," Tariah muttered under her breath, "you didn't."

Dragons had good hearing. The Elders' eyes slowly widened as a group. "Pardon us?" the Fire Elder asked.

Already kicking herself mentally, she crossed her arms. She hated proving her brother right. "I just said that technically, you didn't look for us. *We* looked for *you*." She ignored Dominic's clear amusement, and Jazz's quick grin. "*You* sat on your butts and lamented the sad state of the world!"

For a moment, not a single Elder could find a word to say. Carefully, the Water Elder said, "Well . . . that may be but . . ."

"No buts!" She threw her hands in the air. "Okay, you couldn't track us. Okay, you were afraid you'd go around eating Magi for their stupidity. But you could have done *something*. By doing nothing, you ensured nothing got done!"

"Yes'm," the Elders said as one. The hint of pink bloomed across all four faces.

She continued, "Morgan and I went through a nightmare to find our Furies. And at least *they* were looking for us! What about Dahlia? And Xander? Confining them to the Isle is stupid when they could at least *try* to sniff out their Chronicles. If *we* can feel them, *you* can!"

"Yes'm."

She crossed her arms. "We've got the Elite to deal with. We've got Sistra. There are kids out there that are being denied the truth of what they are. Are you going to sit on your tails and do nothing?" It was shot at them challengingly.

"No, ma'am."

"Good." She turned on her heel and headed for the doors before she made an even bigger scene. The Furies outside hastily moved out of the way, and all began to clap and cheer as she exited.

Morgan and Jazz followed her, and as Dominic turned to go as well, the Fire Elder called his name. "Yes?" He looked back over his shoulder.

The Elder's face creased into a toothy smile. "I like her. We all do." The other Elders nodded in agreement, and all were grinning as well.

Dominic started laughing. "I *knew* she would somehow cause you to agree on something for once!" Still chuckling, he hurried from the room to find his Chronicle.

There were many things he wanted to show her. So many things that he had waited too long to share with her.

~*~

One week later, Tariah and Morgan stood side-by-side facing their Furies who were in Dragon form. Both Chronicles wore clothing woven of the finest cloth by the greatest craftsman on the Isle. The clothes were the formal type considered the standard style of where they were from. For Tariah, it was clothing of the desert. For Morgan, it was clothing of the snowy lands.

Dominic and Jazz wore sashes in the color of their clans; red for him and green for her. All around them, the entire Isle had gathered. Every Dragon of every shape, size, and age had come to witness the event. Because of it, the event was taking place in the middle of the valley where there was room for all of them.

The only others present were Sparkle and Daylar. They were in formal clothing, too, and riding on Solis and Dahlia's shoulders. Neither Kin would have missed this ceremony for the world. Sparkle couldn't stop sniffling, though, and Solis kept handing her tissue. He didn't mind. Her happiness was shared by all of them.

"This ceremony," the Fire Elder said, for he was presiding over the events, "is an old one. It is steeped in heritage and history. It has been a thousand years since it was performed, and yet all present will remember it somewhere inside.

"Furies, will you dedicate your lives to protecting your Chronicles? Will you always support them, and give them the wings to fly across the skies as Dragoons?"

"We will," both Dominic and Jazz said.

"And Chronicles, will you dedicate your lives to protecting your Furies? Will you always support them, and walk beside them when they wish to see the land as Dragoons?"

"We will," Tariah and Morgan said.

"Then it is with honor that I name all of you full Dragoons and confer upon you the full privileges associated with such a position. I also declare you to be Linked by Magi standards, Bonded by Kin, and United by Dragon. You will stand as one, you will live as one, and you will die as one. For eternity."

"For eternity," all present repeated.

"Let us see our Dragoons take their first flight together on their new paths." He moved out of the way, and the crowd backed up as well.

Tariah belatedly discover that climbing onto Dominic's back in a skirt was near impossible, and her nose wrinkled up. Before she could find a way to use her power, Xander walked up and lifted her easily onto Dominic's back. She smiled down at him as she settled into place. "Thank you, Xander."

He smiled. "It was my honor." He moved back once more and tucked his hands into his pockets.

Morgan had already climbed onto Jazz's back, and the crowd held its breath. The two Furies shot straight into the air with a shower of sparks and light, and the crowd erupted into cheers. Half a dozen Dragons flew up to join them and they trailed behind the Dragoon couples as they flew in opposite directions across the sky. They would circle the Isle before going to their chosen homes; it would be the mountains for both, but the sunny side for Tariah and Dominic and the snowy tops for Morgan and Jazz.

Tariah felt an odd sense of peace and disorientation as she held onto Dominic. A lot had happened in what felt like an impossibly short amount of time. "The Magi are calling us heroes," she said thoughtfully. "The Kin are calling us saviors. I'm not sure I want to be a hero or savior. What are the Dragons calling us?"

Her mate smiled and angled down toward the home waiting in a place where the sun would always shine. "I think they're calling you champions."

"I don't like that either." Her lower lip poked out.

"How about I call you something else, then?"

"Like what?"

"*Ishke.*"

She sighed contentedly and leaned down to hold him tight. She had never been happier in her life. "I suppose I can settle for that." In fact, she thought she could settle for anything as long as she had her Fury by her side.

Finally, she was where she belonged.

Epilogue

Dear reader,

And so ends the Chronicle of Destiny, named for the Chronicles who carried the name of Chronis and the fate it bestowed. Though the battles ahead will be tough, and though no one can say with certainty that the outcome will be one wanted by all, there is no doubt in my mind that no one will ever forget this journey and the part it has played in the story of the world.

Where the next will begin, no one can say. But begin it will, for in the language of the Dragons and Kin alike 'luck' shares a character with 'forever' and 'sphere' shares one with 'story'.

And so, the story of the world shall go on forever.

Xander Journe

Made in the USA
Charleston, SC
01 August 2013